TENACITY

The Completionist Chronicles Book Nine

DAKOTA KROUT

This is a work of fiction. Names, characters, places, and incidents either are the products of the author's imagination or are used fictitiously. Any resemblance to actual persons, living or dead, businesses, companies, events, or locales is entirely coincidental.

ACKNOWLEDGMENTS

To all my family, friends, and all the support structures and groups in my life, and to my Patreons, especially Lilly Hawk and Mike Rylander, thank you for helping me have the Tenacity I needed to succeed.

PROLOGUE

"I feel *warmth.*"

The mountain range began to shake as seven enormous Frost Giants moved for the first time in centuries. Each of them had a single distinct characteristic, the only identifying feature among them. The first among them stood as a giant of a man, different from a baseline human only in his sheer size. His eyes were colder than the snow that blanketed the world, and the sheer number of scars that coated his body told of a lengthy life full of conflict.

The next three stood in quick succession after the first had gained his feet, each of their places in the hierarchy of power nearly equivalent. A frost giant covered in electric blue tattoos, with lightning arcing between them intermittently. Another stood with the help of an arm that sprouted directly from his chest, and he pushed himself perfectly off the ground with a single push-up to secure his footing. His brother adjusted an enormous monocle that covered one of his eyes, which had long-since grown deeply into the flesh of his body.

Finally, the three with the lowest positions stood tall, the first of them standing on four legs like a half spider. Then one that had nearly half his face covered by enormous, bushy eyebrows that dangled in front of his eyes. The last among them stood tall, proudly, enormous tusks jutting from the lower mandible of his jaw.

The Jötunn, thrice as large as the mountainous giants that surrounded him, was the owner of the voice that had roused the seven giants from their otherwise eternal, frozen slumber. He alone had remained motionless while the others had been jolted by the sheer power of his voice. The titan of frost was trapped deep within the surface of Jotunheim, with only his arms protruding out of the planet and preventing his escape even as he strained to break free.

"The bifrost has been activated," he rumbled, his voice carrying across the land. "Its blazing mana is slicing through the swirling storms protecting us from being hunted. The audacity of the outer deities knows no bounds! They have dared to deposit their mortal charges upon the surface of our world. Even as we speak, the bifrost is shifting its location, evading our winter's wrath."

The seven other giants lowered themselves to one knee, casting their gaze well beneath that of their Patriarch. The first to break the silence was the giant characterized by an arm emerging directly from the center of its chest. "Do you believe the hunts will commence once more?"

"Most assuredly, *if* we were to let this infestation take root," the Jötunn stated consideringly.

One of them, adorned with a pair of massive tusks supported by two smaller protrusions, spoke out as soon as their leader's voice had subsided. "If the past behavior of the mortals is any indication, they will exert all their efforts towards *fleeing* this realm. Is it even worth our while to take action?"

"We failed to act swiftly enough last time, and think of what happened. Our world was mined for its resources, the creatures slain for sport!" The giant who spoke looked the most like a human: only massive, blue, and scarred. "I say we set out at once to the seven sectors of the world and uproot whatever *vestige* of civilization has sprouted."

Before each of the other giants could say their piece, the Jötunn's words bowled them over. "We made a *pact* with the Jörmungandr. Having filled this world with ice and death, our Geas calls me to action. As soon as one of them goes beyond the limits the world has offered, *we* will be able to act. For now, each of you must begin the long walk. Spread across this planet. Be poised to strike, to lead the children of the Jörmungandr into battle."

"Summon your lessers and send them in advance of yourselves." The Jötunn's eyes slowly began to close, resembling immense glaciers traversing across vast pools of water. "Wake me only if I'm needed. If the situation becomes dire."

The seven towering giants paid obeisance to their leader as he succumbed to his frigid slumber. With his departure into the realm of sleep, the behemoths exchanged sinister grins, relishing their newfound freedom. The last of the giants to depart, known to his brothers only by the immense glacier that had been shaped into a gleaming monocle, whispered in a voice as cold as the frozen wasteland that surrounded him.

"At last, it is time to satiate our hunger. Let us show those delectable, frail beings from the summer realms that the frost... will bite."

CHAPTER ONE

Joe the Ritualist surveyed the new realm he was trapped in. Compared to the last time he had gone to a new world, this was practically a vacation. No choking to death because he couldn't force air into his lungs, he *chose* to come here instead of being exiled, and he was surrounded on all sides by friends. "Great, now we have all the positives out of the way."

He chuckled to himself as he looked around, finding that the surrounding landscape was aglow with the flickering flames of numerous fires, providing warmth and light to the gathered crowd. Even with their joy being tempered by their loss, the vast majority of those assembled were triumphant Dwarves reveling in their newfound freedom, fresh from their escape of Alfheim. Their society lay in ruins, their old way of life had been torn out by the roots, but every single one of them had grabbed the chance to start afresh in this unfamiliar world.

Being the catalyst for their escape—as they had *earned* survival on their own—Joe wasn't surprised to find himself the object of the Dwarves' gratitude. Every person who recognized him would have their faces light up. This was followed in short order by endless offers of potent drinks being sent his way. Their persistent attempts to celebrate with him touched Joe deeply, filling him with the warm fuzzies, even as he politely rebuffed their invitations.

Still, he was only human. The Ritualist could only hold out so long—eventually the pleading and earnest offers wore him down. Even despite his often introspective nature, Joe understood the significance of this momentous occasion and the importance of bonds forged in the fires of shared struggle. With that thought in mind, he submitted to their desires a single time—joining the celebration in his own way by raising a mug of coffee as a toast to their survival and the promise of a brighter future together.

After escaping the small knot of people who knew him well, Joe continued his observation, his keen eyes surveying the mingling crowd. Approximately eighty thousand Dwarves made up the vast majority of the group after the aggressive escape through the bifrost. That was offset by the smaller groups of humans towering over most of the crowd, their multiple thousands seemingly insignificant compared to the dominant population. They were remarkable in the fact that their stances were stiff, and the expressions on their faces differed greatly from the joyous celebration surrounding them.

There was good reason for it, and Joe felt the same sinking sensation in his own gut. They'd all received the same message—they were trapped on Jotunheim, a world of giants, and the only escape lay in the likely years-to-decades-long task of building a City and dispelling the thick shroud of clouds above them, all in the hopes of generating a new bifrost. Even then, to ensure that they wouldn't need to travel tens of thousands of miles to use it, they needed to complete their project before anyone *else* could claim the prize.

Joe rubbed at his lightly frosted bald head, understanding that this world would be yet *another* zero-sum game. Still, he was trying to focus on the positive portions of their circumstances, so he put a smile on his face and worked to keep his mood light. "Gotta enjoy the successes when we have them, or what's the point of winning?"

Smile firmly pasted in place, his mind shifted from observation to planning, thoughts consumed by the task of building a new city, dispelling the clouds, and most likely being the glue that would bind these groups of surviving Dwarves and advancement-greedy humans together.

As Joe's gaze extended to the distant horizon, daylight timidly seeped in, providing an utterly *incremental* illumination of the world. The creeping wall of light moved at a glacial pace, underscoring the inconceivable vastness of the world they now found themselves on. 'Glacial' was an excellent descriptor of the area, as the abundant snow and ice were the only terrain features the light managed to highlight. Before he could start feeling concerned about the situation, he was grabbed roughly and once more invited to join the celebration of the now-shivering Dwarves.

The Ritualist firmly shook his head and set getting shelter as his number one priority for living on this world as he saw the Constitution-focused Dwarves already turning pale and trembling with cold.

"We're going to need shelter sooner rather than later." With that thought in mind, he turned on his heel and started walking back toward the guildhall, the only permanent structure that had currently been created in the area. His goal was to start putting together some apartment complexes, elevating the number of people who could be protected from the elements. He swept some of the blowing snow that had accumulated off of his Exquisite Shell as he thought about his next move. "If I build the apartments in a circle around the guildhall, will that help with cutting down on wind shear? There's gotta be a city planner here who knows, right?"

He came to a halt as he saw a Dwarf on her knees punching the ground and snarling. Of all of the people around, she was the only one who didn't seem happy in the slightest. "Excuse me… what's the matter?"

She stopped moving, letting out a deep sigh as she looked up at the sky, the tears frozen in her mustache catching the light. "I'm an Expert frozen treat maker, I focus on ice cream."

"Ah. Tough luck on that one. Shaved ice might be popular someday." After a conciliatory pat on the shoulder, Joe stepped around her and entered directly through the entrance of the guildhall, his body instinctively shivering as a wave of warmth enveloped him. In that moment, he became *acutely* aware of the chill that had been slowly seeping into his bones. Whether it was an inherent trait of this world or a peculiar environmental effect, it seemed that the everyday dangers of Jotunheim were going to be even more severe than he had been thinking.

Only a handful of individuals were currently in the space, each of them radiating a palpable aura of power and competence. Among them, Grandmaster Snow stood out, a figure of authority and experience seated at a table, meticulously examining a rough map of the surrounding area. Her poise stood in stark contrast to the other, less *elegant* happenings.

Havoc was arguing with his brother, Grandmaster McPoundy, about the viability of creating a smithy immediately. But the conversation cut off as Joe stepped into the small building, the wind howling in with him before he finally managed to shut the door. "Good, finally you realized that you should put down the stein and get in here to discuss strategy with the adults! Hurry up, there's lots to go over."

Joe approached with a respectful nod acknowledging the Grandmaster he was apprenticed to, though his eyes remained on the rough map that would provide him with a glimpse into the treacherous terrain and potential threats lurking in the vast expanse that was Jotunheim.

"Frankly, Havoc, it doesn't matter if he's here or not." Grandmaster Snow murmured as she stroked her mustache. Her eyes never left the document in front of her. "You know as well as I do that he's nearly empty of resources, having used them up in our escape. Until we're able to secure deposits of minerals and such, there's no point in trying to squeeze blood from the stone that is Major-General Joe Pyrrhic."

"I've seen him do more with less," Havoc countered immediately, giving a rare nod of acknowledgment toward the human in their midst. "Worse comes to worst, I'll have him out there converting dirt into bits of coal to light our forges until he's useful again. At least it'll be good training."

Joe's eyes widened, and he decided to get involved in the conversation before he was assigned an absolutely pointless task as a mandatory quest. "Good to see you as well; I'm glad that everyone got through safely. If you don't mind me asking, is that a map or a preliminary report on the area?"

"Ha! *Coal*?" McPoundy triumphantly pointed at Havoc. "I *knew* you were coming around to the idea of making a forge before anything else!"

Instead of answering Joe's question directly, Snow ignored the bickering brothers and tapped the page in front of her, speaking loudly. "We escaped, for now. Everything is going to be *extraordinarily* difficult for the next several weeks as we rush to survive. You may have noticed that the conditions out there are rather… extreme. Well, get *used* to it! There are constant clouds in the sky, and it'll be blisteringly cold, even during the height of daytime. Which, for your information, looks like it will be sometime near the end of *next* week. Settle in for the long haul, and let's start to build a firm foundation, no matter how long it takes."

Everyone quieted and leaned forward slightly, waiting patiently as though she were about to start reading a story to a group of children. Seeing that no one had a comment, Snow tapped the paper and went over her thoughts on the information.

"Going by the size of the planet, and checking that against the slowly increasing light, we're estimating that each day on this planet is approximately two weeks long on Alfheim. That means we're going to have two weeks of daytime, followed by the same amount of time in absolute darkness as we're engulfed by nighttime. Havoc, as you were just having this conversation with your brother, could you enlighten us on the status of our resources?"

"Yeah. That's easy. In the grand scheme of possessing things, we find ourselves in a stuffless abyss, where the void of stuff knows no bounds," the cigar-puffing Dwarf explained shortly. "It's cold. It's dark. We're already under attack by monsters on the outer fringes of our group. We need metal; we need enough plants and meat to survive. Eh, mushrooms would work. All of this comes together to a simple conclusion: we need to start digging right away and get our society living underground like we always should've been."

"I'd wondered about that." Joe didn't realize that he had spoken out loud until he realized that everyone in the room was staring at him. Instead of apologizing, he leaned into his question. "If Dwarves are so used to living underground, why did you all live on the surface when I found you? On that note, why do you all carry axes and the like instead of pickaxes and shovels?"

McPoundy was the one to speak up this time, "We lived on the surface because it was part of the rules of the last world. Since we were in a state of constant war, living underground would've meant giving up all of the fortresses and the resources they automatically generated for us. As to why we carry axes? That one's easy. Elves live in trees."

That got a chuckle from the assembled group. When they quieted down, Snow gently placed her hands on the paper in front of her, lifting her chin until she was meeting Joe's eyes. Seemingly trying not to get her hopes up, Snow quietly, yet firmly asked the question on her mind. "Havoc seems to think that you might have a few tricks that could help us. Is there anything you can think of that you could put in place to increase our odds of survival?"

"Sure. I'm thinking we–" Joe was about to start explaining his plan for putting up temporary housing, but something outside of the window caught his eye. Several Dwarves were using the oversized metal block that the Ritual of the Traveling Civilization was inscribed on as an ale pong table. One of them had just knocked over a cup of the strong brew onto the extremely dangerous, treacherously vulnerable ritual, sending a warning tingle down Joe's spine as he spun and ran for the door.

"Yeah, hold that thought for a minute. If they break that ritual, I'm not exactly sure how big the explosion would be, but... *big*." He dashed back out into the cold, rapidly closing in on the metal block and waving his arms at the ruddy-faced revelers. "Get out of here! Shoo!"

The assemblage of Dwarves scattered like scared chickens, although their laughter made it clear that this was all part of the fun. Joe cleaned off the surface of the block of metal, and as he did so, double-checked to make sure everything was working properly. He accessed the ritual itself, swiping out until he could see Jotunheim as an astral object on the surface. Joe flinched as a cloud of snow flew past him, and he turned his head to see another human man using the snow as some sort of training.

The man had a huge shovel and was creating walkways even though there wasn't a clear route that needed to be made. "Are you trying to stay warm or something?"

"Nah." The man turned his head and grinned at Joe as he continued shoveling his way to the guildhall. "I just dig snow."

"This place is bringing out the worst in people already." Joe snorted and returned his gaze to the projection the ritual created. He was satisfied that everything was safe and was sure the ritual wasn't about to explode from something as harmless as a simple spill. He started closing everything out, but just before he stepped away, Joe felt his body seize up as a glowing dot appeared on the very edge of the map.

It hadn't been there a moment ago, and was ever-so-slowly traveling across the area he had selected to view. Curious, he zoomed in on it until the dot was in the center of the screen. A few words appeared above it, and Joe's eyes went wide. As he realized what he was seeing, his plans changed, and his heart leapt. "That's Alfheim, this was where we left the Shoe, and this…!"

Joe sprinted back to the guildhall, slapping the door open and shouting at the top of his lungs to drown out all other conversation. "The *pyramid*! We have a chance to save it!"

That didn't elicit the reaction he wanted or needed, as most people simply looked at him as though he had finally drunk one too many mana potions.

"The Alchemy hall! It's still intact! I don't know for how much longer, but if we move now, we have a chance to pull it through to this area!"

Jake the Alchemist sprinted into the building, somehow having heard Joe, even though there was no reason for him to be in the area. He hadn't even stopped to open the door that was slowly closing behind Joe, simply smashing it off its hinges and turning it into several chunks of wood in his haste. "You can save it? *Fool*! Why are you wasting time *telling* people! Bring it across!"

"I need help," Joe explained as rapidly as possible, noting that Jake was peeling a label off a bottle labeled 'failed quest punishment'. "It's going to have a severe mana cost; I'm positive of it. I need as many people as can be spared right away."

He waved for people to follow him and hurried back out to the metal block as orders started flying through the air. There were tens of thousands of Dwarves in the area, and every single one of them had access to their mana even if they weren't spellcasters. The people *not* interested in the rescue of the Artifact-quality building *were* interested in the new and exciting 'party game' that required everyone to gather around in a set of giant circles.

Joe wasn't above tricking a few tipsy Dwarves into losing their mana—and likely their lunch—if it meant that they could jumpstart their progress towards having a city. Happily, there was no end to the volunteers, to the point where Joe needed to start turning people away.

He wasn't idle during this time, focused instead on finding the best placement for the Pyramid of Panacea itself. The Ritualist was practically shouting back and forth with everyone who needed to be involved in the placement process. Amidst the bedlam of differing opinions on the ideal location for the building, it rapidly became apparent that Jake the Alchemist was going to take matters into his own hands, exercising his strange level of authority to the utmost.

He proved this fact when an upstart city planner finally arrived and jumped into the fray—arguing about them needing to take their time and really *consider* the layout of the eventual city—the Alchemist simply blew a handful of powder into the Dwarf's face. The bearded Dwarf's fervently excited eyes shifted into a vacant stare, his demanding noises falling flat along with his now-unconscious body.

That spectacle earned a chuckle from Havoc. "Compliance powder. Gotta love ol' reliable."

With that, the location of the pyramid was firmly decided. Joe began laying out the ritual plates that sprang from the block the Ritual of the Traveling Civilization had been inscribed upon. Circles of ghostly energy sprang out, and the Ritualist began directing the volunteers to fill the open spaces. The ritual had a minimum number of people who could be involved, but they blew past that in an instant as Joe filled every position possible for maximum power generation.

In fact, it got to the point where Jake was nearly ready to start shaking Joe to make him *start the process*, but the Ritualist firmly told the Alchemist to back down. His reasoning was sound, the only reason he didn't get a puff of powder in his face and have the Alchemist seize control. "I can almost *guarantee* that we're only going to have one shot at this. Let's not mess it up by underestimating what it's going to require to bring the pyramid across."

With everything in place, the ritual ready to go, and the

party continuing to rage ever louder and wilder outside the bounds of the intense situation... Joe activated the ritual with a whoop.

His voice choked off as the air above them *screamed*. Space itself ripped open, and lava flooded the icy plain below.

CHAPTER TWO

"Hey! This is only supposed to bring across the building; what's with the lava?"

Joe's startled outburst at the incoherent scene caused a visible ripple of unease to spread across the faces of those participating in his magic.

For a moment, the uncomfortable silence hung in the air, like an awkwardly failed bardic spell. Thankfully, in a fleeting moment of self-awareness, Joe realized that literally shouting his own ignorance for all to hear was a great way to erode people's trust in his mystical prowess.

Forcibly shifting his facial expression to understanding and determination, Joe slathered a smile on his face and summoned the power of… deception! "Right, *right*! The pyramid uses lava as an energy source of some kind! This is what's required for it to function on this planet. Makes perfect sense!"

His loud musing caused the participants to breathe a sigh of relief as the liquid stone continued to pour out of the sky and onto the frozen land below. It sank through the top layers of what Joe had originally assumed was soil, now revealed as a slurry of snow and dirt. On one hand, that was useful knowledge. On the other, it made Joe realize that they were going to have to clear a *monumental* amount of snow from the area if they wanted to have firm foundations for their buildings. "Good thing we have shovel guy. Heh. Digs snow. I shoulda gotten his name."

The Ritualist went silent as his eyes drank in the sight of the inverted tip of the Pyramid of Panacea. Strangely enough, where the building touched the ground was a drill, instead of the vertex of the inverted structure. It was clearly built-in, but he couldn't remember seeing it back when the Artifact had first been created. Joe tried to remember if it had been on the original blueprint, but quickly decided that he hadn't noticed the oddity because the building had been created in a single fell swoop.

The enormous building was lowering out of the sky, instead of disintegrating and being recreated on this world. That in and of itself was different than what Joe had expected, but could easily be explained by the quality of the building itself.

Another protuberance which was *far* more distressing caught his attention.

The enormous talons digging directly through the stone of the pyramid was a situation that could *not* be explained. Those were attached to something that was fighting against the pull of the ritual in an attempt to yank the structure back through the portal.

"Celestial feces, the *World Boss* is still holding onto it!" Havoc bellowed as the fight between the two powers began to affect the world around them. As colossal friction saturated the sky around the rent in space, dozens of bolts of lightning danced and crackled. Seemingly endless flows of molten lava spilling from the portal clashed with the icy expanse of the frozen realm. The opposing forces caused an eerie symphony of searing heat haze and ethereal steam patterns that swirled and melded—reducing visibility to only a few dozen feet at a time.

Then the superheated lava met the shockingly cold air, directly generating air explosions from the sudden change in air pressure. Those blasted the mists into vapor that quickly fell to the ground as snow as it rose past the boundary of its heat source.

"Increasing the mana draw!" Joe shouted the warning to all of the participants, working on the ritual to actively control how much power was being invested. A resounding grumble rose up from the multitude of Dwarves, a trumpet call of effort that heralded the masterful feat of magic. As if heaved from the skies, the grand edifice began a slow, steady descent toward Jotunheim.

The unmistakable displeasure of the World Boss manifested itself as another avian limb emerging from the hole in space, its colossal talons ruthlessly piercing through the glassy surface of the building as though it were made of cardboard. The air resonated with a cacophony of stone flash freezing into ice-coated obsidian formations. A sound like stone crumbling and glass shattering rang out as more and more lava shifted into a solid state. Even the wind picked up, as if the icy world itself were fighting against any increase of the ambient temperature.

Glancing to the side, Joe could see that Jake was staring at the interplay with furious eyes, growling low in his throat as he tossed alchemical reagents into the air. Then he began mumbling under his breath and tracing patterns of mana into the somehow-hovering powders.

Perfectly happy to allow other people to deal with the monster, Joe focused on his own task of bringing the building through and into position. His enormous amount of practice controlling mana and aspects was useful here, as the building shook side to side from the wrenching forces. In his mind's eye, he held the image of the pyramid's final resting place and worked to bring the base of the establishment into alignment with the ritual circle.

Each time it got close to the edge of the spinning magic, the friction in the air multiplied tenfold, sending thick bolts of lightning careening into the world. Most of that energy struck the immaterial edges of the ritual itself, either being absorbed or dissipated, thanks to the protections built into the Master-rank ritual.

What *did* get through didn't impact people; instead, it disrupted the stability of the ritual ever so slightly, causing Joe's mental fatigue to rapidly accumulate. Enormous spell effects—coming off of mages and the assemblage of Masters and Grandmasters—begin rocketing into the scaly limbs of the World Boss, aimed extremely precisely to counter its swaying movements. While Joe correctly assumed that there weren't many weak points that could be targeted, he *was* certain getting a caboose-sized nail driven into a leg by a summoned entity couldn't feel nice. "Almost… to the ground… hold on!"

The Reductionist puppeted the strands of power that were wrapped around the mountainous facility, orchestrating the movement until the moment that the building finally firmly settled onto the ground. He heaved a sigh of relief, only to have additional power ripped out of him in the next moment. Contrary to his expectations, the portal above them *wasn't* snapping closed. Instead, it seemed that the World Boss itself was slowly being pulled through and onto Jotunheim.

His eyes went wide as he *finally* realized where the ritual had gone wrong. "It's connected to the building! Break its grip, or we're going to have to deal with a furious World Boss on day one!"

They had no protections, no buffs scaled up to cover the entire remaining Dwarven populace. If the World Boss came through, they likely had no chance of survival. Thousands of combatants got involved, their weapons reaching out to nick tiny paper cuts into the legs and now-visible body of the thrashing World Boss.

As the damage began to accumulate, eventually reaching one percent of the overall health of the monster, it stopped struggling to pull itself and the building back to the previous world—instead choosing to force itself the rest of the way through to Jotunheim. Joe and the rest of the participants of the ritual were knocked to their knees or backs as the ritual completed, and the remaining power in the air dissipated in a small shockwave. The human forced himself to his feet immediately, thanks to his 'Immovable Object' title granting him an eighty percent knockback resistance, gasping for air as he tried to get his bearings.

Skreeee!

His gaze traveled up, higher and higher until they took in the majesty of the World Boss. Joe was looking at a Phoenix made entirely of stone and lava. It could have been his imagination, but it appeared that it was staring directly back at him. "Pretty and terrifying. Pretty terrifying. *Run!*"

Dwarves scattered in all directions as the bird flapped its wings a single time, catapulting a volcano's worth of lava into the air that spread out in a nova of light and molten stone before slowly cascading toward the ground like a blanket flung wide open. It landed on the ground, but also on people—who were instantly lit on fire. It clung to their bodies like napalm, dealing a surprisingly low amount of impact damage in favor of burning them over the next several minutes.

Here the terrain worked in their favor, as many people were able to drop to the ground and sink into the frozen surface, turning the spot they landed into a miniature ice bath. The lava was rapidly quenched, although this forced them to deal with a secondary issue: as the molten stone cooled, it *hardened*. Many of the people who dove to the ground found themselves trapped in a solid stone coffin, unable to escape. Joe assumed that had something to do with the material being created by such a powerful monster, as almost everyone impacted should have been able to smash their way out of such a thin layer of otherwise-still-pliable obsidian.

Joe simply ignored the attack, letting it wash over his Exquisite Shell and fall to the ground around him. He kept his eyes on the creature, one of the few people who did, and noticed something that troubled him greatly. The enormous Lava Phoenix was lifting its feet and slamming them into the building it was perched on, causing it to crumble with every strike. "If that building is permanently destroyed... I will be, too. Probably."

Damage taken: 0! Debuff failed to take hold!

"*Nice.*" Instead of pursuing the safe, likely intelligent choice of running for his life, Joe ran instead to the side of the safely-landed pyramid. He had a few tools in his codpiece that he hoped would be enough to salvage the situation, and he needed to get them in place.

As he reached the easternmost point of the structure, he dropped a lovely little obelisk that had been inscribed with the Ritual of Repair. Grabbing a random Dwarf, he shoved the unfortunate not-quite-volunteer to the side of the plinth and told her how to use it. Joe activated the ritual, plopped the Dwarf's hands in place, and ordered her act as a battery. "Sorry about the *short* notice!"

"Is that a Dwarf joke?" she yelled back at him, unable to hunt him down as Joe ran along the building once more, dropping yet another stone at the northmost point of the building and this time grabbing a passing human.

He repeated this twice more, controlling the final Ritual of Repair on his own as the Phoenix screamed in fury. Each time it lifted a foot, the stonework and crystal of the pyramid flowed back together seamlessly, repairing the damage at a rate that was *slightly* higher than what the World Boss could output. Joe knew this, as he was carefully watching the durability increase then rapidly drop.

Pharaoh's Pyramid of Panacea: 110,354/1,000,000 durability.

"Staying above ten percent. We can *do* this!" Joe's enthusiasm cut off a moment later as the Phoenix head switched to the side, and its gaze seemed to bore into the human on the north side of the building who was determinedly keeping the ritual active. The bird's beak opened, and a burning ring of fire went down, down, down and settled around the human and block of stone he was feeding mana into. Joe couldn't see exactly what happened, being on the other side of the structure, but from the cut-off scream... he could only assume it was nothing good.

Once more a talon went up then came down and crashed into the building. This time, Joe saw that it was being repaired at a rate slightly *lower* than the damage was accumulating. He tried not to let it dampen his enthusiasm too much. "*Maybe* we can do this!"

The World Boss targeted another of the rituals, only for an enormous finger to poke out of the air next to it at that moment, impacting the side of the creature's head and sending the entire creature shifting and tumbling to the side. A clap of thunder from the point of impact shook the air hard enough that Joe was knocked away from his ritual and sent toosh over teakettle. When he managed to catch himself, Joe hurled himself forward, reactivating the ritual as quickly as possible.

"Abyss, if *I* was knocked away with all of my bonuses to remaining steady, ten gold says the others have been sent flying."

Joe recognized that finger–it was the same summon that Jake had used as a warning attack against Havoc when they first were introduced to each other, only scaled up to a size that was on par with the World Boss. He could only hope the hidden powerhouse had an entire *arm* up his sleeve, because as the bird fell, it kept its grip on the building and started flailing around to get back up. Frankly, Joe couldn't even tell if the blow had injured the beast at all.

The Ritualist gasped as he noticed that the structural durability had started ticking down like an altimeter in a helicopter that had just been hit by a rocket-propelled grenade—a situation he had firsthand experience with. "Go, ritual! Fix, fix, fix!"

As the Phoenix flapped its wings again, it ripped its feet out of the pyramid and sent off another wave of lava splattering out as it lifted itself into the air. It screeched its fury, then its eyes seemed to follow the connection of power between Joe, the ritual, and the building that his ritual was repairing.

Flapping hard and screeching its displeasure, it spiraled in the air, sending liquid stone spinning far enough into the distance to light up the visible skyline. The Phoenix reached hundreds of feet above the ground in an instant… before diving at him with deadly intent. Joe watched his death approach, calm in the knowledge that he would be able to respawn soon.

Then the World Boss imploded, sending stone, lava, and fiery feathers geysering in all directions as though two meteors had struck each other in space.

Congratulations! You have defeated a World Boss!

Joe stood in stunned silence as chunks of the *literally strongest* creature in a world landed around him. Notifications were popping up, each one louder than the previous, demanding his attention. But the one at the very top caught his eye more than any of the others.

As the World Boss was defeated through your actions, which dealt more than 95% of its total Health, its Core has been directly added to your storage device. No one else has received a message detailing this fact. Since the World Boss was defeated using a system bug, no experience is awarded. No other World Boss may be defeated in this manner.

CHAPTER THREE

"How?" That was the question on everyone's lips, but especially Joe's as he sank to his knees, gasping for air as his limbs trembled. He didn't remove his hands from the ritual in front of him, maintaining the presence of mind to continue sending enough mana to repair the building that had been almost completely destroyed by the World Boss. The trembling slowly faded away, though the Ritualist was still recovering from the shock of having survived.

Joe had *known* he was about to die.

Normally, when he was that certain, he died.

There was only one place where he could go to get answers. Pulling up his character sheet, he looked at the information contained in it, followed by the Core in his inventory, and lastly the combat log to get the information his brain needed to stop short-circuiting.

Name: Joe 'Major General Pyrrhic' Class: Reductionist
Profession I: Arcanologist (Max)
Profession II: Ritualistic Alchemist (1/20)
Profession III: Grandmaster's Apprentice (14/25)

Profession IV: None.
Character Level: 23 Exp: 289,193 Exp to next level: 10,807
Rituarchitect Level: 10 Exp: 54,700 Exp to next level: 300
Reductionist Level: 4 Exp: 11,341 Exp to next level: 3,659
Hit Points: 2,121/2,327
Mana: 4,313/8,160
Mana regen: 67.83/sec
Stamina:1,837/1,837
Stamina regen: 6.64/sec

Characteristic: Raw score

Strength (bound): 176
Dexterity: 177
Constitution: 169
Intelligence (bound): 185
Wisdom: 168
Dark Charisma: 123
Perception: 173
Luck: 110
Karmic Luck: 110 → 42

Mythic Core: This Core can be consumed for 40,000 experience. If not consumed in this manner, there are several options for its usage.

1) It can be bound to a single skill or set of skills to move from Grandmaster to Sage. Only one skill or set of skills may be bound per person. This will consume the Core.

2) It can be used as a crafting material for a chance of bringing an item up to Mythical Rarity during its creation. This will consume the Core.

3) It can be used as a temporary accessory to allow an item to act as one Rarity tier higher than it is. It can be removed at any time by any person with direct access to the Core.

Warnings: This Core can be stolen. It is dropped on death if it is being held, even if it is in a spatial storage device. Until this Core is consumed, the World Boss it came from cannot naturally respawn.

Combat log:

You are attempting to use a ritual to open a portal between two distinct worlds. Caution! An outside entity is attempting to resist the ritual.

You have initiated a battle of Might and Magic against a World Boss of Svaltarheim—The Magma Phoenix.

Using the combined power of 11,023 individuals, your struggle was a success!

The Magma Phoenix has arrived on Jotunheim.

The Magma Phoenix has gone into a frenzy and is targeting the item that dragged it through chaotic space.

As the Magma Phoenix did not travel across the Bifrost to reach this world, it has been granted a two-minute grace period to return to its world.

The Magma Phoenix has surfaced. Name changed to Lava Phoenix.

The timer has expired. The Lava Phoenix has expired.

Error. World Boss must remain on its own world. Removing excess awards. Canceling titles. Siphoning Experience points.

Joe had seen enough to get the gist of what had happened. Even so, there were a few standout points that he wasn't sure how to come to terms with. For one, his Karmic Luck had never before been so *massively* inflated. He hadn't even noticed when it had jumped from the low double digits all the way to over a hundred, and he had already lost more than half of it. He desperately needed to find a time to discuss the issue with one of the Grandmasters… or he could wait until Cleocatra showed up and hope he could wheedle the information out of her.

Having thought of the Queen of the Hidden Race, Joe vocalized a half-threat, half-plea: "I am actively thinking about you, cat. Don't mess with me."

Hoping that mini-crisis with the Nyandrathal was averted, he moved back to thinking logically about his current windfall. Joe eventually came to the decision that he must have gained an enormous amount of Karmic Luck from saving so many Dwarves by transporting them safely to this world. He could only assume that accidentally generating a bug in the system and killing off one of the seven World Bosses with it was what had taken such a massive chunk out of that largesse.

Even so, that enigmatic Characteristic was more than double as high as he had ever seen it, and he could only hope that meant good, positive things for him in the near future.

His eyes shifted over to view his levels and experience, which had barely budged in weeks, thanks to his focus on bolstering his skills and ritual abilities. Joe wasn't overly concerned; he would have plenty of time in the near future to gain levels. Now that he was on Jotunheim, where the air was heavy and turbulent with power, the experience points would soon be rolling in.

Slowly, he was able to calm his breathing and return to the moment, even though he was *slightly* distracted with thoughts of what he should use his brand new Mythic Core for.

He squashed a tiny temptation to hold the gem in his hand and let his inner greed gloat over having captured it for himself, but happily, better sense prevailed. Going by how brightly *lesser* versions had shone when he pulled them out into the open, Joe assumed that taking it out would send a beacon to the cloud layer above them and alert every person and monster within hundreds of miles to the fact that an unbound Mythic Core was up for grabs.

He instantly discarded the idea that he could directly consume the incredibly powerful object for mere experience points. Looking at his skills, the highest of which was his Ritual Magic at Master level one, he also understood that he was *far* from being able to use it to boost himself. The same went for creating an item he could imbue with its power—the only Sage-ranked blueprints he had were for his weapons, and it would be a long, *long* time before he was able to craft the Sage-ranked version of his Ritual Orbs.

It should go without saying that there was no way in the *abyss* he was going to give it up. He also couldn't carry it around with him, as that was just asking to lose it and gain no benefit whatsoever. With all other options eliminated, only one option remained: using it as an accessory. Before he could decide what to equip it to, Jake appeared in front of him, looking like a nervous parent whose child was going off to school for the first time.

"Joe. Can you repair this damage? I can't do any work in a building that's so heavily destroyed. How long will it take? What do you need from me?"

The Reductionist had never seen Jake speak this earnestly, and it was making him nervous. He had seen this man put *Havoc* in his place; though Joe did find it a tiny bit funny that the Alchemist was only truly concerned with his ability to *work*, not the actual state of the building.

"I can set up a few more Rituals of Repair, but I'm going to need large chunks of stone like this one. If we can get eight of them set up, four on the cardinal directions, four on the ordinal, that will allow us to repair hundreds of damage per ritual, per minute. With a little over nine hundred thousand durability to repair, it should be up and running in a little over... let's say nineteen hours on the upper limit, just so I have time to actually make the rituals?"

Jake took in a deep inhalation, slowly letting it out over a few seconds. "I suppose that will have to suffice. I hadn't expected to regain access to the pyramid ever again, so if I only must wait two-thirds of a day, I will be able to remain in your service instead of exacting punishments for you failing to uphold your bargain."

"Yeah, I saw the bottle you were getting ready. Good to know it won't have to be used." Joe realized that the Alchemist was already walking away, so he let his flow of words trickle to a stop. No matter how annoyed he was, the Ritualist made sure to keep his mana flowing into the ritual as he swallowed his very dry throat. "*Yeesh.* All stick, zero carrot with this guy."

As much as he wanted to get on with his next projects, he needed to ensure that the repair of the building didn't stagnate. Joe called over the nearest group of Dwarves to take over for him, giving them instructions and making sure they could use the ritual properly before he stepped away. Each of the other rituals had been abandoned, save for the northernmost one, which had been... Joe looked at it and decided that 'vaporized' was a proper descriptor of what had happened.

It took a short while, but soon there were once again three rituals up and running. Fighting against the environment, the Ritualist slowly made five more stable Rituals of Repair before he was able to step away and let the volunteers manage the repairs. Even though he had to combat his desire to micromanage, Joe forced himself to trust that the pyramid would soon be back to full durability, even without his helicopter parenting.

There were plenty of people who could handle simply inputting mana into a ritual. Comparatively, thanks to the utter lack of resources or natural landmarks, there was no one else who could create sufficient shelters for the vast number of people who needed protection from the elements. If Joe wanted to use his time as wisely as possible, he needed to do what *only* he could do.

That made it *triply* annoying when he started the ritual to create a cheap, Common building, and it failed on the spot. His system information gave him only sparse feedback.

Spell stability too low for completion of this ritual!

"Ah, that's right. I just had to work around this... this world is extremely unstable for spells and such. Still... I'm pretty sure this should have worked." Joe closed his eyes and bobbed his head, trying to remember the warning that he had been given before coming here. "Was it that Novice spells wouldn't work at all? Or was it all the way up to Beginner? Either way, I should be at least able to *activate* the ritual, even if the building it makes just falls apart. So, why'd it fail?"

Joe tried to remember the exact wording he had heard about this world. He knew that Novice spells were going to be impossible to use, but he was *almost* positive that he should still be able to complete Beginner-ranked versions.

"I'm sure that I can force it. Perhaps I should just look into stabilizing the area a little bit? Feces, I *completely* forgot that most people are going to need to take their Excommunicated title into account. That's an additional twenty percent instability to spells and skills that use mana? Ouch. Combining that with the inherent issues this world has, people are going to be having a real hard time getting anything done. I don't even have to worry about that title anymore, and I'm *still* failing to create these successfully."

Somehow that allowed him to feel more confident in his capabilities, and the Ritualist was able to devise a plan for moving forward. After going through his skills, he realized that he had the ability to create ritual stabilizing items up to the Student rank, thanks to his Ritualistic Forging skill. Even with all of the environmental debuffs to his greatest strengths, he should be able to create the delicate magics without issue soon. Yet, to create *those* tools, he needed access to a smithy.

Seeing as he was the only person who had the means to get this project moving, Joe realized that, after he finished his project, he could even hand over the workshop to some sucker. The Ritualist quickly amended that thought: he could hand the workshop over to an *entrepreneurial smith* for favors and payment when he was done with it.

Joe was reminded of the conversation that Havoc had been having with Grandmaster McPoundy, and he felt a chuckle coming on. "It's a three-for-one special! I might be able to get on the Grandmaster's good side, make a new ally, and lightly annoy Havoc."

He thought about the very strange day he had been having as he scoped out a good location for the new facility. The Reductionist was on a new world, had been a major contributor to defeating a Mythic monster, and was now planning out how to create the tools that he needed… in order to create slightly improved tools… so that he could accomplish the bare minimum he needed in order to design *specialized* tools.

"Seems like an average Wednesday." Joe shivered at that thought. "Whew, my life sure got strange fast."

CHAPTER FOUR

Joe hadn't corrected Grandmaster Snow's assumption when she had told everyone that he'd used up all of his resources getting them here. The fact of the matter was... that wasn't even *remotely* true. In fact, as most of the work on the escape turtle had been done by Grandmaster Havoc as well as the engineers he had employed, Joe's only investment had been setting up the Ritual of the Wandering Civilization and the bubble beam transportation.

Thanks to his reduction spree with the Dwarves, Joe now had the blueprints, knowledge, and way to his own stability for activating a ritual, along with the materials required to do it quickly and on a fairly large scale.

Aspects gathered
Trash: 130,123
Damaged: 65,061
Common: 21,687
Uncommon: 2,383
Rare: 261
Special: 10,003 (Zombified). 100 (Anima). 111 (Molten)
Unique: 1,719

Artifact: 357
Legendary: 0
Mythical: 0

If he wanted, Joe could invest his aspects into their settlement's expansion, building out the town at a fairly rapid pace. But he had learned from his last attempt, which had culminated dramatically in the town turning into a super volcano and destroying almost all of his hard work. "Eh… to be *fair*, that also melted most of the Elves' capital city. So not a *waste*, exactly."

It had been necessary at the time, so he didn't hold it against Havoc. But after they had left The Shoe, either all of the buildings had been destroyed by the lava, or they'd been obliterated out of sheer spite by whatever Elves who had lived through the cataclysm. Frankly, the fact that the pyramid had been intact enough to come through—albeit almost as rubble—was shocking.

"Okay then, let's take a look." Joe went through the stack of blueprints he carried around in his underwear, finding the version of a smithy he needed at the moment. A Rare-ranked smithy would be ideal in order to build the equipment he needed, and he wasn't going to go crazy with upgrades unless someone paid him for that privilege. This wasn't going to be *his* personal workshop; he would be leaving it in someone else's care. Even without investing to make the maximum-effort version of this building, Joe was certain someone would be happy to at least have something instead of nothing.

He walked back to the guildhall, finding the concerned-looking city planner who had finally shaken off the compliance powder and been freed from a stone coffin, then Joe ran his ideas by the bearded Dwarf. His new conversation partner was *ecstatic* to have something to do, even though it seemed that his mind was on another concern at the moment. The Ritualist thought *perhaps* it was the fact that the singed, bearded Dwarf had suddenly woken up encased in a fitted coffin and missed the arrival and destruction of a Phoenix?

Joe followed the bearded bureaucrat's lead, bemusedly listening as the Dwarf chattered away. "With a structure of this sort, we're going to need to find land that's very stable. That way, as the building settles, everything remains level. As it's going to be a strategic resource—the only place we can repair or create weapons for the foreseeable future—we need to keep it near the hall and the pyramid. That brings me to my main concern…"

Joe was surprised by the abrupt halt in conversation, but waved for the Dwarf to continue. "I'm all ears; what's on your mind?"

"Well, you see, there's an Artifact building right over there." The Dwarf pointed sharply at the pyramid that was slowly reassembling itself as mana washed over it from eight directions—the only skyline-blocking object until the horizon. "For some reason, it isn't counting against the town's building count. I'm uncertain why that'd be the case, but I fear it won't last. I believe that as soon as it's fully repaired, we may be forced into a town upgrade in order to open enough structural slots to build shelters."

The Ritualist went pale as he realized that the city planner was probably correct. "Not only that… but it'll make it impossible for us to build anything else until we reach the next settlement level! *Quickly*! Where should we put the smithy?"

With a sudden sense of urgency seeping into them, the duo swiftly scanned their surroundings for the nearest appropriate location for a smithy. After quickly coming to an agreement on a suitable— if not ideal—spot to put it, the city planner turned in preparation of dashing off in search of assistance to clear the plot of land of the slurry of snow and churned dirt. Joe intercepted him with an impatient gesture, then simply sank to his knees and extended his hands outward.

A Field Array sprang into existence, his intimate knowledge of the spell–bolstered by mana manipulation–allowing him to expand its range to what he considered an impressive eleven meters on each side. He squinted slightly as he focused his will on the cables of power he was creating, and an enormous chunk of detritus simply vanished as it was converted to Trash aspects. Sweeping the area with his gaze a single time to ensure that his plan to clean up the space had gone perfectly, Joe replicated the effect three additional times in rapid succession.

Now standing on ground that was firm, laser-level straight, and a perfect cube, Joe pulled out his survey tool and touched the blueprint to it. A ghostly image of the smithy projected onto that space, and he adjusted its position fractionally until the city planner was finally happy with it.

Joe activated the ritual, needing to suck in a breath as the circles and carefully designed diagrams attempted to warp and distort under the ambient energetic fields. Thanks to his experience dealing with the mental weight of aspects, the Ritualist had a firm grasp on what he needed to do to correct the situation. Correcting the instability with his willpower and Mana Manipulation, he held firm and fully activated the ritual, *forcing* the power to move along the swirling pattern he envisioned.

He was slightly curious as to what the process looked like in terms of his character sheet. When the strain became manageable, Joe shifted his focus ever so slightly to watch the notifications of his crafting attempt. His eyes widened, and he sucked in a sharp breath of surprise at just how *badly* it was going.

Ritual activation commencing.

Caution: Enhanced instability is leading to loss of aspects—40% increase—as the aspects are not properly contained in an aspect jar.

Aspects drained!

Trash: 20,000 → 28,000.

Damaged: 10,000 → 22,400

Common: 4,000 → 5,600

Uncommon: 1,600 → 2,283

Rare: 800 → 1,120 Failure! Insufficient aspects!

Joe was hit by a wave of nausea as the ritual began to fail, mana pouring out of him as he did everything he could to stabilize the situation—all while panicking and trying to think of a way to salvage everything. Hitting upon an idea, he barked out a command: "Substitute insufficient Rare aspects with Special Aspects: Molten!"

Determining... request accepted! 100 Molten aspects converted into 1,000 Rare aspects, Unstable Molten energy, 3,000 Common aspects, 10,132 Trash aspects. Unstable Molten Energy is automatically imbued within the construction!

Heaving in a deep breath as the pressure on his mind alleviated, Joe refocused on his task, completing the smithy over the next few seconds. He collapsed to the ground as the strain vanished, then took a few moments to collect himself before looking at the information of the building that he had just erected.

You have created: Smithy of the Unstable Student.

The Smithy of the unstable student is a volatile center of forgecraft suffused with unstable energy! Create items where the laws of metallurgy intertwine with the whims of chaotic chance! Within these walls, a remarkable phenomenon will occur. For every creation brought to life in this forge, there is a 20% chance that the resulting item will express the extraordinary ability to repair minor damage over time!

This fortuitous gift comes with a warning to be mindful of the mercurial nature of this establishment! A 40% chance of failure hovers over the surface of each attempted item, and upon its completion, it may inexplicably return to a molten state.

"Not ideal, but to be fair... that was really pushing it. I'd bet money that failure chance is my fault for letting the energy go wild. If I had been able to *only* use Molten aspects, I bet I would have gotten the twenty percent chance of items being repaired without the possibility of losing them." Joe wiped the sweat off his brow, flinging his hand to the side and watching as the small droplets of water turned to beads of ice before hitting the ground.

Walking into the building, he paced directly over to a smithy station and pulled out his aspect ingot hammer and gave it a test swing. It flickered in his hand like a cartoon during a quarter-second power outage. "*Whew,* this instability is absolutely insane. We need to fix that before anything else can get done."

Luckily for him, as he was working directly with aspects and mana, he didn't need any fuel for a fire. Joe didn't need to heat anything up, he just needed the correct area and tools to work with his materials. Since he was attempting to make a Student-ranked stabilization item, he decided to make cubes instead of tiny pyramids. He voiced his reasoning to himself, used to working alone at this point. "Cubes are more stable, right? Pyramids are stable, and cubes are a couple of those melded together. Yes. Solid logic. Cubes it is."

The first one was made in only a few minutes, as he had practiced making plenty items of a similar nature back on Alfheim. Yet, just as the first cube was completed, the properties of the building he was working at kicked in, reducing the completed item to molten metal.

Joe helplessly considered the smithy he had created and couldn't help but practically *feel* the debuff emanating from its walls. To an omni-crafter like him, this was no better than a cursed place where magical making could easily go wrong. Even *knowing* that he needed to be careful, *certain* that he had executed his efforts perfectly and flawlessly, the two-in-five chance that anything he created within its walls would fall apart had activated, leaving behind an unusable mess of metal.

This caused the Ritualist to realize that even though what he had just created was still reusable to others, it was *unutterably* worthless to him. Since the item was reduced to goopy metal instead of aspects, it was no longer a crafting material he could work with. "Hopefully, I'll be able to hand that off to a smith who will put it to use. Feces… I didn't think this through."

He *could* try to reclaim some of the aspects he had put into the object by using a Field Array, but since he was using his spatial storage device instead of an aspect jar, there'd be a loss of potential both on the way in and on the way out. Joe sighed heavily, realizing that the time and effort it would take to restore the object to its former state was simply not worth it.

"I need at least seven of these, and now I'm down to one hundred thirty Rare aspects. At ten aspects per try, I can only fail seven of these before I'll need to go find something to break down." Happily, by maintaining his consistency and careful attention to every detail of the process, he only failed another two times over the next hour and a half, completing the set of seven stabilizers he needed for most of his everyday work.

Joe looked over the seven cubes, trying to convince himself that this was *all* he needed for now. "Two in a straight line with me as the center, five in a pentagram around that to make the prime of seven. Yeah, sure, I bet it'd be more stable with a set of three forming a triangle within the pentagram. But this'll just have to do for… for… *no*! I have forty more aspects; I can at least try!"

The next cube that he attempted to make melted into a puddle of metal as soon as it was nearing completion, but with his remaining resources, he created three in a row that gained the bonus that this building could impart, becoming able to heal from minor damage automatically. "Just like that, I'm down to only a single Rare aspect. Yikes and yay! Success!"

It seemed that his intense concentration on his task or perhaps the difficulty of fighting through the shifting energies in the air was acting like a skill gain multiplier. As he finished the last cube, he received a notification he had been craving.

Ritualistic Forging has Reached Student II!

It hit him suddenly that everyone else must be feeling at least as stifled as he was at this moment. Joe at least had the benefit of being a willing traveler, someone who took practically everything he owned with him, or was okay with leaving it all behind when he got the urge to move around. Now he had invested a huge amount of time into creating a settlement, only to see it destroyed, then he'd needed to flee to this world with practically nothing. The Ritualist was swept up in an uncharacteristic amount of empathy for all of the Dwarves that were suffering more deeply than he was.

He fought off the invasion of empathy and got back to work. "Only way to help them is to help myself!"

His mind *definitely* didn't turn toward another person, a

person who left him confused by his own thoughts. Someone who had helped him, kinda, but also had been lying to his team since the moment they met on the last world.

"Stop it, Joe... Daniella betrayed us!" He fumed for a second, but his anger was held in a sieve, and drained away faster than it could build up. "But... she *did* also save me and Jaxon."

Frankly, he wasn't certain which action he was affected by more. On the plus side, she wasn't on this world, and he had no way of leaving it to go find her to work through his thoughts and gain closure or... perhaps something else. At least, he didn't have a way to leave until the City was complete.

That realization had absolutely *no* bearing on why he was suddenly working faster, whistling through a slowly growing smile as he worked.

CHAPTER FIVE

After leaving the smithy, cubes cheerfully jangling together until he dropped them into storage, Joe heard a commotion in the distance and changed his heading to see what was happening. As he arrived at the scene, he was confused by what he saw at first—all the way until he realized that the World Boss hadn't simply *disappeared*. It had been crushed, yes, but its remains had been scattered all across the area. The commotion was opposing groups arguing over who should get what, or if there was value in keeping the remains at all.

"Listen up, you daft lot! All this foolishness is going to do is attract *monsters*!" one outraged Dwarf was bellowing at the milling crowd. His voice was already hoarse from shouting, and one of his fists was waving in the air while the other was clenched around his beard hard enough that he was pulling out beard hair. "What do you mean *cook* it? Are you out of your minds? Do you have the slightest inkling of whether that creature's flesh is safe to eat, or if it's *poison*? From what I can tell, the meat is a flexible stone, and its blood is flame in liquid form!"

"Don't listen to him! Embrace your inner poultry lover and

savor the taste of success!" Joe wisely decided to duck at that moment, pretending that someone else had spoken as he stifled his chuckle. His mission of stirring up the crowd complete, the Ritualist took a moment to inspect the huge pile of carcass chunks. He spared one glance back at the wild-eyed Dwarf who had been shouting at his brethren. The fellow was now clenching a fistful of loose hair in one hand as he hopped up and down in fury.

As Joe got closer to the piled corpse, the ambient temperature was noticeably and sharply increasing. He was learning exactly what the Dwarves had already discerned: the body still had all the properties of the Lava Phoenix. Specifically, it was blazing hot, enough that the bare stone below it was ever-so-slowly melting. "Err… maybe we should scatter its body around and use it to get this area warmed up?"

"Bald bro! Yeah! That's what *I* was saying!" someone chimed in on his accidental utterance. "But that scaredy bro is wimping out about the monsters 'round here. He already stopped me from hucking a chunk of this into a fire pit. *Twice*!"

Joe winced as he realized that he'd just gained the attention he was trying to avoid when he had been pouring gasoline on the fires of their shouting match, but luckily someone else was nearby to make an executive decision.

Havoc strolled up to the melting zone, a wide grin on his face and smoke puffing out through his nostrils. "That's pretty bold of all of you, putting together the remains of a Phoenix like this! I don't know if I *like* our chances against it if it manages to go through a rebirth cycle. But, ya know what? I applaud your fearlessness, and I'm ready to die together in a blaze of glorious fire."

Joe hastily backed away from the corpse mound, and he wasn't the only one. It appeared that no one else had considered the possibility of a fresh, furious Phoenix showing up while they were trying to figure out how to eat its original body. It took mere moments for the arguments to die down to nothing. Then, all at once, everyone was clamoring for the remains to be destroyed or scattered.

Havoc just shook his head, pointed at Joe, then pointed at the immense hill of what could generously be called 'meat'. The Ritualist nodded happily, understanding perfectly what Havoc wanted him to do. He moved over to stand next to the remains, set up a Field Array—as well as each of the aspect jars he had on hand—and began converting the carcass into his personal crafting materials.

He stopped almost immediately as he felt the magical *weight* of the incoming aspects. Eyes flaring wide, Joe softly groaned, "*Legendary*."

The Ritualist couldn't help but feel a touch of frustration at the fact that he was going to be getting a less than perfect conversion ratio, but Joe grit his teeth and continued the process. As he was being careful to get every single portion of the Phoenix—while also pretending that he was merely doing so out of good will and not greed—Joe stayed there far longer than he probably should have. Yet, the payoff was absolutely worth the effort. The flaming bird had been the size of a small mountain, shown in its ability to grasp the Pyramid of Panacea in one talon and drag it into the ground.

Every *speck* of it was powerful, and if he'd had an aspect conversion area set up with all of the aspect jars correctly put together, Joe likely would've even been able to gather a few *Mythic* aspects. However, as he was working with subpar collection tools, anything that may have been Mythic had been broken down to a lower form.

Joe had no complaints in the slightest about the windfall. Four and a half hours after he began, the final feather of the bird had been converted into aspects. Only the talons had been claimed by the council, deemed safe from causing the apex avian to respawn, and those were no doubt slated to be shaped into weapons.

Aspects gathered
Trash: 210,123

Damaged: 52,234
Common: 25,687
Uncommon: 4,577
Rare: 4,388
Special: 10,003 (Zombified). 100 (Anima). 111 (Molten) 688 (Phoenix)
Unique: 6,879
Artifact: 5,518
Legendary: 12,902
Mythical: 0

The Ritualist was practically *quivering* in excitement as he checked over the massive influx he'd been able to earn off of a single corpse. He had expected something to the effect of… perhaps a burst of additional Molten special aspects, maybe a *few* Legendary aspects, so earning a full five figures of the nearly-best aspect in a single sitting was an extremely pleasant shock. "The new aspect has me all excited… what's a *Phoenix* aspect, and what does it do?"

Filled with eager anticipation, Joe could only fervently hope this new material was going to be nothing short of extraordinary. The meager quantity he had acquired wouldn't allow him to have any margin for error to spend in frivolous trials across multiple items. Instead, he would need to invest these precious aspects into creations he already had extremely high hopes for and cross his fingers for a favorable outcome. "Celestial feces, I got almost thirteen *thousand* Legendary aspects, yet I'm more excited about less than seven hundred of the Special? My brain likes to mess with me."

Joe finished his project with a great sense of satisfaction and looked around the area expectantly. A moment later, slightly perplexed at his own actions, the Ritualist realized he was waiting for someone to come bellow demands or whisk him away to tackle yet another task, now that he was free to do something else. To his surprise, as he began slowly walking away, the only interactions he had were other people offering him a nod or a customary greeting.

It was a delightful departure from his new normal, and Joe decided immediately that he liked this shift in his daily dynamic. Still, his out-of-sorts reaction made him slightly introspective. "Have I gotten so used to being barked at, to following orders and instructions from someone else, that I feel a little bit lost now that I'm charting my own course? Or... could it just be that I haven't had coffee in a while?"

Burble! AutoMate poked its head out of the Ebonsteel mug Joe wore attached to his belt by a carabiner, looking at him expectantly with the coffee beans that it had instead of eyes. A moment later, it began to quiver in place as a layer of frost covered the now-exposed portion of its body. Joe quickly dismissed the elemental and lifted his coffee mug to his lips. It was filled with cold brew, something the elemental had never been able to produce before.

"Oh, shoot! I should figure out how to repair this mug without accidentally unsummoning you." Sucking down the drink, he looked over the damage the mug had accumulated rescuing him from a heavy attack. Joe let out a satisfied sigh, nodding to himself as he practically skipped back to his guild-hall. "Yep, that was the problem! Thanks, buddy, I will make it up to you soon. Good, what else should I get done...? I can build practically any building I have in my stack of blueprints now. Maybe we should start with-"

As if the universe was conspiring to thwart his enthusiasm about doing his own thing, at that moment, a notification went out to everyone in the area, evidenced by the sudden cessation of movement and multitude of vacant gazes.

Congratulations! You have founded a Camp-

Congratulations! You have founded a Hamlet-

Caution! You are attempting to increase your town level from a tier one Hamlet to a Village! As this is the first time this message has been sent out, you will receive slightly more information than otherwise would be available. In order to increase your town ranking, your Hamlet will need to meet certain requirements.

1) Surviving Beast Waves. (Hamlet → Village: 5 waves.) — Condition not met.

2) Filled building slots. (Hamlet: Trash: NA, Damaged: NA, Common: 20, Uncommon: 5) — Condition overridden due to extreme rarity. (Artifact ranked Alchemy Hall, Rare Smithy)

3) Morale modifier: 0+-25. — Condition met.

As conditions two and three are met, the Beast Waves will begin sometime within the next 24 hours. Each wave at this town ranking will occur once per 12 hours. If, at any time, the Town Hall or guildhall is destroyed and a new one has been rebuilt, the town will revert to a Hamlet and need to go through all Beast Waves once more.

Trying to understand why this message had appeared at this moment, Joe searched the area for what had changed, gaze landing on the pyramid which had been fully repaired in a third of the time he'd been expecting. The facility was once again a beautiful, shining beacon of hope for everyone.

It also filled him with a deep sense of dread as the ground began rumbling the very instant the message vanished. Looking out to the horizon, he tried to determine if the Beast Wave had come early, but there was no sign of any monsters whatsoever. "Does anyone know what's happening?"

No one had enough knowledge to formulate a proper answer, but as Joe walked closer to the pyramid, he noticed that the shaking of the ground dramatically increased. Over the next few minutes, it grew more intense, then slowly began dissipating; almost as though the source of the shaking were moving into the distance. With no answers to be found, Joe simply had to shake his head and toss his hands in the air. Clearly, the Artifact building had done *something*, but he had no idea how to figure out what that 'something' was. "Abyss, *I* built it! If anyone should have answers, it should be me."

He needed to leave that mystery alone for now, so he decided to join the war meeting that was almost certainly happening in the guildhall. Joe hurried over, only to find his path blocked by countless Dwarves conglomerating around the guildhall, each of them having had the same idea about how to gain an answer to this dilemma.

Initially uncertain of how to skip the line and gain entry, Joe smirked as an idea blossomed in his mind. Activating Omnivault, the Ritualist effortlessly propelled himself over the crowd. Gently pressing off of—and inadvertently blocking—a Dwarf, Joe executed a flawless front flip, crossing into the cozy entryway just before the door was fully closed to block off the cacophony of sound.

A hand *slapped* him out of the air, sending him spiraling through the air until he smashed into the wall. Moments later, those same hands were grasping his shoulders and helping him to his feet. Jaxon looked at Joe with great concern, an apologetic expression plastered on his face where a red handprint was already forming into a bright bruise.

"Joe! Oh, my friend, I'm *so* sorry. Truly, I didn't realize it was you coming in right behind me! I thought it was a giant mosquito after my blood again. You were moving so fast, and Joe… you were *horizontal.* Just like those pests flying around! Even after taking the initiative to swat you, I didn't realize it was *you* until a grinning, bald shadow struck me. That's always been you, so it slapped some sense into me!"

"Careful over there! We just had the door fixed, and humans clearly don't make for good wallpaper. Just *paint,* but you need to hit them harder. Much harder," Stu Sarcasm, Dwarven Master of Sarcasm jeered as he reluctantly allowed Joe into the ongoing meeting.

Technically, the Ritualist had proven his worth by defeating him in a competition between masters and should've been on the Council of Dwarven Masters. That technicality was likely the only reason he wasn't attempting to send the human through the wall himself at this point, but he was now clearly eyeing Jaxon as a possible target.

The fact that he had slapped Joe was likely the deciding factor in allowing him to stay in the room.

A notification pinged in Joe's ear, and a message suddenly

arrived in front of his eyes. Then a couple dozen more, and he looked at them in confusion. "Mail? I wasn't getting emails… oh, shoot! Come to think of it, I've only ever opened these in my respawn room or at a coffee shop. Do I not have… whatever passes for internet service in this world, if I'm not the guildhall? Or maybe it's just any specifically designated area?"

Seeing as the ongoing conversation was currently focused around small talk, Joe took a moment to skim the top few messages. "One from mom, I'll read that in just a minute. This one is definitely spam; glad to see that some things never change. But this…?"

His eyes narrowed as he read the subject and first couple lines of the letter.

Subject: Bittersweet Safety.

Joe, I hope when you get this letter you are somewhere safe and far away from the Elven theocracy. I've managed to secure my position in the Architects guild, and I'm sure you are thriving on Jotunheim. I know that I was not totally honest with you, but I hope that saving you at great risk to myself was enough to-

"*Daniella.*" Scowl distorting his face, Joe slapped the message away, his finger hovering over the 'delete message' button. Taking a few breaths to get himself in a calm state of mind, he simply closed it out and decided to deal with this issue later. Refocusing on the conversation, he realized he had already missed some important tidbits.

"-saying we aren't *ready* to handle monsters. We're finding attrition with the few random animals around here. I say we should just tear down the pyramid and be done with it." Master Dreamstrider was saying, earning himself a dirty look both from Joe and far more ominously from Jake the Alchemist. "We could get far more buildings, set up a few walls, actually get *prepared* for this place. Right now, we're still recovering from leaving our world and people behind; we shouldn't have to dive straight into the next survival situation."

Snow took his words seriously, not scoffing or insulting him for making such a self-sabotaging suggestion. She even nodded slowly, earning a considering look from Jake as he sized up the room, clearly intent on destroying everyone in it if they tried to mess with his precious baby. “I understand your concerns, but… think about what you’re saying, Dreamstrider. We're the *Dwarven Oligarchy*. We don't flee from a battle that we have the means to win. I think Havoc is correct, and I’m going to stand by that choice. We just need to buckle down and prepare ourselves to weather the storm. To that end, I’m ordering a hard ration on any drinks that impair judgment as we speak.”

There was a round of groaning from outside the building that shook the water glasses on the table and drowned out Snow’s next murmur, a quiet and considering, “Besides, that monstrosity has a million points of Artifact-ranked durability. I don't know if we even *could* break it down in only twelve hours without going all-out.”

A Dwarf that Joe recognized from the reception area of the guildhall pushed through the crowd and handed Master Stu a folded note at that moment. The Master of Sarcasm opened it, cupping his hands to ensure no one around him could read the words, and allowed a smirk to grow on his face.

Jake coughed into a closed fist with a clear intention to be heard, earning dozens of eyes on him in the next moment. “On that note, I am uncertain if you have noticed, but there was a slight shaking of the ground-”

Havoc quirked an eyebrow and pointed at the wall, where two of the windows had shattered. Ignoring him, the Alchemist continued his train of thought. “As you should have seen when the pyramid was being drawn to this planet, the base of it contains a massive drill. I believe it is currently descending deep into the crust of the world, looking for a source of lava that it can use to empower itself as it did in the… previous area we had settled.”

Jake was being careful not to say ‘Alfheim’, as that was a grim reminder that this society was now a Shattered Race. Even though he should be listening carefully to the Alchemist, Joe's gaze was drawn to Master Stu as he pushed the folded note he had received across the table to Grandmaster Snow. She opened it with a sigh, then seemed to read and reread the contents, a frown rapidly developing on her face. "When the drill has breached the mantle, I believe the Alchemy building will become even more durable, thanks to the flows of magma that will funnel through it."

"Do you think that's why it was able to survive for so long in the clutches of the Lava Phoenix?" Joe's academic curiosity was piqued, and once more, the Alchemist had his undivided attention. "Did it have a secondary layer of protection which was constantly refreshing, since it was submerged in the superheated stone? That would also explain why we didn't notice the drill when it was first built… it didn't have to go farther than a few feet before reaching magma–"

"Nerds." Havoc hooted at them, forcing the two 'humans' to nod at each other in acknowledgment that they'd continue this conversation at a later time. "Here's what I say. We all have our answer. Let's get the word out; it's time to put the pedal to the grindstone. The Legion should start digging trenches, the civilians should contribute wherever they can, and the rest of us need to play to our strengths."

"I can rally the engineer corps and Earth Mages to start building walls to protect the core of our location, providing a fallback point," Bauen called out, allowing Joe to release some internal tension he hadn't noticed before this moment. He hadn't been sure if his favorite Dwarven engineer had survived the escape to this world, or the World Boss, until he had stepped out of the press of people in the room. "They'll be rough, but we all know that walls don't count toward our building slots. Any protection is better than nothing at all."

"Good, we have a rough plan." Snow's gaze shifted toward Joe, a slight chill in them that the human couldn't make sense of. "I know that you're likely considering going out there and setting up traps, or doing some other magical malarkey. Happily, we don't need strange, creative solutions to this situation. Killing monsters is something that we're extremely well acquainted with, and I have a request of you… if you're willing to work with us on this project. We can trust you to put in your best effort, yes?"

Joe's head tilted to the side, not quite certain why she was speaking to him as if he didn't have as much skin in the game as they did. *Literally* every building that existed in this world currently was—he amended that thought before he finished it. Jake was technically the owner of the pyramid. Still, he owned two-thirds of this Hamlet at the moment. "Of course, I am willing to help however I'm needed. What can I do?"

"We need you to solve the housing crisis that we're undergoing at the moment. The environmental debuff is insidious, slowly increasing over time while numbing our minds to how severely it's impacting us. If something doesn't change soon, we'll start to take losses. Also, morale will be impacted, which may cancel out our ability to undergo this event."

By the time Snow had finished speaking, Joe had already generated and discarded three and a half ideas on how to handle the issue. With a wide smile on his face, he threw out a grandiose salute. "I'm *on* it."

Snow sighed and closed her eyes as he turned on his heel and started walking toward the door, pushing gently through the crowd. She called after him in a slightly calmer tone, "Something *normal*, please."

CHAPTER SIX

Joe sat in the smithy that he had created, waiting for some brave Dwarf to come over and ask to use it. Until then, he figured he could work on his plans for the area. "Something normal? *Normal?* If you want normal, you need to talk to some construction-focused Dwarves. Hmph! Well... at least she was polite about it."

He let out a quiet chuckle and allowed his dramatic acting to seep away, leaving behind a stone-sober, focused Ritualist. Dozens of ideas were flashing through his mind, but almost everything that he'd done up until this point had been nearly the opposite from what could work in this area. Previously, Joe had needed to create enormous heat sinks in The Shoe to keep the area from melting down, but that was a simple matter of taking the ambient thermal energy and converting it into power for a magical air conditioning unit.

Cold was literally a lack of energy, so he couldn't as easily solve this issue by converting it into a useful power supply.

"If I could get volunteers to sit around and pump mana into some oversized rituals that would generate heat, that'd work," Joe mused quietly as he looked through his currently available options. "Can't imagine anyone would be really willing to do that, though. Not for any length of time. Oh, you're a powerful, mystical warrior who's survived centuries of conflict? Can I use you to replace propane for a few months?"

That forced a chuckle out of his mouth as he realized how hilarious he was. "Yeah, that probably won't go over too well. Maybe I should focus on a slightly larger picture? The wind is going to be stripping away any heat we do generate, so maybe I adapt my Ritual Bubbles? Put a large dome over our population center. That could work for blocking the wind, though I'd need to make it semi-permeable to allow air through."

Ever so slowly, Joe refined the key requirement areas his project needed. His hope was that, as the tasks were laid out, a single guiding principle would take over and let him solve all of the issues at once. Eventually, he had a rough version of what he needed, but still no ritual designed to implement his concepts. "Comes down to the fact that I can either make one enormous bubble that covers a specific area, or I can make a ton of bubble 'tents'."

After a significant amount of consideration, Joe decided that a single, enormous dome would essentially be an invitation to destroy their only protection against the elements. It would also require significant upkeep, mana investment, and multiple other factors that he likely didn't even know about at the moment. "If only I could figure out how to harness the wind, it wouldn't be such a huge jump from collecting thermal energy to collecting kinetic energy. But… that'd probably make it a lot harder for us to enter or leave, at least without destroying the fragile bubble structure."

He groaned and stretched his back, rubbing his bald head as he tried to decide how he could make everything as autonomous as possible. Eventually, Joe gave up and just started scribbling notes. "Tons of smaller rituals it is. If I set up a ritual on a Ritual Tile, I can make it generate a ten-foot bubble that will block the wind. As long as no one's poking the outside or inside with sharp objects, they should be able to move through the bubble, if they go slow enough. That way, everyone can be in charge of their own comfort."

Drawing out a rough design, he placed two different handprints in the center of a circle. "Pumping mana into the right-side activation sequence will create a bubble tent; pushing it into the left will convert their mana to heat. If a couple people at a time are in each tent, they can share the cost, so no one gets too low to defend themselves if there's an emergency. Good. I like this. Simple. Effective. Also, not *my* problem after I make it. I like that part best."

Since what he was making was actually two distinct rituals, he was able to keep the design as a simple Beginner rank. Creating a prototype, Joe placed his hand on the right outline of a hand and began imbuing it with mana. Sparks flew off the original tile, and the entire stone item shattered as though it'd been made of glass.

Damage taken: 73 penetrating damage.

Exquisite Shell: 11,596/11,669

"Well. Right. Gotta account for our location." He needed to make the design at least Uncommon, also known as Apprentice rank. Thinking it through, Joe realized that there was a simple answer: first, he'd combine the two rituals, keeping it as efficient as possible. Second, he added the patterns needed for the bubble to be reflective on the outside. That way, those resting within would also have privacy from anyone who wasn't meant to be part of the small group.

Those simple changes brought it up right to the edge of what could still be considered an Apprentice ritual, while still keeping it compact enough that he could rapidly rattle these off. After laying out his stabilization cubes, Joe felt a subtle shift in the air. That was his cue to get to work.

Apprentice Ritual creation complete: +100 Reductionist experience.

"Ah, that's right. Experience from crafting is always nice. Now, let's see. Takes about fifteen minutes for each of these to be created." Joe muttered to himself as he let his Aspect Inscriber flow across tile after tile. "Let's assume that four people can comfortably stay in each bubble, and we'll set up six rotations of four hours apiece for sleep—thank goodness everyone has massive Constitution scores—I'll need… only about three hundred and sixty of these to make sure all of the eighty-five thousand people in the area get a chance to recuperate. Wow, that's a lot less than I'd expected to need to make."

Then he realized that, even if he was able to continuously make these until he had everything he needed, that was still nearly ninety hours of work that had to be done. "I can get close to forty-eight of these done before the Beast Wave hits, but then I'll probably be pretty useless. Luckily I had some coffee, but I have no idea when the last time I slept was."

The **scritching** of his inscriber burning aspects into stone was the only sound that reached his ears over the next few hours, until someone politely knocked on the door. He looked up as it opened, meeting the eyes of a slightly surprised Dwarf. "Ah, sorry about that. Didn't know anyone was in here. Am I correct in thinking that this is a smithy? Would you mind if I…?"

Joe nodded to a stone bench that was a part of the building, not wanting to split his attention further until he'd finished on his current Ritual Tile. As soon as the last line had been drawn minutes later, and the aspects were stable, he pushed himself to his feet and stretched. Then he turned to address the Dwarf. "Thanks for your patience; those suckers tend to explode pretty violently if I don't finish them in a single sitting."

That earned the haphazard pile of stone next to Joe a casual glance, the Dwarf merely nodding in acceptance. "These things happen when you're pursuing your craft."

Her nonchalant understanding of the situation put a light smile on the Ritualist's face; Joe enjoyed finding like-minded individuals. "As it turns out, I was looking for a manager for this building. You interested? You'll be able to use the workshop as much as you want for free, so long as everyone else who wants to use it gets charged. To be fair, I'm not sure what exactly we're going to be using as currency on this world, but I'm sure we'll figure something out."

"Of course we will! There's no way to tax us if we don't have a standardized way of paying those taxes." The resignation in those words made Joe cackle, and it put a small smile on the till-now-stoic face of the mustachioed Dwarf. "I'll take the job. I assume everyone needs to figure out their own fuel and ingot source?"

"You know it." Joe extended a hand to shake on their deal. "I'm Joe; what can I call you, Ms...?"

"Just call me Smitty, everyone else does." Now her smile was extremely wide, causing the ends of her mustache to be level with her pointed chin. "Ya gonna finish up what you're doing there? Do you mind if I start heating up the forge?"

"Yes, and no, in that order." Joe dropped back down to the floor, waving for her to do as she pleased. "Any word on the Beast Wave, or what else is going on out there?"

"Kind of." She shrugged as she walked over to the closest forge and pulled a sack out of some storage device, producing lumps of coal in the next moment. She arranged the first few, then pointed her open palm at the black chunks and concentrated. An instant later, they began smoldering, and she nodded approvingly. "The scouts have been shouting at each other for the last hour or so. I guess living on an enormous, flat wasteland has a few benefits. One of those is that you can see the monsters *waaay* before they get here. Far as I can tell, we've got about a hundred minutes until the first of them closes in on our warriors."

"Any concerns about pulling through?"

"Not unless a *whole* lot more monsters show up than we expect." Smitty scoffed as though the question was directly offensive. "Almost everyone was told to stay back and go about our business. So, here I am."

"Fair enough." Joe considered his pile of tiles, deciding to work until he'd finished seven more. He should be able to get through six and two-thirds before the first group of monsters showed up, which meant he'd only be five minutes late to the battle if he wanted to see how it was going. Getting back to work was tough after finally having someone new and interesting nearby to break his focus, but this was important. The Ritualist pushed on, completing all of his work and managing to ignore the sounds of battle until his ritual was completed.

Then he jumped to his feet, swept everything into his codpiece, and hurriedly waved at Smitty, who was just starting to heat up the first ingot of metal she was going to be using for her craft. Just before he rushed out the door, he came to a sudden halt and looked back at the Dwarf with a cheeky grin. "Sorry, forgot to mention, this building is unstable. There's a forty percent probability that anything you make in here turns back into molten metal just as you finish it. Don't worry, there's also a one in five chance that it'll gain the ability to self-repair… slightly."

He heard a light curse, which was bit off as Smitty recognized the potential value of the second option. As he closed the door, the swearing was reduced to mere grumbling instead. Joe had no problem with grumbling. So long as the work was getting done and getting done well grumbling was something that happened in every industry.

Rushing out into the cold, he followed the bellowing and sounds of combat. As he took in the view of what his allies were fighting, the human's mouth dropped open. "This is the *first* wave? You've got to be kidding me! Those things are massive!"

He inspected them as he hurried closer, wondering if he could figure out an easy counter for the monsters.

Defeatist Fluttering Penguins. These are the world's standard prey animals. At the bottom of nearly every food chain on Jotunheim, the Defeatist Fluttering Penguins fully expect that their assault is going to fail. Typically, upon taking 30% losses, they will scatter in all directions. During a Beast Wave, they are compelled to attack their target: the Town Hall or guildhall governing the rank of the settlement.

The flightless birds were able to hop enormous distances, flapping their fin-like wings to allow them to hover slightly. The smallest of them was fifteen feet tall, and there had to be at least four hundred of them in this first wave. Strangely enough, they didn't surround the area and attack from all sides, instead following the bird in front of them as if they were sheep following a shepherd off a cliff.

It was a *slaughter,* to the point that Joe couldn't remember when he'd ever seen the Legion have such a collectively good time.

CHAPTER SEVEN

The Penguins didn't have much in the way of defensive options nor offensive capabilities. Just as the system had informed them, these were essentially prey animals. They were the equivalent of rabbits or level one rats on another world. Even so, they had an extremely dense outer layer of blubber protecting them against the ravaging cold of Jotunheim, which at least gave them excellent natural defenses against blunt attacks, while also slowing down any edged weapon that parted their flesh.

Truly, the only reason they hadn't been completely destroyed yet was their sheer size. Since they were so tall, the Dwarves needed to jump into the air or be on a raised embankment to target their heads directly. Since none of those were great options, they were forced to carve their way through the rotund bodies of the squawking Penguins swing by swing.

Contrary to Joe's expectations, the Dwarves were loving it.

"Annoying things... they just ignore the trenches! Good thing I had my spear ready to greet this one!"

"Look! I carved out a little house for myself... it's so *warm*!" The words of this particular Dwarf were slightly muffled, as they were emanating from a gaping wound in the side of a bird that was shrieking and flapping wildly.

Joe blinked several times and shook his head as he tried to wrap his head around what he was seeing. The Dwarves weren't taking this threat seriously, and it showed in the strange, over-the-top methods they were using to kill off the creatures. Another Dwarf had a different mission in mind, but it wasn't any better. "Get out of there! You're going to make the meat all sweat-salty, bro!"

"What a surprise, you see monsters, and your stomach starts rumbling, dudette." That comment got a multitude of laughs and jeers at the expense of the Dwarf in full plate armor. Joe couldn't tell for certain, but there was likely some serious blushing going on under that helmet.

The Ritualist looked at the situation at hand with new eyes. Pieces started clicking into place in his mind, and he realized something extremely important. "Wait, I think these Beast Waves actually *are* our food supply. The ground is completely flat, and until the Beast Wave started, we had no idea where any monsters were. *Hey*! All of you, stop playing with your food! Jokes aside, I think these are the only meat we're gonna be able to eat for a good, long time!"

His words rippled out through the too-relaxed encirclement, and the truth started dawning on many faces, his words being repeated over and over. Then someone looked back at Joe and scoffed, "Yo, bald bro... why should we listen to you? I say buzz off, rando."

Joe felt that comment as a physical blow, as he instantly gained a notification from the system.

Title lost: Major-General Pyrrhic, Noble Candidate for Baron. The society that granted you this title has been shattered. Remnants of the Dwarven race have shown their disapproval for your attempts to assert control, and the system has recognized that your continued usage of this title is erroneous.

"*You*...! You made me lose a title!" Joe sputtered as he tried to make sense of what was happening. He had no idea that his hard-earned rewards could be taken away so easily. "I was a Major General! I had a massive capability to help us succeed! Abyss, if I *died,* you'd do fifty percent more damage until I respawned!"

The Dwarf he was bellowing at by the end of his rant had the good grace to look slightly shamefaced for a moment, though his eyes hardened a moment later. "Guess you should've thought about that before trying to tell us what to do, *civilian* bro."

Joe lost sight of that particular Dwarf in the next few seconds as the death of the Penguins had apparently reached a breaking point. With a terrified squawk, the line of birds scattered into the distance, some of them running away, some of them circling the troops and looking for a way through. With their enemies no longer coming along and cheerfully throwing themselves on their weapons, the Dwarves suddenly had to struggle to chase them down and remove them from existence.

The Penguins were surprisingly fleet of foot, moving faster as more of their number was exterminated. Then, when there were only fifteen percent remaining, they dropped to their stomachs and slid across the frozen earth at twice the speed they'd been moving. The Dwarves started cursing as they switched to longer range weapons and began relying on their spellcasters to take down the sliding targets. "Abyss! Finish them off!"

It wasn't difficult to find them, as they stood fifteen feet tall and hopped like crazy. None of them should be able to do too much to cause issues for the Hamlet. At least, that was what Joe thought until the system informed him of the next piece of unfortunate news.

The guildhall has been destroyed! Town upgrade canceled. Caution! All remaining Beast Waves will still be targeting this location! If you rebuild your guildhall or build a Town Hall, the Beast Waves may overlap.

"*What?*" Joe bellowed as he turned and raced to the center of town. Sure enough, as he got closer, he could see the remnants of the building scattered across the ground. A half dozen of the Penguins slid, bounced into the air, and blasted through the walls. An instant later, a hair-thin tendril of mana shot out and sliced each of them perfectly in half.

A very displeased Grandmaster Snow stepped out of the rubble, shoving a falling wall in the other direction. "Somebody *please* tell me this is a joke. We lost our guildhall in the *first wave*? To *Penguins*?"

Her eyes darted over to Joe and narrowed slightly. The human crossed his arms to showcase his own extremely disgruntled expression. "Don't look at me; I'm not in charge of anything. The Dwarves on the front line made sure to make that *eminently* clear to me. They refused a *warning*, and it made me lose my title with the Legion."

Snow looked slightly above his head and squinted, which would make his name and currently equipped title appear. As he'd always made sure to keep his title as a Major General visible so that the Dwarves would know where he stood, it being replaced with 'Despised by Humanity' was quite obvious. "Well, this is a right mess. No one's going to believe it was lost that easily, so there goes your support in the council. Great. Just… hold off on rebuilding this; let's figure out what happened and make a plan to take care of it."

"What! You can't blame me, I didn't do anything to lose my title. The system-"

Snow held up a hand, not looking at him. "The fact that the system took your title away is going to be used by some as a word of caution against you. There's already been a few… allegations. We can't know the truth of the matter, so let's just deal with the issue at hand."

He wasn't happy about it, but for the moment, Joe didn't know what else to do.

Lapsing into silence, he waited until the rest of the wave had been cleared. As soon as someone shouted that there weren't any more monsters, the system confirmed it with a notice that the wave was over. It hadn't sent a word until they'd confirmed it with their own eyes, making him wonder if that was going to come back to bite them at a later date. Several scouts went around, gathering information and asking eyewitnesses what they'd seen just before the guildhall was attacked. Soon enough, they had a preliminary report on how it had fallen.

"Reporting to the Grandmaster!" a Dwarf in light armor shouted as he sprinted over to the listless group of leadership. "The reason behind the failure to defeat the enemy in a timely manner, as well as the subsequent events, has been distilled into a report. May I offer that report publicly, or would you like to keep the information private?"

"Make sure everyone can hear it, Chief Scout," Snow loudly stated, apparently not wanting anyone to think she was trying to be anything but transparent.

"Ma'am!" The Scout saluted and began recounting events in a loud voice. "Beginning with the enemy! Each of the Beasts followed the one in front of it, moving in a single line from a point in the distance where they'd staged themselves for the assault. Their linear path suggests that they were targeting the fifteen-foot opening in the stone palisade that had been erected around the wall over the last half day, going by standard time-keeping."

"Just tell us what's going on; you don't need to qualify every statement." Snow informed him primly, her patience waning thin.

"Understood. It almost seems that the creatures were guided to this particular location, as they moved in a perfectly straight line without original line of sight." Joe heard what the Scout was saying, and a sneaking suspicion began to form in his mind. Still, he waited to interject until the remainder of the report had concluded. "Upon reaching approximately thirty percent losses, that straight line of enemies broke down and scattered across the area."

The Scout coughed lightly, looking slightly uncomfortable. "Upon reaching eighty-five percent losses, they doubled their speed and were also able to jump higher than had previously been accounted for. This allowed several of them to directly go over the currently completed sections of wall with a single bounce. Once inside the fortifications, they directly targeted the guildhall with no deviations."

"Why did no one inside of the walls defend the building? How were *Penguins* able to avoid eighty-five *thousand* battle-proven people? Surely someone stepped forward to block them?" Grandmaster McPoundy rumbled ungraciously as he glared around the area.

"That's..." The Scout hesitated, clearly not wanting to speak up and make enemies for himself. Even so, he was the one in charge of giving this report and managed to spit out the words. "No. By the time most of the people had realized that a threat had entered the area, it had already passed them. All eyewitnesses questioned on this gave approximately the same answer of 'I thought someone else was going to deal with it'. I believe that there's a heavy debuff affecting their initiative as the cold sets in."

"Objection, relevance." Havoc called out softly. "Your next excuse is going to be that your dog stepped on a bee."

Snow glared at Havoc, as absolutely *done* with his strange references to Earth culture as Joe was at this point. "Thank you for reporting the findings. If anything else comes to light please let us know."

"Okay, here's what we do." A Dwarf in the crowd started calling out to the people around him, earning lots of attention as he started speaking out before anyone else had a chance. "We start with really big walls. Like, absolutely *huge*. The best walls ever. That way, no one can get through if we don't want them in."

Havoc's eyes narrowed as he looked at the crafter who was trying to grab fifteen minutes of fame by offering an inane solution instead of a proper plan. "You! What's that on your shoulder?"

The Dwarf wilted slightly under the smoldering glare that he was receiving, looking on each of his shoulders frantically to figure out what Havoc was talking about. Seeing that his shoulders were empty, he responded with evident confusion. "Um. Nothing?"

"Exactly. Now what do you see on mine?" The Major General stood proudly, crossing his arms.

"It's… four stars?" The Dwarf seemed to know where this was going, and his reply came out flat.

"That's right! Four star-" Havoc cut himself off, looking down at his shoulder. Glancing up at the people standing ankle-deep in rubble, he slowly lowered his face and licked a crumb of broken cracker off of his shoulder, slurping it into his mouth and chewing quickly. "*Three stars*! Question. Know what that means? Answer! Keep *your* blasted mouth shut when *I'm* talking!"

"So!" With the crowd thoroughly cowed, Havoc spun on his heel and lowered his tone to speak softly to the others. "Hate to say it, but that guy had a point. Really big walls might be the way to go."

"No." Snow cut him off with a swipe of her hand. "Not right away, at least. We need more information."

Joe stepped into the silence, releasing his realization into the wild. "I think I figured out the trick to this. I can't guarantee it's correct, but it's pretty easy to test. First off, to make sure we aren't defeated by abyssal *Penguins* again, instead of a single wall, we should set up a double wall. That way, even if they hop over the first, they won't have enough room to build up speed to jump the second."

"Eh. Fair point." Havoc let the air fill with smoke as he hissed out the reluctant agreement. "What's this trick you're talking about?"

"I think this entire world is a specific scenario. Enormous, flat landscape, building a large fortification, and at minimum a City is the end state goal. The big clue is that the monsters come in waves." Joe took a deep breath and nodded as he became sure of his thoughts. "If I'm correct, back on Earth, we called this kind of scenario a 'tower defense', and it plays by some very specific rules."

CHAPTER EIGHT

The Ritualist started outlining his explanation to the people in the area who could actually make things happen. "If this is what I think it is—a tower defense—having perfect walls is actually going to be a detriment. If there isn't a space where the enemy can come walking through, they'll attack and destroy the walls before continuing on, forcing us to allocate time to rebuilding."

"I certainly hope you don't... *expect*... us to remain unprotected." Snow spoke on behalf of the assembled Masters, who nodded at her words.

Joe shook his head and waved his hand to have everyone hurry past that comment. "Not at all. Again, this is very easy to test, since they're such low-powered monsters right now. But you can't think of this world as exactly like the one we just left. The rules are different, even if it's subtle. What we need to do is essentially build out an extraordinarily large labyrinth around the city. The walls can't be fully blocked, because, again, they'll just be smashed through. Instead, we need to wrap the walls around and find out what'll keep the monsters moving along the path we set. We need multiple layers to make sure that, if they manage to get over one wall, there's another one blocking them from pressing forward."

"A labyrinth? Not a maze? Is there a difference?" Havoc interrupted as Joe took a breath.

Considering that for a moment, the human bobbed his head back and forth as he realized that, yes, there *was* a difference. "Pretty sure that mazes have their entrance and exits at the perimeter, whereas a labyrinth has an entrance at the perimeter, but the exit goal is the center. So… yes, I used correct terminology there."

While Havoc seemed ready to jump on board, Joe could tell with a single glance that his specific language wasn't enough to convince the others of the need. That was fine with him… if they wanted to let everyone die. "Look around and be realistic, people! We need to figure this out *now*. Do you actually think that the walls that you used to make to hold out wimpy little Elves are going to be effective against fifty-foot-tall behemoths? Or do you think it's more likely that there are hidden win conditions, and the reason this place has no population whatsoever…"

"…is that no one tried a new way of surviving the onslaught of monsters?" Joe's argument was finally enough to make them reluctantly nod as they slowly came around to his way of thinking.

Havoc pulled on his singed beard a couple of times as he ordered his thoughts then gestured at the rubble that was the guildhall before speaking. "At the very least, we're at a point where we can take a little chance. Pretty obvious that we need to figure out a new way of doing things, isn't it? Joe's right. Failure to adapt is what killed off millions of our brothers and sisters in the last world. Let's board this train and set sail."

"Thank you for the information, Joe. We'll take it from here and start putting these ideas into place. Once we have a layout determined, I hope you'll be willing to build a *Town Hall* on our behalf. I no longer think a guildhall would be appropriate." The Grandmasters' words were polite, yet firm. Once more, Joe looked at her quizzically, uncertain why she seemed to be pushing him away. "By chance, have you come up with a solution to the environmental factors?"

Nodding slowly, he pulled out a Ritual Tile and placed it on the ground. Quickly explaining how it worked, he activated the bubble, continuing to add mana to the system until a mental gauge **clicked** into place. Only a few moments later, the air warmed up enough that they could see their breath. Previously, it had been so cold the vapor leaving their mouths instantly turned to frost crystals and either collected on facial hair or dropped straight to the ground.

"It might take a while, possibly even another refill of mana, but pretty soon this bubble will be warm enough that you might mistake the area for a balmy coastal destination." Joe's words were met with cautious smiles as the layers of debuffs began ever-so-slowly being removed. Between the warmth and Joe's Neutrality Aura, the people assembled inside of the bubble bowl were soon blinking rapidly and moving much less carefully.

"That cold is... insidious." Stu Sarcasm still shivered slightly. "I think you should begin deploying these immediately, instead of waiting for your full quota to be complete."

Joe looked over at Snow, who was still maintaining a neutral, pleasant expression as she stared at him. "I'm happy to distribute these for free. For... for now. Something seems to have changed between all of us. I hope it changes back, or if I need to figure out a different way of interacting."

Snow's pleasant smile faded into a slight frown at that, before she turned away without a word. Joe looked at Havoc, who merely shrugged and rolled his eyes. Having nothing else to say, Joe left the Ritual Tile where it was, as the bubble slowly heated up the ground and caused a thin layer of water to appear. "Oh! A new feature that I wasn't expecting! Great, now we can secure an easy water supply. I guess if people decide to sleep in these, the beds are going to end up being boat-shaped."

That got a few uneasy chuckles, as everyone was now aware

of the strange dynamic that was evolving before their eyes. Deciding that it wasn't his problem, the human stalked away, slightly grumpy over how that interaction had gone. "Guess I'm off to make free housing for the last vestiges of the Dwarven Oligarchy."

Grandmaster McPoundy stepped out with him, expectant eyes staring at the Ritualist. "So… you made a smithy. I'm wondering if I could entice you to make a, well… *better* one?"

"What's wrong with the Smithy I already made?" A tiny smile graced Joe's lips. He knew that the building was practically cursed, but he wanted to hear the Grandmaster's reasoning. "You know what, while we are on the subject of buildings, why did Snow say that a guildhall wasn't enough? I don't get it."

"That's easy enough to explain. A guildhall is enough for a town to be built up around it, but it leaves whoever is in charge of that Guild as overall owner of the settlement. You can't have a Town Hall built in a town built around a guildhall, but you can have as many guildhalls as you want in a settlement centered around a town hall."

The Dwarf sent an annoyed look into the distance, where smoke was billowing out of a chimney. "As for the smithy you made? Too low of rarity. Ignoring the extra features you put into this one, fact of the matter is, if I try to make a *real* item in there, I'm going to end up turning the little workshop into a crater the first time it fails."

"Snow wants other guilds to be available? Or just wants to ensure they have control of the town?" The smile had long been wiped off of Joe's face. It only deepened into a slight scowl as he recalled that Grandmaster McPoundy had done all of his work in a Subspace *within* a smithy, not at an actual forge that anyone else could use. He reluctantly nodded, having no choice but to shrug his shoulders helplessly. "Sorry to say, I have nowhere near the resources to put something like that together right now. I'm guessing you want at least an Artifact-rank building?"

"If it won't be too much trouble." McPoundy nodded a few

times as though it were a casual exchange. "You're great, bald human friend. I'll leave you to it, then!"

Joe watched the Dwarf go, his left eyebrow raised high in the air. Murmuring to himself, he rolled his eyes and started walking away. "Yeah, *that's* not happening until I get an official Quest from him. Going to make him supply all of the necessary resources, too. 'If it wouldn't be too much trouble'. Pah. He doesn't just make tools, he *is* one!"

With the guildhall destroyed and Jake still refusing access to the pyramid for anyone, Joe had only one other option if he didn't just want to drop a bubble where he was standing and get to work. He trudged to the forge McPoundy had just casually insulted and plopped down onto the floor, ignoring the ringing blows of hammer on metal as Smitty and a few unfamiliar Dwarves continued working on their own projects.

He pulled out his Aspect Inscriber, stared down at a Ritual Tile, and shook his head. "Nope, too sleepy to do free work right now."

Joe stepped outside of the building, walked over to the back corner behind the front door—where he should be hidden from casual view—and activated a Ritual Tile. A bubble appeared around him at once, barely distorting or obscuring his view at all, though no one else would be able to see in. Knowing that there was going to be quite a bit of water generated, Joe considered going off and finding some sort of tarp, chunk of wood, or other item that would allow him to float. Then he remembered that they were in a wasteland, and the only things that existed were whatever anyone could carry on their backs during their escape.

With a groan of frustration at his sleep being further delayed, he quickly set up a ritual to collect the water in the area. As it was a Novice-ranked ritual, Joe was able to create it in midair, and instantly. One quarter of a second after the ritual was complete, it exploded in his face. The potential damage was completely mitigated by his Exquisite Shell, being mostly unstructured mana and wind. He blinked once, twice, then pulled out his stabilization cubes and set them up. Using a Field Array to dig a square well one meter wide by ten meters deep, Joe recreated the ritual in midair above his makeshift cistern.

The ritual activated with little fanfare, though it flickered concerningly at first. Then it did its job perfectly, running smoothly and without any issue. As the icy ground he was on began to melt, droplets of water collected in the center of the ritual, only to drop into the opening. The Ritualist had ensured that it was designed to only collect water that was *above* the surface of that hole, so it wouldn't create any issues with grabbing the same water over and over. "I wonder if a Student-ranked stabilization setup is overkill for a Novice ritual?"

Completely unable to make his curiosity quiet down, Joe took one of the cubes and tilted it a fraction of an inch to the side. There was no change in the ongoing ritual, so he took away the outer five cubes and waited to see if anything would change. Then he poked the first cube in the triangle, receiving a blast of mana, wind, and water for his trouble. "Noted. Don't mess with the ritual while it is in place and active."

It was the work of a moment to replace the cubes and the ritual, so he settled in for a nap as the land he was laying on slowly shifted and warmed. Even though Joe was laying directly on the ground with only his Robe of Liquid Darkness for a pillow, he slept deeply and well. Hours later, his eyes fluttered open as the sound of bladed edges meeting flesh reached his ears.

The squawk of pained, enraged Penguins clarified what was happening. "Musta slept all the way to the next wave. Well, hope they can handle it."

Joe realized that he must have been far more exhausted than he'd realized, as his mind was now spinning and whirling with its usual speed and efficiency. A quick glance in his makeshift cistern showed him that only a couple feet worth of water had been collected, and he had an oversized ice cube down there to show for his efforts. Just for fun, and because he needed them for more useful rituals, Joe pulled the cubes away and let the detonation of the Novice ritual wash over him. "Ah… probably the closest I'm getting to a shower for a long time."

When he walked into the smithy, Joe found a bright smile on his face, so he set about his work with gusto. "I forget sometimes that, even though a high Constitution can let us delay getting sleep, that doesn't mean we need *none*. Let's see if I can get the creation of these Ritual Tiles down to ten minutes a pop."

This time, instead of creating all of the circles by hand, Joe set up the stabilization cubes around himself and directly imprinted the first two circles onto the Ritual Tile in an instant. Then he only needed to draw out the Apprentice circle to maximize his speed of creation. If Joe wanted, he could push himself to be able to create that third circle instantly as well, but didn't feel like he had a good enough grasp on the intricacies of his Somatic Ritual Casting to be able to hold the ritual in his mind perfectly and cast it with the instability of Jotunheim working against him. "Maybe by the time I've finished the first hundred?"

Fun little challenge in mind, the stack of ritual bubble tents on his left began growing precipitously. Joe soon found that he had been overly optimistic: it actually took until the one hundred *fiftieth* creation of the tiles before he was comfortable imprinting the ritual directly with his thoughts. Then he was able to make one of the bubbles every minute, though he needed to take a short break every fifth one. The mental strain and heavy focus on each individual detail was incredibly taxing, but the much-enhanced speed made it worth it.

Working in the flow state, Joe only stopped when he reached for a fresh tile, only to have his hand touch the floor. His eyes focused on the ground, and he blinked a few times to moisten them. "Would you look at that? Went a little overboard… I think I have four stacks of a hundred instead of only the bare minimum. Well, I'm sure there's going to be a few people out there interested in privacy. Doesn't hurt to be over-prepared."

Pleased with his progress, Joe looked over his notifications, specifically the experience notifications that he'd been ignoring in favor of completing each of the tiles as quickly as possible. "Sum up the experience gain as a single notification, please."

The slew of messages rapidly condensed, turning into a final, single message for him to stare at as his smile grew wider.

Reductionist class experience gained: 4,000!

Congratulations! Your class, Reductionist, has reached level five! To commemorate this momentous occasion, you have been granted a token. At any time, you can choose to exchange the token for the blueprints to a Monument! Hint: There will be times when exchanging the token will result in a better blueprint. Keep your eye out for monument-worthy events!

"That's... nice. Kind of underwhelming for a milestone level? I'm certainly not going to complain, though. I *could* have only gotten a notification that I'd reached level five." Joe looked around the workspace he was in, finding that Smitty was patiently waiting for his attention.

He waved her over, noting the slightly guilty expression on her face. Words spilled out of her mouth as soon as she was at a conversationally appropriate distance. "Sorry to say, I just don't know what to collect from the other smiths. They've been creating stuff, but I'm not sure if I should take a finished project as a tax, or if I should-"

"Don't worry about it for now." The Reductionist firmly cut her off. "Until we have a system in place, all we can do is frantically work together without trying to squeeze blood from a stone. I know most of us have a whole lot of nothing, so until we're all earning some income, I'm not going to hold your feet over the fire for something that's not costing me anything. Tell you what... give it seventy-two hours, then start taking every fifth item created as payment. That's essentially a twenty percent tax, and pretty high, but we kinda have a monopoly going here."

After agreeing to the change, they exchanged a few other pleasantries before Joe politely excused himself and went out to see what changes had been made while he'd been sleeping and working. There was a thick, black smoke rising in the distance, and he began trudging toward the smoky beacon while shaking his head. "Seriously, what're they doing out there? Burning Penguin blubber for heat? Did they somehow figure out how to light the walls on fire?"

Joe decided that he'd simply go and seek the answers out for himself, instead of waiting on a second or third-hand account of the situation. Even as he began Omnivaultin closer, he realized that something inside of him still wanted to be actively engaged in what was going on, instead of being a passive civilian. "You know what, Mate? I don't care that I'm no longer a Major General, and I've got no idea what bug crawled into Snow's nose, but the next time there's a monster wave, I'm going to get some practice!"

Burble! the coffee elemental excitedly cheered him on. Joe wasn't certain if the summoned creature really knew what was going on, or if it was just matching his energy. Either way, having a conversational companion was important. The Ritualist had been getting too many sidelong glances as he muttered to himself while working. This way, since he was talking to his coffee cup, Joe was certain no one would think he was losing his mind.

CHAPTER NINE

"*There* you are! I've been looking around for you everywhere. Do you have any idea how out of alignment all of the spines of these Penguins are?" Jaxon merrily hollered at Joe, accidentally fracturing the back of the monster he was riding on in that moment of inattention. "Ooh! *Crunchy* one, aren't you?"

Joe watched his friend somersault off of the creature's back as it fell forward, the beast landing heavily on the ground—only to be slain with a single strike from an oversized axe as a Dwarf ran past. The Ritualist had seemingly joined in on the final wave that had yet to be cleared, making him wonder exactly how long he'd actually slept. The assumption was that it was only a few hours, but between his work and his sleep, he realized that he must have been out of touch for days. "Any issues out here, Jaxon? I like what they've done with the walls so far."

"I heard that was your idea? Why *wouldn't* you like it?" The counter-charismatic chiropractor chuckled. "Have you seen the other monsters yet? These Penguins are great, good eatin', too, but the Hoardlings are something *else*, you know?"

That captured his attention, and their conversation died off as Joe eagerly scanned the blood-coated battlefield, hoping to catch a glimpse of the creatures Jaxon was hinting at. His gaze roved around the expanded killing field, drinking in the sight of the casual wall design he had proposed—even now being able to witness it slowly expanding outward under the skillful craftsmanship of a multitude of Dwarven Engineers, Geomancers, and Earth Mages.

His mouth set in a flat line as he realized that, even with mages' skill in creating the layout, the walls themselves were still simply raised bulwarks coming directly from the ground, and they didn't have any quantifiable durability. "Those might as well be paper, for all the good they're going to do if the monsters decide to bust right through."

It took him a few moments to notice the creatures Jaxon was talking about, even though they were at least as tall as the Penguins and significantly wider. The Hoardlings looked like a bipedal cross between some kind of draconic creature and a silverback gorilla. Its muscular, four-limbed stature exuded an aura of primal strength. Each of the beasts had numerous scars across their body, hinting at countless battles against not only the unforgiving cold, but the other powerful creatures that roamed this planet.

Although they had somewhat lizard-like features, they were covered in a thick, shaggy coat of icy white fur, which likely provided protection from the biting chill, as well as allowing them to have near-perfect camouflage as they roamed this frozen tundra. Strangely enough, the thick fur was held close to their body beneath a sheath of ice, and Joe just *knew* that they would have some kind of first layer of defense against slashing or piercing attacks, which would shift over to protections against blunt attacks when the ice was broken and out of the way.

One major standout on the creatures were their eyes. Piercing, keen orbs stood out like frozen sapphires dropped in the snow, and were locked on the warm-blooded creatures in front of them with a hungry stare. Powerful limbs ended in razor-sharp, icicle-coated claws protruding from its padded paws, once more seeming to have a strangely flawed combination of both lizard and ape. As they ran along, their feet would clench, allowing them to hurl themselves forward powerfully, but clearly not giving them the dexterity afforded a true primate.

What truly concerned Joe was the fact that, if they *hadn't* been pointed out carefully, while also moving at a continuous rapid pace through the gaps that had been intentionally left in the walls, he wouldn't have been able to see them. The Ritualist shivered and muttered softly to himself, "Looks like I'm going to need another big boost in my perception for this world."

"Just for clarity's sake, I should tell you that their name *isn't* what it sounds like." Jaxon winked at Joe with a broad smile on his face as he blindly lashed out at a passing Penguin, punching it perfectly in the paunch. "I know how your mind works, and when I say '*Hoard*ling'..."

"Please don't." Joe tried to cut his friend off, only for Jaxon to barrel on with his thoughts.

"...you probably guessed that they go around carrying a bunch of loot, but they don't. I think the 'Hoar' part means 'Hoar*frost*', as every attack they make deals some kind of cold damage. Even when *I* hit *them*, they give me a 'chilled' debuff." Jaxon cocked his head to the side and looked at Joe quizzically. "Hold on, what did you think I was going to say?"

Joe shook his head and refused to answer, instead changing the subject. "I should start collecting a few of them and see if they're worth breaking down. You'd mentioned that the Penguins are a good source of food; I'm wondering about those now. Has anyone tried the meat off of these?"

"Nah, it's bad dragon meat." Jaxon's face contorted into a disgusted expression. "Apparently, even the most diluted dragon bloodlines make it so the meat isn't just a *little* poisonous, it's 'you'd rather go to respawn than finish out the debuff' poison. Yet, initial tests show that it's useless as a weapon enhancer. It doesn't even make *us* sick if it gets into an open wound. Must have something to do with breaking it down and trying to feed it to our system? Don't worry, I'm sure there will be at least ten academic papers on this in the next year or so. We'll figure it out for sure by then."

"Well, maybe the skin and bones will be useful for crafting, I'm sure the fur will be useful in this cold-" Joe's head snapped to the side, and his eyes zeroed in on a blurry monster in the distance that had just screamed. "What was *that*?"

Notice! Every five Beast Waves contains at least one elite or boss monster! As this is the first time this message has been shown, you have been given this information in advance of the monster reaching your walls. Good luck, and stay warm!

As far as Joe could tell, this monster was an oversized version of the Penguins. Unlike the others that had come before it, this one was sliding on its stomach at high speed from the moment that it came into view. If he had to make a comparison, Joe was almost certain that this bird was approaching highway speed limit speeds, and it was tossing up snow and packed earth in a huge wake—like a shark speeding through the ocean. It didn't seem to care if it slammed into allies or enemies; it was on a mission: the destruction of this invasive town.

"There was quite the change in how the monsters behaved after the guildhall went down." Jaxon offered the information to Joe offhandedly. "When the guildhall was there, they mostly ignored people and stuff in their way. Now, as soon as they get someone in their sights, they try to take them out. Frankly, I prefer this version more! Makes everything so much more *exciting*!"

Before Joe could say another word to him, the chiropractor launched himself into a mid-air somersault, landing on a passing Penguin's back. Then he rode it like a surfboard deeper into the Hamlet, shouting in glee the whole time as he punched down.

"Bye, I guess? I suppose he had places to be." The Ritualist watched as the elite monster got closer, only to be met with a wall of Dwarves that reduced it to ribbons in only a few moments. Frankly, the fight over who got to claim the kill lasted longer than the monster itself. Knowing that he didn't have much to do here, Joe simply tossed his hands up and started walking back toward the city as the final remnants of the wave were fully cleaned up.

They soon got a notification informing them that the Beast Wave had been cleared, but Joe gained no personal rewards or other data beyond that. With the additional waves cleared, it was time for him to return to the destroyed guildhall and rebuild it. The Ritualist moved with a cheerfulness that only having a purpose in life can bring.

He was met at the location of the demolished building by a small cadre of Dwarves, including one who was carrying a rolled case. That Dwarf stepped forward and gave a respectful salute, pounding his fist into his chest. "Mr. Joe, it's been requested that you use *this* blueprint for the Town Hall. The building you had made before, the guildhall, was equipped more for… shall we say comfort? This'll be a small, squat building with nearly triple the durability, and it should only become more durable as it grows along with the settlement rank. It'll be nowhere near as luxurious, but we shouldn't lose it to a couple of Penguins on their first attack."

The Dwarf ended his small speech with a chuckle as he looked at the rubble. Joe took the package, though he stared at it for a few long seconds to work through his thoughts on the matter. "Grandmaster McPoundy gave me a brief on this, but can you clarify for me a little more why the change? This won't be a guild town, if it isn't started as such, and I suppose that makes sense since we're attempting to create a fortified city. Tell me this: can a town hall and a guildhall exist in the same city?"

"Very much so," the Dwarf replied with a firm nod. "A city can have a large number of guildhalls, so long as the main governmental building began as a Town Hall. Otherwise, it can't support both."

"That's what McPoundy had mentioned. I guess I'm just wondering *why* the town needs more guilds? Are there a lot of Dwarven guilds? Do we *need* more guilds here?"

"I'm certain that the council has a plan in place that I'm unaware of." The Dwarf's voice was cooling by the second. "I was also told that this is the *only* facility that will be accepted."

Understanding the implied threat, if not the reasoning for it, Joe could only let his internal dialogue chew on the issue for a while. He had no way to test the truth of that matter, but he didn't see any reason why they would lie to him. Knowing that the only path forward was to get this building up and running, the Ritualist cast aside his concerns and pulled out the blueprints. As he went over them, making small, cursory notes as he adapted a Ritual of the Architect to fit the plans, the Dwarf who had given him the design watched on like a particularly vindictive hawk.

Finally, Joe nodded at the small contingent of Dwarves to indicate he was ready, idly wondering why the Masters weren't the ones to meet him here. The group of Dwarves encircled him, spreading out to fill the role of providing mana as the Ritualist set up his stabilization cubes. It was strange to him how much the simple placement of metal stilled the area around him, as though a tornado had been churning the air in the distance, only to be replaced with a cool breeze coming from a single direction.

Just before he could activate the ritual that would create the bureaucratic center of the Hamlet, the city planner stepped in and flapped his arms at them, arguing incessantly until they agreed to move to a slightly different location, which he *insisted* would help with the flow of the city when it had finally been completed in the future.

For some reason, the angry demands were the final straw for Joe. His frustration began to boil over, and he slipped slightly into malicious compliance mode. Savagely, the Rituarchitect looked over his gathered materials and decided that he *would*, in fact, be testing out his recently acquired Special aspects. Along with all of the other resources, the Rituarchitect silently imbued fifty of his Phoenix aspects into the design.

From his previous testing, that seemed to be a nice, even

number that would be effective for a Common-tier building like this. Joe hoped that, as the building grew, so would the magic inside of it, then he'd eventually learn what the aspects actually did.

Under his breath, he muttered quietly enough that the Dwarves around him couldn't hear over the strange electrical discharges of the Town Hall being built in front of them, "Then again, if the building comes out covered in feathers, I think they might notice. Meh, at least I'll have answers."

The Special aspects were accepted by the blueprint without question. Joe had been expecting that there'd be a notification if he'd put in too many, and he had seen what happened when he went outside of the upper bound of a safe range. Since this building was not self-destructing immediately, he figured that he'd made the correct call.

As the last of the crown molding materialized onto the building, and the ritual slowly spun to a halt, Joe couldn't tell if anything was different than what he'd expected, based on the blueprints alone.

Building completed: Phoenix-Aspected Town Hall (Common). Congratulations on building a Town Hall for the first time! +50 Rituarchitect experience.

Class Quest updated: Apprentice Rituarchitect III. Meaningful monument-class structures created 1/3.

Joe considered the information he'd just gained. Until now, he had never guessed that the Town Hall would be considered a monument. He supposed it *did* make sense: monuments were structures that could increase in power over time as they became more meaningful to the community, as well as typically only being able to be created when it made sense to make them.

Even if he had a monument that would automatically record the names of friends killed in battle, it'd be impossible for him to actually create the structure and have it work if all of his friends were healthy and hale.

"I'm not going to lie to myself; I think I've been feeling pushed aside by Grandmaster Snow ever since I lost my title."

Joe had left the group of self-congratulatory Dwarves behind and was now murmuring into his half-full coffee mug. He took a deep breath, inhaling the generously thick aroma AutoMate was creating for him, and he continued on with his moment of self-realization.

"I fully recognize that disallowing the Masters to work with me was just another power play, meant to ever-so-slowly make me lose influence over the area. If I'm unable to play a meaningful part in combat and am relegated to background tasks where the credit can easily be taken by the leadership of the Dwarves… yeah, I can see how I'd rapidly fade into obscurity."

His searching glance swept over the monument that he'd just created. "But… I might be okay with that. If they did it openly and asked me to stay out of the limelight, I'd probably jump at the chance. You know what? That's *exactly* what I'm going to do. I'm just going to quietly do my work and let my success be my noise."

With a sharp inhale, Joe threw his shoulders back and straightened out his pose, standing in the strong, domineering posture that Jaxon always recommended for correct spinal alignment. Slapping a wide smile on his face, he turned on his heel and walked away from the Town Hall without even bothering to go in and inspect his work.

He *knew* it would be perfect. As always.

CHAPTER TEN

"Knowledge, Ritual Lore." Joe used his ability to increase his skill rank for the third time since coming to Jotunheim, having either been too busy to make full use of the perk… or asleep. He'd missed out on a few opportunities to activate it in perfect sequence, but he could only do his best. Over the last few days, Joe had still managed to increase his Alchemical, Architectural, and Ritual lore to Student rank one, two, and three, respectively.

Joe's chosen purpose in life was to gain immense magical potency and knowledge. It was very difficult to have one without the other. In a place like Jotunheim, it was incredibly difficult to gain a deep level of insight from the environment. He couldn't just go to an established magical university, which left him with only two options. The first, which he was utilizing at the moment, was to do his own research and use his skills and spells to directly boost his understanding.

Other than that, he could only go out and find a tutor on a world with zero population besides what he'd brought with him.

With the Dwarves focusing inward, apparently becoming more insular and less friendly—at least, in his opinion from when he'd been sleep deprived—Joe's best option was likely to extort smiths for training. He could trade knowledge for the ability to work for free at his smithy. Or… Joe eyeballed the enormous pyramid and realized he could go ask Jake the Alchemist to fulfill the obligation to train him. "You know what? I'm sick of seeing facial hair. Let's go learn some alchemy."

The pyramid was only a double-Omnivault away from the new Town Hall, but Joe still had the great pleasure of seeing a couple hundred reflective bubbles glinting in the slowly brightening daylight from his midair vantage point. While he'd committed to staying under the radar on this world in general, it still brought him great pleasure to see other people relying on his research and innovations. The Ritualist knocked on the door of the pyramid only a few moments later.

Several minutes after his first knock, the door opened, and Jake ushered him into the building, slamming the door behind the Ritualist in order to keep the chill of the day outside. "I'd say it's a pleasure to see you, but you only ever seek me out when you want something. So, I will happily skip directly to the important bits. Are you here for training? Or do you need some concoction? You reek of self-doubt; do you need a love potion, perhaps?"

"Please don't analyze my… I'm guessing it's my pheromones?" Joe realized at that moment that he'd allowed his Neutrality Aura to slip, and he snapped it back into place with a thought. If nothing else, that would make it impossible for someone to sniff him out, in a literal sense. "Training is what I'm after. I've been considering binding another of my attributes with my Ritual Orbs, and I'm a little bit too far away with my skill levels to be comfortable creating the binding agents I need."

"You could just *ask*," Jake informed him blandly. "It would make my day far easier to take three and a half minutes to create it *for* you, instead of several hours of instruction. Not to mention that the Alchemist Hall is still only functional by the barest of margins. Enough to make *Philters*, at best. I cannot get the cauldron over five thousand degrees until I have a steady supply of energy being collected and coalesced from the core of this planet."

"Seeing as my Ritualistic Alchemy skill is only at Beginner five, I don't think that will be necessary." Instead of waiting for what he was certain would be a noncommittal minor insult, Joe pushed past the Alchemist, knowing that he wouldn't refuse to help. Seeing as they had made a bargain, if the Alchemist was the one to break the deal, he'd suffer immense consequences. "I could probably use a standard kitchen oven for what I need to make, right? Any chance you know what a microwave is, and if so, would that work?"

Joe's lips curled into a subtle smile as a choked noise of vexation resounded behind him, followed by the hurried shuffle of footsteps as Jake caught up to him and directed him around strange, bubbling experiments. Sending a few nervous looks at the boiling brews, Jake brought Joe directly to the focal point of the building: the main cauldron.

No matter what else could be said about him, Jake had a great enthusiasm for Alchemy. While he was perhaps not the best teacher, the Alchemist could still turn the low-level lecture into an enlightening discourse, explaining each of the intricate properties Joe needed to craft to create whatever binding agency he desired. As the rapid instruction came to a conclusion, Jake meticulously wrote out a detailed, comprehensive recipe, then gave Joe a few minutes to convert the information over to an aspect version.

"I know you are set on this path right now, but I would once again urge you to consider learning Alchemy as a whole, instead of merely this small subset of skills." Jake was the first to break the silence as he watched with begrudging envy while Joe finished the newly altered recipe. "It's narrow, too specific, and you have a surprisingly large grasp of the basics. With such a firm foundation, as well as the ability to ignore the need for rare or nearly extinct reagents, seeing you wasting your abilities on such a small target irritates me greatly."

"Mmm," Joe hummed noncommittally, "I *do* have my Alchemical lore in the Student ranks, even though it's low-level. The problem is, before I focus on such a broad topic, which would take me potentially decades to achieve Mastery in, I need to pursue my current path, just as you'd mentioned."

No further words were exchanged as the Ritualist attempted to create a Vial of binding agents. 'Vial' was the specific name of this rank of alchemy item, and Joe had more than once gotten on Jake's bad side by casually labeling everything they made as a 'potion', which was actually a Trash-ranked alchemy item. Unfortunately, over the course of the next few hours, that was the only thing his efforts produced. Trash.

It seemed that, no matter how Joe spun aspects in the cauldron—attempting to heat, cool, contain, and mix as needed—each time he approached what looked like a viable product, the aspects would convert into a liquid, immediately blacken, then release noxious fumes. Eventually, the Ritualist grew sick of the smug, condescending look on Jake's face and slapped his hand down on the edge of the cauldron. That would've been a *terrible* idea, were he not covered in a scintillating layer of magic protecting him from the superheated surface.

"Please, just tell me what I'm doing *wrong*! We've been at this forever, and I haven't made a single passable item." Joe's seething fury cooled in an instant as Jake shrugged.

"Nothing."

"I'm doing *nothing* wrong?" The Ritualist narrowed his eyes as he watched for any sign that the Alchemist was teasing him. "Then I should've succeeded by accident at this point, if nothing else!"

"No. You shouldn't have." Jake took a deep breath, centering himself and pursing his lips before trying to speak words that would make sense to the alchemy-curious human. "If you had the requisite skill level, you would have succeeded on your third attempt. Do you perhaps recall that I gave you guidance until then, and I then stopped talking as you continuously repeated the same failure? Your actual Skill level is that of a Beginner, and you are attempting to make something that can only be created consistently by an Apprentice."

"*Ah.*" Joe let out a sigh and got back to working to beat the odds. "Is there anything I can be doing to increase my chances of success?"

That put a smile on Jake's face. "Hooray! You are asking the correct questions. Wonderful. In every industry, the most difficult thing to do is know the *terminology* of what you need. If you at least know that much, you can search through tomes of information for that particular keyword. If you don't know it, you need to ask someone so that you can get the nomenclature correct. With that life lesson out of the way, in this case, the issue you are running into is the incredible instability in the magical matrices of Jotunheim. There is something about this world that actively disrupts the lowest ranks of magic and skills."

"I should set up my stabilization cubes?" Joe pondered hopefully, even as the cubes started popping into his hand. "I suppose this makes sense—*hey*!"

Jake had whisked a cube out of his hand and began curiously scrutinizing it. After giving them a thorough inspection, he shook his head and handed them back. "Great for smithing, useless for alchemy or spellcasting. Those only stabilize the surroundings so long as magic is being imbued within the bounds of its containment. They will do nothing to stabilize the reagents that you are using. It may sound arbitrary, but it is a fact of the matter that those are simply outside the realm of the craft of alchemy."

"You're wrong." Joe's instant refusal caused Jake to clam up and cross his arms.

"*Am* I now? Please, *enlighten* me."

"I've used them for smithing *and* creating rituals. In both cases, the cubes have been enough to stabilize everything I'm working on. I even tested it by slowly moving them away, and they have a clear and undeniable impact on my rituals."

Jake pondered that for a moment, sharply nodding a single

time. "I think I have determined where your confusion stems from. But first, I will inform you that, while I *do* have to teach you via the terms of our agreement, I don't need to do it in a room *not* filled with itching powder that could make a World Boss scratch its own skin off. If you won't respect me enough to mince your words into a palatable smoothie, you will suffer for every *minute* of the education I provide you."

They stared at each other for a long moment, Joe's mouth working as he tried to rein in his surprise at the sudden chastisement. "I'm… I didn't realize I was moving past the bounds of polite conversation. Sorry about that. Sometimes I fall back into old habits, and I tend to spend quite a bit of time alone. It can impact my social niceties. Please, allow me to try again. As far as I'm aware, these cubes should work for any craft, as they're currently already working for two of them. To my knowledge, it seems that should extend to other professions, and if I'm wrong, I'd truly appreciate your guidance on that matter."

"Better," Jake allowed, seeming pleased that he didn't need to create greater tension or push the limits of their deal. "I have a good thing going here, what with having control of the Pyramid and all. I'd hate to risk that because you let your anger at the treatment of the Dwarves come between us. To answer your original question, if you want alchemical stabilizers, you need to make them. Look around you. What do you see?"

"You've seen that, too? What's up with them?" Jake shrugged and waved his finger around the room as he waited for an answer. Joe, reassured that he wasn't reading into the situation with the Dwarves, that someone else was seeing their standoffishness, felt his mind relax fractionally. He took the time to study his surroundings, not wanting to give a flippant answer after having annoyed an entity that could slap someone like Havoc around, if he wanted to. "I see all sorts of alchemy things: equipment, empty space, storage, bottled reagents, finished products."

"How are you seeing it?" The Alchemist slowly began guiding him toward the answer.

"With my… eyes?" Joe had unease etched on his face as he attempted to speak the seemingly casual answer with great sincerity. There were just too many potential replies, so he had finally opted for the most literal response. To his relief, it appeared to have been the correct one, since Jake seized upon his words and launched into an explanation as soon as his words had left Joe's lips.

"Correct." Waving around the room, Jake pointed out various recessed sconces built into the building itself. They exuded light without releasing any residue, such as soot. "This room always has perfect visibility, but even with that being the case, you will notice that there are scores of candles throughout the room, each of them burning brightly and steadily. If you look closer, someone with your aptitudes should be able to notice the fact that those same candles are set in specific patterns, each of those patterns containing specific meanings."

Now that Joe knew what to look for, it was readily apparent that the candles were set in prime number sequences, exactly as he used his stabilization cubes. He could also tell where high-level alchemy was being performed just by the fact that some of the experiments had candles numbering in the hundreds around them. "I see. Thank you for the explanation. If you don't mind me asking, it seemed to me that you'd noticed something that might be relevant to why my cubes worked with multiple professions? Would you mind…?"

"After your attitude adjustment, I am *more* than happy to explain. I enjoy instructing polite, eager Alchemists." Jake waved Joe over to the center of one of the rings of lit candles. "Go ahead and create a Novice ritual circle. Light or something equally easy, as I have seen you make those by the hundreds."

Figuring that the powerful Alchemist knew what he was doing, Joe didn't waste time asking questions, instead forming a ritual in the air and activating it immediately. Unlike the flickering that happened when he was using his cubes, the ritual was solid and perfect from the moment he'd started placing the aspects. "Candles stabilize my rituals as well? Why does it work for them and not other things?"

"Unless I miss my mark…" Jake let his head loll to the side. "Your ritual skills encompass more than just rituals. In fact, I'm certain that you could achieve the same effect with your stabilization items made in a smithy, candles from alchemy, enchantment foci, and potentially even calculated matrices—specifically placing your rituals in formations so that, as one becomes stable, it stabilizes its neighbors. You can speak with your Dwarven friends about that. Their race is known for their impeccable formations, part of the reason they are such a terror on the battlefield."

"You know… I'd heard of that." Joe scoffed at his own naivete. "Here I thought they were just talking about how they aligned their troops, and it was actually about the magical resonance of their placement."

"In other words: yes, but also no." Jake reached out and patted Joe on the shoulder comfortingly. "The multiverse is a vast place, and the waters of magic have never been explored to their deepest depths. For now, I think you should focus on the fact that you have a *handful* of ways to boost the stability of what you can create, while everyone else has only *one*. Here is your homework for the night: think of how you can use the additional stability to your advantage. Now get out."

CHAPTER ELEVEN

Joe walked out of the door unassisted, a pleasant surprise as Jake had threatened to bodily hurl him out of the door if he didn't leave to 'ponder his few advantages and many disadvantages'. That was fine with the Ritualist, as he'd been unable to create a single alchemical compound of any rarity. Well, technically he *had* been able to generate lots of Trash-rank items, but he shouldn't count that.

Jake would know. Somehow.

Even so, going through the motions and doing everything correctly had been somewhat beneficial. The Alchemist had given him excellent instruction, to the point where Joe had received skill levels in the lore incredibly quickly.

Ritualistic Alchemy has reached Beginner VII!

Alchemical Lore has reached Student III!

Calculus and Number Theory has reached Beginner VIII!

"Two lore levels in one training session..." Joe shook his head at that thought, even though a wide smile was plastered on his face. "If I'm able to keep that speed up in my next few lessons, I should focus my Knowledge spell on other areas. I guess the Math skill came from all of the super intricate fractions of aspects he was making me contain in various patterns. I bet, if my Magical Matrices skill had been lower, that would've gone up as well."

Joe took a moment to go over the entirety of his crafting skills, as they were what he'd been mostly focusing on and what he hoped to bring to the highest heights while he was stuck on this world.

Crafting/gathering Skills

Enchanting (General): Beginner V

Field Array: (Maximized)

Herbalism: Novice VI

Message: Novice VII

Natural Magical Material Creation: Student 0

Ritual Magic: Master I

Alchemical Rituals: Beginner 0

Enchanted Ritual Circles: Beginner VIII

Ritual Circles: Master I

Ritualistic Forging: Student II

Magical Matrices: Journeyman 0

Ritualistic Alchemy: Beginner VII

Somatic Ritual Casting: Student VIII

Spellbinding: Student 0

Words of Power (Written): Student 0

"Almost unbelievable that I technically only have ten different crafting skills, since Ritual Magic breaks down into five distinct subskills. Crazy how, with just this much, I can literally change the face of this planet when I get powerful enough." He looked over each of the other skills, noticing with a grimace that a few of them were practically useless to him. "When was the last time I used herbalism? Not like I need to be able to tell plants apart anymore. Kind of wish there was some way to get rid of it."

Permanently delete skill 'Herbalism'? You will be granted one free skill point for each novice level, plus five for the skill itself. To regain the skill, you will either need to pay the same amount of free skill points or complete enough herbalism-related tasks to regain the skill and level as it currently is. Yes / No.

The Ritualist read over the message several times before he closed his eyes and took a deep breath. "I just *know* someone close to me knows about this and never bothered to mention it for some reason. I bet it's something class trainers use all the time to help their students focus all of their abilities into a useful, cohesive whole. I can't even get mad, since I'm the only class trainer for Ritualists and will absolutely tell them. I'll just need to make sure this goes in my notes for when I train people again."

Only taking a few more moments to bemoan the fact that there were still so many fundamental things he didn't know, Joe cheerfully converted the skill into free skill points… then he went looking for more useless skills.

Herbalism permanently removed! +11 free skill points!

The only other skill or spell that he found that he might be okay with giving up was 'Wither Plant', but he'd already increased that to the Student rank. At this point, he felt he had invested enough time into it that he should hang on to the spell, just in case there was some enormous plant that needed to die. He felt it was a fair concern, as he was in a world of giants.

Just before he closed out of the skill sheet, Joe realized he'd overlooked one of his skills because it was technically listed under his combat skills. Usually, he wouldn't consider getting rid of one of those important abilities, but Intrusive Scan tended to make more issues than it solved.

First of all, anything at his level or higher could easily tell that they were being scanned, and they would know exactly where he was. As he progressed through the worlds, he was certain he wouldn't get much use out of this ability. He decided that it was appropriate to cash it in for additional points, figuring that it would be easier to assume everything was much, much stronger than he was. If he wanted to know a non-hostile entity's name, he should just ask for it.

Removing the skill brought him an additional fifteen free

points, and he double-checked his skills more carefully to make sure he hadn't missed anything else. "Nope… everything else is as close to perfect as I can get it."

Seeing that he'd optimized his abilities to this degree even without knowing this shortcut returned the smile to his face. "At least I know what to do with useless skills now! Where should I put these skill points…? Let me see… when I got my Reductionist class, I remember it telling me that I wouldn't be able to use skill points for my ritual magics anymore."

He tried, just to be on the safe side, and got instant confirmation that he couldn't place the skill points on anything to do with his class skills. That left him plenty of options, but his eyes kept returning to his Combat Ritual Orbs skill. It had been stuck at Beginner five for a long time, and he had to consider the fact that it was going to be harder to use them at all on this world. Just to find confirmation that he wasn't worrying about nothing, Joe flicked open the bandolier he was wearing and attempted to take control of the orbs.

One of them came out with ease, but as the others lifted from their placements, they dropped to the ground as if the gravity of this world was ten times stronger than he was used to.

"Oh look, found confirmation!" Not hesitating for a moment, knowing that this was an important skill even if it wasn't going to be the main focus, he put five of his free points into his Combat Ritual Orbs skill, four points into Artisan Body, and kept the last seventeen until he found a place where he was particularly in need of a rapid boost.

Congratulations! Combat Ritual Orbs (Exotic) has reached Apprentice 0! You are now able to easily control three Ritual Orbs with great finesse. The durability of all orbs bound to your Characteristics is increased by 25%!

Congratulations! Artisan Body has reached Apprentice 0! You are now able to devote a set amount of your Stamina Regeneration to this skill, to automatically begin training a physical Characteristic (Strength, Dexterity, Constitution, or Perception). Would you like to do so now? Yes / No.

Both of those rank bonuses were extremely beneficial. Joe

hadn't yet had one of his bound orbs destroyed, but it would be a painful experience if it were to happen. Going by the warnings on his weapons, one of his Characteristics would be effectively halved until he was able to recreate and rebind the item. An automatic durability boost was always appreciated. The next bonus was even more exciting.

Joe had a *ridiculous* amount of trouble increasing his Characteristics at a rapid rate. The speed boost that his Artisan Body gave him would still require forty-eight minutes of continuous training to increase any of the offered Characteristics by a single point. "How much stamina can I set to be used?"

Up to 50% of your Stamina Regeneration can be diverted into automatic Characteristic training.

"Good enough." Joe decided to allocate that full amount and watched with excited eyes as he chose to increase his lowest physical Characteristic: Constitution. A notification popped up, and he read it out loud in absolute disbelief. "Time until Characteristic increase is… one hundred eighty hours? Are you kidding me? That's over a week! System, what's with that number?"

*Calculation is as follows: Characteristic is at fourth threshold (above 150 but below 200). Stamina Regeneration allocated is 3.32. 150*4 = 600 stamina hours required. 600/3.32 = 180.72 stamina hours.*

"So, I need to be at half stamina regeneration for more than a week in order to…" Joe stopped talking, simply waving it all away. "You know what? I'm not using my stamina very much anyway, and incremental gains are still gains. Fine."

For a very long moment, he was sorely tempted to dump an additional ten free points into that skill and bring it up to the Student rank, but he decided that he needed to keep those in reserve just in case—even if it was aggravating to be patient. Joe peeled his mind away from thoughts of increasing his physical capabilities and turned his attention to the enormous, mostly empty wasteland he was standing in.

Thanks to reducing the remains of the World Boss, he was in possession of a hoard of raw materials that he could transform into anything. Joe's gaze landed on the Town Hall that was the center of bustling activity. He grimaced slightly, amending his thoughts. "I can make almost anything. Locked out of *buildings* for the time being."

There was one major benefit to having a large, wide-open space that was mostly safe. Joe chose a mostly unpopulated corner of the Hamlet and cleared an open space for himself. Far away from the center of activity, from the oncoming Beast Waves that were sure to attack now that a town hall had been built, he activated a Ritual Tile and was instantly hidden behind a reflective bubble.

"If no one wants me to take care of their issues for them, that works out perfectly for me. Just means I have all the time in the world to figure out what I want to be doing and make it work. Hey! I can also make some progress on my Class quests. Killing a thousand monsters with a ritual I've never used before isn't going to happen by itself."

Short-term goal fully embraced, Joe pulled out his reward from completing the second part in the Student Ritualist questline: The Ritual of Slaughter.

CHAPTER TWELVE

Despite being classified as a Journeyman rank, internally, Joe nearly regarded the ritual as a Master rank due to its overwhelming complexity. Not wanting to damage the original containing document, Joe held up a piece of paper that he'd been transcribing the beast of a diagram onto, gently slapping it with the back of his right hand. "This is *ridiculous*! I can't even activate it manually, I have to meet *each* of the activation requirements? Mate, pop your head out, so I can complain to someone!"

*B-*burble*!* The coffee elemental bravely poked its head out of the mug, expecting to be met with the same frigid environment as the last time it had materialized fully. Noticing with relief that the temperature of the air was only *slightly* below zero, the coffee bean eyes focused on Joe as he began his rant.

"Look at this! First off, the ritual is just abyssally *expensive*!" Joe tallied up the requirements in his head, spitting to the side as he figured out a useful comparison. "I could build *two* Rare apartment complexes with special attributes for the same price as just setting this up. Then, *then*? Right here! These are the activation requirements. Do you know what it says? Of course not. You don't actually have eyes; you can't read this."

AutoMate nodded in dignified agreement. The entire mug Mate lived in waved back and forth, seeing as Joe hadn't unattached it from his belt. The human was completely lost in his own thoughts, and stopped paying attention to the summoned being. "Basically, it goes like this. I get to set the activation requirements. There have to be at least five different requirements, since it's a Journeyman ritual. The 'more specific' I make them, the better the end result of 'power released'. What does that even mean? That's like telling a chef to add a pinch of salt and a dash of paprika! Where are my hard numbers? I love numbers."

Burb-

"That's not even dealing with the sheer purple prose that goes into the design of the ritual. Mate, I kid you not, there's a haiku built into it. Right here, on the third circle." Joe started laughing as he read off the words that he'd translated. "Magic flash at start. Monsters fall with a thunder. Victory is now."

His chuckling continued for a long few seconds, until he finally trailed off in thought. "Maybe it's actually being literal. If I go over this section for usage again, I *suppose* it could be very generously interpreted as 'only when all of the requirements have been met will the ritual activate'. If that's the case, then putting in requirements that are easy to fulfill would result in the ritual activating prematurely, and... not building up much power? But where's the section on *how* it builds up that strength?"

Without the Ritualist realizing it, Mate sank back into its cup and unsummoned itself. Joe had a bad habit of going off on a tangent and forgetting to release the elemental, so he'd granted it the ability to send itself home when it knew it wasn't needed. The sound of pages flipping and incensed muttering were the only sounds for the next long time, as the light outside of Joe's bubble ever so slowly increased. "Ah-*ha*! I've got it!"

Storing his original document in his codpiece, Joe started

writing down his insights into the ritual. "The cost of the ritual is so exorbitant because of the potential for destruction. If I used this correctly, I could complete my quest in a single activation, slaughtering a full one thousand monsters. Let me see... right here! The final damage dealt to the target of the ritual is based on how many creatures have fulfilled each of the activation requirements. But right here, it shows that the ritual is activated as soon as *one* of the targets fulfills *every* requirement."

That gave him plenty of ideas on how to make this work for best effect, but unless Joe had an extremely accurate metric of how each of the monsters in this world reacted, he could create a Ritual that could never be activated. For instance, if he were to set one of the requirements to be that a creature 'flew' over a wall, it wouldn't activate if something 'jumped', 'hopped', or 'was thrown' over that same barrier. Not that he would ever use that as a requirement. Seeing as this world produced massive creatures, Joe was guessing that very few, if any, of the monsters on this world would be able to fly.

"If I make the activation too stringent, they'll never activate, and the ritual will have practically no power at all. If I make it too open, there won't be enough power input into the ritual before it's activated. This is actually kinda fun." Joe was scribbling furiously at his paper as he tried to decide what he should make first. "This is such an interesting logic problem... where will I have the best effect, and where will I have diminishing returns?"

Eventually, he had to slow down on his research, as the ritual itself was an extremely dense piece of magic. It was going to take him hours, possibly days to set up the final product, once he got started. There were far too many things to do before he could let himself get sucked down the rabbit hole of setting it up. "I'm betting that this round of Beast Waves is going to be taken care of fairly easily, since we have so many defenses set up, and I figured out the trick right away. That means I should start planning for the next stage, going from a Village to a Town."

The Ritualist was less excited about this portion of his work, as there was no direct benefit to it… other than *eventually* escaping this world. It didn't afford him personal power, he wouldn't be able to take the buildings with him when he left, and once again, any currency he gathered would be rendered useless as soon as he left Jotunheim.

At this point, he was so sick of having to deal with accumulating wealth and losing it that he was actively opposed to making an 'income'. "I bet this is what vampires felt like on Earth, if there were any. They work really hard and build an empire, only for the country that they had their money invested in to fall. Eventually, perhaps everyone realizes that the pursuit of money is useless, if they live long enough. Need to build my tower somewhere and spend a few decades learning. Knowledge is the *true* currency of the universe."

Wisdom +5! You have stumbled onto a great personal revelation, even if that insight is only a small part of a greater pattern.

Joe was too deep in planning for the next stage of the town to pay much attention to the notification. "Forget buildings, I've got everything I need to make those and whatever we need for them. We need to focus on the morale modifier; that was what always held me back in The Shoe. What were the big things there that I needed to take care of? I think it was heat, light, shelter… no, living spaces. That's the right one. Water sources, air quality, and resources."

"Let's break it down into the easiest ones to fix." Joe's finger lightly trailed across the paper and came to a stop on the word 'light'. "I've already done this one, so I should be able to do it again. I learned my lesson last time; it's not enough to just have light, we need a proper circadian rhythm. Day and night cycle. I don't think people will appreciate a full two weeks in either the sun or the dark, but the challenge is going to be how to make sure we've enough light to take on any monsters that manage to make their way into the area?"

For the next few hours, Joe was content to sketch out his plan on an oversized piece of paper. When it was done, he had a drawing that a five-year-old could've made, but it had been enough for him to get his thoughts in order. "Perfect. If I create a flat barrier half an inch thick directly above our heads, I can set it to let in light only half of the day. Then it'd be easy to set up 'street lights' in the form of circular points in the air where I *don't* block the light. That way, we still maintain excellent visibility without having to sacrifice our vision."

The next step was going to be figuring out how much space he needed to cover with all of this. That was how Joe found himself walking from one end of the walled-in area to the other, taking careful, measured steps. He tried to tune out any distractions and was extremely thankful that the Dwarves had defaulted to planning a grid pattern for the city. Even though he got quite a few strange looks as he moved along, loudly counting each step, it was nothing he wasn't used to. Still, whenever anyone asked him what he was doing, he took the time to pause, carefully remember where he was, then answer their question with a smile.

One of the most important factors in maintaining a low profile was ensuring that he was cheerful and pleasant to anyone that he ran into. If he wanted to make a building extremely sneakily, pretending that it was for something exquisitely specific, he resolved to ensure that he invited everyone to help build an 'ice block storage center' and ensure it was painted beige. That way, he could be assured that people would leave him alone, or else they'd be put to work. "Boring is the best camouflage."

Charisma (Dark) +3! As your charisma has been aligned to darkness, by plotting to manipulate and deceive, your Characteristic progression has drastically increased!

That gave Joe pause for a moment as he reevaluated his actions. After carefully thinking through it, he found no fault in his logic. If the system wanted to characterize what he was planning as manipulative, that was *its* problem, not *his*. He was just trying to be careful and intentional with his plans. Then again… it was rewarding him for this behavior, so perhaps he should lean into it?

When his calculations were finally complete, Joe went back to his secluded corner and started creating the design. His Calculus and Number Theory came in exceptionally useful at this point, as he found that not only did he need to calculate the square footage of the day-night barrier if he wanted to leave what were essentially flood lights in it, he needed to determine how large of a cone of light would pierce through the darkness based on the circumference of the unblocked area. It was a different challenge than he was used to, but nothing was trying to eat him at the moment—a positive spin that Joe could put on nearly everything these days.

"Sheer size and complexity is going to make this a Student ritual," Joe muttered gently as he continued his process. Checking over his inventory, he found ten Uncommon Cores and a single Rare. Then, of course, there was the Mythical Core shining brightly and practically *begging* him to use it for such a simple, throwaway ritual. "That's… very strange. It wants to be used. Of course it does; otherwise, the World Boss can't respawn back on Alfheim."

He resolved to get it out of his inventory at the soonest possible moment. Happily, he only needed the Rare Core. Taking that out of his codpiece so that he wouldn't be tempted with the sight of its much more powerful companion, Joe placed the flat tile he was working on into the ground, added the last variables that would determine the location of the ritual manifesting, ensured that he had a secondary repository so that he could keep this ritual going with injections of mana or the use of a Mana Battery—then, checklist complete, he began to alter the sky.

It only took a few moments for concerned citizens to start shouting and pointing at the sky, which was rapidly darkening as circles began swirling in the air, shifting into what appeared to be low-flying black clouds. They quickly spread over the entirety of the town, from wall to wall, then reverted into a matte black, as if the sky had been deleted.

Class experience gained: Reductionist +200.

Moments later, that blackness filled with stars, constellations, and the view of the worlds floating in the distance. Joe walked along the perimeter of the open area to make sure that every part of the darkness lined up perfectly, wincing in annoyance when he saw that he'd missed three inches on the Eastern side, allowing a large flood of light to brighten that area enough to overpower his false stars. "Still… got pretty close, for just eyeballing it."

"Joe! Bring the sky back!" Havoc's voice rolled over the area. "You're going to mess us all up; it's supposed to be daytime right now! Nighttime starts in seven and a half hours!"

Blinking a few times, the bald human went back to the Ritual Tile, reached down, and scratched a few markings over the top of the active diagram. Instantly, the night was replaced with day, and he was *pretty* sure the gap issue was fixed. No more shouts or commands were sent his way, so Joe took a moment to surreptitiously scoot some loose dirt over the top of the tile. Someone looking for it in earnest would be able to find it, but after a few days of blowing snow, this would be more than enough to hide the ritual near-permanently.

"I should probably get a dedicated vault to hold my active rituals. Sure would be a shame if someone stepped on this, and it went off like a landmine." That made the Ritualist chuckle for a second, until his smile froze in place. "Then again, I'd bet money it'll be me. Yeah, maybe we take some time to sink this into the stone. Eh… tomorrow."

CHAPTER THIRTEEN

Having set up a proper day and night schedule for the Hamlet, it was time to go and figure out how he was going to be getting paid for his services. Between the temporary housing and the floating light barrier, he'd invested not only a significant sum of aspects, but he had needed to break into one of his last few remaining usable Cores.

He understood that without having 'Reputation' backed by a higher group, such as the Oligarchs, it wasn't going to be useful to try and trade that now-outdated currency for goods. No, the only system that would work until they had an extremely stable civilization up and running here was that of bartering. Without access to mineral deposits, forests for lumber, special plants for alchemy, or anything of the like, the only viable option was monster corpses.

Joe was completely fine with being paid in flesh and blood, as he could take anything and turn it into anything *else,* thanks to his class. As he'd proven with the World Boss, there was even the possibility of getting extremely powerful aspects or special bonuses from the raw components.

As he was walking toward where the corpses were being

collected, Joe amended his thoughts. "I can't turn them into *anything* else… I still need Cores to complete the energy requirements of my rituals. Also to make high-end aspect jars."

Slowing down, he tried to think of anything else that he might need, but beyond training, which he could trade for, those were his only needs. "Cores and corpses. I guess I'm going to be turning into a C and C machine. Ha. Now the only question becomes: who do I talk to about this?"

The first option he'd normally go with was to simply find the Dwarven Council and make a proposal. He was certain they were holed up in the Town Hall, but he didn't want to get himself annoyed by forcing himself to speak with them again so soon. Instead, Joe walked over to a Dwarf that seemed to be managing the placement of slain monsters and waved him down. "Hi there! How can I go about getting a bunch of these for the work that I'm doing? While I do love working, I don't love doing it for free."

That startled a laugh out of the bearded Dwarf, who looked up with a smile on his face until he saw the hairless man in front of him. Then he winced in sympathy and directed Joe to stand closer to him. "You look cold, hairless human. Come, stand by a warm-blooded Dwarf while we discuss what you're talking about. What're you doing, and why do you feel that you should be paid for it?"

"Bubbles, light barrier." Joe pointed sharply at the examples in the area, and while his finger was in the air, he noticed something else. "Also, my light barrier is trapping heat, so I'm warming up the area and will be able to eventually fully remove the 'chilled' debuff everyone is suffering under."

To his credit, the Dwarf only nodded, checking his ledger against Joe's words. "What sort of payment do you want? We can offer labor in return for labor, and… yeah, that's about it."

"Cores and corpses," Joe stated easily, having firmly decided on what he wanted. "That's all I need to continue working at a decent pace for a good long time."

However, by the time he was done speaking, the Dwarf was

already shaking his head in the negative. "No can do. Sorry, bald bro. Cores are still considered a strategic resource for our continued survival, and we've got nearly ninety thousand people waiting for a grilled penguin steak."

"No way for me to get them?" Joe sighed gently, a twisted smile appearing on his face. "Are you *sure*?"

Nodding firmly, the Dwarf confirmed his previous statement. "By order of the council, all Cores are to be handed over for distribution to the most worthy causes. All edible meat is necessary for our short-term survival."

Joe considered the nuclear option of simply canceling every active ritual in the area until his demands were met, but decided to keep that card in his back pocket for now. "I see. Well, I guess I'll need to set up shop, then. I assume that no one's going to come knocking on my door trying to grab monster meat or Cores that I haul in?"

"Nobody has time for that. You kill 'em, they're yours. That's how all of this works. I swear, everyone's trying to get these." The Dwarf waved Joe off as yet another petitioner stepped forward to demand access to the giant pile of stagnant resources, proving his point nearly instantly.

Seeing that he wasn't going to be getting bodies without a fight—one way or another—Joe decided then and there to go out and join in the fight against the next Beast Wave. To that end, he needed to upgrade his weapons if he wanted to be an effective fighter, and *that* meant going back to the Alchemy Hall and binding his next Characteristic to his orbs before joining the front lines of the fight.

Shortly after making that decision, the Ritualist was admitted into the pyramid. Jake showcased his annoyance over being interrupted by slamming the door shut behind him as he stalked back to his work.

As he wasn't here looking for instruction, Joe simply got to work practicing his binding agents. As the second round of aspects in a row turned to goop, the Ritualist closed his eyes and let out a gentle growl. Then he went still as he remembered the spare skill points he was holding onto. Knowing that Jake would likely not appreciate him skipping steps, Joe made sure he was alone before adding the three points he needed in order to get his skill up to the Apprentice rank. "Heehee… technically Ritualistic Alchemy's not a subskill of my ritual magic—that's Alchemical Rituals—so this shouldn't be an issue, right? *Yes*!"

Congratulations! Ritualistic Alchemy has reached Apprentice 0! You have gained a Tome of Alchemic Ritual Adornments (Small)!

Joe eagerly flipped the book open and began perusing its pages. There was an abundance of items he could potentially create, and he had to keep himself from thrusting his fist in the air when he turned a page and saw the exact item he needed: ritual candles. The book was going to be extremely beneficial to him, as amidst the options, there were plenty that he could not fully comprehend at the moment. A few examples were things such as aura-erasure incense and dao-seeking serums.

The final item was likely to be extremely useful someday in the far future. It had caught his attention by lacking a proper explanation, and that usually meant 'hidden powerful thingamajig'. Making a mental note to try and casually drop it into conversation with Jake, he finished acquainting himself with the variety of options the book gave him, carefully closed it, and lifted his view—only to lock eyes with the Alchemist directly.

"I'll only say this once." Jake's voice was warm and pleasant, only highlighting the underlying oddly sibilant and menacing undertones. "Shortcuts are only permissible once you fully understand the material you are working with. If you try to change the game before understanding how to play the game, all you are doing is cheating yourself. Certainly, there is the possibility that you create an entirely new game, but how would you even *know* if you were successful?"

Joe didn't answer him, merely nodding along and profusely thanking his past self for only adding the bare minimum required. There was a difference, at least in his mind, between throwing your skill levels super high and just bringing the system recognition up to the level he had already demonstrated mastery over.

Following Jake's next instructions, instead of going directly into making binding agents, he first started by creating Apprentice-rank alchemy candles to increase his stability. He could infer from Jake's incomplete information that attempting to bind himself to his Ritual Orbs with an unstable binding agent would have… *unfortunate* side effects. To that end, unlike with his stabilization cubes, Joe hadn't been planning to stop at the bare minimum of ten.

But as he was making his eleventh candle, Jake looked at him as though he'd been dropped one too many times as a baby. "You do realize that you are only stabilizing your ingredients up to the rank of *Vial*, correct? Creating another circle of Apprentice candles in the position of Student Apprentice candles will do nothing to help you and will only waste your resources."

"Doesn't hurt to have extras!" Joe decided after a long moment of wavering between finishing or letting the candle turn into mushy wax.

"Good." Jake showed a rare approving half-smile. "You will go far in life if you have the proper tenacity. Without your desire to remain firm and unyielding, you will bend too much… perhaps even one day finding that you are serving as a quest reward for someone barely worthy of it, even if they are intriguing."

"Um." Joe couldn't say another word before Jake whisked himself out of the area, going off to stir a cauldron in the distance that was beginning to hiss and, if Joe wasn't mistaken, scream at them in French. Jake looked back a single time, arching a brow at the Ritualist, who decided that he had plenty of his own work to focus on. "No need for me to worry about someone else's strange items."

Having practiced the motions so frequently and accurately, Joe was able to complete his binding agent on the first attempt, nearly an anticlimactic event for him after so much failure. "No, I can't think that way! Success *should* be boring. It should be what I do every day with no deviation. Why would I *want* life to be harder, when I could instead be using that time to do fun things?"

He made a couple spare binding agents, just in case his first attempt failed. As he was walking toward the exit, planning out which of his Characteristics he should bind to himself, Joe's knuckles brushed against the metallic girdle of his codpiece. As his attention had been drawn to it, he remembered once more that he needed to do something with the Mythic Core. "What did that description say again…? I could use it as an accessory to any item? Does that mean, hey, could I attach it to this building?"

Returning directly to the room that he'd just exited earned him a deep sigh and a 'patient' expression from his instructor. "Welcome back *yet again*, Joe. What can I do for you now? You know, instead of completing the formula for this Injection that I can only hope to someday be able to mix up?"

"I have a proposal for you…" Joe stated slowly, biting his tongue before launching directly into his offer. "But, before I say anything, I need your solemn oath that you won't attack me upon hearing it. That anything I've brought into this building is mine, and you won't attempt to take or keep my items from me by any means other than compromise and mutually beneficial negotiation."

"You have my interest and a larger portion of my attention than I usually give you." Jake leaned forward aggressively, eyeing Joe up and down. "What if I grab on and *shake* you really hard right now, just to see what falls out?"

Joe didn't say anything, counting on his Neutrality Aura to remove the sweat that was beading up all across his bald head. "If you don't want to hear the offer, just say no."

"Oh, I *am* interested. You never get this cagey unless there is something *very* interesting on your mind. For the remainder of our conversation, until you walk out of the door, I officially swear an oath to the terms you have offered me."

The Ritualist was already shaking his head. "Not good

enough. I need you to swear that you won't attack me, *ever*, based on the information I'm about to share with you."

That earned a much longer pause before Jake ever so slightly inclined his head. "I suppose I will agree to that. If you had not planned to do something to my benefit, I'm sure you wouldn't have brought this up in the first place. Which means I would have never known about whatever it is you are about to tell me. Yes, I so swear."

"What would you say if I asked you to guard an item for me? That so long as you did so, and gave the item back to me when I asked for it, I could grant you a Legendary version of this building?"

Joe gulped as Jake stayed silent for *far* too long. That wasn't the concerning part. The true issue came from the fact that the Alchemist's hands kept shooting toward his own pockets, only to stop and move back to their original position, his fingernails extending into claws then retracting like the paws of a tiger.

"If you said something like that... *you*? You, who seem to have enormous gaps in the foundational knowledge of this world? Why, I would accuse you of holding onto a Mythic Core." Jake's voice was hoarse, as though he had just finished screaming for half a day. "I would also mention that, had you *not* extracted the oaths that you did, I would be claiming it from whatever remained of your steaming corpse. At the very least, I would be sifting through the ashes to see if I was correct in my assumption. I suppose I finally have irrefutable proof that my tutelage is not being wasted on a dullard. I'm probably glad, very deep down."

"Great. Here I just thought I was being paranoid." Joe wiped his forehead and showed a relieved smile. "I knew people would kill for this, but-"

"You actually *have* it, don't you?" Jake chuckled lightly, though the sound was anything but humorous. "I thought that, when *I* was the one to deal nearly five percent of its health in a single blow, I would have the Core placed in my inventory. It counted your ritual as the main damage dealer, didn't it?"

"Yes, although I got a notice that it was a bug, and I wouldn't be able to defeat a World Boss like that again."

That earned him a searching look from the Alchemist, who finally muttered a question at him. "I'm not detecting any new curses, though?"

"Curses? Why would I get cursed?" Joe absentmindedly rubbed his bald head.

"Mmm." Jake seemed to be looking over all of Joe's equipment, trying to find where he was hiding the Core. "You don't just get to trigger balance-breaking events and walk away unscathed. Wait! All of the Dwarves that you rescued... everything that you gave up without expecting a reward...? Was that it? Your Karmic Luck took the hit instead of you, didn't it?"

Now it was Joe's turn to go still. "Can you explain that stat to me? I lost something like sixty points of Karmic Luck as soon as the World Boss was defeated."

"*Sixty*?" Jake gasped sharply, though it turned into a deep belly laugh after a long few moments. "You also didn't get cursed, which means you're still positive in the stat! Oh, I'm certain you have some moderators absolutely *furious* with you right now. Still, I'm not a Karmic Race. Therefore, any attempt I made to explain the Characteristic to you would only confuse you and most likely lead you to an incorrect assumption. My own knowledge is lacking in that area. Back to the issue at hand... I *want* that Core."

"No." Joe held up a hand to forestall any further remarks, launching into his explanation as soon as he saw the deranged look on Jake's face, along with the fact that the previously human teeth in his mouth had turned needle-sharp and shark-like. "*Abyss*! Jake, I have the option to use it as an accessory, and by equipping it to any item I have, it can be considered one rank higher. I figured this was the safest place, and we could really use a pseudo-Legendary Alchemy Hall."

"You would just... leave it here? So that I could reach higher heights in my profession? Why? You already have a deal secured by me." Jake looked away and up, trembling and apparently not trusting himself to not attack Joe if he looked directly at him any longer.

"I believe this is the safest place for it," Joe explained humbly. "Since only you have control of this building and have the means to defend it, and I've told no one else of its existence, the Core would be safe here. If I took it with me, there's a chance I could lose it."

"*Lose it?*" The words tore themselves from Jake's throat as though he had just eaten a handful of fiberglass and his organs were being shredded.

Joe shuddered softly before continuing. "As to what I want from you? Keep it safe, willingly and *peacefully* return it to me when I'm ready to make an attempt at the Sage rank or need it for something else, and… you'll owe me a favor."

"Counteroffer." Jake's eyes snapped to meet Joe's. "A minor favor if I have it for less than six months. A medium favor if I have it for up to a year. A major favor if I have it for more than one year, but less than five. A grand favor if I have it for more than five."

"I didn't know there were actual classifications of favors, but let's call it a deal." Joe reached his hand out, and the two shook hands. As Joe tried to let go, he found that his appendage was being held in an unshakable iron grip. Knowing what the other man wanted, Joe had the Core appear in his off hand, palm facing downward.

For a long second, as he waited to use the Mythic Core, Joe felt that he was in the center of a lightning bolt the thickness of a tree. His world was light, pure light so bright that it physically hurt. Somehow, although the Core itself was making no sound, Joe couldn't hear his own words as he shouted for the Core to be attached as an accessory to the Pyramid of Panacea.

Attach Mythic Core to this building? This will set the effective rank as Pyramid of Panacea (Legendary). You will require the building owner's permission to unattach the Core being used as an accessory. Yes / No.

Even though Joe knew he was saying the word, the sound didn't reach his ears. "*Yes.*"

CHAPTER FOURTEEN

As soon as his role in attaching the Mythic Core to the building had been completed, Joe was unceremoniously cast outside of the pyramid. Until the door finally firmly closed, Joe had to watch in utter bemusement as Jake ran to the central cauldron while squealing in glee until the door finally firmly closed. It wasn't a sight he'd ever expected to see from his stoic, menacing mentor, but he could understand the sentiment. Frankly, he *perfectly* understood Jake's attitude at the moment. If he had access to a Grand Ritual Hall, he'd be doing the exact same thing.

Even though he landed on his feet, Joe felt the need to brush off his shoulders as though he had dirt on them. Perhaps it was just the fact that bruises were forming where Jake had been holding on to him when he chucked the Ritualist out of the entrance. Luckily, those were already fading, thanks to his constant healing aura. Joe took a moment to view the notification he'd received, shaking his head in wonder.

Pyramid of Panacea (Legendary). For all intents and purposes for the creation of items, this Alchemy Hall will be treated as a Legendary structure. It will allow for the creation of Injections of the Legendary rank at a

5% greater success rate. Sage-ranked Concoctions can be attempted with a 0.5% greater chance of success. Other functions exist. See the building owner for a full description.

"Not a huge fan of the information being stuck behind a paywall, but if that's how it's got to be, I get it." Joe let out a small exhalation containing every last drop of jealousy he was feeling at the moment, remembering wistfully the Grand Ritual Hall back in the previous zone. He still didn't have the bonafides to own or control that building, but the sheer fact that it allowed him to create things greater than his personal skill level meant that he could progress at a monstrous rate. "As soon as I can grab my building from Midgard, I'm taking that Core back, favor or no."

If nothing else, the fact that the Mythic Core was safe for the moment was a huge weight off his shoulders. As it stood, Joe didn't have the method or means to protect it on his own. Now he would feel comfortable pushing forward with his plans to fight and collect his own resources. As he lamented the fact of how few people had the tools or workstations they needed in order to complete their own tasks, the Rituarchitect realized that he could likely create a profitable feedback loop if he was the first to make those displaced workers some hope—even if that might step on the toes of his erstwhile allies.

"Am I okay with ramping up the friction with the Dwarves? I guess… yeah, I am." Taking a breath, Joe found that he was filled with a newfound resolve. With the Hamlet's upgrade likely drawing to a close soon, he was going to start creating as many buildings and businesses as he could get away with. "I need to ensure a steady supply of resources, if I want to execute my new plan: 'Nibbled to death by ducks'. Long code name, amazing results."

Each now-confident stride he took was accompanied by a resounding crunch. The snow and frozen earth submitted to the weight of his feet as he pushed himself forward with renewed vigor. A lack of planning was the largest detriment to his overall success, and he'd once more allowed himself to get swept up in doing what others needed from him or thought of him, instead of seeking and achieving his own goals.

No longer.

Now, he'd fight for every ounce of what he believed that he deserved, and if anyone had an issue with that… well, he could always start another settlement somewhere else.

Soon, he had crossed the tundra that this Hamlet had been built upon, reaching the wall and directly Omnivaulting to the top. Joe did a flip, pushing off a Ritual Orb that he'd thrown out at the last moment to execute a mid-air double jump. Landing on the top of the battlements with a whoop of excitement, he looked into the distance—where he could see monsters swarming toward the very walls he was standing on. "Let's go get my hands dirty!"

Accelerating directly into a sprint, he ran along the top of the wall until he found what appeared to be the smallest gap between the stone protections. He pumped mana into his Omnivault, launching himself across the distance and easily landing on the next wall over. "That's a bad sign. If I can make that jump, a monster three times my size *definitely* can. I'll let someone know, and… I guess I can only hope they'll listen!"

There was something freeing about *knowing* he was no longer in charge. He could focus on his character build and just have fun for the first time in a long time, and Joe was going to chase that. At least until he was inevitably drawn back in when the Dwarven Council realized that they simply couldn't expand quickly enough without his assistance. "Either that, or they'll want to move as slow as possible, losing all the momentum we've gained from diving right in. That seems like a very Dwarf-civilization thing to do. Only allow the *possibility* of a city after a hundred years or so? Nah, forget *that.* I've got to make sure that doesn't happen."

Omnivaulting another three times was enough to bring him to the end of the walls. Even if that was a concerningly short amount of distance in his own mind, Joe reminded himself that these walls surrounded a vast area of land that they were planning to build the last bastion of Dwarven civilization in. The fact that they had already made multiple rings of walls around the city was to be commended, and they clearly had plans to expand further. There was nothing to do but not worry about it for now.

Joe looked out over the edge of the defenses, taking stock of the situation and holding himself back from his initial plan of throwing himself over the edge and straight into the fight. "Throw myself in…? *What?* Where'd that thought even come from? I can do so much more from up here than I could down there, surrounded by enemies. Go, Ritual Orbs!"

Currently, he only had two of his orbs bound to individual Characteristics: the first to his Intelligence, the second to Strength. Happily, he had another option for dealing extreme amounts of damage to large, single targets. Thanks to increasing the rank of his Ritual Orb skill, he was able to lift each of them into position before having them unspool into the Ritual of Summoning. Just before he activated the ritual, Joe remembered to set out his cubes in a formation to offer the ritual additional stability.

Pushing mana into the orb, in his mind called orb five, Joe activated the spell that had been captured. Planar Shift flared to life as the preset ritual began drinking in power. Moments later, the orb was surrounded by a desiccated skull with oversized fangs. "Welcome to Jotunheim, Morsum."

He wasn't expecting an answer, which was perfect as the summoned Pseudo-Lich skull merely contemplated the fleshy human, hunger the only feeling it exuded. Joe wasn't concerned, as the skull had only ever spoken in times of intense emotion, such as being offered a contract so that it could fly, or after draining a particularly delicious enemy of their life essence. Controlling his first two orbs, one of which was shaped like a dumbbell, and the other like an oversized needle, the Ritualist targeted the closest of the monsters and got to work taking them down.

Thanks to his skill reaching the Apprentice rank, the base

damage of his attacks with a skillfully used orb was two hundred and two points of damage. In the case of the Intelligence orb, that was automatically converted to piercing damage. The Strength orb gained a hefty bonus, dealing two hundred *ninety* points of damage per strike. When he was using his remaining weapons in a non-skillful manner, they took a slight hit to their output, only managing one hundred fifty-one damage per hit.

Even with throwing everything he could at a single creature at a time, Joe realized that it was going to take on average fifty strikes to bring just one of the Penguins down. "These things have something like ten thousand health? That's *boss* level on any other world so far!"

"Morrr-yum." The Pseudo-Lich skull groaned at him, eyes locked on an oversized Penguin speeding toward them.

"Yum? Oh, you see the elite out there. I thought we had more time before the final wave." Joe gave up on his current target, deciding that it would be more fruitful to take the resources from an elite monster than a standard one, anyway. As the extremely oversized avian was speeding toward them at double the speed the lesser Penguins could achieve, he didn't need to wait long.

He pulled the orb with Morsum attached back, lining up the shot and shoving forward with his hand and mind at the same time. The summoned creature was launched forward as Joe shot-putted it at the bird in the distance, his control over the orb allowing him to account for sudden shifts and turns. Joe dropped a Dark Lightning Strike on the beast, interrupting its concentration and allowing Morsum to nestle into place unimpeded.

The skull struck and stuck just behind the left wing of the bird, teeth digging in and beginning to drain the creature just as it let out its first cry of pain for this round of combat. Joe spread his arms to the side and brought his fingers together to cut off the view of anything other than his target in the center of his makeshift sight picture. The remainder of his orbs blasted out, slamming into the creature one after another. Damage notifications began accumulating, but Joe ignored them in favor of controlling his orbs in a parabolic arc upward, followed by a straight-line slam into the Penguin from behind.

The elite Penguin didn't even attempt to avoid them—except for the Intelligence orb. Each of his orbs were like tiny rockets, but the sharpened one? Even though it was faster than the others around it, the Penguin took great pains to dodge it. Joe fully understood that this was due to the thick layer of feathers and blubber mitigating blunt damage, and the orb in question was able to pierce directly through that and inflict all of the intended damage. "Abyss, I just realized that Cone of Cold is going to be practically useless in this world. I should unequip that and put something else in its place…"

Only the fact that Joe was safely ensconced far above the creatures allowed him to take the time to think through future combat even while being embroiled in it at the moment. "Acid Spray *could* work; it should be able to deal more damage than a frost-based attack against a creature seemingly immune to the cold. Feces, it sped up!"

Joe hadn't been the only one with the idea of claiming the rewards of the elite monster for themselves. Half a dozen Dwarves conglomerated around it, their axes, swords, and spears lashing out in an attempt to be the one to achieve victory. This made the human grumble slightly, but happily or concerningly depending on how he thought about it. Even with all of the enhancements to their bodies, the Dwarves were simply not able to keep up with the elite monster in its own frozen domain. For a long moment, as the Penguin raced toward Joe's location, he didn't quite understand what it was attempting to do.

Then his eyes widened. Joe mentally called his Ritual Orbs back to himself, finally abandoning them at the last moment as he sprinted away, Omnivaulting to the next wall over. Even as he was jumping, the Penguin had launched itself off the ground and shot over the barricade like a dolphin breaching the surface of the ocean. The odd sight typically would've made Joe laugh, but as the Penguin reached the apex of its overhead arc, it angled itself to its fall with a sharp beak, clearly intent on penetrating his soft human flesh in passing. "Jumping was a terrible idea!"

Just before Joe gave into despair, his Strength-bound orb reached him, and he pushed off the metal rung in a second Omnivault. The increased speed, and slight shift in angle meant that the Penguin zipped by him with a mere half a foot of clearance, instead of going directly through his chest. Morsum and Joe locked eyes for a split second that seemed to last a full minute, thanks to the dense adrenaline pumping through his system. The Ritualist could've sworn that the Pseudo-Lich was smiling.

"At least one of us is happy right now!" Joe grumbled to himself as he scrambled to land on the wall and keep himself in position. Just after he got his feet under him, the wall shook from an intense blow, the elite having rammed it. A section of wall crumbled immediately, the hastily constructed protections failing under the first direct strike from a monster.

Only half of his orbs had made it back into his hands, but that was all Joe needed for the moment. As the Penguin flapped its wings, jumping roughly twenty feet in the air and slamming its head into the stone wall like a woodpecker into an apple tree, the Ritualist tried to figure out why it was furiously attacking instead of joining up with the main group and hunting the Town Hall.

In an instant, Joe discerned that the stretch of stone he was standing on now formed a self-contained box, entrapping the Penguin on all fronts. Evidently, a stone-headed geomancer had failed to understand that creating barriers without an exit meant the destruction of everything in the monster's path. Now devoid of the enigmatic signal directing its course, the feathered menace would plow forward relentlessly until it achieved its goal or entered a section that would reignite that odd compulsion.

Until then, Joe could only start working to grind its health down, seeing as no one else had access to the monster at the moment. "Note to self, complain about the sandstone walls and make sure someone yells at whoever is making these, until they all connect back to an opening that goes to the Town Hall."

Nom nom.

"Yeah, yeah, I get it! Glad *you're* enjoying yourself, Morsum."

CHAPTER FIFTEEN

The elite broke through the wall on its seventh strike, giving it direct access to the next corridor of space leading to the town. The entire time, Joe was peppering it with various attacks, seasoning his strikes with the occasional Dark Lightning Strike. To his dismay, as soon as it made it through the wall, the Penguin was once more enthralled and began scooting along the open space at high speed. "Abyss, most of the defenders are at the entrance. This is going to have another straight shot at the Town Hall, if I don't block it off!"

Happily, all he needed to do to catch up was Omnivault to the next wall, and in a handful of minutes, the elite Penguin had circled the entirety of the town and was once more approaching him at high speed. Joe threw everything he had at the creature, ever-so-slowly battering its health down. Now he was thankful that a few of the Dwarves had landed some attacks, as this creature had a solid twenty thousand health. If he had needed to rely entirely on his own efforts, Joe would have needed to close in on a hundred total blows before taking it down.

Even after he'd gotten in another thirty hits, the Penguin

completely ignored his existence and shot past him, vanishing into the distance like a race car on an open highway. Joe winced as it failed to control its speed. Instead of making a perfect turn, the Penguin slammed into the wall at the end of the straightaway, causing a section of it to disintegrate from the sheer momentum. "Good thing that's leading out and not in. Still going to let a bunch of monsters skip the line, so not *all* good."

Jumping to the next wall over, Joe once more got into position. He'd learned from the creature's previous movements, so he placed himself directly at the end of the path. Practically holding his breath, he lifted his weapons into the air and prepared to cast his spells.

Thirty seconds had scarcely elapsed since Joe had taken his position, and a blur crossed his vision. The Penguin materialized before him in a cloud of dust as it impacted the wall, tearing it apart in the process. As it struggled to change its course and regain its momentum, Joe took advantage of the fact that its frenzied dash had been slowed—unloading all of his spells and orbs once more. He scored a direct hit with his Intelligence-bound orb and punctured a fist-size hole all the way from the front to the back of the monster.

A strangled scream-squawk told Joe that he was making good progress, and he furiously battered the creature as it began to pick up speed once more. Seeing that its health was rushing towards empty, Joe activated the spell contained in his Strength orb and let the spell Corify take effect just before it got out of range of his attacks. He watched it go, planning his next assault… when the Penguin suddenly flopped forward, its beak slamming into the ground and sending the monster tumbling through the air.

You have slain an Elite Defeatist Fluttering Penguin!

Experience gained: 500.

Morsum feels satiated!

Corify has caused a guaranteed Core drop from this monster.

Not taking a break to catch his breath, Joe sprinted over to the monster to ensure that he was able to claim his spoils of war. When he got to the fallen beast, he held his Intelligence orb in the air directly in front of him, slowly inching it forward as it spun like a drill to penetrate the thick hide of the beast. It took him a full minute of searching, but he emerged victorious, if coated in gunk, holding the Rare Core triumphantly. As the blood and gore was whisked from him and his acquired goods, he stored the treasure in his spatial storage codpiece, the very instant a half-dozen Dwarves began congregating on his location.

"Hand that Core over, bro!" the lead Dwarf bellowed at him. "By order of the council, we're collecting those!"

Deciding against arguing, Joe spared a long glance at his slain enemy with slight annoyance before Omnivaulting to the top of the wall and running into the distance. "Looks like they aren't going to give me much time to handle my own collection of goods… am I in the opposition now, somehow?"

A vision struck him: sneaking out at night, being a reverse Anarchist as he created beautiful buildings in a perfect grid square, enriching and enhancing the town as his detractors attempted to keep him from making the town close in on an upgrade. It seemed incredibly bizarre for a moment, earning a chuckle before Joe realized that this might eventually be an event that came to pass, if the Dwarves were unwilling to rapidly reach for a City tier. That put a wince on his face, but he'd already decided how he was going to handle things if the situation got to that point.

Joe pulled out the Rare Core, trying to think of how best to use it and absentmindedly unsummoned Morsum. He was down to one full Rare Core and ninety percent of the other one, which he'd used to make a schedule for day and night. With such a hard limit on what he could create, Joe needed to build up his personal reserves and make sure he didn't fund things for free going forward. "Didn't that resource management guy tell me that no one would try to claim my goods? Something shifty is going on, and I don't like it."

Beast Wave complete! Congratulations, your Tier one Hamlet has met all of the conditions required to be recognized as a Tier two Village! As you are no longer actively attempting to increase the rank of your town, you will only need to deal with wandering monsters as well as a Beast Wave approximately every 48 hours.

New building slots have opened up.

1,000 slots for Trash-ranked are available!

500 slots for Damaged.

50 slots for Common.

25 slots for Uncommon.

1/10 slots for Rare remain.

The requirements for reaching a Tier three Town are as follows:

1) Surviving Beast Waves. (Village → Town: 25 waves.) — Condition not met.

2) All pre-modifier Common and above building slots filled. (0/50 Common, 0/25 Uncommon, 9/10 Rare) — Condition not met. (Artifact ranked Alchemy Hall is counting as 8 Rare, Rare Smithy is counting as 1)

3) Morale modifier: 200/500. — Condition not met.

4) Population: 92,412/1,000 — Condition met.

5) Uncommon Town Hall (Upgrade in progress.)

Every 100 points in positive morale allows for an additional 10 Common buildings, or one Uncommon. Every 500 allows for one additional Rare along with the others. Every thousand allows for an additional Unique structure.

Originally, Joe had planned to run back to where he'd leveled the ground and perhaps claim that space as his own. But instead, he slammed his feet into the stone and reversed course, realizing that what he actually needed was easy access into the entrance of the defensive corridors. He assumed that nobody would be jostling for that position yet, and he had many uses for such a space.

After making the sudden decision, only a few minutes in total passed as he sprinted, Omnivaulted, and finally allowed his feet to collide with the ground, causing him to sink to his ankles in the snow and blood-ice slurry next to the entrance of the walls.

Instead of digging himself out, Joe simply leaned forward

and created a Field Array at ground level, ripping away the top layer of soil and filth in an instant. He did this two more times, clearing a large amount of space. Then he pulled out his survey tool and measured his distances, leaving three inches of space between the two projects he had planned. "What I *need* to do is make an Anima Supported Prodigal Entrepot Containment Tower, but that's a Unique building. I can't get that in place until the town upgrades at least one more time… or I get the morale modifier up. Better leave room for it to go right up against the wall and snag the last Rare building slot."

He needed a workshop where he could set up a permanent stabilization station and contain some of the more dangerous rituals he would leave running at all times. Joe's fingers were flashing as he searched through all of his blueprints. After finding what he needed, he set up his stabilization cubes. Somehow, he just *knew* there'd be someone seeking him out to stop him from doing exactly what he was doing at this moment: grabbing every benefit he could. In fact, Joe was certain he could hear someone shouting his name in the distance, but he ignored them in favor of dumping mana into the ritual.

As soon as the circles flared to life, he let out a quick exhale. Anyone who interrupted him now would be endangering people's lives. With that concern out of the way, Joe took direct control of the ritual, having it move as slowly as possible. He was the only one supplying it with power, and if he went too fast, it would collapse, destroying the ritual, wasting the aspects, and most likely sapping the life out of Joe before fully expiring.

Ever so slowly, the building came together. Joe almost lost control during a flinch as Havoc let out a long, smoke-filled sigh. The Dwarf was standing right next to the Rituarchitect, critically eyeing the building being raised. "You know that Snow wants me to stop you, right?"

Joe kept his silence for a long moment, but it didn't seem that the Dwarf was going to press the issue. "What's going on with that, Havoc? I literally just saved everyone here from extinction. It'd be nice to have a little bit of leeway before the leader I just rescued turned on me. Some advance notice, perhaps?"

"You're a smart kid. I'm sure you figured it out by now. At least part of it." Havoc shrugged noncommittally, not taking his eyes off of the workshop that was nearing completion. "Humans are used to working in a different time scale. Snow is thinking a lot more like I bet the old monsters on this planet are. The likelihood of the bifrost coming anywhere near us in the next century is close to zero. That means that the Elves who're pursuing us have only two options. The first, and least likely, is that they're going to come to Jotunheim and try to build faster than us, then eventually slowly spread out across the surface of the planet in order to find us and finish us off."

"By then, you'll be so deeply entrenched, and have such impressive defenses, that you're ready for them, I assume?" Joe had worked out what he would be worried about and decided to test the water and see if they were aligned with the Dwarves' concerns. "You think that the only other possibility is that they wait for us to create a city, opening the bifrost directly into the heart of the city, and wipe you out from there. That sound about right?"

Havoc nodded solemnly. "That's about the gist of it. As to why you're getting edged out? The fact that you lost your status, your title, could be as simple as our people becoming a Shattered Race then our people refusing to work with you. I believe you, 'cause that's what you *said* happened. But, as the paranoid faction keeps reminding our not-so-fearless leader, it *could* mean that you officially decided to work against us and betrayed our people. That would definitely also explain the lack of an Excommunicated title."

"I'm not directly or intentionally working against your people," Joe stated quietly, even as he finished the building he knew the Dwarves were unhappy about. "I'll say this. I played a major part in saving the Dwarven race. As it stands, do you think that I'd throw away the goodwill that came from doing that? Last thought… you've seen what I can do. I bought freedom for your people; now I'm expecting my own freedom in return. I haven't asked for favors, awards, or high positions. I fully intend to remain a good friend of the Dwarves. Can you guarantee that your people feel the same way? If not, I just need to be left alone to work things out."

Havoc stayed silent for a while, thinking about what answer he wanted to give. Joe knew that the exceedingly paranoid Grandmaster wouldn't give him a quick answer and expect it to be trusted. Therefore, when the Dwarf did speak after nearly ten minutes of consideration, Joe listened well.

"There's a faction that wants us to create our own city, inside our own walls, where humans aren't allowed to tread. They want an outer city, the trade quarter, where others can do their business without putting the main body of our people at risk. I tell you this, though, Joe. You're *my* Apprentice. Both of us know you deserve better than you've been shown since we got here, and I *will* make sure you get your due. Could take a while. I'll try to make them be polite to you while they figure themselves out."

Joe slowly nodded then started walking toward the entrance to his new workshop. "That's not asking for too much, is it?"

"Nah," Havoc told him in a deep tone. "To be straight with you, lad, I think that's the problem. The *real* problem. Every single one of my people owe you a heavy debt. The worry warts are afraid that you're going to come and collect. Even if you ask for something absolutely outrageous… at this point, how could they *possibly* say no?"

That made Joe realize a possible *true* reason the Council of Masters was avoiding him so heavily. If he walked up to them and made a demand, their honor would dictate their response. But if he could never get close, Joe could never ask for anything, could he? Against his own expectations, that put a smile on the human's face. He gave Havoc a nod and stepped into his workshop. "Lots of work to be done, if we're going to turn this Village into a City in under a year."

"That's the spirit, human." Havoc quietly murmured, the

ashes of his cigar catching in midair and swirling in a loop around the new building. Unbeknownst to Joe, bright letters formed on each of the walls in a spectrum the human race couldn't see. The Dwarf winked at the closed door, then turned and started walking back toward the Town Hall, his mouth forming into a firm line.

"Abyss, I hope I can slap some sense into these shiftless fools before that bald guy loses his temper and turns this place into a crater."

CHAPTER SIXTEEN

"I figured out light for them for free, but what should I do for water?" Joe didn't want to actually set everything up for the community without some form of clearly stated and agreed-upon payment, but he figured he could get started on the work before they finally broke down and absolutely *needed* it. Then he could have an answer instantly, and Joe didn't mind looking extremely competent.

Using a variety of spells, he could always maintain homeostasis for himself. As an example, his aura allowed Joe to remain well-hydrated and in perfect health. That meant that figuring out this issue on behalf of the people around him was more akin to a riddle he was determined to decipher. Thanks to his previous experience, it was less challenging to source water than it was to tackle issues of air quality or heating such a colossal unprotected expanse.

Granted, he could easily solve the issue of living areas by constructing residential structures such as apartment complexes. But without a clear quest and reward offered, he wasn't going to undertake such a monumental task using his own resources. In fact, Joe wasn't entirely certain if homes and the like were going to be a main focus at *all*, thanks to the temporary housing that he'd managed to get in place in under a day. "You know… that's a good point. What if we built only structures that were useful for research, item creation, storage, and the like? Would we be able to advance up the technology tree faster?"

Again, it was an interesting thought experiment, but it was unlikely that he'd be able to convince tens of thousands of people to live in literal bubbles for upwards of a year. He snorted and let a rueful chuckle escape his upturned lips. "Then again… I'm not in charge. *I* don't need to convince anyone."

Just like that, Joe decided that he was going to fill every single building slot with useful facilities. When they reached the level of a city, he was certain there'd be plenty of slots available for the use of housing: he could likely even make enormous skyscrapers that could contain the entirety of the remaining Dwarven race in a single building. Blinking away the daydream, Joe returned to the issue of water.

It was a profoundly simple issue. Water was all around them. This was a world of ice, and a simple step outside would put him in the snow. But any water that was collected needed to be maintained at a temperature that allowed it to *remain* a liquid.

That meant any water collection needed to include a source of heat, and if they wanted to pipe that water to individual buildings or cisterns, the entire route would need to be warmed somehow. Even then, not only would the collection points need to be heated, but the pipes would as well. With no visible source of wood, the only easily accessible flammable material was Penguin blubber. Joe was certain that using that resource for that purpose would drastically reduce the air quality in the Village, meaning they'd just be trading one problem for another.

"The solution is absolutely going to be mana and magic." Joe had been going down his checklist piece by piece, and this was where all paths led. "If we don't want to just hire a massive workforce of people dedicated to pumping their mana regen into rituals or enchantments, I'm going to need to start converting Cores into Mana Batteries. Then the next step is… figure out how many of the monsters drop a Core. If it's a whole bunch of them, we can make a self-sustaining civilization and economy entirely off of the monsters that are trying to destroy us."

He tapped on his paper a few times, slowly nodding in acceptance of his own thoughts. "Yes… I like that. It's elegant. The monsters don't want us to have a city. The only way we can possibly have one is by harvesting the monsters that are trying to stop us. I guess the only question is, does that make us symbiotic with this planet or parasitic? Follow-up question: why do I care?"

Joe's remaining checklist was fairly straightforward at this point. Once he got confirmation that there was an abundance of Cores thanks to the Beast Waves, he'd invest in creating an exceedingly stabilized Ritual of Enchantment for the production of Mana Batteries. Using those as a base for his construction and rituals, he'd be able to remove the bottleneck of gathering people and having volunteers work with him.

With his path determined, Joe pushed himself to his feet and darted out the door. Running toward the large mound of slowly freezing corpses in the distance, he thought about how he was going to phrase all of his questions and propositions. After much thought, he settled instead on a crude strategy. Joe resolutely steeled himself for the possibility that, if he failed to obtain what he needed from the Dwarves due to their obstinance, he'd start working to stockpile an exorbitant amount of resources.

Then, he would go and build a city in one fell swoop… *after* turning the surrounding countryside into an absolute death trap of rituals. It might take a long time to build a city on his own, but Joe had faith that he could do it.

Approaching the Dwarf that was in charge of cataloging

everything in the pile, Joe made sure to keep his posture firm and unyielding. "I need a report on what sort of resources we can acquire from each of the monsters. What their body parts are good for, what the rate of Core drops is."

"Ah, Mr. Joe. Major General Havoc told me to be expecting you." The bearded Dwarf, who had recently offered to warm up the bald human, handed over a sheet of paper and started going over it line by line. "As you can see here, the Penguins are excellent for fuel as well as meat. The feathers that they provide will have a range of uses, from the design of clothing to ward off the chill to fletchings for ballista bolts. They're too large for regular arrows, though we have some industrious Dwarves hard at work creating oversized feather blankets."

Moving down, he pointed at the section detailing the Hoardlings, "These nasty beasts have a few tricks up their sleeves: even after death, they exude cold. If we weren't on this frozen planet, I'd say that we should use chunks of their body to refrigerate foods and drinks. Their bodies are *lightly* toxic, and samples have been provided to the Alchemy Hall for further study. As far as we can tell, their leather will be useful for armors; once again, we hope to see a benefit against the cold by using them."

Joe opened his mouth to speak, but the Dwarf pushed on without giving him a chance. "To answer your last question, we see an Uncommon Core from the Penguins in one out of every five bodies or so, one out of four of the same for the Hoardlings. We didn't get a Core from the first Elite Penguin, but our information states that you managed to extract a Rare Core from the second. Can you confirm that for me?"

Having worked himself up into a fervor, Joe felt slightly put off by the fact that each of his questions was answered in a clear and succinct manner. "Oh. Yes, I did get a Rare off that, but I also used a spell that guarantees a Core being formed if the target is killed within a few seconds of its casting."

"I see. Thank you, that helps with the knowledge of its

worth. Unfortunately, it doesn't give us much information on its drop rate." The Dwarf marked something down on his own sheets of paper, looking up and studying Joe a moment later. "There was approximately a twenty percent increase in each wave of monsters. Four hundred for the first, a little over seven hundred on the fifth wave. That included an elite Penguin, bringing us to approximately two thousand, eight hundred monsters for the entirety of the assault. We weathered two full assaults, which means we're expecting approximately fourteen hundred Uncommon Cores, after we're able to fully process each of these."

Joe stood there for a moment, mind whirling as he took in all of this information and tried to find the best way to use it. "Thank you, that was... very helpful. Is there any chance I could request a large number of these for my own uses? The Cores especially would be great for my work."

"Yours and everyone else's." The Dwarf told him dryly. "Not to mention the thousands of noncombatants who want to find a way to purchase the Cores for experience in lieu of risking their own neck. I will also note, the group that chased you away from your kill have been reprimanded, and the body is en route to your workshop as we speak. We guarantee that any of your kills will remain your property from this point forward. Is there anything else I could help you with at the moment?"

Joe could tell that Havoc must've been hard at work since their meeting, and he felt a wave of relief that the not-so-subtle shoving of him to the side might have been firmly halted. "For now... that will be all. Thank you for the information, and let me know if there's anything I can do for the people around here."

"Are you... perhaps *looking* for things to do?" The blandness of the Dwarf's tone was what truly caught Joe's attention, and he turned around with a gleam in his eye.

"To *think* I was just about to walk away! Do you, perhaps,

have a *quest* for me?" Joe chuckled as a slight smile appeared on the Dwarf's stony face.

"Well… I don't have any official authorization to make this *request…*" the Dwarf started evasively, making Joe's smile go wider. If they were making a deal under the table, he could get paid in the same way and charge a premium for it. "You may have noticed the enormous pile of over five thousand bodies behind me. You may also notice that they're out in the open, promoting disease, unease, and spoilage. In this cold, I wouldn't usually consider that last concern as a possibility, but since they're so resistant to the cold, I've already noticed signs of decomposition on some of the earliest-gathered of them."

"Would you perhaps be interested in having a warehouse devoted to the storage of the creatures we'll be getting *all* of our resources from for the foreseeable future?" Joe pretended to think long and hard about what he would ask for, but he'd already decided on his path. The Ritualist mumbled to himself as he placed a salesman's smile on his lips. "I see it's already time to enact 'Nibbled to Death by Ducks'."

"Sorry, missed that last part?" The Dwarf leaned forward, hoping for clarification, but Joe merely waved him off while keeping a broad smile on his face. "Erm, yeah. Without proper storage, all of this is going to be trash in no time flat. We don't have a hollow mountain to dump all our waste and failed projects into anymore, and I don't think most people have realized that yet."

"I can make that happen." Even as he was speaking, Joe whipped out his notepad and made a note to create several large-scale rituals for 'Little Sister's Cleaning Service'. That would be a constant source of low-rarity aspects in the near future. "Storage, that is, not a mountain. In fact, I can make it happen *right now*. But I want one percent."

"Say that again; I can't have heard you correctly." The Dwarf rubbed at his ears as though Joe had just said something extremely offensive. "You want me to pay you in a *percentage*? Have you never *met* a Dwarf? Our entire society is based on creating and following Oligarchs! I'm not about to be swindled like this."

"Don't be too hasty!" Joe's wide smile had never wavered. "You didn't hear the rest of the offer."

He paused, letting the silence entice his negotiation partner, who finally cracked. "Well? Spit it out, human!"

"I'm not going to charge you for the building, but I'll directly transfer ownership of it to you. Not to the council, not to a group... *you.*" Joe only paused for a second this time, knowing better than to let an idea marinate when it was supposed to be flash-fried. "Instead of paying me for an Uncommon warehouse, all I ask is that one percent of what gets stored there gets tossed out a little bit... early. Instead of just sitting on the materials until they rot because no one can use them fast enough, only ten out of a thousand of the corpses that need to be processed get sent my way. Anything given to me as payment for another job does not count against this number, of course. We'll keep the details just between us?"

"Of course." The Dwarf was rubbing at his beard thoughtfully. "I suppose no one's going to look into one... percent... *urgh.* At least, not too hard... agreed."

"Just make it an official quest, and I'll start building right away." Joe loved seeing the wince the Dwarf didn't even try to hide. Much like a magical contract, a quest meant that the percentage would be seen as his quest reward, and the system would enforce the payment—and lash out directly against the Dwarf if the deal wasn't followed to the letter.

The Dwarf agreed, with the caveat that the warehouse had to be ready to use in under an hour. Joe accepted, much to the relief of the Dwarf, who apparently had no faith that Joe would be able to perform the miracle of getting an audience with the Dwarven Council and acquiring permission to build.

But Joe didn't mind skipping that step. Fifteen minutes later, feathery bodies were being transported into a brand new warehouse, and an excited—if slightly crestfallen—Dwarf was shaking Joe's hand.

As the human walked away, he kept an eye on his surroundings, hoping he'd find yet another need he could handle. "Hmm… those craftsmen look *really* cold, working out in the open like this. Let's see if any of them are interested in leatherworking in a toasty workshop instead of around a fire that keeps going out."

CHAPTER SEVENTEEN

"It's a pleasure doing business with you." Joe shook the hand of the mustachioed Dwarf. She was interested in creating a scented soap company with the tallow she would render from the Penguins, as well as somehow being able to produce crystallized lye from burning hair from the Hoardlings. Apparently, her business partner would use the excess tallow for candles or food preservation, so realistically, it was going to be a two-for-one special.

While that was great, Joe's focus was on what he could acquire as an investor. Since this company was going to be creating actual goods, and he didn't really *need* much of anything, his bargain was for two percent of the final products instead of materials.

"Please come visit us soon! The Joy of Pleasant Scents looks forward to delighting our guests in the near future, and we are very excited to have our items featured in your constructions in the future."

Joe could only admire the business savvy and Charisma this Dwarf exuded. If she weren't going to open her own shop, he would try to hire her as a salesperson on his behalf. As it stood, he could only nod and graciously accept her thanks. There was no reason to explain to her that he would never use the scented soap or candles for himself.

Smelling good never hurt anyone, but his goal was to have small gifts and such to offer to guests and friends in the future. As for Joe, his protective magic was so effective that not even a trace of the smell would be able to linger in the air around him. Sure, he enjoyed nice-smelling things as much as the next person. But experience had taught him that, as soon as he let his guard down, someone would get a bloodhound or other mythological analog to hunt him down—or perhaps figure out how to use the skin cells he shed for a nefarious spell.

As he left the new workshop behind, Joe looked around at all the progress he had managed to force. The area was filling out nicely, and even though he didn't have actual access to the Town Hall at the moment to see the area development metrics, he was keeping a running tally in his head. If he had to guess, at this point, the chart in the Town Hall would look something like:

Building slots remaining:
1,000/1,000 Trash slots remain.
500/500 Damaged slots remain.
35/50 Common slots remain.
12/25 Uncommon slots remain.
0/10 Rare slots remain.

The nice thing was that he didn't even *need* to keep an actual list if he didn't want to, as his class experience for Rituarchitect went up by a set amount for each building he made. That was indication enough for him to be able to remember everything. Between the Common, Uncommon, and Rare buildings, Joe had already pulled in two thousand, two hundred and fifty experience, pushing him over the edge into Rituarchitect level eleven.

For a few minutes after gaining the new level, he'd waited and hoped that the system would give him some small accolade, perhaps an item that would be useful to him. Then he remembered that he'd earned a *massive* reward at level ten—the Ritual of the Traveling Civilization at the Grandmaster rank—so he shouldn't expect to be given anything more until he reached… perhaps level fifteen?

Still, that called into question for him the last time he had actually earned a level in the Rituarchitect class. After thinking about it for a moment, he shook his head and chuckled. "I got to level ten all the way back on Midgard… that was two worlds away! This class *really* needs some love, and luckily, I have a whole empty world to fill up. Time to find the next sucker—whoops, I mean the next person who needs a building, who I can generously help."

He'd already secured supply chains for all kinds of luxury goods, everything from embroidered satchels to completed weapons and armor to base materials gathered from monster waves. Joe's eyes alighted on a group of Dwarves who each had a pickaxe, shovel, and various other tools with them. With a smile on his face, he walked toward the group of miners that had no mineshaft, prepared to start offering his usual deal.

"Joe!" The human turned toward the familiar voice, nodding in acknowledgment as he realized that the Dwarven Council had sent a familiar face to do their dirty work this time. "You've got to know that you can't just outright own the whole Village and expect that there won't be some pushback."

"Major Cleave! So good to see you as well." Joe started the conversation with a bit of tightness in his voice, annoyed that she'd skipped basic pleasantries. Then he reassessed his feelings, recognizing that she had always been efficient to the point of being abrupt. "Can I ask what you're talking about?"

The Dwarf grunted as she came to a stop in front of him. "The council saw what you were doing, called a vote, and created the first law for the village. Do you know what the first law in any new settlement *usually* is? Almost always, it's something to do with not stealing or protections for the people, something to that effect. Not here. No, they needed to waste the limited number of laws that they can make by starting with 'no individual can own more than five percent of the total buildings in this Village'. They told me to come get you and bring you in as a favor, so that you can choose which of the buildings you're going to be giving over to the council directly."

"What a nice favor!" Joe shrugged helplessly as he waved. "Unfortunately, I can't help you with that. I only own one of the buildings in town: my workshop. If I do the math… I only own one out of the thirty-two buildings here… that's nowhere *near* five percent! Man, what a strict law to put into place and affect no one at all, when they can only make a few total laws. Bummer, there. Sorry to say, I can't help you out."

"I just *saw* you make that shop. What do you mean that you don't own it?" Cleave pointed accusingly at the shop where two Dwarves were painting 'The Joy of Pleasant Scents' above the door with smiles on their faces. The greataxe-wielding Dwarf furrowed her brow as she realized what they were doing. "I see. You're subverting this law already, and you didn't even know it was being made."

"How could I subvert a law that didn't *exist*?" Joe's professional smile was fading rapidly, and he let it go in favor of watching the Dwarf with a stony stare. "It does seem like a *strange* law for people who revere Oligarchs. I can't say that I disagree with that proposition, as I believe allowing people to run their own businesses and make their own way in life is the path toward prosperity. In fact, I truly hope that it's *incredibly* difficult to change that law or get rid of it."

"It's nearly impossible, unless the Town Hall is destroyed." Cleave informed him, a considering look on her face as she let her eyes rove the human up and down. "Something about you has changed. I can't say I don't like it. You seem overall calmer and happier. Good. I'll go and inform the council how badly they messed up just now. For your information, I did put forward an opinion on the matter before the vote, stating that it seemed they were targeting a single person with this law. I'm pleased that you had the forethought to disrupt their plans."

"Aww, is someone liking the company of humans?" Joe

shook his head as a conspiratorial smile appeared on his face. "Never thought I'd see the day."

At first, the Dwarf didn't answer him, merely nodding and starting to walk away. She slowed to a halt and spoke over her shoulder without looking directly at him. "Our time together showed me that I was misguided on many things, and I'm sad to know that time has drawn to an end. Not only am I impressed by you, and in a lesser way humans in general, but I no longer hold an innate disgust for bald, clean-shaven people. You've shown me that sometimes what matters is the beard you grow on the inside."

Joe didn't have anything to say to that, chalking the strange compliment up to cultural differences as his once-teammate walked away. With a lighter heart, he moved over to his original target: the group of miners having a fierce argument nearby. "Good day, fine Dudes and Dudettes! You seem to be having an issue, and I was wondering if I could offer my services?"

At first, only scorn-filled glances were sent his way, but then one of the Dwarves grabbed the apparent leader by the shoulder and whispered something sharply into his ear while gesturing at Joe. The human waited patiently, pretending that he couldn't hear exactly what was being said, just like every other member of the group who had third-threshold Perception. "That's the human that was a Major General! You know, the one that got us to the Bifrost! He's a magic bro, maybe he *can* actually help!"

The Ritualist was glad his reputation was starting to precede him again, this time in a positive manner. As strange as it felt to him that so many Dwarves had no idea who he was, he understood perfectly. For one, he'd lost his title, which would give them an inherent knowledge of who he was. For another, there was no reasonable way to expect that every person in a group of nearly a hundred thousand people would recognize him on sight. That would be sheer narcissism, and Joe couldn't think of *anyone* humbler than he was.

A short back and forth followed, as the chief miner grumbled at his subordinate, only for that Dwarf to point at the sky, then at all of the buildings that had been popping up in the area. Finally, he threw his hands into the air and stomped over to the human, jumping directly into their issue. "We need a mine, if we're going to last here for any length of time. Metal tools are what makes civilizations thrive, and all of us have the ability to find ore deposits. There's a Minor tier one metal vein over here, but every time we start digging toward it, we get a nasty warning."

The Dwarf that had been whispering on Joe's behalf filled in the information. "The warning tells us that, if we dig more than ten feet underground, Beast Waves in the future will include burrowing monsters! Also, large monsters moving through the area have a chance to cause mine shaft collapses. Since every monster is a large monster here, we don't know if it's worth the risk."

"We need metal to survive!" The chief miner seemed to have made up his mind at this point and gestured for the others to start working. "We'll just let the council know that they need to plan for underground incursions in the future. That's their problem, not ours."

By this point, Joe was slack-jawed as he watched the Dwarves get ready to put the entire Village at risk just so they could get some work done. "You guys can't be serious about this, right? We're going to just have to figure out a different way for you to mine metals. Seriously, a couple of *Penguins* got in and destroyed the Town Hall once, and the current defenses in place are barely enough to hold off the lowest *prey* for the real monsters. If you add burrowing monsters to what we need to defend against, this place is going to be destroyed by the next wave!"

"Well, what do you suggest we do, mister fancy pants mage?" the Dwarf snarled at him. "Start learning a new career three hundred years in?"

"No, but we've been here less than a *week*." That earned him a few strange looks, and Joe paused as he considered how much time he'd been spending on his own recently. It was entirely possible that he had lost a few days somewhere in there. "Just give it a little bit of time? Or maybe we need to set up a mine outside of the city walls? Will that still cause underground monster attacks?"

There was a bit of hesitation at that, and Joe realized what was going on. "I see. None of you have checked if building a mine outside of the city is possible, as that would be too dangerous. Is that about right?"

"We specifically chose not to stay in the Legion and to pursue our craft." The Dwarf blustered, refusing to back down on behalf of his subordinates. "We can't be expected to expose ourselves to the elements and every random creature that wants a taste of us."

That was met with nodding and a few outspoken agreements. Slightly annoyed, Joe tried a different tack than he'd been pursuing until this moment. "You won't put yourself at risk, but you're willing to put the entire... *okay*. Just... give me a couple of days to look into a better solution than this. You *do* understand that opening the mine here will put the whole Village at risk, and you're a *subset* of that group, right?"

Quieting down, the group talked amongst themselves for a few moments before their spokesman turned and shrugged at Joe. "I'll give you one hundred and twenty hours to come up with a better solution, or we're breaking ground."

Quest gained: Don't dig your own grave. The Dwarven Mining Guild is getting antsy, wanting to hunt for higher rank metals and materials. Their excitement about digging into the depths of Jotunheim could be the undoing of not just them, but the Village they are attempting to build the mineshaft in. Find an alternate solution within 120 hours. Reward: Access to various-ranked metals. Failure: The Village will be attacked by burrowing monsters during all future Beast Waves, even if the mine is closed.

"Why that time limit? Can't you just say five days?" Joe was reeling from the information the quest had given him. The Dwarves were ready to start this very moment, even with the knowledge that they would truly cause issues for their people.

"Made that mistake once already." The Dwarf scoffed as he pointed at the false sky, which was showing darkness at the moment. "Turns out that five days here's what we think of as five months. Nothing like *not* getting your request fulfilled for nearly half a year."

"Got it." Joe shook his head and walked away, only fairly certain they wouldn't start digging as soon as his back was turned. His next stop was the Town Hall, to share this news and get some outside help finding a solution.

CHAPTER EIGHTEEN

"If you've come to complain about the new laws–"

Joe brushed past the smirking Dwarven receptionist trying to block him from getting farther into the building. However, the Ritualist was intimately familiar with this place, having been the person to build it. Simply Omnivaulting off the walls twice at odd angles was enough to put him past the fleshy blockade, allowing him to gracefully stride into the main meeting hall.

He was met by a group of wary-eyed Dwarven Masters, and Joe gave a respectful salute before outlining the issue that he'd run into with the miners. The looks being sent his way shifted away from concern and directly into incredulousness. Having explained the issue, Joe turned on his heel and started walking out of the building.

"Wait! Where are you going?" This question was startled out of Grandmaster McPoundy, who went silent as Joe turned around with a slightly annoyed demeanor.

"Grandmaster, with all due respect, it's been made clear to me that I need to work around you all, not *with* you. I'm confused by the sudden lack of trust and graciousness that was granted when my services were absolutely required for the survival of your people." Joe shrugged, but it wasn't a helpless gesture. It was pure resignation. "Seems strange to me that I've been silently ostracized, but what do you expect me to do? Come here and beg for attention? I've found my niche, and I'm going to run with it."

Prepared messages sent!

You have new mail!

Eyes flicking to the notifications, he realized that the letters he had written to his mother, a few friends, and even the *tentative* agreement to remain friends with Daniella had been sent off as soon as he had service, which he assumed was a function tied to the teleporter in the building. With a smile on his face, Joe gave another salute and walked out of the building, ignoring any feeble protests sent his way.

When he was alone, the Ritualist shook his head and voiced his true inner thoughts. "They're old and afraid. Just need to stay off their radar until they get their feet under them again, or I'm going to be turned into a scapegoat."

Oof!

Joe was sent tumbling to the ground as Havoc suddenly rammed into him from the side. Then the terrain was flashing by underneath him as he was swept up and carried along by the Dwarf, who sprinted into the distance as if his legs were pistons. "Found someone you gotta meet! This is too exciting to let you walk there at the speed of a child!"

"Havoc! What-!" Joe cut off as the momentum roughly shifted, and they came to a stop. Trying not to let the vertigo turn into nausea, he pulled himself upright and looked around at the small group he 'had to' meet. At first glance, he was completely unimpressed. He already knew Bauen, the engineer, which was his first clue to take the initial meeting of the others seriously.

The first new face was a human, who was currently dressed in a wrinkled, filthy robe, only somewhat covered by a large coat obviously meant for a much shorter, stockier body. Although the man was standing there shivering, Joe could see a fierce intelligence in his eyes. Havoc began introductions, "This is Sucker–"

"Socar!" the man retorted instantly, clearly used to this joke. "Hello, Joe. We've heard a lot about you, and we think that you're going to be instrumental to our project."

Havoc interjected immediately, "Yes, yes, we're all very excited. Introductions first. How do you ever expect to build up your Charisma if you cut straight to the heart of every matter?"

The Mage looked like he'd been slapped with an astounding truth and bowed at the waist as the words percolated in his skull. "Thank you for your guidance, Grandmaster!"

"You know Bauen, so we'll skip talking about him." The engineer mockingly shook his fist at Havoc for those words, but the Grandmaster was already on to the final introduction. "Lastly, this is Heartpiercer Mcshootypants."

"Before you ask, I didn't know names would be locked in," she interrupted with a longsuffering sigh. Joe looked at the heavily customized visage of the bow-carrying, twenty-something-year-old lady. Everything from the bleached-white hair flowing around her in the wind to the eyes as pale as the snow that capped the highest mountains of Jotunheim practically *screamed* that she'd started in Eternia with a mouse and keyboard. Her complaint finished with a low growl, a reminder that even those with the most enchanted, customized appearances were still beholden to frustration and impatience. "*Or* that they would say the entire name every time they talk to me."

Frankly, Joe was surprised that Heartpiercer hadn't decided to side with the Elves when she got to the second world. Between her unrealistic appearance and clear disposition toward archery, he assumed she'd have fit right in. Joe rubbed at his own bald head ruefully, reminding himself that perhaps he shouldn't be one to instantly judge people by their appearance.

"Heartpiercer Mcshootypants is an expert on targeting sequences and has been studying the field of overlapping fire with a Dwarven Master. Socar has been studying Formations and variant architecture, and as you know, Bauen is an expert in engineering and logistics."

Havoc took a breath, waiting to see if Joe would be able to use the incomplete information to understand the project at hand. Joe, having gotten used to the Grandmaster, simply waited patiently. "Pah! Fine, I'll spoon feed you, just this once. Together, you can set up some designs for rituals that can assist in the annihilation of the Beast Waves that are coming in."

"You can figure out a ritual and tell them what sort of range it has." Havoc pointed at Socar, Heartpiercer Mcshootypants, and Bauen in order. "Then this one can tell you the best placement of each ritual in sequence, to assist in destroying the enemy without damaging our defenses or defenders. *She* can help you fine tune your range and account for the movement speed and dodging abilities of monsters. Then, my Dwarven minion here can assist you in getting whatever you need to set all of this up and ensure that you've access to what might otherwise be restricted areas. Figure the rest out yourselves; I've got my own issues."

A crater appeared where Havoc had been standing; the snow underneath him shot into the air as though an artillery shell had landed next to the group. Each of them was sent stumbling away, slight concern in their eyes as they tried to see if the Dwarf had just taken a spell directly to the face. After a moment of careful examination, Joe rolled his eyes.

"I'm not seeing any blood… or oil. I guess if there's something out there that could disintegrate *him* from a distance, without any warning, there's nothing we could do anyway. Most likely, he just ran off at his top speed, so we couldn't ask him any questions. He does that."

"Dude pulled a batman without even waiting for us to turn around!" Socar shook his head in amazement, a wide smile on his face. "I can't wait until I can do something like that!"

The Mage's enthusiasm was infectious, and it broke the ice enough for the group to start getting to know each other. After pleasantries were exchanged, Joe realized that each of them was getting fairly chilled, but Socar especially looked like he was about to die on the spot. Cursing himself for missing out on that fairly clear issue, Joe pulled out a Ritual Tile and erected a bubble around them. As mana converted to heat and filled the enclosed space, each of them was soon able to loosen their outermost garments.

That led to a moment of great confusion as the Mage took off his overcoat, revealing that what Joe had assumed was a fur scarf was actually a cat wrapped loosely around the man's neck. He leaned closer, studying the animal closely for a moment, before subvocalizing, "*Nyanderthal.*"

He could see the cat's eyes widen, then the 'pet' winked at him a single time. Joe assumed that meant they would speak privately another time. He knew better than to expose the cat, as members of the Hidden Race were very *touchy* about their status. Heartpiercer took over the conversation, pointing at the ritual that had given them a small workspace. "I didn't know these things could generate heat! I thought they were just for blocking the wind."

That put a frown on Joe's face, and made him wonder how many of his other creations were being underutilized. Before he could dive into that thought process any further, the bright-eyed archer started picking out portions of his ritual diagram and talking about vectors. Deciding to humor the archer-not-a-mage, he let her ramble for a few moments, but his smile dropped off as her terminology took a turn for the eloquent.

"-then, if I'm not mistaken, this section is what you're using to create the bubble. I'd looked at the one in the bubble I'm sleeping in, and I see the same issue hasn't yet been addressed on this one. This is clearly intended to create a full dome, but streamlined energy usage is contraindicated by the full sphere—as it constantly tries to form, even while impacting the ground. Adjusting this to one point two radians should decrease mana consumption enough to be a significant improvement." Finally finishing her thought, she looked up to see each of the other members of this strange group watching her with admiration. "What?"

"I'd never thought to look at this section in terms of radians. I've only been using degrees and parabolic arcs." Joe started laughing at himself. "Just by adding in that much, you've probably saved me hundreds of thousands of mana over this upcoming year alone. I was watching in shock because I didn't think someone in such a different field of study would be able to pick apart my formulas like that."

"Archery *is* math," she stated with an easy shrug. "Adjusting for the curvature of the earth, wind speed, penetration necessary for damaging your target, applied force and vectors. It takes people a long time to realize this; that's why you're not going to see very many human archers on Jotunheim."

Socar jumped into the conversation at that point, eager to prove that he was equally as valuable to the group. "Joe, this isn't an official assignment, Havoc just told us to try and figure something out. I've a bunch of ideas for what we can do to not only boost the power of your rituals, but also to grab a bunch of resources for ourselves. Before I get into that, I need a few guarantees. One, all of the blueprints or patents for devices I help create become open-source. In a world like this, we don't need to bottleneck ourselves by gatekeeping information. We need as many people creating our defenses as possible, if we are going to survive and thrive. Two, I want a quarter of whatever monsters we take down."

The entire group dove into negotiations, with Joe pointing out that the two requests were mutually exclusive. "I'm just saying, if you say that everything we design is going to be open-source… as soon as it's public, *why* would I give you a portion of whatever I'm killing? Royalties come from exclusivity."

Eventually, they agreed on a much more limited scope, but so long as each of them was working their hardest to make their defensive project a success, they agreed to split everything evenly. With that agreement hashed out, Socar finally started explaining what he was bringing to the table.

"Do all of you know what I mean when I say that I've been studying Formations?" The Mage smirked slightly as he got the exact answer he'd been expecting, although Bauen rolled his eyes as though it were a question meant specifically for children.

"It's where you put stuff for maximum effect, right?" Joe offered his thoughts, thinking back to his time in the military, both on Earth and working with the Legion. "For instance, a Delta formation is used for specific types of attacks, specifically aggressive ones where you're trying to punch through an enemy-held location. I know there's a magical variant that you're referencing, but I'm not familiar with it."

"You are correct; that *is* called a formation." Socar languidly stated as the Dwarf in their group chuckled softly. "But I think the closest analog from Earth would be feng shui–using the environmental, ambient energy of the world around us to enhance what we are attempting to do. When we combine that with Heartpiercer Mcshootypants' expertise in overlapping fields of fire, we will be able to see a massive increase in everything from accuracy to destructive potential."

Not completely convinced, Joe leaned back and tried it to keep the disbelief out of his voice, even as he reconsidered the deal they'd just struck. "I don't mean to sound *too* skeptical, but how much of a boost are we talking? If you're going to tell me that we're going to get a one to three percent boost, I'm going to ask if your studies involved burning a *lot* of 'incense'."

"They did. In fact, I can name one hundred and seventeen different types of incense that are useful for the practical application of Formations." Socar chuckled as Joe's face distorted. "But no, following the principles of the Dragon's Nest Formation, and going by the sheer space that we will be setting up, we should be seeing one to two *hundred* percent, at the low end. If we build with expansion in mind, by the time this place is a city, that should be in the low *thousands* of percentage increases."

There was silence for only a moment before Joe leaned forward and offered a hand. "I'm in."

CHAPTER NINETEEN

After discussing with the others for a few hours, Joe realized that each of them had extremely deep insights into their own professions. Even the Dwarf among them seemed amazed, as he had only been able to achieve his level of success thanks to hundreds of years of practice. As they were preparing to disperse, Joe hesitated and asked for one last favor. "Could any of you look at this ritual and offer advice on how you'd set out the parameters?"

He set out the full diagram of the Ritual of Slaughter, as well as his notes on the subject. Each of them took turns analyzing the Journeyman ritual, which was for the most part incomprehensible by each of them. Heartpiercer dragged a fingernail lightly along several points of interest, showing how each of them converged in a specific manner. Frankly, it had looked like squiggles even to Joe until that moment, and that was with his Master rank in Ritual Circles. "If I'm reading this correctly, this part details how the energy will be dispersed."

"I'd been wondering about that." Joe leaned in and traced along the lines, looking as closely as he could to ensure he understood each part of whatever she was about to say. "What

I'd gathered from this was that the first of the targets that fulfills all conditions will be the first hit by the buildup of power."

"That's accurate, I think, but it also shows how much of the energy will continue on." She tapped at the spot again, showing how every single line that mentioned direction and discharge connected to this point in the ritual, even if the lines were extremely faint. "I'm almost certain that this means *all* of the power will hit the lead target, and what remains after the creature is destroyed passes on."

Joe's eyes brightened as he realized what that would mean. "Then this is equally effective against a single target or multiple targets! No, hold on, hear me out. If the first creature to meet the requirements is some little Penguin, then that means there are likely hundreds of Penguins that are about to be slaughtered. But, if *thousands* of creatures are meeting the requirements, and one supermassive monster sets it off, all of the damage will be focused on that single target. All of the damage will accumulate on the one who fulfilled the requirements, making them far easier to defeat, even if it doesn't outright kill them."

"But *also* not allowing any of that damage through to the rest of the swarm." Socar cautioned him carefully. "You know… this has aspects of a Formation. I bet, if you set your flags at these trigrams—Black North, Southwest Big Earth, Center Square, West Small Metal, and East First Son—you will create an *incredibly* impressive single-target piercing effect when the ritual activates. Then again, we could also exchange the East First Son with Center Everyone, and West Small Metal with South Fire for a superheated effect that would be extra effective against the swarm of Yin-aligned creatures of this world. Sorry, ice-aspect creatures."

"I say set *all* of those up and see what happens!" Bauen slapped his knees and stood up as if the conversation was over. "Hard to know what's going to be the best to use if you don't have a control case and a few use case tests."

Socar winced and immediately refuted what the Dwarf had

to say. "Ooh, *ye~eah*, I can't recommend that. The problem is, by having your flags out in these formations—by the way, when I say 'flags', I mean the requirement points of your ritual. Like… tripwires, landmines, actual flags. Sorry, went on a tangent there, but having the 'flag' in one sector, then having a secondary ritual that has the same effect and flags in opposing sectors won't just *dilute* the effect, they'll likely *cancel* each other out. For maximum **oomph**, only one of these on the field at a time."

The Ritualist nodded along with what the Mage was saying. Privately, he told himself that, after the first test—unless this information was perfectly accurate—he'd be setting up as many of these rituals as he possibly could. They had too much potential power, and using only one at a time would feel wasteful. "Thank you all for your thoughts on this… I think I have a good understanding of what I'll need to make all of this."

"First thing tomorrow—let's call it eight hours, actually—we're going up on the walls and planning our auto-turret emplacements?" Heartpiercer wondered aloud to confirm their plans, and everyone nodded enthusiastically about setting up what would, with minimal maintenance, eventually become a passive stream of raw materials.

"Can we meet at my workshop, right near the entrance to the outer walls?" The group separated after agreeing to his request, leaving Joe wondering what he should do with his time. Having his Constitution past the fourth threshold meant that he required very little time for sleep, usually only every couple of standard days for a few hours. He loved this because it meant that each day was worth twice as much as it had been when he was closer in stats to a standard human.

"My quests are kind of hard to complete right now, but so long as I'm working on setting up this ritual, at least they'll get some progress soon. Actually, what do I have going on right now with those?" He rummaged with his character sheet for a moment, pulling open the tab and reading over his currently active quests.

"Let's see… Student Ritualist three, need to kill a thousand creatures with the Ritual of Slaughter. We'll call that one 'in progress'. Journeyman Ritualist, all I need to do there is have someone from my coven back on Midgard reach the Student rank. Nothing I can do there except wait. Unless I wanted to establish a new coven here…? Nah. Apprentice Rituarchitect three. I need to make two more 'meaningful' monuments. What counts as meaningful? Useful?"

Pondering that for a few moments brought no enlightenment, so he simply shrugged and looked at what else he had going on. "Apprentice Reductionist two wants me to make Apprentice-rank items then reduce them. We can knock that one out pretty quick, probably. But Student Reductionist two tells me to make five Unique crafts…"

That tickled something in the back of Joe's mind, as he considered the open building slots. At this tier of town level, there were no options for having a Unique structure, which meant he was going to need to work on his other crafting— "Wait! That's what it was, didn't the upgrade notification include bonuses for morale? Let me see, let me see… yes! Every thousand points in the morale modifier allows for an additional Unique structure. If I want a permanent reduction center, another A.S.P.E.C.T. tower, I need to earn that Unique slot at the bare minimum. Boom, just like that, I have an actual reason to get basic systems that make people happy in place for the city."

This put a smile on Joe's face, as he'd been feeling extremely hesitant about building up the town further. "I don't mind making my own meaning and generating projects to give me responsibility for them. With over half the possible buildings in the area offering me a small amount of tribute, combined with my class quests, I've got some serious incentive to go and make cool things happen."

So long as he could keep up this pace, creating buildings and making bargains that cost him very little but gave him extremely long-term benefits, he wouldn't have to care about what the leadership of the area had to say. As Joe increased the quality of the area, boosting the conditions for people to live and work, everything he made that was earning him passive income at this point would be well worth it.

"Finally, I can start saying that I went out there and took charge of my life instead of waiting for someone to hand me things to do. Let's go figure out the water issue."

As he cheerfully strolled along toward his workshop, Joe pondered the other non-class quests he had at the moment. "Still have that reputation quest going from Occultatum. I guess that means not all of my shrines have been found yet. Or maybe they were, and the explorer got dissolved in a bubble of acid? Heh. Couple of quests I can't do unless I can open the bifrost, so I don't need to worry about those, then of course figuring out the mining situation… even if it's just a 'miner' problem, I think I'll still need to dig into it."

The Ritualist could only hope he'd get some assistance in that quest from the Dwarven Council, even if that only came in the form of the Dwarves getting an order not to start digging within city limits. He didn't particularly care about the quest reward, only about the punishment for failure. They were nowhere *near* equipped for burrowing monsters.

"Water." With his priorities in order, Joe stepped through the door of his workshop and closed it behind him, so deep in thought that he didn't notice his favorite chiropractor standing in the room waving at him until he'd nearly run into the man. "Jaxon! Good to see you; what have you been up to?"

Ever-present grin in place, the chiropractor swept Joe up in a hug and tossed him side to side, cracking his back in eight places. "Learning new techniques, as per usual! Do you know that the Penguins in the area have one of the same issues that was affecting humans before we came to this universe? They have a terrible hunch, and I have no idea how they're finding cell phones large enough to use with those fins."

"Phones?"

"But of course! Why else would they be hunched forward

and looking down all day? Are they book editors? I doubt it—no fingers. Now, to be fair, I haven't seen anything with a touch-screen that they could be using, but all that tells me is they leave them at home before they come to attack us." Jaxon sincerely nodded at that, tapping the pads of his fingers together in a constant undulating motion. "Perhaps that's not the *only* possibility, but going by historical data, it is the most likely."

"If they were *humans*." Joe stressed that last word, but it didn't seem to be getting through to his friend. "Why am I even participating in this argument? No. Anyway, *bye*, Jaxon. I'm trying to figure out a good way to handle the issue we're running into with water."

"There's plenty of snow out there." Jaxon waved toward the door uncaringly. "It's easy enough to heat it up and drink what we need."

"For *now* it is." Joe consented with a dark undertone. "But what's it going to look like when we have extremely large buildings with a need for indoor plumbing? I'm looking forward to a hot shower, even if I'm constantly getting cleaned by my magic. A soak in a tub? Water coming from sprinklers for when we eventually set up a greenhouse in order to grow food? Large-scale industrial projects that require water for any reason? Scooping up a handful of snow isn't going to last us very long."

"How very interesting! You're considering problems so far in the future, and I have no interest in them. I'm not going to say that I only come visit you when I'm coated in hot, sticky blood, filthy as a pig, and feel like having clean underwear again… but I'm feeling rather fresh and ready to get back out there. Have a lovely day!" Jaxon swayed back and forth as he sashayed toward the exit. The last hints of the bloody footprints he had made on his way in vanished under the scouring of Joe's Neutrality Aura.

Joe watched him go, unable to stop a small chuckle escaping his lips. "At least *he's* having plenty of fun here."

With that, he pulled out some parchments and began writing down his thoughts, making notes, and trying to determine what the best solution was. As he broke the large-scale water problem down into smaller and smaller pieces, time seemed to pass ever faster. Now completely absorbed in his task, Joe only spared a single passing thought outside of his work.

"Good thing I told everyone to meet me here. Probably wouldn't look too good if I was late for our first agreed-upon meeting."

CHAPTER TWENTY

**Wham!*

"Wahh!" Joe was startled from his focus, tossing himself back from the table and throwing his fists in the air as the horrendously loud sound came again. "What *is* that? Was there an attack? Or... someone's just knocking, aren't they?"

Hoping they hadn't been trying to get his attention for too long, the Ritualist rushed over to the door and threw it open, revealing the smug face of Bauen and the slightly exasperated faces of the humans who had been waiting. The Dwarf chuckled at Joe's flustered expression. "Were you asleep in there? Took me knocking on the door with ol' reliable here to bring you running. Just like old times."

There was a crowbar in the engineer's hand, which he was lightly tossing up and down. Joe's eyes shifted slightly to the side, accessing his building's information. He grunted slightly in annoyance as he realized that his door had taken five points of durability damage. "Pretty sure you never needed to use a crowbar to get my attention in the past."

"Well, I'm pretty sure I've never been standing waiting on

you while my beard hair froze to my chest," came the immediate counter.

Deciding against getting into a verbal spar at the moment, as his mind was still half on his water cycling project, Joe joined the others in the bitter air—instantly feeling apologetic about making them wait for him. "Thank you all so much for being patient with me; I've been trying to figure out some quality of life things I can do for everyone living here. Still, I didn't mean to take so long. I know we all want to get this up and running before the next Beast wave."

No one had actually complained about being kept in the cold, but his words definitely helped melt the frigid expressions on their faces. Bauen pointed up and into the distance with his crowbar. "The best view you're going to get of the walls is over there. I've arranged for some porters to walk with us today. They're bringing a few sets of ladders we can use to get up there, then pull up and lay over the gap so we can walk between the walls."

Moments like this reminded Joe exactly why it was so important to have a group of people with different skill sets, strengths, and weaknesses. If he needed to be the one to get people up top, he probably would've grabbed a long rope, jumped up there, and dragged people to the top. As to getting them across the walls? Joe thought about that for a few seconds, faintly smiling at the images in his mind of attempting to leap across while holding someone in his arms, causing them both to slam into the ground anywhere from thirty to forty feet below them.

The porters were waiting for them, and as soon as the group arrived, they were on the move. When the entirety of the group was atop the wall, they began walking along it, planning out their positioning. To Joe's surprise, he had very little input at the moment. Socar asked him to provide a variety of the rituals he could create, their effective range without any additional boosting, and the type of Elemental Affinities each of the rituals would possess.

Not completely comfortable about revealing the entirety of his arsenal, Joe still presented a solid dozen options. From there, Socar and Heartpiercer begin discussing, arguing about various placement, targeting ability, whether they should rely on a potential range boost or not, and how they could pack in as many rituals as possible without disrupting the formation the Mage wanted to employ to set everything up. As the conversation grew more heated, Joe and Bauen took a few steps back.

Their communication was silent. Joe held up an empty coffee mug at the Dwarf, raising an eyebrow before having AutoMate appear and fill it with a near-boiling brew. There was only a moment of hesitation to be polite, and the Dwarf nodded firmly. By the time he took the cup, it had already cooled down enough that it could be carefully sipped. Joe felt a tap on his shoulder and turned to see the two porters looking at him hopefully. Always happy and ready to share the joys of coffee, the Ritualist pulled out a couple of coffee-elemental-rejected Ebonsteel mugs and handed them over as soon as they were filled.

The four of them sipped their coffee and enjoyed the persistent daylight, watching as the conversation between the other humans reached a strange point. Heartpiercer shoved Socar in the middle of jabbing her finger at a corner position and shouting how the ritual *needed* to have a slowing effect so that the other rituals could target creatures from all angles, but Socar's reflexive retaliation in kind sent her stumbling backward and off the edge of the wall.

"Abyss! *Retrieve*!" The Mage pointed at the falling woman, and a laser pointer created a red dot on her chest. The cat that was draped around his neck leapt off, zooming through the air like a stinger missile and landing on the Archer. An instant later, the two of them were teleported back to the top of the wall, where Heartpiercer landed heavily. The cat jumped off of her, resuming its position on Socar's neck.

"That was amazing!" Joe called out in awe. "You have a 'Teleport Other' spell? I don't even have a 'Teleport *Self*' spell!

Can you teach me? Also, if you two can't be professional about this, we're going to have some serious issues. Seriously, either one of you could've been falling there, and we're what? An *hour* in?"

"Sorry." Socar's apology was heartfelt, and the mumbled reply he earned from Heartpiercer could have passed for the same word. The Mage turned to Joe, and the Ritualist carefully ignored the trembling in his hands, as the adrenaline of the moment was clearly washing over the man. "Unfortunately, my magic is bound up in my companion animal. I provide instruction and power, then the spell is cast through Nimue here."

"Ni-*mew*?" Joe waited for a reaction, but the Mage only nodded in agreement that he'd said the name correctly. "Isn't that the witch from Arthurian legend that bound Merlin for all time?"

"Yup. I was struggling with what to name her, but that came to me in a dream. I thought it was fitting." Socar reached up and pet his cat, earning a loud purr. In fact, it was *very* loud, almost as though it was a hint to Joe that he should stop speaking.

"Pff." Heartpiercer stood up and brushed the dirt off her clothes. "Sounds like your *cat* is the Mage, and it's just humoring your power fantasy of being a wizard."

Joe looked away, pretending to admire the morning daylight so he wouldn't give anything away. After composing himself, he looked back and noticed that the cat appeared to be glaring at him. He was certain it was just a coincidence.

From there, the next few hours were much more calm. They crawled about the tops of the walls, making notes and setting points where the rituals would be placed. When they had enough determined that Socar guaranteed the formation would activate properly, Joe found the nearest mark and started setting up his ritual.

"Ritual of Dark Lightning." Joe had been able to create this version at the Student rank, which gave it plenty of power, range, and reusability. The only downside was that he needed to use approximately one-tenth of a Rare Core each time he set up a Student-rank ritual. Even though that efficiency was up from his previous best of one-sixth of a Core, he only had two Cores at that rarity at the moment, and he had been hard at work making buildings.

Joe needed to carefully choose which position he'd place these higher-powered versions in. They'd decided that, until they could acquire better Cores, they would focus the stronger ones on rituals that would damage an area, instead of a single target.

Between the four members of this group, it was easy to decide on the positioning, set it up, and empower the circles. After only a minor back and forth on morality, they decided that it would be perfectly acceptable to let this magic strike out at any living creature that walked through the walls along the ground; so long as it wasn't a human or a Dwarf. Anything outside of that category was fair game at this moment. Flush with feelings of success, they moved to the next part of the wall they'd marked for getting a ritual.

Joe realized an issue that he was going to be having nearly immediately. Student-ranked rituals were powerful enough, *stable* enough, that they could operate in Jotunheim easily. The requirement of having a Core for the initial creation was a bottleneck, but it otherwise wasn't a huge issue. Yet, now that he wanted to make lesser versions, he'd need to account for stabilization. Making a Novice or Beginner ritual would be at least as expensive to place as setting up an Apprentice rank. His previous tests had shown him that they needed to be stabilized to the Apprentice rank, or they would violently discharge.

After explaining this issue to the others, he earned a few looks that he wasn't sure how to interpret. Smarminess, perhaps? Socar clapped him on the shoulder, illuminating him with his next words. "I suppose that means the rest of us are done working on this for the day. In fact, we can just leave you this map, and you can come back and finish the job on your own when you're ready, right?"

Joe was lost for words, but only for half a second. Then he crossed his arms and sighed. "You guys *suck.*"

"Eh, this way *you* get to be cold for a while while we wait on you to finish up," Heartpiercer jokingly told him, letting Joe know that she was still not perfectly happy about that. He hoped that completing the work without further complaint would erase that debt.

Bauen's face fell into a contemplative expression as he eyeballed the walls, raising a hand to gauge the speed and chill of the air. Pressing his hand to the stone, he closed his eyes. "Quiet down for a moment. I'm attempting to sense the vibrations generated by people walking around and scale that up to what will be felt as supermassive beings stomp about. Have you considered how you're going to keep the stabilization cubes in place?"

Joe was uncertain how to answer that. "You know, I'm not sure? I've never needed to make defensive emplacements that had to last for any length of time. Usually, I've just used my rituals as traps: one-off consumables that I was perfectly fine losing if they were destroyed or ran out of power. With these? I guess I'll need to figure something out. Do you know anyone down there who makes glue, maybe tape?"

"Yeah, I'm with Bauen on this one." Socar had clear unease in his tone. "I don't know how I feel about the idea of relying on the monsters being beat back by powerful magical effects that are literally held together with duct tape."

"I could get a spray bottle and freeze the cubes to the top of the wall with a few spritzes?" Joe looked around the group, counting up the number of winces he saw. Still, no one had anything better to offer, so he tried again. "I'll see about getting an earth Mage that can close the stone around the cubes-"

"No," the Dwarf interrupted. "You probably haven't run into this issue yet, but that would nullify the stabilization effect of the cubes. They need to have a perfect line of sight to each other."

Joe offered a thumbs up, his bland facial expression not

shifting in the slightest. "Oh, look! I'm all out of ideas! I'll try to think of something, but maybe you guys could help me out on that? If I have to fix *this* on top of everything else, I guarantee you I'm going with glue."

He didn't mention that he was perfectly fine with them having to work while he was working, and he tried to keep his lips from curling at that thought.

Bauen nodded at Socar. "I'm an engineer, and I remember Havoc mentioning that you had experience with variant architecture. If Heartpiercer Mcshootypants chips in some advice, I'm sure the three of us can figure something out. Let's continue this conversation around a heat generator in a tent bubble."

"Then I'll go make more cubes." Tasks decided, the group split up. Joe looked into the distance and found the smithy, then Omnivaulted directly off the wall—greatly enjoying the gasp of shock from someone behind him.

"No matter how often I hear that, it never gets old. At least Socar didn't panic-send his cat to retrieve me."

CHAPTER TWENTY-ONE

One of the perks of owning the smithy was that he was able to skip the line. Even so, standing over the cold forge and doing math was causing the Dwarf that he'd budged in front of to ever so slowly turn dark crimson as he tried to contain his vitriol. Which made Joe move extra *carefully* on his calculations. Absolutely because he was… nervous. Yes.

"If I want one hundred rituals under the Student rank, that means I'm going to need a thousand cubes." Joe paused in his calculations as he realized that this would be a perfect test to see what his percentage bell curve looked like. As he needed a perfect one thousand of these cubes for his short-term plans, and there was a forty percent chance of the item he created being turned into goo by the unstable building, he could assume that at least four hundred of his projects would fail. "That's not great… time to kick this into high gear."

After talking to Smitty for a few minutes, Joe was now the proud owner of half a dozen smithing-specific blank blueprints. He carefully recreated the technical specifications of the cubes that he needed, eyeing them critically as he finished each one. He was no artist, but luckily this wasn't considered art, seeming to be governed more by his mathematical abilities than anything else.

"I'm going to start making this item. If there are any smiths in here that can create this stabilization cube, I'll give them free usage of this building for a month if they help me complete a large order."

"It's already free to use this place!" another Dwarf brusquely growled at him. This made Joe's head snap to the side, and he glared at Smitty, who gulped and couldn't meet his eyes.

"It's not *supposed* to be free. Your free trial has *expired*. The use of this building requires that every fifth completed item is handed over to *me*." At that moment, Joe realized that he hadn't made it an official quest with the Dwarf he left in charge, but he didn't want to accept the blame for this. He stared Smitty down until he got an answer.

Eventually, she cleared her throat and seemed to find her voice. "You see, Joe, when people are used to doing things a certain way, change is really difficult. I hadn't been charging them, so a sudden shift of one in five completed works coming over-"

"I understand. It's difficult to be in charge, but don't worry. You don't need to think about that anymore." With a mental **click*, Joe removed her as the manager of this building and took full control back. "Whoops… I think I forgot to count this building as one that I owned back when Cleave was warning me about the new law."

He did the math and realized that *technically* he owned six percent of the buildings in the area. This caused him to break out in a light sweat, and he cast around for a suitable… his eyes landed on Smitty once more, who seemed appropriately flabbergasted by her rapid shift in fortune.

Immediately, he saw a way out of his predicament. "I'll gift you ownership of this building, not just management, so long as you create an actual contract or issue me a quest to get you ownership of this building, for my percentage. I understand metal is extra-precious here, so we'll drop the fee to one in twenty items, a mere five percent."

Every person in the room who was listening flinched, though it was noticeable that no one jumped in to offer him a different deal. Smitty considered her options for a moment, nodded, and Joe gained a quest alert in the next moment. Quickly scanning it to ensure it covered all of the pertinent details, he transferred ownership of the building back to her and completed his portion of the quest instantly.

That small issue taken care of, he got back to the offer he was trying to make in the first place. "Back to my offer to the group at large. If you help me with what I need, I'll give you the right to come in and immediately get to work without having to wait in line. For whoever works with me on this, I'll grant permission for Smitty to let you keep the percentage of goods I'd otherwise take."

Although they were slightly malcontent, he still had three Dwarves take him up on his offer. Then Joe got to work immediately, creating his cubes and handing off any of the failures that melted down into misshapen lumps of cold metal. The Dwarves could work with those, even if he could not. Since the metal was perfectly pure, thanks to being created directly, they simply needed to melt it down and reshape it.

Hours passed, and the artificial nighttime that Joe had created for the town shifted to daylight, then ever so slowly back—then did so again—before he finally stepped back from his forge. Between himself and the other smiths who had cycled in and out, he'd finally been able to complete the first one thousand cubes he needed for his project. Looking at the tally that he'd kept, Joe realized something interesting. "My approximation was off…? With a thousand cubes to make, we should've had a nearly perfect distribution of two in five failures. But it only failed three hundred and three times?"

Looking through his skills to see what could've affected that, Joe decided it was due to his Ritualistic Forging. As it stood, the skill *specifically* gave him a thirty-one percent increased chance to succeed when creating items for stabilization. "One in three of my failures was forced to succeed... interesting. If we were to put that in terms of a dice roll, all of the fours that should've been failures turned into fives, meeting the minimum requirements to let it be created. Interesting."

He had also kept a tally of the number of cubes that had gotten the ability to heal from minor damage, being pleasantly surprised at finding that two hundred eighty-six of his personal creations had been successful—slightly higher than expected—and ninety of his failures had been completed with that bonus after the Dwarves reworked the metal that kept failing to hold its form upon completion. "Not sure what I'm going to do with three hundred seventy-six cubes that can heal themselves, but I don't think there's going to be any *detrimental* effects from using them."

Thanking the other Dwarves for their help, Joe dragged himself out of the smithy and over to his personal reflective bubble. On the way, he noticed that he must have missed at least one general Beast Wave, because there were dozens of groups hauling bodies toward the warehouse he'd made for their storage.

"See, that right there is the issue with using bladed weapons to kill these things. Giant creatures like that are basically giant sacks of blood." Joe hopped over the near-literal river of monster juices that led from the entrance of the city all the way to the warehouse in a straight line. Getting to his bubble, he wrapped himself up and immediately fell asleep.

Sleeping was always an interesting experience when thought of from an academic perspective. The mind refreshed itself, chemicals and hormones were rebalanced, and oftentimes people were able to make intuitive leaps that had been evading them. When Joe woke up an unknown amount of time later, his eyes flew open, and he sat bolt upright, shouting, "The blood! It wasn't *frozen*!"

He dashed out of his tent-bubble so rapidly that the entirety of the structure popped, but the Ritualist couldn't be bothered to fix it at the moment. He sprinted to the warehouse, noting that the ground was more frozen, but was still a thick, stomach-churning mud. Pushing through the open doors, he ran around like a basilisk with its head cut off until he found the owner of the warehouse.

"You! We never exchanged names!" Joe shook his head wildly, sending the filtered light in the area reflecting as glistening rainbows off his bald pate. "Nevermind, that's not important right now. There's an enormous trail of blood out there!"

"Yes, it's a hazard of needing to collect every body that's produced," the building owner stated dryly. "You're welcome to send your complaints to the complaint department. Oh *wait*, somehow none of them managed to survive our cities being destroyed. Crazy how that happened with them, lawyers, and anyone holding a political science Profession."

That made Joe blink and close his mouth in surprise as he attempted to think of how the logistics of that would have worked out. "What did you all do, send those people to the front lines at the last minute? No, wait, never mind. The blood! What is it being used for?"

"Beyond providing job security to my janitors?" The Dwarf slowly shook his head in confusion. "Nothing. Samples have been sent to the Alchemy Hall for testing on if they have uses in the creation of remedies or the like, but as far as I know, it's inert. Useless except as decoration and lowering morale, in other words."

"Now *there's* a specialty shop I'd only want to window shop at. Bloody good decorations!" Joe laughed at his own joke, which was good, because no one else did. "That's all I needed to hear. I'll see what I can do to clean all that up for you and the city, free of charge!"

"Thanks?" The Dwarf shrugged non-committedly. "You worded that somewhat suspiciously, but I just don't care enough to pursue it."

Not saying anything else, as he didn't want to give his plans away, the Ritualist simply flounced out of the building as mysteriously as possible. As soon as he was outside, his pure white garments—the set of the Silkpants Mage—practically made him invisible in the lightly blowing snow. Only when he leaped over the bloody trail did he stick out as a stark contrast, but only for a moment. Then he was sprinting toward his workshop.

Quest complete: Don't dig your own grave. You gave the people in charge the information they needed to save the Town from nambly-pambly civilians, and they figured out how to get an off-site mine working properly. As most of the work was completed by a separate group, your only reward is not having monsters pop up from the ground while you are walking. Within your city walls, at least.

That was perfectly fine with Joe, as the rewards for completing the quest had been essentially the ability to shop for metal. Not particularly something he cared about either way, but having his eventual defensive rituals ignored wasn't something he wanted to have to figure out a workaround for. With that small, nagging concern out of mind, Joe got to work putting his inspiration into a ritual.

"All I really need to do here is shift the water collection into blood collection, then add a secondary circle *here*… that'll separate the water out from everything else in the blood and plasma. Bring it up to the Apprentice rank by having it pulled over to a specific location… bring that *ri~ight* to the upper edge of Student rank by having the liquid and solid portions fill different containers. Okay. Last part, cleaning it up and testing it out!"

Knowing exactly where he wanted to put it, the Ritualist hurried out the door… and stopped. "I *knew* setting up my workshop right next to the exit was an awesome idea. Great thinking, past Joe!"

CHAPTER TWENTY-TWO

After tearing a hole in the ground on either side of himself, merely long, vertical shafts created by his Field Array, Joe activated his ritual and set the cavities as the target for his ritual's output. Making sure everything was well-stabilized, he activated the new ritual and eyed it carefully as it slowly spun into effect. "Hmm… snail's pace at ramping up. I'll need to find a way to streamline that portion."

Notepad out and fiercely scribbling, Joe continued to observe the progress of his new, active ritual. The snow and dirt rapidly became visible as sanguine fluid was leached out of it. To the untrained eye, it appeared as though two crimson snakes were slithering across the ground toward the human, lifting their heads up out of the snow only to be ever-so-slowly disintegrated.

Blood was sloshing toward him both from deeper into the city, where the warehouse was situated, as well as a small tidal wave speeding through the killing ground where the monsters had originally been butchered. The fluid flowed into the set point in midair where the ritual effect was being manifested. Liquid was coming in on one side, a thick powder and clear water pouring out the other. After only a few minutes, the water cistern was completely filled, and Joe paused the ritual without ending it.

As an unintended side effect, all of the blood that had been drawn toward him sloshed to the ground as a rapidly spreading puddle—moving right toward his holes! Cursing softly, he dropped to his knees and generated a Field Array over the top of his clean water. Then he pumped mana into it, instantly converting any blood that would have fallen in into aspects. After the strangely warm flood had subsided, he double checked his handiwork and confirmed that none of the blood had tainted the water. Breathing out a sigh of relief, he settled in to see the results of his experiment.

"Forgot a control case!" Joe cursed himself for a second, but eventually could only shrug. He'd already seen water freeze in one of these holes in only a few minutes when he had made his bubble tent, so he could safely assume that it would be the same here, unless this water was different, for some reason. Ten minutes later, he dipped his finger into the collected fluid and was relieved to find that it was still fairly warm. Pulling out his notes, he worked on another project, only dipping his finger into the hole in the ground once every half hour after that.

Three hours had quickly passed as he worked his observations into a new version—completing a variant updated ritual—and the water was starting to get cold enough to freeze. As soon as he noticed frost beginning to form, he scooped out roughly a gallon and brought it into his workshop. Applying heat to it in a pot brought the fluid to a boil in a fraction of the time he would've normally expected. Still, no matter what test he ran on it after that, it appeared to be pure, clean water.

"Looks like water, tastes like water, the system says that it *is*… but it doesn't freeze as rapidly as water does." Joe could only assume that this was magic shenanigans, some intrinsic property of the monsters on this world that persisted so long as the material he was using had been taken from one of them. "If it does this with the water that was once blood, what kind of clothes are we going to be able to make? Weapons? Will they absorb heat so well that bringing them to another world will require us completely changing into another outfit so we don't burst into flames?"

Deciding those problems were best suited for someone else to figure out, the Ritualist finished up and walked closer to the Town Hall. As he approached it, he noticed that there were now guards stationed outside of the doorway. Surprisingly, he walked directly past them without being stopped. This time, he let the receptionist block his path, though the Dwarf was watching him extremely warily. "I'm here to get a quest!"

New mail has arrived!

The jovial tone Joe was using seemed to be unexpected, and it took the receptionist a few moments to compose himself and determine how he was going to reply. "That's an interesting... *assertion.* If you want a quest from the village, even if we don't actually have any to offer you at the moment, I need to make sure that you're a person in good standing. That means that you have no negative titles with the council, you're in compliance with all of the laws of this Village, and that you qualify for whatever the quest will be. Are you okay with signing off on letting me run a background check for those qualifications?"

Joe was twice as glad at this moment that he'd remembered to offload the ownership of the smithy before coming here. Without Cleave informing him about this law, he might've not only lost out on a chance to get paid for his services, but he could've even been charged with a minor crime. "Absolutely! Unless strange new, *specifically targeted* laws have been put into place, I should absolutely be in compliance with everything that you just rattled off at me."

In an instant, Joe felt a *very* unpleasant tingling wash over him as the receptionist's eyes glowed a swirling purple. The Ritualist had given up his own Intrusive Scan, but Joe decided that, if he was going to feel uncomfortable, so was this receptionist. He touched a finger to the ritual orb that had captured his Essence Cycle skill, which turned his eyes a disturbing, stygian black.

The Ritualist could see the flows of power around him, the collections of energy that represented people, more intense around some than others. Peering deeper, Joe could also see how this building in particular connected to the village as a whole. Strands of sympathetic energies reached between each of the buildings that fell under the purview of the village. The world itself was saturated in dense, roiling–

"*Sir*!" What appeared to be the fifth or sixth time the receptionist had called out to him was accompanied by a light shove that broke the contact Joe's finger had with his orb. The human blinked several times, his eyes instantly returning to their normal coloration. "Good, for a moment there, I thought you'd been… never mind. As I'd told you already, but somehow doubt you heard, everything seems to be in order. Did you want to submit a request for review?"

Composing himself, Joe gestured toward a large, constantly shifting chart that was in plain view for the public to see, so long as they stood within this room. "I'm working to boost our morale modifier to exceptional heights. I've solved the issue with water freezing and want to offer the Dwarven Council first option on securing the rights to the services I'm providing. Otherwise, I'm perfectly happy to create a utilities company they have no control over."

The human paused for a long moment, then realized what he was saying and chuckled to himself before walking toward the door. "Actually… never mind! I just realized I *don't* need a quest."

"Wait! That sounds like something they would be *very* interested–" Joe let the door fully close behind him before the Dwarf could finish speaking. To his surprise, the receptionist followed him out. "That's something I'm sure they'd be very interested in generating a quest for!"

Joe flashed a smile over his shoulder, "I'm really glad to hear that. Unfortunately, a better opportunity has arisen, and I am going to pursue that. In the future, the best way to get a deal with me is to take what I offer right away, instead of trying to delay me with pointless bureaucracy, thereby giving me a chance to think of a solution that's better for my personal success and happiness. Because, from now on, *that* is what I'm focused on. Toodles!"

As he jauntily walked away, Joe opened his new mail and found a reply from Daniella that seemed to have been hastily jumbled together. In fact, there was a counter next to it, showing that there were multiple letters.

Subject: You replied!

Celestial feces! I can't believe you wrote back so quickly! Seriously, you have no idea how cheerful I'm feeling at this moment—it's like a burst of confetti in my stomach. I've missed chatting with you, how is Jaxon doing? Just trying to get my thoughts in order right now, I'll send along—no! Don't send!

The message cut off there, and Joe snorted as he realized what must have happened. "Gotta love autocorrect and auto-send functions. She said 'send' twice; that must have been enough to have the mail go out."

Exactly as he expected, the next letter was much better put together, and he could practically feel a wave of embarrassment rolling off of it.

Subject: You replied! (Ignore the last one)

Dear Joe,

I hope my letter finds you well! If you got a different letter with the same subject line before this one, I hope you ignored it. It sent before I had a chance to edit it. That will teach me to drink 20 oz of coffee and try to put together a letter entirely with voice-to-text.

Anyway, let's focus on the positives! I'm super grateful that our paths have crossed again. The thought of being friends again is the only thing keeping me going right now. Work has gotten… strange and difficult over the last few days, and I'm not sure what has changed. My boss is looking at me with furious eyes, as if I'm guilty of a crime I didn't commit.

Hopefully, we can be great pen pals over the next few years, until we are finally able to meet up again.

The letter continued in that vein for quite some time, and Joe put together his own draft, which he would include more details on over the next few days. Luckily, he didn't have to worry about the mail sending on its own, as he could only find connection to the outside worlds when he stepped into the Town Hall. He detailed some of the challenges they had been facing and some of the most comedic moments that he had been a part of.

"Next time I see you, I'll have a giant penguin beak for you to keep as a super bizarre token of our friendship. I will *absolutely* expect to see it as a centerpiece on your table anytime I come to visit. Save message as a draft." As soon as he was done speaking, he found that he couldn't stop chuckling about his mental image of Daniella throwing a beak into a cupboard, only to have to reluctantly put it out as a decoration whenever he came to visit in the future. It would be satisfying, if petty, revenge.

Feeling much more lighthearted, Joe began flipping through his options for creating a water containment facility. Thanks to his spree in the human capital city back on Midgard, Joe had a plethora of building blueprints he'd never bothered to look at before. At least *one* of them had to be a fairly straightforward and simple water tower. In a city of hundreds of thousands of people, these had been so common that he hadn't needed permission from anyone to scan it. "New plan: I'm going to need to build and 'sell' enough buildings that there are forty total when I make the water tower, at least if I want to stick to the five percent or fewer requirement."

Pulling open the note he'd made, and Joe reviewed his options for rarity.

35/50 Common slots remain.

12/25 Uncommon slots remain.

0/10 Rare slots remain.

"Seven more buildings, then the eighth one can be my water tower." There was only one small issue with that: between all of the buildings he'd created so far, and his cubes for stabilization, Joe was running extremely low on low-end aspects.

Aspects Gathered

Common: 3,373

Uncommon: 122

"It's *astounding* how quickly I can go through those." The Ritualist could only sigh as he realized that his crafting abilities were currently running on fumes. He could always convert higher-ranked aspects to lower, but that came with issues of its own. First, the rarer an aspect was, the harder it was to collect, for obvious reasons. Wasting it on something like this just wasn't worthwhile. Luckily, Joe had a simple solution. "Time to go collect rent!"

The first thing he did was unload all of his stabilization cubes in his workshop in a hail of ringing metal that poured out of his codpiece while he sighed in contentment at the feeling. Then Joe went to each of the buildings to which he'd transferred ownership, picking up the percentage of complete goods that he was due. His final stop was the warehouse. Upon walking in, he was led to a side room with annoyingly noticeable subterfuge.

Once he was tucked away, it was the work of merely a handful of minutes to set up a Field Array in the room and convert his percentage of corpses directly into aspects. As a fringe benefit, as the bodies vanished, the Cores contained within them clattered to the ground, unable to be converted into any other raw material. His embezzling partner watched this with great interest and didn't even complain as Joe scooped those into his spatial storage. They wouldn't be much use to the Ritualist, as he didn't particularly need Cores that were under the Rare rank. "Suppose I could eventually turn these into batteries, though. Better to not waste them."

Then the human turned on the Dwarf with a bright smile. "Hello, kind supply manager! My name is Joe. I'm here to purchase a large batch of unprocessed corpses. May I ask your name and what you'd be willing to accept as payment?"

"I don't understand what game you're playing at." The bearded Dwarf brushed off his beard in a sharp motion, something Joe understood was a sign of either confusion or contempt in his society. Possibly both, given this situation. "Carpe Commeatus Maximus is my name. As to the price–"

"Hold on, your name is 'seize the important supplies'?"

"Strange. Is that how it translates in your language?" The Dwarf moved on quickly. "As I was saying, until an official currency has been generated, we don't have any good metric for exchange."

"I'm going to call you Max." Joe loudly interrupted, taking the opportunity to splay out dozens of samples of the goods he had access to. "Any of this catch your eye? I bet the soap especially would be well-received by your workers. Always getting covered in goo and such."

As he looked over the goods on the floor, there was a subtle but clear shift in both the Dwarf's posture and temperament toward the situation. "Can you get these in bulk?"

"Yes, I can get these finished products in enough bulk to make trades for raw materials. Unprocessed raw materials that will require lots and lots of work before they're useful to anyone else." Joe knew that the negotiations had already begun, and he was ready to drive the hardest bargain he could.

"Well. In *that* case," Max stated with a twinkle in his eye as he twirled his beard with one finger. "I suppose you can call me anything you want, and Max is close enough. As payment for that favor, I'm thinking I'll take seven of those, three of this, and at least a dozen of those bars of soap per Penguin, but if we want to discuss *Hoardlings*–"

As they bickered back and forth on the final barter agreement, Joe realized that this was the longest stretch of fun he'd experienced in a long time. Maybe it *wouldn't* be such a terrible idea to set up his Wizard Tower somewhere nearby, then spend a few decades just growing and exploring this immense, frozen world.

CHAPTER TWENTY-THREE

"There's only a couple of hours until the next Beast wave commences." Socar alerted the group with a hint of trepidation in his voice. "Are you certain we can't wait until afterward to begin production of our defenses?"

"You're the one who said you had something for us." Heartpiercer scoffed lightly at the fear the Mage was expressing. She wouldn't admit it, but as the cat rubbed its face against his, obviously an attempt to calm its human down, she was slightly jealous. "Plus, if we miss this opportunity, it could be up to forty-eight hours before we get another chance at earning a decent chunk of supplies. I don't know about you, but I'm running *real* low."

"One of the downsides of coming here with only what we could carry with us." Joe demurred as she looked to him for support. "I was able to make a few solid trades, but I'm still too low on supplies to really be useful or get ahead of the Dwarves who might want to make houses or apartments."

"Get ahead of them? What do you mean?" Bauen had known Joe for a while now, and he was correct to be suspicious. The Ritualist wasn't about to explain to him that his plan was to block any and all attempts at making living spaces. To that end, the human merely stared at Socar and relied on the cool temperature and his magic to keep any sweat from appearing on his forehead.

The cat-clad Mage didn't need much in the way of stimulus in order to produce his plans. "Here's what I was thinking. We have walls, and we know that most of the creatures are going to follow set patterns moving through those walls. If we're going to be playing a tower defense, clearly we need *towers*."

From there, the Mage produced several different options, which would have corresponding differences and difficulties in creation. "Joe, I'm going to need to rely on you to figure out what you want to build, as well as what's going to be the best for your magics and such. These are base templates, and I drew them up pretty quickly. If you and I spend a little bit of effort, we can incorporate your ideas fairly quickly. But these ones and this one have edifices similar to the talons on the Phoenix World Boss that would hold each cube. I noticed that you're using a prime number for each ring of them, so I incorporated that in the design all the way up to the Journeyman rank."

"You did this quickly?" Joe was suitably impressed, although his eyes did land on a few dates on the page that were quite a bit older than the last twenty-four hours. "You sure you haven't been working on these for a while?"

"*Ahem.*" Socar blushed slightly and rolled one of the papers up. "You see, ever since I saw the Mage's Tower, I've wanted to make something like it. What's more magical than a spire surrounded by magical defenses that reaches to the sky? It's not going to be exactly that, but… with your help, I think we can get close."

Joe threw an arm around the man's shoulders, "I knew we were going to be best friends as soon as I heard you were an expert in 'variant architecture'. I'm going to have to pick your brain on all of this."

"What about these ones? You excluded them from your earlier explanation." Bauen was looking at the squat structures with great interest. "I see doors and… is this a bunker? I've seen many bunkers in my day, and that's one for certain."

Socar leaned forward and tapped the paper. "Yes, that's what I'm calling a melee tower. Since these monsters are so huge, I essentially went with a design that's more turtle shell than turret. We can set these up along the walls, using them as places for Dwarven warriors to fall back if the monsters are too strong for them. Then they'll offer them extreme defense while still providing the opportunity to attack. Obviously, if they have a ranged option, that'd be for the best."

"I like it." The Dwarf started tapping the paper excitedly. "Getting my people to abandon a battle is not… easy. But we could sell this as a way to take down more and larger enemies instead of as a hidey hole. Perfect."

"Why are they listed as 'Special or Unique'?" Joe questioned as he compared the magical and melee towers. "The ones that you've set up for me are only up to Special towers. That's Journeyman level, but two of the three melee towers are rated as Expert?"

Socar hurriedly nodded. "That's just for the sheer durability and protection values. If there are people in the buildings, I care about them a lot more than I care about the autonomous structures. Technically, I think you can set up your rituals on any surface, so there shouldn't be any conflict here. The reason these ones for you are Rare is so that I can add a modular component, in case we think of something to add to the towers in the future."

He made a fair point, so Joe simply focused on the actual structure's design. "I'm guessing that their surfaces are shaped like this for your formation plans? Otherwise, this one that looks like a needle with a spoon at the top doesn't make any sense."

"Correct!" Socar's eyes lit up as he began talking about one of his favorite subjects. His nervousness over being so close to the front lines of the Beast waves dissolved like a morning mist under the sun. "Each of them has to be placed correctly and carefully, so I can ensure that the energy flows of this area are moving smoothly and without turbulence. That's a zero-point scoop… or I want it to be. We'll see what actually happens."

The Ritualist silently decided to use his Essence Cycle skill before and after placing the towers and rituals, just to see how much this actually would impact the world around them. In a land of magic and giants, he certainly wasn't about to discount the notion that it truly mattered.

The conversation ground to a halt as each person expectantly looked over at the Ritualist. Joe cracked his knuckles and let his smile spread. It was finally time to shine.

He internally praised himself for his decision to create only Uncommon or better buildings in the village and resolved to use only Common-ranked towers for the moment. While they'd have the option to upgrade these in the future, he didn't currently want to give up any of his higher-ranked building slots, knowing that it would impact the village and his plans too much.

"I can make fifty Common towers in total right now, if I want to save the morale bonus for Uncommons, but if I'm reading these plans correctly, right now I only have enough materials to make about ten of them. Let's get farther away from the village, so we can maximize our contribution against the monsters."

Because they were going to be making towers instead of simply placing the rituals on the walls, as had originally been decided upon, Socar tagged along and slightly adjusted each placement of what he called the 'feng shui flags'. Thanks to Joe's Rituarchitect Survey Grid, they were able to shift the final product into the exact position Socar demanded with perfect accuracy, sending Socar into ecstatic outbursts each time they *perfectly* placed one.

As the tower itself was going to sit on the wall and was a very simple, Common building, it was the work of only a few minutes for it to be fully formed. Joe watched as his aspects dwindled further, but this was a worthwhile investment. "I'm glad that you included a ladder in the design, otherwise I'm not sure how I'd get up there to place these cubes and the ritual."

"I tried to think of everything," Socar humbly deflected, even as he smiled happily at the ease with which his design had been brought into reality. "I'm sure I missed a few things, but these are early designs, so… I guess I'm fine with that. Please feel free to offer guidance on how I can improve in the future."

Extremely pleased with the start of their business partnership, Joe rapidly scaled the tower and placed the cubes in the edifices that had been designed for this express purpose. Looking closely, he realized there was quite a bit of detail on the metal talons that would close around the cubes as soon as they were placed. "Huh. Those really do look like an accurate representation of the talons of the Lava Phoenix. He has a good eye for this stuff."

Before he placed his ritual, Joe lightly brushed his finger against the orb containing Essence Cycle and found that, even with one building, there was a noticeable, if slight change in how power flowed through the area. Similar to placing a spoon in a sink and turning the water on, the energy would strike the top of the tower and be deflected in what seemed like random patterns. However, as he looked deeper, comparing the flowing power with his knowledge of the area, and the map that Socar had already adjusted, Joe realized that those deflections would be caught by the other towers, likely creating a laminar stream of flowing, ambient energy.

Just like that, he started to understand what Formations were all about.

You have met the qualifications for earning the skill Basic Formations at the Novice level. Unfortunately, the disruption in the area makes it impossible for the skill to be quantized. Seek instruction from a higher-ranked Formation trainer in order to gain this skill.

"Hold on, I earned it and I *didn't* earn it at the same time? Lame." Joe shook his head as he was pulled out of Essence Cycle by the intrusive notification. He didn't mind missing out on the Formations skill for now, since he knew that, as his insights into the use of Formations became deeper, he'd likely gain the skill at a higher rank. Perhaps it would even have a positive effect on the skill growth that he knew more before actually earning it.

There was still plenty for him to do, so he tried not to linger on the missed opportunity. With the cubes in place, Joe was able to set up his ritual. Since this was going to be the ritual closest to the exit and the monsters would be bunched into a large group as they tried to enter, he went with his highest damage, largest area-of-effect ritual. "Hard to go wrong with acid-filled bubbles that hone in on your enemies."

The downside was, if any Dwarves came in range of the effect, they would take damage as well. He could only hope they would remain in a better, safer position. With that in mind, he also adjusted the whitelist of the ritual, ensuring it wouldn't target humans or Dwarves. That was the best protection he could put in place with the materials on hand and this particular ritual. Once it was complete, he slid down the ladder and took a look at the final product.

"Is it just me, or does that look like a scoop of ice cream about to be launched to start a food fight?" Socar chuckled quietly as he examined the building, though he shrugged and started walking away immediately. "I suppose if it works, it's not stupid."

"I *promise* you… both can be true." Joe laughed as well, though he choked slightly as he realized that the small tower had already taken durability damage. Looking closer, he could see that the chaotic energies of this world were essentially working to dissolve the tower. "Abyss, look at that. Entropy at its finest. I'm going to need to point that out to someone. I bet these walls are starting to melt from the inside out."

Shaking his head, the Ritualist realized that the towers weren't going to be quite as low-maintenance as he'd hoped. If he wanted them to last for any real length of time, he was going to have to swing by on the regular with a Ritual of Repair. Otherwise, just by existing, the towers would slowly collapse. "I think I'm going to have to renegotiate my portion of the gains from this…"

"We already have a deal!" Heartpiercer Mcshootypants called before Joe could start bringing any other issues to light. "No take-backsies!"

CHAPTER TWENTY-FOUR

With each tower they put into place, Joe realized that the energy in the area was truly being impacted at an astounding rate. As the decuple of structures completed their creation, Joe felt a sharp static tingle along his skin, almost as though he were standing in a place where lightning was about to strike.

"Excellent!" Socar called out with barely-contained excitement as he watched the tip of the tower briefly glow with energy. "I see that the Formation is in place. Unfortunately, it's only a basic Formation, meaning it would only qualify as a Novice rank. That's not going to do much in this world, but we *could* still see a few percentage points of increase."

That made sense to Joe, as none of his Novice-rank abilities were useful or easily forced into being on this world. Deciding against getting into a long-winded conversation—the Beast wave was imminent—Joe hurried to the top and set up a Ritual of Dark Lightning Strike. When it was finished, he took the opportunity to watch the flow of essence in the area, noting that there was now a clear outline of a decagon between each of the buildings. The energy passed along the scoops moved back and forth in waves, creating a two-dimensional film of power in the air between them.

"Amazing…" Joe pulled his hand away from the orb, having finally gotten the knack of how to actually force the skill to release him. Shaking off the odd lethargic feeling that always seemed to settle over him after using that ability, he climbed down from the tower and began his trek back to the start. The Ritualist was excited to see if his rituals would have as much effect on the hundreds of monsters as he hoped they would, and he also wanted to be present to see how rapidly the towers would degrade over time.

Getting into position next to the first that he'd created, Joe scanned the building and realized that it had lost about six percent durability already. "What's that… two percent per hour? Yikes, until we get these up to at least the Apprentice rank, keeping them from falling apart is going to be practically a part-time job. Which… I can hire out."

Letting out a cackle that *barely* qualified as maniacal, Joe silently tried to determine how many bars of luxury soap it would take to hire someone to walk the walls once a day and use the Ritual of Repair to keep the towers in good form. "It's not quite like a banana for measurement, but currency is getting *weird*."

Scrutinizing the monsters in the distance, Joe calmly watched as they went from the size of an ant to the enormous creatures that they actually were. The ground was rumbling from the synchronized sprinting, and dust began falling from the walls below him. As he wasn't the owner of the walls, he had to trust that someone was keeping them in good shape and lamented the fact that he didn't have a way to assess the durability of them at the moment. "If they made Common walls, these suckers are going to fall just from the creatures coming toward them. Maybe I should found a company that's focused on repairing low-ranked buildings…?"

Shhzzz… splash!

The first of his acid-filled bubbles erupted away from the

tower at subsonic speed, spinning through the air and distorting from the resistance. It hit the front ranks of the monsters, erupting into a geyser of acid that dropped down and splattered scores of creatures at a time. The Penguins that had been directly impacted by the bubble had their momentum broken, generating a pileup of monsters that stumbled and fell all over each other.

Four seconds after the first of the bubbles had been sent, another one was approaching full. On the fifth second, the attack repeated itself. With so many monsters moving around the slower ones, when the bubble hit this time, it drenched nearly double the number of beasts.

"Oh, yeah. It's all coming together." Joe quietly patted himself on the back as the front ranks of monsters got too close to the ritual for it to target them. That was fine with the Ritualist, as he knew there were nine more opportunities for his towers to deal some damage. This first one was only really intended to break their speed, start damaging the group as a whole, and make them more susceptible to the effects farther in.

Acid wasn't an ideal choice if he wanted to preserve the pelts of the monsters, but it allowed him to break through the first barrier that would otherwise block some of the damage potential. The corrosive fluid was already causing patches of feathers to fall out and skin to show. This would allow for the human and Dwarven defenders to strike deadlier blows and his magical effect to better compound with each other.

Lastly, as the Penguins met with the forces defending against them, Joe realized why he wouldn't be earning a higher percentage of rewards from these creatures.

A Defeatist Fluttering Penguin has been slain! You earn 3 exp for your contribution to its death!

"I... I completely forgot to account for earning experience off of these!" Joe looked at his towers with even greater happiness filling him. "It's not much, but I am damaging every single one of those beasts. This'll add up over time, and there's only a little over ten thousand experience to go!"

He couldn't even remember the last time he'd gained a Character level, but with these rituals and an endless number of enemies to slay, he finally had a chance. With nothing else to do for the moment, Joe decided that he should be working on his weapon control, so he started sending his Ritual Orbs into the fray.

Morsum soon made an appearance. Since the summoned creature did more damage to creatures that were low on health, Joe sent the Pseudo-Lich skull flying after them as a finisher. The orb that summoned his creature wasn't bound to him via a Characteristic, which meant that if Joe lost track of the orb, it could be permanently lost. He resolved to bind that orb as soon as he was done here, but for now, he simply retracted it whenever it was about to go out of range—much to Morsum's annoyance.

The Beast wave only consisted of approximately eight hundred total monsters this time around, and upon defeating the last of them, Joe got a notification that another would be attacking anytime within the next forty-eight hours. As the bodies were collected, Joe saw how slow and inefficient the process was, adding a note to his to-do list.

Happily for the people collecting the corpses, any blood that flowed out of open wounds was drained away and sent washing across the ground, no longer staining clothes, armor, or skin as it was sucked in by his original, inefficient ritual and converted into water and powder.

A standard Beast wave was crushed with no casualties or loss of structure! Your Village's morale modifier gains a temporary 2X boost! Current morale modifier: 1110/500.

"Ahh… so that's how it works." Joe watched that number hungrily, knowing that, because it had touched five hundred, he would get access to another Rare building slot. "I guess it makes sense. Do things that make people feel happy and secure, and they'll have better morale. I wonder, if we're able to have a flawless upgrade from Village to Town, would a temporary boost like that become permanent? Wait…! Forget a *Rare* structure, the morale is over a thousand with that boost! That means there's a *Unique* slot up for grabs!"

Before he could panic and rush off to create a new building, Joe calmed himself with the realization that there was no possible way someone else in town could create such a strong building before *he* took the opportunity. It would take weeks on the low end to create a potent edifice, whereas he could do it in under an hour, with proper preparations. Resolving to take the time to do some research, as well as make sure they had a flawless upgrade when they went to make a Town, Joe followed through on his plans and made his way back to his workshop.

He had a Ritual Orb to bind, and the collection and division of resources from the slain monsters was going to take *quite* a while. Three minutes and a half dozen Omnivaults later, Joe stepped into his workshop and gently closed the door behind him. Ensuring that he was alone in the room, Joe started laying out the ritual that he would be using to bind his weapons to his Characteristics.

Every part of this process was going to be different than what he had done before, the ritual as well as the alchemical components. The ritual, at the Journeyman rank, was most certainly going to be the easiest portion for him to control and properly utilize. Even so, the alchemical components, the binding agents, were at the Student rank. He couldn't think of a single instance when he had used such a potent component from a different magical field in his rituals. He was sure that it was going to be fun, but trying a new thing was always at least a little bit nerve-wracking.

"The main stabilization items are going to be the candles, although that will only provide additional stabilization up to the Rare circle." Joe fretted over whether he should try and push for higher-ranked candles, eventually deciding that the powerful outer layer would be sturdy enough on its own—so long as he managed the instability of the lower circles. With that thought in mind, he placed each of his candles… then, after a moment of hesitation, placed stabilization cubes in the open spaces between the already-melting unscented wax.

"If my cubes work on blacksmithing and rituals, and my candles work on Alchemy and rituals… it would make sense to use them to *greatly* stabilize where they overlap. Right?" Joe was hoping this was what Jake meant when he said that he should play to his strengths with these items. Just before he lit the candles, the Ritualist paused and decided that he could make it even better.

"Technically, putting them in circles like this had some kind of mathematical reasoning, right? Even if I don't have the skill for Formations, I can calculate what their position *should* be by using Calculus and Number Theory, then cross-referencing that with my Ritual Lore."

Thanks to already having a near-perfect understanding of where they should be placed for best effect, it took merely half an hour to design what he thought would be the ideal placement of the differing stabilization items. After shifting them slightly, mostly a simple twist instead of an entirely new spot on the floor, Joe took a moment to look at the design using his Essence Cycle.

Congratulations! Calculus and Number Theory has reached Apprentice 0! Item gained: Local area topographical map.

"That's promising." As soon as Essence Cycle was active, he sucked in a breath in shock at what he saw.

Energy was running back and forth between the candles, between the cubes, then finally commingling and creating an umbrella effect as the distinct items harmonized with each other. "It's *beautiful.* I can even already see how I can improve it! If I were to adjust this entire setup to be in alignment with the patterns of the constellations, thereby bringing my Ritualist class effects into play, I don't think there would be *anything* that could disrupt this."

Feeling confident and powerful, Joe took a moment to pull out the map he had just gained as a reward. He unrolled it excitedly, his smile falling as he took in the information the map provided. As far as he could tell, it was a plain sheet of white paper. "I don't know what I was expecting from a topographical map, when we can see hundreds of miles in the distance and know there isn't a single landmark or terrain feature. Does this update if I move around? No? Perfect. Back to it, then."

Unfortunately, without the ritual either being outside with a view of the night sky or in a Grand Ritual Hall that directly showed him the positioning of the stars around himself, there was no way to safely set up a better version of this ritual. Still, Joe was extremely happy with the current placement, so he activated it immediately. "I've already used the opposing Characteristics of Strength and Intelligence. What do I need to grow to a higher height?"

Silently, he was asking himself another question: which Characteristic could he afford to sacrifice if it were destroyed? As this orb was the one he summoned Morsum around, it had the highest chances of being singled out for destruction by a powerful monster. To Joe, countering that danger took priority, so he wanted to boost the capabilities of his summon and his orb to their maximum potential. With that in mind, he chose to bind the orb to his Constitution.

Ritual prepared, alchemical binding agent at the ready, Joe tossed the orb forward and let the magical effects resonate with the images, diagrams, words, numbers, and intent that he'd etched into the ritual itself. Binding a Characteristic was extra difficult because he needed to align all of those concepts with his own physical being, as well as what his conscious and subconscious understanding of Constitution truly was. The instructions had warned that, the more he left to the magic to fill, the weaker the result of the binding would be.

This process went smoothly and was so comparatively gentle that Joe almost didn't realize when it was over—he'd been braced for pain. Unlike the previous binding, this time, Joe didn't get a message informing him that he would need stronger rituals or binding agents. That meant he could do another one in the near future without having to increase his skills to crazy heights, and he resolved to do so in short order.

Whether it was true or not, Joe credited the maximized stability of the ritual for his well-being and comfort. The first thing he did after his successful ritual, even before reading the final effects, was write down *exactly* how the ritual had been stabilized, noting the positions, even drawing pictures to accurately capture exactly how everything had been placed. Finally, with that out of the way, he looked at the notification he'd received.

Ritual Orb of Constitution (Masterwork). This Ritual Orb has gone through an Alchemic treatment as well as an extra round of enchanting via rituals.

Characteristic assigned: Constitution. Any spell assigned to this Orb will have the primary durability or duration effect greatly enhanced. Base durability of this orb is increased by 50%.

Automatically grants Orb the 'recall' ability. It will return to you after five minutes if left behind, forgotten, or stolen.

Core assigned: 890/20,000

Spell assigned: Planar shift (Student IV, awaiting unbinding for skill upgrade).

Ritual Diagram captured: Planar shift (Focus).

"Exactly what I was hoping for!" Joe exulted as he recalled the orb to his bandelier. It was already slightly shifting its shape, and if he was correct, it would end up looking similar to a heart. Not a perfect anatomical mirroring, but more like what a child would draw on a paper to portray love. His eyes looked over the statistics on the orb, and a small frown appeared. "I need to replace the Mana Batteries in these and adjust the bound spells."

Since there was no time like the present, Joe started laying out the next ritual diagrams immediately, a wide smile on his face.

CHAPTER TWENTY-FIVE

With a simple Ritual of Unbinding, Joe was able to remove the currently bound spells from his orbs. He started with Planar Shift, as was his intention, but the notification he received as soon as he did so made his eyes go wide, and his hands begin flying as he created a second ritual.

Delayed spell experience allocated!

Planar Shift (Student IV → Student VI)

That was rapidly followed by a series of additional notifications as he pulled the spells off of his orbs. The longer they'd been attached, the more drastic and dramatic the final results.

Delayed spell experience allocated!

Cone of Cold (Beginner V → Apprentice VII). Congratulations! The spell has broken through into the Apprentice ranks, gaining a 100% chance of inflicting 'Brittle' upon use!

Corify (Beginner V → Apprentice II).

Lay on Hands (Student VI → Journeyman I). Congratulations! The spell has reached the Journeyman ranks. When using the spell to heal other people, there is a small chance to bless them with a small random buff!

"How long has it been since I first equipped those spells, that almost all of them were able to jump at least a *rank*?" Joe rubbed at his bald head as he thought it over, realizing that he'd never unbound *any* of the spells until now. "Now I know to do that more often, I guess."

Still, it was difficult for him to be unhappy with the results of waiting. As he worked to unspool the metal wire mesh that was within the orbs, Joe tried to determine if it would be worth it to figure out a Mana Battery recharging station. It was something he'd been thinking about, and he even had a rudimentary diagram for one that he had guessed at, but he knew that creating a real version would take an extreme amount of effort and the assistance of an outside enchanter. "That means… I'm going to have to figure out a way to bribe Havoc into helping me out with that."

A Mana Battery recharger would need to be a pure enchantment. While he could eventually create a ritual to then create the enchantment, that would necessitate a completed, working version with a carefully constructed blueprint diagram. Not only that, but the recharge station would need to scale with the size of the Mana Battery he wanted to fill.

Creating a Rare-ranked version meant that an Expert-ranked battery would charge at a substandard rate, possibly even causing the enchantment to fail as it worked to overcome the denser power of the higher ranked material. Using a high-rank charger on a low-ranked battery would cause explosions. "I'm going to need one for each tier, aren't I?"

He thought about it for a few moments, realizing that he *really* only needed a few to start with. Uncommon Cores were the most common ones he'd seen on Jotunheim. Rare came from elites, and he had a sneaking suspicion that Special or Unique ones would come from bosses. It was *highly* improbable that he was going to be using his best Cores as batteries, so he decided to plan for a Rare, as well as an Uncommon station.

For the time being, he simply held one of his batteries in his hands as he walked along, devoting his mana regeneration to it. The process was slow, inefficient, but at least he could slowly fill it up without fear of causing it to explode. As he walked toward the warehouse to start collecting his materials, he shook his head at his past self. "I just had to put a twenty-thousand-capacity battery in that orb, didn't I? It's going to take like… three hours to fill up!"

That gave Joe pause. He lifted the battery in front of him and watched as his mana regeneration pumped into it. With a regeneration of nearly seventy mana per second, he should've been able to fill the battery in under an hour. Yet, the charge it gained was a mere fraction of what he pumped into it. "Forget three hours, that's closer to ten!"

Doing some quick math, he realized he'd be able to invest two hundred fifty-one thousand, four hundred sixty mana per hour. But, at the rate it was being converted, the battery would only accept two thousand and twelve per hour. "Where's it even getting that number from?"

For the time being, he could only shake his head in confusion and allow the power to naturally accumulate. Walking into the warehouse, Joe found several lines of fighters, porters, and craftsmen waiting patiently for their allocation of goods. Max saw Joe and moved directly over. He had been wandering the floor, assisting his employees each time there was a question or confusion. Once more, Joe was pulled into a side room, though this time there was a substantially larger piles of bodies.

"This looks pretty good, Max. Smaller than I was expecting?" Joe let the question hang in the air, hoping the Dwarf would become flustered and give him more. Instead, he was met with a firm shake of the head.

Pointing at several charred places along the corpses, Max explained his reasoning. "You did lots of damage to lots of creatures. Unfortunately, acid and other effects ruin pelts and meat, while only counting as superficial damage. Overall, your contribution was already increased by nearly thirty percent because of the assistance you provided by creating critical hit strike points. No one can deny your effectiveness, but most of the work to finish them off was still completed by the legion, which is why you earned this much."

"I think-"

"*No.*" The Dwarf cut him off sharply. "There are no discounts or bonuses right now. Respect my expertise in this field. I've spent three of your lifetimes learning how to properly calculate contribution, and I'll not have my craft disrespected by *haggling.* We already have a deal; we already have established additional payouts for you. I guarantee that none of this is a cheat, on my honor. Question *that* at your own peril."

"Abyss, Max." Joe took the corpses into his Field Array without another complaint, only the minor grumble to show his reluctance at accepting what someone else told him at face value. Soon, he was back out in the snow and decided to check in at the Town Hall to see if he could figure out why the morale modifier had reached such an inflated height before getting doubled during the Beast Wave.

"Joe!" Jaxon came slithering through the snow like a cross between the Penguin attackers and a giant anaconda. "Look, I created a new movement technique!"

"That's great, I hate it." Joe backed away from his friend as he slithered up to him, rearing up like a cobra and transitioning into walking on his feet like a regular person. "I've barely seen you since we got to this world! What have you been up to?"

"Oh, this and that. More of this than that, if you know what I mean!" Jaxon rambled as they stepped into the small center of bureaucracy for the town. "With such large monsters, my hands have been eating well. I've been focused on advancing them from T-Rex Head Hands to T-Rex Head Hydra Fingers. Joe. Do you have *any* idea how much meat ten dinosaurs eat on a regular basis? At least, if I'm trying to rank them up, which I am. Precious babies."

"Uh-huh." Joe looked at the morale modifier diagram that was constantly in view from the reception area, trying to line up the numbers he was seeing with what the system had informed them of upon the completion of the most recent wave.

Jaxon lightly gripping his shoulder caused Joe to give the man his full attention, and he found himself staring deep into his friend's eyes. "I just want you to know that I have not been ignoring you for no reason. Both of us are busy, and at some point, I'm certain we will resume our forays into the unknown. Until then, I'm not just going to sit in your office and watch you read books and alternatively frown, curse, or giggle."

"Is that what it looks like from the outside?" Joe blinked a few times as he realized that, yes, that was probably *exactly* what he looked like while lost in thought. "Don't worry about me, Jaxon. I know you're working hard so that we can both move on to the next world together, when we're ready for it."

"Exactly!" The Chiropractor patted Joe's back, adjusting his spine before turning, dropping to the ground, and slithering out the door. "Sssee you sssoon!"

"You're not a snake!" Joe shouted after his friend, who didn't seem to hear him. "I know you can't taste the air; you're just sticking your tongue out at me! Celestial feces, I really *hope* he's not actually turning into a snake."

"Is there something that I can help you with… that will get you to close the door?" The receptionist called over, the passive aggressiveness of the Dwarf never failing to get under Joe's skin immediately.

Biting back a caustic retort, the Ritualist managed to put a pleasant expression on his face. "Yes, I'm wondering if you have certain knowledge that I seek. I noticed that the morale modifier has grown exceptionally well, and I am wondering what factor has affected that the most."

"Bro. Speak regular words, will you? If I need to get a thesaurus for every time you show up, I'm going to lock you out." The Dwarf gave a long-suffering sigh and started explaining the situation to Joe as if he were speaking to a child. "You see, human, when a bearded Dwarf is very happy, he's more productive. When a mustachioed Dwarf is more productive, she's more happy. When both of them are happy and productive, they make little morale babies."

"You know I can burn this building down with a single word and a half-formed gesture, right?" Joe's intrusive thoughts finally got the better of him, slipping out of his mouth before he managed to force his teeth together with a **click*. "Let me try that again... what's the direct correlation here? What specific action increased the modifier?"

"Well, someone out there's been extra industrious and built a whole lot of buildings." The receptionist shook his head as if he were confused as to who it could have been. "Those facilities by themselves give us a base morale increase directly correlating to their rank. Trash is a negative twenty-five, Damaged is worth nothing, Common gives us ten, Uncommon is twenty-five, increasing by twenty-five until we reach Artifacts, which are worth two hundred. You may have noticed that we had a base two hundred back when the town was founded, right?"

"Kinda." That hadn't been something Joe had paid much attention to, but when he thought back... nope, he hadn't seen that anywhere.

"Well, it should've been a *lot* higher than that!" The Dwarf actually gained a grin when he saw Joe flinch away from the guttural roar he'd just let out. "*Somebody* set down an Artifact in place instead of a whole bunch of other, more *useful* buildings. A Town Hall and utilities are all worth fifty morale *by themselves*. Then, of course, there are all the individual choices of the people living here, which just means everything is impacted by the kind of day someone's having. Everyone's individual thoughts on how things are going will adjust the modifier accordingly."

"That... sounds like a nightmare to try and track." Joe was just glad that he didn't need to sit on a computer somewhere and individually account for everything that was going on. "I guess I'm glad the building does it for us automatically. That's all, thanks for the information."

"Hey! Where are you going? Did you come here for a reason?" The receptionist called after Joe. "Every time you show up here, things get weird."

The Ritualist tossed a dramatically sad face at the receptionist, though his eyes were dancing with glee. "Don't worry about what I'm doing! I'm just going to go and fight monsters until I've enough resources to make a Town out of this hole in the wall."

The Dwarf rolled his eyes, then looked down at a paper on his desk as Joe was leaving the Town Hall. Words were appearing on it, and as the page continued to fill out, his expression deepened into a scowl. The door closed fully, and the Dwarf couldn't hold back his mutter at what he was reading any longer, his head already shaking in frustration and rage.

"-'let me tell you about these crazy huge Penguins'. This human is *such* a traitor. Giving foreknowledge of this world directly to our enemies?"

CHAPTER TWENTY-SIX

Despite his bravado with the receptionist, it took more than a week's worth of hours to gather enough resources to complete the final building required for tiering up. Although he had attempted to ensure that every building he made was entirely useful, there was only so much he could do. To his delight, the water tower where his filtered blood-based water was deposited was considered a monument, advancing his Apprentice Rituarchitect class quest. Now there was only one monument to create before that quest would be considered complete.

Joe had caused quite a stir by snatching the Unique building slot and creating his A.S.P.E.C.T. tower. By a 'stir', he supposed that it could have been considered closer to a riot than anything else. Their argument was that, if he had devoted that building slot to something else, such as single-family apartment complexes, nearly a thousand Dwarves would have a place to call home currently. Frankly, the human didn't understand what the issue was with living in bubble tents.

It was an adventure, something fun and new!

At least, that was how he sold it to the crowd. Eventually, he had to make a small concession, offering to hand over the water tower—in combination with the blood-filtering ritual—to the Dwarven Council before the mob finally backed down and returned to their own pursuits.

All pre-morale building slots have been filled! Commencing countdown until the first of twenty-five Beast Waves occur for settlement rank increase. As your Village is attempting to upgrade into a Town (Uncommon to Rare), you will be subject to a set of elite monsters every five waves, with one boss monster per ten. Monster waves will occur, at maximum, eight hours apart and, at minimum, four.

Feeble mortals from the summer realms! Your insignificant Village's audacious growth has gained you the unenviable attention of your Superiors. Rumors are spreading of the pathetic nest you build, where even a pigeon would be too ashamed to roost. Tremble before us as we gather to strike you down, you foolish invaders, you blight upon our domain!

The flavor of the message was completely different between the two sets of notifications, almost as though one was just a simple chatbot sending information their way, and the second was a direct message from a high-end barbarian General of this world's forces. Still, Joe felt confident that he was going to be able to weather anything sent his way. Over the previous week, he'd set up a permanent Aspect Array, recharged and rebound his ritual orbs, and created dozens more buildings—mostly ritual towers for defense.

He was even a good chunk of the way into designing the Ritual of Slaughter, though he was taking his time with it. Mainly, Joe was uncertain what qualifiers he should use as the requirements for activation. It wasn't enough to assume that every monster that came through would be two-legged, as only the Penguins had so far had that attribute as they waddled along the open spaces between walls.

Struck by inspiration at that moment, Joe whipped out a quill and started writing down his thoughts. "What if it's all about the points in the maze out there that they walk through? What if, instead of saying 'it has this attribute' the ritual simply says, 'it isn't a human or a Dwarf, and it went through this point in the maze'."

Scribbling furiously, he pared that down slightly further. "It's so much easier to decide what *not* to account for, instead of saying what it must be. How could I possibly make a set of all characteristics that'd be needed, otherwise? Yes… I think this is exactly what I'll be doing. If monsters pass in front of a Ritual Tile, let's say within forty feet northeast of it, that puts all monsters between that section of the walls in range. Then, if I can set it up where they have to circle the entire city another time in order for this second condition to be met, that'll make an even more stringent requirement! That means a more powerful activation sequence!"

As the inspiration swept away, a broad smile remained on Joe's face. He jumped up to the top of the walls, moving to find the position he wanted for the oncoming tide of monsters. Inspecting the towers, he found that there was only minor damage currently. That was simply a result of *existing*, so he couldn't fault the Dwarven bakers he'd hired. They hadn't been able to set up shop yet, so Joe had been able to offer them the job of running his Rituals of Repair, and they were glad for the work. "They sure did drive a hard bargain, though… the next Unique building I make'll have to be a greenhouse, or they might *actually* start a riot."

As a compromise between the fulfillment of Socar's relentless demands for perfection in the placement of the towers, as well as Joe's insistent need to construct them in sets of prime numbers, a grand total of twenty-nine common ritual towers now stood poised to unleash their lethal magics upon the savage beasts that would be churning the ground between the walls of the village. Unwilling to completely trust the human who was creating so much opportunity for them, the Dwarves demanded the right to assume responsibility for the defense of the city itself.

In a bid to find a solution that both groups could agree upon, the towers had been strategically positioned along the outermost walls where the concentration of monsters was highest—therefore minimizing the risk of inadvertent harm to their allies while maximizing the damage Joe would be able to do against the onrushing horde. This was perfectly acceptable to the Ritualist, as he'd be able to claim the greatest number of monsters as they attacked. The fact that his allies wanted to be the final say on if they succeeded or not was understandable, if frustrating and concerning.

The Dwarves didn't fully trust him, and Joe, in his own way, found the distrust to be mutual. There was always a chance that the Dwarven Council would order the ranks of warriors to simply step aside, allowing direct access to the Town Hall. It was a *low* chance, as there would be an uproar, and Joe had made his position on that matter perfectly clear.

He'd leave.

The Ritualist was uncertain if that was as much of a caution-inducing fact to them as he hoped it was, but he also wasn't going to fully burn that bridge by declaring that they would become his enemies.

"Only a few more hours, and I'll be able to start claiming aspects by the thousands, Cores by the hundreds, and planning out the final vestiges of my Ritual of Slaughter," Joe was murmuring to himself as he approached the small group that he'd joined. They'd gotten used to coming to this spot at the start of each day, and with a new upgrade being announced, they'd all hurried here to see if there were any last-minute events they needed to plan for.

The Ritualist started explaining his new plan for his ritual to Socar, who was happy to help adjust the placement of the 'flags' to maximize their effect.

"Still trying to figure out why you're always calling them flags. In this case, it's a motion detector, isn't it? Let's just go with that," Joe gently teased the Mage, who furrowed his brow as his mouth twisted into a frown. The bald human started chuckling immediately: Socar didn't like using modern terms for his work, and it was easy to rile him into a tizzy.

"Thanks for the help, friend," Joe added more seriously. "We have about eight hours still before combat should begin, so

I might go and start putting these in place. I only have… probably a couple hours of work remaining on making the ritual?"

"What are you going to use as the fifth and final part of the activation?" Heartpiercer suddenly interjected into their conversation. "That's the one that's going to be the most important, right?"

Joe nodded agreeably, even as he scrambled to find a reason *not* to tell her. He'd gotten so used to his rituals being mysterious in everything except the final effect that he was extremely reluctant to share the details of this hopefully powerful version. Still, she'd earned enough trust from him that he managed to force himself to share. "I think I'll have it hold off unless something manages to land a blow on the Town Hall. That'd make the most sense to me. If something manages to get past all of our defenses, defenders, and last resorts, it'll find one last surprise waiting for it."

"Smart…" Bauen tugged at his beard consideringly. "With such a stringent final condition, the excess power should clear out any other monsters that have broken through. Not only would that give us a good opportunity to regroup, it might be strong enough to clear out all of the low-level monsters that are still moving through the killing corridors."

"My thoughts exactly." Joe was the first to leave the group at that moment, but each of them scattered to either take a position for themselves or finish a completely different task. Hurrying to his workshop, which was now dwarfed by the gaping maw of the A.S.P.E.C.T. tower directly adjacent to it, Joe got to work figuring out how to convert his thoughts into diagrams and formulae for the ritual.

By the time the unpowered ritual was ready to go, and Joe stepped out of his workshop, he realized that the amount of light in the sky had noticeably started to dim. Under the false sky he had created, that was something that he hadn't really needed to account for. "Would you look at that…? We're approaching the night of our first day on Jotunheim. It's been an *eventful* day."

He considered the event he'd just initiated and the fact that it would likely be full dark by the halfway point of the waves. "Well, abyss. I suppose I could've planned that better. Now I need to go find some 'volunteers' who can help me get this ritual up and running."

Over the next hour and a half of arguments, pleading, and various threats directed toward him, Joe was informed in no uncertain terms that the Dwarven Council didn't appreciate his attempts to place an unknown, untested magical effect on the Town Hall. Certainly *not* while a flood of monsters were closing in on them this very moment.

The human could only slink away with his gathered group, tail tucked between his legs to show his understanding and consternation. When he was alone with his followers, he turned to them with a morose expression… which vanished in an instant as he clapped his hands. "I'd *completely* forgotten that we don't need to be over there in order to activate this! I'll just set it as a key point for activation *later*."

Utterly nonplussed, the assembled humans and Dwarves tried to think of an excuse they could use to back down. Joe could tell that a few of them were even considering running and informing the council what he was up to. Before anyone could move, he activated an enormous ritual that placed a bubble over them and hid their actions. With a glint in his eye and a lopsided grin on his face, Joe finished preparations for getting the Ritual of Slaughter in place.

"Shall we get started?"

CHAPTER TWENTY-SEVEN

As the ritual began, Joe could tell immediately that it was different from almost anything he'd made before. To start with, instead of the clear, blue-white coloration that his ritual circles typically took, this one was alternatively green or purple. Watching it spin up put imagery in his mind of what it would be able to accomplish: namely, the death and destruction of those who activated it.

The Ritualist felt slightly sick to his stomach as he realized what memories this ritual was dredging up. "It feels like that tainted war ritual that got me banished from Midgard… or that twisted ritual I used to put an eye on the back of my head, the one that backfired and killed a bunch of Dwarves. Not a great association."

He was already reconsidering the use of this powerful magic, but there were three things stopping him from backing down. One, the most important, was the fact that he needed to slay a thousand creatures with this ritual in order to progress his class quest. Two, he needed to create the most potent defenses he could for the city. Three, least important but still hard to let go of, was the fact that he'd already invested all of the materials into its creation. Lips set in a firm line, he powered on as the ritual finished drawing out all of the energies it required.

Congratulations! You have completed the War Ritual: Ritual of Slaughter for the first time! As this is a Journeyman ranked ritual, you gain 400 Reductionist class experience. Don't forget to take all the parts and set them up correctly!

The notification washed over him, but Joe's eyes were on the ritual itself, which had begun to shift and pull apart. The smallest circle, the Novice rank, embedded itself on a small Ritual Tile, followed by each of the others in turn. When it was the fifth circle's turn, the Journeyman-ranked one, it hovered closer to Joe while remaining free-floating. He dashed over to the tiles, scooping them up and carefully storing them away. Then, using the mental powers that he'd honed with his Somatic Ritual Casting skill, he took control of the floating portion and slowly started moving it.

With every step he took, it moved incrementally faster, until he and the swirling energy were walking along at a rapid pace. Many eyes turned his way as he moved, and anyone in his path quickly cleared room for him to pass. The small crowd of people who had helped him create this impressive piece of magical artwork followed along, their numbers swiftly growing as he approached the Town Hall. The murmurs of confusion shifted to alarm as the circle didn't stop, moving on a collision course with the building.

As it touched the stone work over the door, the power was sucked into the building, and a small ring of glowing energy began swirling above the entryway, almost as if it were an LED sign from before Earth fell to monsters. Making sure that piece was in place, Joe turned to the people who had followed along and addressed them grandly, striking a heroic pose. "Thank you all for witnessing this glorious event! Now we should all run away as quickly as possible; before the council gets annoyed that I ignored them and put magical protections in place!"

So saying, he swiftly Omnivaulted away even as the metal barrier separating indoor and outdoor for the Town Hall was slammed open almost hard enough to deal damage to the building itself. He wasn't sure which of the Masters it was, but whoever it was… they were displeased. "Joe! We *told* you to leave this building out of whatever you're doing!"

"Muhuhaha!" Joe laughed as he rubbed his hands together in midair, pleased that his diabolical plan was moving toward fruition. "Now I just need to get the other four tiles set up, and we'll be rocking and rolling."

For this first version, he was planning to follow Socar's advice, putting the plates together to create the formation that'd be most effective against a large number of weak enemies. If the Mage was correct, the unaspected magical damage would instead be converted to fire damage, and be significantly more threatening to a large group of icy beasts.

As he approached the walls, a warning horn was blown. Shouting immediately followed that sound, then Joe could hear the rushing liquid noise of his ritual bubbles being filled with acid, then launched. "They're *already* at the walls? How? We were supposed to have *hours*!"

The answer came in the wind the next moment. "Camouflaged beasts are leading the way! Everyone, prepare for combat!"

"Well, that'd do it," Joe grumbled to himself with great annoyance. "On the plus side, my rituals don't have eyes and won't be fooled by something so simple as 'blending in'. I love it when my work speaks for itself."

He didn't pause in his movement, though he did adjust his plans on the fly. Joe knew that he would have to somewhat shift his plans for the Ritual of Slaughter, as the Ritual Tiles had been planned for placement near the entrance to the walls. With creatures already in there, he didn't particularly care to risk his neck by jumping into their midst and carefully, accurately, *methodically* placing the tiles. That was basically begging to be frozen and casually torn to shreds as enormous monsters wandered past him.

Luckily, he knew where Socar was going to be, and the Ritualist could count on the Mage to help him adjust the placement on the fly. He found the man in the next few seconds, landing next to him, scooping him up in his arms as the Mage let out a yelp of surprise, then launching both of them upward. Joe kicked off his ritual orb of Strength, gaining the height he needed to land safely on top of the wall. Socar smacked him on the chest as Joe let him down. "Give me *warning* next time, you brute! Wait a second, *why* are you a brute? Aren't you a mage?"

"I have fairly well-balanced Characteristics." Joe waved off any further questions, pulling out the not-very-detailed map of the walls. "I have four Ritual Tiles to place, and our original plan isn't going to work with the creatures getting here ahead of schedule. Where else can I put these so that I can achieve the same effect?"

By the end of his question, his counterpart was already shaking his head. "I've already given you the ideal placement for creating that formation, anything else is going to be subpar at best."

"Then let's *do* subpar! We can always change it later, but I'd rather have something in place than nothing at all." Joe's assertion was punctuated by a long, warbling scream as someone was caught by a camouflaged monster and, by the sound of it, stomped flat. Without any further complaints, the two of them quickly sketched out the placement and positioning. As soon as the last mark had been made on the page, Joe pushed off the ground, completing a backflip Omnivault as he plunged into the pathway between walls.

Approaching the ground at terminal velocity, he punched the ground upon landing, converting his momentum into a small shockwave that would knock away anything that was around him. His title, 'Superhero Lander', only converted half of the terrain damage that he would typically take, and the passive effects of Omnivault negated the rest of it. Everything around him was still, as the residents of the village had evacuated as soon as the horn was blown. "Yet another reason we should take the time to put bunkers throughout the walls."

Grumbling quietly to himself to make sure he could hear any creatures creeping up on him, Joe rushed along the empty walkway until he found the spot that Socar had designated for him. "This goes on the west wall, facing east, at a twenty-two-degree angle. *Abyss* it, Socar! Who carries a protractor around with them?"

Eyeballing it as best as he could, Joe placed the Ritual Tile and started sprinting through the open area. Approaching the wall, he Omnivaulted upward, kicked off to go the opposite direction, then hopped atop the wall. "That's the east side done; let's go do the south."

As the entrance to the walls was on the north side of the city, Joe was able to place the second and third tiles without issue. As he rushed to the north, the ground beneath him began shaking, and the air was filled with screams, the scent of blood, and a dense energy from the spells of the defenders and the spell-like abilities of the creatures assaulting the village. Knowing that he was rushing into a fight, Joe focused on where he needed to go and shoved off the ground.

He was coming from the westernmost position, and as he took a sharp right to get in the open area of the walls just north of the village, he pushed off the wall once, twice, then rocketed through the air above a mostly empty area which was shimmering like a mirage from the unbearable cold. It was a reverse heat haze, as warmer air came out of the village and reached the aura of frost exuded by whatever creature was hidden beneath the camouflage.

Even at this close range, Joe couldn't tell exactly what was attacking. The walls were visibly starting to take severe damage, the frost penetrating deeply into the stone and causing cracks to form. "Abyss, abyss, *abyss,* that's bad."

His target was in sight, the center-most position, exactly halfway along the wall where east met west. Preparing himself for pain, he leaned forward and dove directly at the wall. Just before impact, he twisted his body so that he met the stone with a meaty **slap**, distributing the force across his entire body instead of only his face. Then he slid down the rime-coated stone, and the thin barrier generated by his Exquisite Shell was the only saving grace keeping the exposed flesh of his body from fusing to the deadly cold rock.

Joe was breathing heavily as he landed, already feeling the strain of his magics attempting to hold off the area damage. With shaking fingers, he placed the final Ritual Tile and lightly brushed against his orb with the recaptured Essence Cycle. An indistinct pyramid had been formed with the outer Ritual Tiles creating a base and the centermost ritual imbued into the Town Hall being above them by an appropriate amount. "I-it's g-gonna have to be enough."

Teeth chattering so hard that they felt like they were going to shatter, Joe invested a single point of mana into the ritual to have it begin working to mark each of the creatures that it would exert influence on. He flinched away as the activation shattered the Ritual Tile that the circle had been stuck to, panicking for a moment as he thought it had failed. Closer inspection revealed a tiny swirling circle attached to the wall at the exact angle where the tile had been placed.

Releasing a sharp exhale of relief, Joe attempted to Omnivault up and away, to safety. Blinking in surprise, he realized that his legs hadn't moved. Looking down, he saw the issue: his legs were frozen solid just above the knee and down to his feet. A blast of cold air coated his head as a creature hissed directly next to his ear, and the world went white.

CHAPTER TWENTY-EIGHT

Only a fraction of an inch from Joe's eyes, a thick sheet of ice had appeared. No matter how he struggled, his entire body was utterly immobile. From the outside, he was certain he looked like an ice sculpture, but his Exquisite Shell had collected the dense ice along its edge instead of allowing the attack through.

Damage taken: 9,065 frost damage! You have been Immobilized! Exposure to absolute cold is sapping five Health per second!

Exquisite Shell: 2,604/11,669

Health: 2,322/2,327

Luckily, he was in no danger of suffocating, as his Neutrality Aura constantly refreshed the air around him and in his lungs. Still, even struggling with all of his strength didn't allow him to budge a fraction of an inch. He wasn't certain if the monster was going to follow up the breath weapon with an attack to shatter him or if it'd assume that he was dead and would walk away. Either way, he still needed to escape from this immobilization as quickly as possible.

"I don't have any spells that will help me get out of this," Joe mumbled against the ice, which had frozen against him so perfectly that it shaped itself around his lips and ever so slightly into his mouth. He had to be careful not to accidentally overextend any part of his body past his protections, or his tongue would instantly freeze against the shimmering frost in front of it. With his spells failing him and his body too weak to make a difference, Joe realized he could still rely on his mind.

Concentrating carefully, he gripped his orb of Intelligence with his thoughts and set it spinning then launched it out and away from his body. It shredded the leather pouch that contained it, but the spinning, drill-like orb blasted through the ice, shattering over half of it in an instant. Joe forced himself forward, breaking his way out where he could and shimmying his body out of each opening where he couldn't.

Since he'd be under attack from the moment he emerged from his frozen cocoon, Joe wasted no time in launching himself forward and upward. As his feet touched the ice that the ground had been converted into, he lunged and struck the wall and fell into a squatting position like a leaping toad. The air behind him crackled as a breath weapon was unleashed once more, and he forced himself to continue moving without pause.

His dangling shoes and robe gained a flash-frozen sheet of solid frost as he barely evaded the upper portion of the attack, and he flipped in the air to gain some additional momentum. Looking down at what was coming after him, all Joe could see once more was the shimmering haze and mist that formed where warm air met cold.

"What *are* those things?"

There was no time to find out; he needed to get to safety and reset his shield. The fact that he'd survived a perfect sneak attack while he'd been distracted was a testament to the power of his defenses as well as a hefty bit of luck. Enough so that he half expected to gain a stat point for it or *possibly* lose a point of Wisdom for his foolishness in diving into the active combat zone.

When nothing changed, he assumed that the system had considered it a wash, and he was perfectly fine with seeing no change at all.

Now that he didn't need to circle the Village, it was the work of only a few minutes to return to the populated central area. He landed next to a large group of Dwarves and snapped out a sharp request for information. "I need a situation and damage report! Somebody get me numbers on those things, and-"

"Hey, calm down *civilian* bro!" A sergeant of the Legion shouted him down. "That's on a need-to-know basis, and we don't need you running back to the others with a wild story and causing a panic while we're busy. Why don't you get to a bunker or something, since you're clearly not open to getting involved in the fighting!"

"What're you even talking-" Joe's hands clenched into claws, and he let out a snarl of frustration as he recalled the fact that he'd lost his Major-General title. "I'm the guy setting up the automated defenses! I need to know an estimate of how many monsters are coming in, because the walls are already starting to fail!"

Apparently he was the first person to come back with information of that nature, and after a moment of hesitation, the sergeant acted on the new data and began snapping out orders. Yet, Joe was completely left out of the conversation and was even regarded with hostile eyes as he tried to eavesdrop on what was going on.

In an effort to get information for himself, Joe pulled open his character sheet to start calculating how much experience he'd gained, checking it against the combat logs to figure out how many creatures had already been slain by his defenses.

Name: Joe 'Despised by Humanity' Class: Reductionist
Profession I: Arcanologist (Max)
Profession II: Ritualistic Alchemist (1/20)
Profession III: Grandmaster's Apprentice (14/25)
Profession IV: None
Character Level: 23 Exp: 298,158 Exp to next level: 1,842
Rituarchitect Level: 11 Exp: 57,000 Exp to next level: 9,000
Reductionist Level: 5 Exp: 15,541 Exp to next level: 5,459

Hit Points: 2,121/2,327
Mana: 5,957/8,160
Mana regen: 69.85/sec
Stamina:1,837/1,837
Stamina regen: 6.64/sec (3.32 reserved for Artisan Body)

Characteristic: Raw score

Strength (bound): 176
Dexterity: 178
Constitution (bound): 170
Intelligence (bound): 185
Wisdom: 173
Dark Charisma: 126
Perception: 173
Luck: 110
Karmic Luck: 42

"Looks like my Artisan Body was hard at work. I didn't even notice when I got that point in Constitution." Joe's mind had gone off on a tangent because he was comparing the value of the experience he'd gained against the combat log. Finally, he couldn't ignore it any longer. "Accounting for the bursts of experience I got here and ignoring the tiny amounts I earned in previous Beast waves… I've only killed thirteen total monsters so far this wave? Sure, they're worth six hundred apiece, and that's great, but how tanky *are* these bad boys?"

Just then, an additional notification rolled into his view. This time, he didn't need to push it to the side to focus on his surroundings.

You have slain an Ancient Ice Salamander!

Just reading those words was enough to make Joe facepalm. "They have a frost aura! What am I doing sending acid at them? I bet it does a tiny bit of damage, then freezes into a slush and falls off and to the ground. How much do I need to revamp my rituals in order to have them be effective here?

Thank goodness I gained a fire affinity for adding that Berserker deity to the Pantheon… *gah*! I've forgotten to build even a local shrine here!"

Twisted up in his self-reflection and annoyance, Joe failed to hear the first time an outsider began speaking to him again. Only when they tapped his arm hard enough to cause his Exquisite Shell to flare did he sharply look up from the ground and meet their eyes. He faintly recognized the Dwarf in front of him; her mustache was a hot pink instead of a standard red. Two blinks later, he remembered that she was often in the company of Bauen, which should make her an engineer for the Legion Corps.

"Joe! They told me that you saw the walls failing. I need specifics on that and an action plan to deploy geomancers to reinforce the damaged sections." For a moment, the human stiffened as he took in the authoritative demands that were being sent his way, then he shook himself out of his affronted mindset; remembering that they were in a deadly situation at the moment.

He shoved his finger at the walls nearest them. "The ones that I saw starting to crack were the third and fourth set north of the Village, not too far from here. I'm guessing they're not the only ones that are starting to go. Anything under Uncommon ranking rapidly degrades unless it's maintained, thanks to the entropy the chaotic energies of Jotunheim inflict. Combining that with the frosty aura these Salamanders are emitting is only speeding the process up."

"The walls are failing even without being attacked?" The Dwarf gasped in shock, making Joe frown slightly before he realized that he'd failed to bring that tidbit of information back to the council and have it shared around. "The geomancers have just been focused on building the walls out farther and farther… I don't think we've done *any* preventive maintenance checks and services! Why would the walls fail without being attacked? No, don't answer that; I understand the situation."

Without another word, she turned and sprinted away, a blur

of chrome and pink to his Perception. All Joe could do was hope she could handle the situation: his Rituals of Repair wouldn't work for this problem. Since the walls were only raised stone, not a proper structure, targeting them with his ritual would be the same as targeting the ground in Arizona and hoping he could fix up the Grand Canyon. "If we make it through this, I'm making them implement a *proper* wall."

Joe paced back and forth, scanning the threshold of the towering stone walls that protected the village. Every nerve in his body was on high alert as he risked himself by entering the field and meticulously arranging a network of ritual traps and barriers; each designed to be deployed only in the direst of circumstances. Closing off the entrance entirely was a risk, for it'd only entice the ravenous monsters to seek another path—potentially letting them bust through the defenses that currently protected this not-so-safe haven.

His only hope was that, if they *did* need to activate this last line of defenses, it might grant them precious minutes to fortify their position and brace themselves for the impending onslaught.

As always, it was the unseen that troubled Joe the most. Humanity had long felt that monsters lurked in the darkness; they had felt their palpable presence at the edge of their perception. Here, it was all too real. The uncertainty gnawed at him, a relentless torment that infected him, passed along by the ranks of Legionnaires standing in defense of the fragile Village behind them. As time continued to pass, tempers flared like sparks in a dry forest threatening to ignite into a conflagration that would weaken them all.

Just as tensions reached their most dangerous peak, a gust of freezing wind swept through the opening, throwing a layer of frost over the stifling heat of their fears. The clash of the contrasting fronts of air—one frigid, and one warmed by the invaders of this world—spawned a veil of chilling fog, shrouding the approach in an ethereal haze. That icy whisper of winter tamed the fiery passions of the prepared warriors, pushing them to come together as a cohesive group.

In that moment, as they stood united, shivering in the numbing embrace of the wintry fog, they believed they were ready to face whatever horrors Jotunheim would send their way.

A set of eyes glowing a white light opened in the fog, so intense it stood out against the snow. The low **hiss** accompanying the striking visage announced the arrival of the Salamanders.

CHAPTER TWENTY-NINE

Just as he prepared himself to dive into the fray, Joe received a series of notifications that gave him pause. A quick glance confirmed that they were kills of monsters, and they were racking up faster and faster. By the time he looked over, a half dozen of the messages had appeared, with more arriving every second.

Defeatist Fluttering Penguin defeated!

Hoardling defeated!

"The rest of the first wave must've just gotten here." The Ritualist took solace in the fact that his defenses were more effective against these weaker creatures, then stopped himself before he could feel too much pride. "Ugh… now that I think of it, is it really so impressive that my defenses work exceptionally well against the *weakest* of our foes?"

His ritual orb of Intelligence had already been recalled and reappeared in his hand, as he'd forgotten it in the maze during his recent escape. Tossing it into the air, he focused on making it spin faster and faster, before lifting his other orbs up behind it, setting the orb of Constitution just behind the end of it, and slamming the orb of Strength into the one in the middle, coinciding the moment where the leading orb was struck with sending it forward. Joe had used this combination before, but it put a strain on his weapons, so he'd not felt too comfortable using it until now, where he was able to use the most durable of his weapons to accept the strike.

The drill-like orb flashed through the air so quickly that it left afterimages in his vision, striking the third Salamander that emerged into the open area. Even with his careful preparation, the speed of the monsters in this world was something his mind couldn't currently keep up with. He'd aimed at the leading ice lizard, but luckily the entrance was narrow enough that another one had taken its place by the time his attack arrived.

Unfortunately, he hadn't accounted for the angular, frost-coated scales of the creatures. Instead of striking and drilling directly into the monster, his orb hit the creature's skull and rebounded up, into the wall. A large chunk of stone was blasted out of the wall itself, and Joe earned himself dirty looks from everyone who knew where the attack had come from. "Oh, come on. I didn't *try* to do that; it was straight-up bad luck."

In a practiced formation, the Legion's defensive line advanced a single step in perfect synchronization. Holding axes, swords, and polearms high, they surged forward. Deadly edges pierced through the air or cleaved monstrous foes, depending on the accuracy of their attacks.

Joe's Characteristics promised him remarkable physical prowess, and he *should have* been able to match at least the slowest of his adversaries. Unfortunately, his Perception was simply not up to the task, transforming the unfolding clash into a melange of light, gleaming blades, frozen droplets of blood that splashed into eyes and mouths upon exiting the protection of flesh.

At least a dozen members of the Legion targeted each beast, their concerted assault proving devastating as the Salamanders shattered upon impact as if they were made of fragile ice. As the reptilian forms crumbled under the barrage of countless blows, the battlefield became a chilling canvas of frozen remnants, a testament both to the combined might of the Legion and the deadly threat of the Ancient Ice Salamanders.

Only twelve of the beasts had escaped the labyrinth that'd been designed around the city, and Joe was shocked to find that he'd secured over half of the kills before they'd entered into melee range. "There were only twenty-five of them? *Total*? That few managed to threaten our defenses to this degree?"

His incredulousness was shared by dozens of people around him, going by the over-loud conversations that always occurred after the adrenaline-filled moments of combat. An hour later, after the last penguin had been cut down with a lamenting **squawk**, they received the notification that this Beast wave had ended successfully. Very few people were quick to leave the scene. Most milled around in confusion, waiting and hoping for direction and information.

Eventually, it became clear that none was forthcoming, and small groups began to band together and spread out, some moving to walk through the walls, some to return to their tasks in the village, but most to collect corpses and turn them over for refining into goods. Joe was among the latter group, and he was eager to find the remains of the Salamanders his defenses had managed to bring down.

His smile was extremely wide, as he'd taken down the vast majority of the wave by himself. "I get to keep a quarter of those for myself and split the rest with my group. Celestial feces, I *love* the fact that the Council wasted their first law trying to block me. That's probably the reason there isn't a tax yet. Inadvertent anarchy-grown oligarchy, here I come."

Instead of diving into the killing ground, Joe collected a large group of porters and the like who would haul the slain monsters back for him. After he had a solid twenty temporary employees, he began marching forward. They trailed along behind, collecting bodies each time they stumbled upon one. Each time they came upon a Dwarf working to secure materials from a body, Joe chased them off with a smile and a reminder that the current rules of the Beast Waves was that whoever earned the kill got the material.

In under an hour, every single one of his helpers had their storage devices completely full and were carrying a string of enormous monsters on their shoulders or dragging the bodies behind them with a rope. The Ritualist himself was no exception, and he made sure he was working just as hard as the people he was paying with luxury goods and promises of ritual-based services. They returned to the open area of the village, depositing a mound of several hundred bodies next to his A.S.P.E.C.T. tower.

Once more, Joe was exquisitely pleased with how he'd managed to snag what had seemed like an undesirable location and turned it into a profitable, highly sought-after workspace. Then there was the fact that, if they'd needed to go farther into the city, there would've been dozens of complaints over him hoarding resources, possibly an edict from the council forcing him to give up his earned materials, and certainly a general loss of positive feelings toward the shiny-headed human.

He had all of the types of creatures divvied up, even taking one Hoardling fewer to make sure he didn't go over his allotment. Then, he sent the porters away with those portions with instructions to deliver them to his temporary teammates.

As the energies spun up, Joe began bodily throwing corpses into the opening of the building, which he'd created at a ninety-degree angle, compared to his previous version. Now, they did not go into the top like it was a hopper, instead simply needing to pass through the opening on the side to start being reduced to aspects. Joe's reasoning for this was simple. He could always set the building upright, if he got a working ritual set up to drag the bodies in for him.

Until then, he'd be having other people toss enormous monsters into this, and Joe didn't want to have it get clogged and backlash against him if someone stepped into it in an attempt to push the monsters through. Even thinking about what it had felt like to have a living creature in the tower while it was active made Joe's stomach painfully clench in anticipation of pain. He shook that off, reaffirming his decision as he set out the aspect jars and ensured only materials for breaking down remained within the walls of the building.

As mana flowed into the reduction chamber, the bodies simply vanished, and the aspect jars rapidly began to fill. Every few seconds, Joe would hear a **plink** as a Core was dropped out of the array and onto the metal floor. When the final portion of his allotment had been reduced, Joe powered down the array and stepped inside to collect his goods. "That's a pretty good haul... two Rare Cores? Those must've come from the Salamanders."

It was a shame that all of the Uncommon Cores and lower were essentially useless to his pursuits at this time. He paused on that thought and amended it, recognizing that perhaps they would be useful for other crafting purposes or to advance his Professions further. Joe shrugged off that thought and turned his attention to his aspect jars, getting an updated amount of aspects he'd collected with this venture.

Aspects gathered

Trash: 615,539

Damaged: 312,268

Common: 58,131

Uncommon: 19,484

Rare: 6,388

Special: 10,003 (Zombified), 100 (Anima), 111 (Molten), 638 (Phoenix), 44 (Stellar Ice).

Unique: 8,309

Artifact: 5,518

Legendary: 12,902

Mythical: 0

"Approximately eight hundred total monsters, and I got the kill for almost half of them. I might've only gotten to keep a quarter of that for myself, but so *what*? Abyss, even my Unique aspects increased, although that's just thanks to my Natural Aspect Jars." In fact, it'd have been even higher than that, if he hadn't needed to invest two hundred and fifty aspects into the permanent array.

He shook his head as he took a moment to bask in the effectiveness of his rituals against the monsters. "I've got to hand it to Socar; the output of those rituals must have actually been boosted by an enormous amount, thanks to his Formations. Otherwise, there's no way all of those would've fallen to my rituals."

He stiffened in surprise as he realized that he'd not yet received a notification for experience and excitedly opened up his character sheet to see what sort of massive benefit he'd gained from his ultra kill spree.

Calculating Experience gained…

Joe stared at that message for a few moments, but it didn't change. His eyes slowly narrowed as he realized that there must be some malarkey going on behind the scenes. "I'm not going to get the full experience credit for slaying them, am I? This is Midgard all over again, but at least this time, I *intended* to kill all of those things!"

The system had the good grace not to make a joke about the situation, remaining silent throughout whatever internal debate was occurring. Eventually, Joe could only shrug helplessly and continue on with his day. It wasn't like the world would listen if he whined at it to give him what he wanted. "They can balance and rebalance all they like. So long as my personal power continues to increase, it doesn't *matter* what numbers they assign to my power. I'm not just going to sit around and wait for it to be handed to me. I'm going to go out there and *force* the world to work overtime."

For a bare moment, his entire body was covered in dark black lines, archaic symbols that had been placed there upon receiving his class. "Just *try* and stop me."

You have been cursed with-

"Wait, no, it's just a turn of phrase! Don't *actually* try to stop me!"

Curse canceled.

CHAPTER THIRTY

"We have a handful of hours until the next Beast wave, and you're choosing *now* to be stingy with sharing the resources we will need to survive?" Master Stu Sarcasm scoffed and folded his arms in front of him. "How very like a *human*, pretending to be all friendly and useful until they can war profiteer off of us."

All that earned him was an amused stare as Joe continued writing out the notes for his next project. "I think lack of visibility was the biggest source of frustration, at least in terms of knowing where the monsters were during the most recent attack."

Stu wasn't happy about being ignored, but Joe didn't particularly care. The council was trying to make him come to them and stand around, waiting anxiously for them to finish their deliberations, but the Ritualist wasn't interested in their politicking. He stayed at the entrance of his A.S.P.E.C.T. tower as his workers tossed in bodies, making sure no one could come and force them to stop without dealing with him directly. He *was* interested in experimenting to see if he could create some kind of... maybe a drone that would wander the killing zones and send back images? Or maybe a kind of crawling camera?

But now that Stu had actively sought him out and was attempting to annoy him, he wasn't going to get much in the way of work or planning done. Not with the constant interruptions. Joe let his quill pause, quivering in the air as he formulated a proper response.

"Tell me something, Stu." Joe chose his words carefully before fully committing to the conversation. "Your entire society and currency system was based on reputation, which was accrued by collecting resources, training to higher skill levels, and trading off finished products. Correct?"

"I don't see where you're going with this, but yes."

Joe waved one hand at him, as if he were indicating that the Dwarf should calm down. "Just hear me out. Let's do this as a rapid-fire back and forth, okay? When a Dwarf collects a lot of goods, then charges a large premium of reputation to give back the final product, they're esteemed members of your people."

"Yes."

"Many of the oligarchs who used to be the leaders of your people earned their reputation based on funding battles, building fortifications, and supplying weapons to the Legion. They didn't do this for free but for an excessive amount of reputation."

Stu rolled his eyes and nodded. "Yes, that is correct."

"So, when a Dwarf is shrewdly collecting lots of materials and goods, then making a huge profit, even during times of conflict and strife, they are to be commended. Yes?" Joe was smiling gently at this point, but it seemed that his Dwarven conversation partner didn't understand where this was going.

"Absolutely. If they do extremely well in managing their assets and subordinates, they've proven that they have what it takes to be in charge of larger and more important things." Stu looked around at the other Dwarves who were finishing with the last of Joe's corpses. They had paused to listen in, and seemed to be just as confused as the Master was. "This is a basic tenant of the Oligarchy."

"Okay. Now…" Joe tucked away his notebook, lifting both

hands into the air as he spoke, gesticulating in hopes that, somehow, he'd be able to force the concept into the Dwarf's thick skull. "So when I, a human, take the resources I've earned and collected, train to a higher skill level, and trade off the finished products-"

"War profiteering." Stu firmly stated, causing Joe to throw his hands in the air and turn away. "We won't *stand* for this, Joe! You forget that you're not a Dwarf! You don't *get* our benefits."

The Ritualist didn't bother looking back, simply raising his voice as he walked into his workshop. The bodies were almost completed, and if Stu caused problems, the loss would be minimal. "All I've done is take what I'm owed for my work. If you don't like how many of the creatures I get to process, you're welcome to go and face them in open combat yourself. I'm sure your *sharpened wit* will be enough to slay thousands of the monsters that want to tear everyone here into shreds."

He closed the door behind him, not bothering to wait for a response to his words. "Seriously, did losing that title truly drop their estimation of me that much? Was all the work I did for the Dwarven people only given consideration because I was an officer of the Legion?"

There was no easy answer for his question, and as he thought about it, he realized he'd never had a discussion with another human who was working with the Dwarves. There was no way to tell if his experience was unique, or if this was the standard. He had seen how the *Elves* treated humans but had generally expected that they were just terrible, pointy-eared sacks of feces. Were the Dwarves just as bad? Was this just a cultural difference that he didn't understand? It was possible that this was just how they treated outsiders, but it felt *extremely* personal to him.

"Whatever. Right now, they're just bitterly complaining that I'm doing better than they are. No one's made a direct move against me." Taking a deep breath in and closing his eyes, he let it out after a long moment, trying to imagine all of his annoyance going away with the outrushing air. When that was complete, he felt more energized and determined to succeed.

"I need to figure out how I can make actual, defensible walls instead of these... large rock paths." In his notebook, he had set that as a medium priority, because there was no way he could take complete control of that project. Something at that scale had to be managed by whoever was in charge, else he would be pointed at as the reason for losses if the walls were destroyed. "Yep, no reason to assume that liability, unless I have some other assurances in place."

Happy that he'd clarified his needs, Joe flipped his pages until he got back to the issue of generating visibility for himself as well as everyone else. This was a tough nut to crack, as he'd never needed to create a ritual that would do so many complicated things on its own. Almost all of his most powerful constructs to this point had a very specific purpose, and they did that very well. "Only way to eat a whale is one bite at a time, so let's break down what it needs to do... first, it needs to travel a set path. Then capture images and somehow project them back to a command station?"

Eventually, he merely shook his head and set the notepad down. "I've got to be overthinking this somehow. Most of these, *individually*, seem doable... you know what? I've already figured out a way to capture images and project them. The barrier I put above the city is a prime example. What if, instead of making camera-like rituals that crawled along, I just made reflective barriers at an angle over each of the open kill zones? Then we could see what was going on in there, and they wouldn't be able to see us watching them!"

He already had everything he needed for that project, even if it would require multiple people watching the projections for them to work correctly. "Sometimes the low-tech option is just the way to go. I could over-engineer the abyss out of this, but for what? A single issue that I might never have to worry about again?"

In a flurry of focused activity, Joe dedicated an hour's worth of work to assemble several of the prototype rituals. Understanding the need for a measured approach, he chose not to create everything required for the entirety of the maze in one sitting. Instead, he spent his time testing the effectiveness of his preparations and put together a proof of concept. Gathering his newly prepared tiles, he rushed out into the bitter cold and ventured directly into the maze.

Filled with a mixture of excitement and nervous energy, Joe activated the first of the tiles, unleashing its magical effects. Watching the sky and the enormous rectangle of reflective energy above him, he swiftly traversed the open space, strategically positioning the tile to cover the maximum area it could affect. As he hadn't precisely measured the walls, it was an imperfect fit. He didn't mind that so much. "Perfect is the enemy of good, and I can always improve on this later!"

Even more determined, now that he'd seen his ritual in action, he quickly pressed onward, navigating the maze and diligently documenting the outcomes, mind already racing with ideas on how to refine and optimize these rituals for future use. "If I'm going to have these at each of the openings, I'll have to place them carefully, so that whoever is watching can see each of them. That means that, the farther out I go, the higher the ritual will have to be placed in the air. Probably would've needed to do that anyway, otherwise the view would just be blocked by the wall."

After setting up the few rituals he'd designed, he hurried back into the Village to inspect his work. Joe looked at the actual view that was created, comparing that with his notes and writing down what he would need to do to adjust their angle and reflective properties. At one point, he stepped directly into the focused light reflection, and his eyebrows shot up. Joe quickly wrote down his observation, murmuring to himself the entire time. "Even with the sun completely blocked by the thick clouds, the reflection *does* generate some small amount of heat. If I set one up at each of these walls as they're built, there's a good chance that I could treat this like solar heating for the area!"

The last ritual that he was able to set up before receiving notification of an impending Beast wave was a large reflective mirror placed directly in the mouth of the maze leading into the Village. This one he angled so the defenders would be able to see directly down the entire corridor, and the monsters would see the line of defenders as if they were coming in a straight shot.

"If I play this correctly, there's a chance that the monsters will build up a ton of speed and try to ram the ranks of the Village." He chuckled darkly to himself as he struck a line through one of his notes. "Of course, they won't realize they're attempting to slam directly into a reflection… and there's a wall there. Right, I think my best option would be to just place an enormous chunk of metal there, sink it deeply into the ground to make sure it remains stable, then cover the side they'll ram in spikes, possibly other nasty surprises as well."

The Ritualist understood that such a basic trap would only deceive the frontrunners of the approaching wave, but that didn't diminish its value in the slightest. In fact, that was likely to be the most important aspect of this illusion. Only the fastest or toughest of the wave would make it through all of his ritual towers, especially when those had been augmented by the network of future defenses he'd planned. There was only one obstacle to his plans: he did not *have* an obstacle to put in the way.

Undeterred by this fact, he improvised and adapted to the situation at hand. Joe exploited the ritual he'd just set up, ducking behind it and angling his Field Array to create what could either be considered a serrated edge that the largest of monsters would tear themselves up on, or enormous spikes that would impale hopefully dozens of smaller creatures.

Joe exercised much caution, mindful not to excavate a pit deep enough to provoke burrowing creatures. When he was finished, he looked over his work and was… merely satisfied. It wasn't the grand solution that he envisioned, but it did represent a solid starting point for his future plans. He had barely tapped into his plans of starting off his expansive network of traps and protections he would be designing to assist his ritual towers. Still, a few low-tech traps might be exactly what they needed.

The most recent Beast wave had been eye-opening in the fact that sometimes, relying on a magical solution was just flat-out going to fail.

"I do *love* a good challenge." Joe chuckled as he prepared for a long haul of innovation, meticulous preparation, and—hopefully—successful solutions.

You have slain a Defeatist Fluttering Penguin!

"Ahh! Time to leave." If his towers were already killing off the fodder beasts, that meant the more powerful creatures mixed among them would almost certainly be rushing through the walls at this very moment. Joe turned and high-tailed it out of his position behind the illusion he had created, dodging a half-dozen arrows loosed at him. At that instant, the gathered defenders flinched in surprise as someone appeared out of nowhere.

"Abyss! Same team, *same team*!"

CHAPTER THIRTY-ONE

The frigid wind that consistently blew across the flat landscape of Jotunheim picked up in intensity, howling over their heads and through the corridors as the newest residents of this world braced themselves for another relentless assault which would only end with the death of their enemies or the destruction of everything they'd accomplished up to this point.

Joe critically eyed the walls they were relying on to keep them safe, having been assured that they had been reinforced with additional stone, especially the closer to the Village they were. He wasn't sure what they would have been able to accomplish in only a few hours, but... to be fair, working on his *own*, Joe was able to accomplish enormous feats in that same amount of time. With a cadre of hundreds or even *thousands* of powerful, centuries-old Dwarves, who could say for certain what they could accomplish?

As the sun ever-so-slowly continued to dip below the far distant, icy horizon, a deep, bellowing howl shattered the frozen air. As the call ended, the only thing Joe could hear was the creaking of leather as Dwarves and humans alike gripped their weapons more tightly, faces filled with determination and readiness… and perhaps just a hint of trepidation as the fear of the unknown brushed against their minds. Still, Joe was feeling extremely confident—until the system notification appeared for everyone, accompanied by gasps a moment later as everyone digested the information it contained.

The Boss monster of the first ten waves has decided to join the vanguard! It will be accompanied by a group of elite monsters!

"What in the blue blazes?" someone nearby shouted with deep concern. "This is only the second wave for the upgrade! Elites are supposed to come every *five* and the boss every *ten*!"

Joe was sure everyone else was doing the same thing he was at this moment: digging through the old messages until he read over the actual text that had appeared when they began this challenge. He found it, murmuring it out loud as he realized that he'd been complacent. "You will be subject to a set of elite monsters every five waves, with one boss monster per ten. It… that doesn't say that they *must* come on the fifth wave or the tenth. It implies that, at any point in five waves, the elite can come, and the boss can come any time within ten."

Fifteen minutes passed slowly, then he was starting to gain notifications that Penguins were being defeated, followed by Hoardlings. Yet, the cold air had gained a sharper edge to it, pushing Joe to assume that there were certainly going to be Salamanders amongst the monsters as well. As for the elites, let alone the boss? He had no idea what to expect. Not yet.

The air began snapping, flash-frozen in an instant, once more creating walls of fog that billowed down the open killing zones. There was an additional sharp sound, so loud it could've been a sheet of metal being hit with a baseball bat, if not for the earthy undertone. Joe recognized that sound, and he winced as he realized that at least one wall had likely just cracked, if not outright broken. His only solace was the fact that the sharp sound hadn't been accompanied by an overbearing rumbling of stone, signifying that, at least, the barrier hadn't fallen.

Yet.

"Those Salamanders are going to be a real issue, unless we

can figure out a way to harden the defenses against their magical effects." Letting out his own annoyed **hiss** of air, Joe let go of his orb and let it hang in the air as he reached for a quill, quickly jotting down a note to find documentation about materials that were resistant or immune to cold. It would be pointless to spend a huge amount of effort raising an effective wall around the city only for it to break because it got a little *chilly*.

In that moment of inattention, a Penguin shot past the startled defenders with a **trill** of success, only for the sound to cut off as it sped directly through the reflection at breakneck speed and impaled itself on the spikes hidden behind. A geyser of blood fountained out through the illusion, splattering across the walls and ground. There was a collective inhale of surprise, as a few people stepped forward to see if they needed to finish the beast off. However, it didn't make a reappearance, and Joe had already been informed of its demise.

"That's a bad sign." the Ritualist finally determined after considering what had just happened. "If the prey beasts of this world make it through my rituals, that means there must be an extremely dense hoard approaching."

The first ritual tower, which sent bubbles filled with acid, was supposed to be able to handle large groups. In fact, in general, the denser they were packed, the better the result would be. The only way it would be *less* effective was if there were just so many that they were layered on top of each other, possibly even bouncing off each other or simply being protected from the acid bath by a multitude of bodies blocking it. Joe looked up, checking the mirrors that had been set up and watching as creatures tumbled into view, one after another.

As the tiny trickle turned into a swarm of monsters practically crawling over each other and tumbling into view, Joe recalled with great annoyance the agreement he had made with the Legion. In order to be allowed to create his defenses without interference, Joe had offered not to set up any ritual towers that would be directly adjacent to the town, so long as they'd leave his towers alone. He resolved to absolutely ignore that tacit deal in the future. The entire Village was in danger of being overwhelmed because Joe had been trying not to step on too many toes.

Jaxon slithered up to the Ritualist in that moment, going from a prone position and up to his feet in one smooth motion. "This looks like it'll be fun! I'm looking forward to seeing what sort of behemoth those things are running away from."

"Running *away*?" Joe watched as the Penguins and Hoardlings drew closer, realizing that Jaxon had a point. They weren't moving in the rapid, controlled patterns that he'd witnessed thus far. No, they were actually fighting each other as they moved closer, only those at the lead of the pack ignoring those around them in favor of gaining additional speed. The Ritualist followed his mirrors, searching for the issue all the way until his eyes landed on the reflection that would show creatures at the maximum range from the entrance of the Village.

By this time, his kill count was approaching the mid-hundreds. Unlike every Beast Wave to this point, it seemed that the entire assault had moved as a single unit—explaining why their defenders were already in danger of being overwhelmed by the press of weighty monsters. Another heavy **crack** of stone resounded through the air, still with no indication of what was causing the ear-splitting sound. That didn't stop Joe from shooting a contingent of Earth Mages a dirty glance.

Their attention was ripped back to the entrance of the area as a half-dozen Penguins overshot the turn, creating another extremely gory sight. That caused the creatures following them to squawk in concern and attempt to abate their momentum. Some bounced up and out of the press of bodies, but dozens were shoved into the opening behind the reflective surface, adding to the cacophony of shrieking. That wouldn't be enough to kill most of them, nor even damage them heavily, thanks to their thick blubber and feathers. Still, it slowed them down enough for a large group to gather.

A red dot appeared in the center of the flock of flightless

birds, only visible thanks to the darkening skies the extreme focus Joe had on that group. Its sudden appearance was followed by a cat leaping in a straight line, covering a hundred feet in a second. It shattered the sound barrier a second before it struck where the dot had been placed. The creature it landed on must've had every bone in its body broken from the force impact alone, but that was hidden behind a sudden, *massive* fireball that filled the area and continued slightly down the open tunnel.

Blinking away spots from the sudden intense light, Joe watched as the fire clung to every surface. It severely burned the birds, filling the air with the scent of crispy feathers and cooking chicken. The pained squawking cut off as the Legion stepped in and filled the beasts full of arrows, but Joe was just relishing the fact that the spell had created enough heat that he could feel how cold he actually was at the moment. The Ritualist leaned closer to it to warm up. "What was that? A cat-based fireball?"

"Nya-palm bomb!" Jaxon brightly suggested an alternative, surprising a bark of laughter out of Joe. His mirth died down, even if the fire didn't, since the Penguins continued to throw themselves into the flames, turning into blazing torches that then shot at his comrades-in-arms. Contrary to his expectations, being on fire *didn't* make the Penguins more dangerous, merely greatly distracted. They were mowed down by the merciless line of defense, creating a flaming wall of flesh that slowed the advance of the following monsters.

A dense cloud of fog erupted at the edge of the sudden heat wave, roiling higher and higher, until it suddenly started flowing forward *into* the flame. To the unobservant, it would appear that the dense mist was smothering the fire, but Joe could tell that the temperature was simply dropping so far, so fast, that the flames couldn't continue their combustion. The Salamanders were there, hidden behind the shifting curtain of condensation, and moments later, the cold washed over Joe.

He'd never been quite as happy *not* to be wearing metal-based armor as he was at that moment. Frost began accumulating on most of the members of the Legion, inhibiting their movements and debuffing their motivation. Just as before, the eyes of the lizards were the first things that could be seen, then they charged into the blender of Dwarven melee combat.

As battles raged that he couldn't be a part of due to his too-low Characteristics, his gaze was instead drawn to the exit the monsters were pouring from. A deep, rumbling sound was filling the area, punctuated by sharp **tinkling** noises that he couldn't quite place. Dust, snow, and even the lighter humans began bouncing around violently as the ground began to shake. Joe's gaze shifted up and away, watching the mirrors, completely aghast as the cause of the vibrations drew closer.

The thick fog that had covered the corridors was being shoved away by the air pressure of a huge… *something* that was moving at high speeds. It was large enough, fast enough, that it created an air barrier in front of it as it ran, enticing the mists to swirl and blow up over the top of the walls before waterfalling down the other sides. At first, he caught merely a glimpse of what *must* be the boss monster, but as it slowed at a corner and resumed its charge headlong down the next, he was able to fully examine it.

"Is that a *Rhinoceros*?" His low gasp of a descriptor drew the eyes of many people in the area, as all but those most active in combat quickly turned to see what was happening. If it wasn't a rhino, he assumed it was certainly the Jotunheim analog to it. As it opened its mouth, he realized it wasn't *just* a rhino, it also had a hairy body and sharp teeth. The beast had to be at least nine meters tall, and it was covered in thick plates of ice. "A seal combination? A Rhinosealus?"

Its horn expanded out to triple its actual size, thanks to an insanely dense icicle that had grown up and over it. A maelstrom of elite Salamanders clung to the sides of the creature, greatly enhancing its frozen defenses. The combination of the charging beasts created a swirling cyclone of frigid air that not only surrounded the boss monster, but the storm preceded it as what Joe could only guess was a relatively short-ranged, frost-based area of effect.

Before they could make any plan to handle this creature, it turned on the final approach to the Village, barreling down the path. The monster splattered any creature that got in its way below its feet—which appeared to be spiked like cleats in order to allow it to run on icy surfaces. Any of the lesser monsters that were slain in this way turned to ice behind its rampage, shattering into frozen motes that followed the Rhinosealus, catching up and somehow being added to the armor it was coated in.

For the first time since making the small reflective ritual, Joe fully regretted setting it up. The Rhinosealus trumpeted its triumph as it hit the wall like a stellar ice meteor, ramming it with such immense force that the walls were demolished by the impact and shockwave. Physics came into play, as the dozens of feet of earthworks had been frozen, rapidly heated to extreme heights, then dropped below Neptunian temperatures. For hundreds of feet in every direction, the walls crumbled into an avalanche of gravel.

For a long, drawn-out instant, the defenders could only watch in shock and awe as the cataclysmic events unfolded in front of them. They were only broken from their stupor by an agitated grunt, a blast of icy air erupting from the Rhinosealus' nostrils as it turned toward them… pawing at the ground as it prepared its next charge.

CHAPTER THIRTY-TWO

Wasting not a single moment, Joe clapped his hands together to bring his right palm into contact with the tiny Ritual of Activation that he was holding in his left. Sparks flew as his magic bounced off the magical diagram, and he sucked in a breath as he shook the lingering power off of his hand. "*Feces*! It's too low-ranked to activate without stabilization!"

He started dropping cubes around him as rapidly as he could while ensuring they were in their proper place, but he was still far too late to do anything about the Rhino's initial charge. Instead, the hefty beast met with a shield wall, sending Dwarves flying like bowling pins as the second, third, and fourth ranks interlocked their shields and drove their heels into the ground. The mighty surge of the armored creature was brought to a standstill, the stocky warriors proving that, together, they were far more substantial than any mere stone wall could hope to match.

Joe finished his setup, once more slapping his Ritual of Activation, this time succeeding in his attempt. A half-dozen barriers sprang into existence behind and to the sides of the boss. Originally, the Ritualist had been concerned that this would incite the wrath of the unending horde, but with the walls broken and a gaping wound in their protections, his magic barely even *slowed* the tide. The surging Penguins and Hoardlings were funneled through various points, and a mix of shouting humans and bellowing Dwarves stepped forward to meet them.

Realizing how dire the situation was, Joe made sure to activate each of the last resort rituals that he'd put in place around the breach.

Ritual of Proximity (Wind Blades) has activated!

Ritual of Proximity (Dark Lightning Strike) has activated!

Ritual of Force (Barrier) has activated!

Ritual of...

Over a dozen rituals clashed with the monsters head-on, but without a tower to allow these rituals to rain down magical damage on his enemies, the series of contained spells could only attack the nearest target that met the requirements. The barrage blasted the lesser creatures, allowing the Legion to focus on the greater threat of the grunting Rhinosealus as it swung its horn back and forth. The massive protrusion sheared through any shield or armor that it even managed to *brush* against. Between its incredibly durable armor, which continuously regenerated itself thanks to the efforts of the Salamanders, and its flashing horn weapon, the Rhinosealus slowly gained momentum once more.

An arrow that looked more like a ballista bolt *shrieked* through the air, slamming into the skull of a Salamander and bursting through it, pinning the lizard to the frozen plates it clung to. Joe chanced a look back along the trajectory of the assault, briefly managing to get a glimpse of Heartpiercer McShootypants before she shifted locations to attack another of the oversized geckos.

The results were apparent immediately, as the armor the Salamander had been boosting began to show signs of wear, cracks appearing on its surface as it failed to regenerate any further. A voice that Joe recognized but couldn't quite place bellowed out from the ranks of the Legion, right up against the Rhino where the attacks were crashing against the ice. "The Salamanders are buffing it! Slay them first, then target the boss, or we'll get nowhere with this thing!"

Even with as enormous as the creatures were with their mountainous numbers in their Constitution, against the concerted efforts of thousands of hardened warriors, they were slain with three motions each instead of only *one*. Then came the arduous task of continuing the assault, tens of thousands of points of damage merely going toward breaking through the armor on the creature before it saw a single point of health loss.

When they finally struck true, and a deep purple stream of blood splattered off of the creature, Joe saw a chance.

He Omnivaulted forward, catching a handful of the substance before his still-active rituals could drain it away to be converted into water. Then he pressed off of the surface of the Rhinosealus, barrel-rolling through the air until he landed near his original position. With no time to prepare further, Joe didn't pull out his inscribing tool, Ritual Tiles, or any other implements that would assist yet slow him. Sucking in a deep breath, he pressed both hands forward and tried his hand at Somatic Ritual Casting mid-combat.

Even with his stabilization cubes around him keeping the backlash from coming into effect instantly, Joe could feel the heavy distortion of this world fighting to *punish* him for his attempt.

The Ritualist believed in himself at this moment. His skill was approaching the Journeyman ranks, but it had been bottlenecked at Student eight for a long time. The ritual he had in mind sprang into existence in front of him as mana and aspects poured out, finishing by feeding the blood into it as a targeting mechanism. As the ritual flared to life, a matching set of rings appeared around the berserk Rhinosealus.

"Keep it within the rings for a minute! Just *one minute*!" Joe's voice rang out in a clear, concise commanding tone. He wasn't sure if his companions were listening to him, or if they were simply doing their duty and attempting to push the beast back, but each time the Rhinosealus surged forward, they would shield-bash it back as a unit, twenty to thirty Dwarves at a time in perfect synchronization. The entire time, spells were flying, weapons were singing through the air and flesh… and monsters, humans, and Dwarves alike were dying.

"...fifty-seven... eight… one minute!" The Ritual of Containment that Joe had desperately mustered snapped into place around the boss, ethereal tendrils of mana seeping into the flesh and blood of the colossal creature as well as the bones of the world underneath of it. A blood-curdling scream of rage erupted from the creature's mouth as it sensed the unfamiliar magic taking hold, causing it to convulse in a movement pattern closer to the seal portion of its makeup.

The twisting, undulating motion forced the Dwarves to reposition, and the Boss escaped the encirclement. Despite the ritual's insatiable appetite for its stamina, mana, and vitality, the creature pressed on, undeterred by the draining effect that constantly intensified the farther it strayed from the containment circles. "I absolutely cannot *believe* that worked…!"

"Really? If you had no faith in it, why did you do it?" Jaxon gently tapped Joe's chin with his fist. "You need to believe in yourself more! Now pardon me, I'm going to see if I can fix that Penguin's back, since I have so much experience with their bones."

The job wasn't done, and the Rhinosealus was on the loose. Hundreds of Dwarves abandoned their post, chasing after the rampaging creature and leaving a hole in the back lines of defense. Joe went with them, most of his time chasing spent in the air as he reactivated his Omnivault off of every surface he touched. The creature was making a straight-line shot at the Town Hall, building up momentum to the point where Joe was unsure if they'd be able to stop the juggernaut, even if they *did* manage to get in front of it.

"Come on, come *on*! Go down already!" He could practically *see* the Stamina drain, as the trio of energies steamed off the beast with every step that it took—siphoned back into the ritual itself to further empower it.

Even having failed to hold the rhino among the Dwarves, Joe felt a cocky grin arrive on his face unbidden—pride filling him at that moment from the fact that he was able to call upon that ritual while having last studied it two worlds away.

"One of my oldest ever rituals, but that one really stuck in the ol' noggin. Maybe I should rename this one to 'Ritual of Reliability'. First saved my rear when I captured Cel, then against the warden at the Well of Shadows, and it even stayed useful enough against Gameover that I could provide a constant power source for Tatum."

Still, agitation replaced his exultation as they quickly neared the only building this creature had to destroy. Joe's mind raced, seeking a solution that could turn the tide of this battle. The melee had devolved into chaos, and his risky gambit of precise timing and coordinated efforts was failing to produce results. At this point, he could only hope that the Rhinosealus would activate the Ritual of Slaughter and get turned into charcoal before managing to outright destroy-

**ZZzt!*

An oversized arrow *slammed* into the front left knee of the creature, penetrating into place just as it came down on that foot. The unexpected wound sent the creature stumbling, arresting a large portion of its momentum. It didn't fully go to the ground, managing to continue its charge at a lesser speed. Yet, it was enough of a reprieve for the front ranks of Dwarves to catch up and begin harassing the creature, attacking its rear legs, the only place they could easily strike while moving at this speed.

For a fleeting moment, the Rhinosealus staggered under the onslaught, its formidable defenses tested to their limit. It roared in fury and defiance, eyes shining with an icy fury. Blow after blow struck with precision, exploiting its weakened state. Even though it possessed a remarkable vitality, something Joe wished he had for himself, the creature's mighty frame quivered, strength and resolve weakening… approaching a breaking point.

A Dwarf used his companions as a launchpad, flying into the air above the boss monster. He reared back with his oversized hammer so far that he nearly toppled backward, before clenching his abdomen muscles and bringing the weapon over, around, then down onto the still-frozen skull of the beast. While the boulder-shattering strike didn't kill the creature, it did force its horn down. The natural weapon caught in the ground, causing the Rhinosealus to catch and flip forward; up into the air for multiple seconds, due to its enormous frame. With a resounding **crash** and a mushroom cloud of snow and dirt, the boss collapsed to the ground. Mere moments later, it succumbed to its injuries as a continuous deluge of attacks rained down upon it.

Congratulations! You have participated in slaying a Boss monster: the Armored Iceberg Rhinosealus! Rewards will be calculated at a later date, now go and finish this A.I.R. raid!

Silence descended over the immediate area as the warriors relented in their assault, heaving for breath and allowing cautiously optimistic smiles to appear on their faces. Joe even heard one of them scoffing as though they hadn't all just gone through a rigorous trial. "Hah! Only one more of those in this entire assault? Or something like it, I suppose. Why'd we ever worry about upgrading to Town rank?"

Those words were met with a roar of approval as the majority of Dwarves shoved their weapon-bearing hands into the air.

It was simply a matter of poor timing that one of them used his offhand, and the tower shield he was raising was able to be used as a jump-off platform for a lone Penguin. The squawking beast had managed to maneuver past the less-dense group of defenders and approach the otherwise occupied Legionnaires focused on the Rhino.

Joe watched in horror as the Penguin spiraled through the air, its beak striking the stone of the Town Hall. The whip-crack sound of stone breaking filled his ears, even as his heart sank. Not because he was worried about the structure. No, there was no way a single Penguin would be able to take it down before they destroyed it. The Ritualist inhaled deeply and held his breath so that he didn't scream as he watched the ritual he'd placed onto the Town Hall spin up and activate.

His last-ditch trap card was being used for the first time, and Joe wavered between interest and intense annoyance. The air crackled with arcane energy over the next three seconds as the carefully crafted, Formation-enhanced ritual hummed with ramping-up collected power. Strange beads flew to it from all around the Village, so fast as to be nearly imperceptible. "What is… could that be the markers that the ritual put on the beasts that went by them?"

Any further questions were forced to be held, as five unaspected circles of magic snapped into position in the air above the Town Hall, their chaotic energies tamed and channeled into a single purpose: exploding into rampaging fire.

Joe fell to his knees, gripping his skull as he didn't have any hair to try and rip out. "*Noooo*! That's so *expensive*! Don't go off now; there's only fodder creatures left!"

The ritual cared not for his petty anguish. Its purpose was clear, and its requirements had been met. Now, there was nothing that could stop it from unleashing torrents of raw power against the marked targets.

Even the sky itself seemed to ignite as a torrent of flame cascaded down, fluid and majestic like molten gold, searing the air around it. With a blinding intensity, the flames coalesced into a radiant beam of heat and flame as it surged forth, aimed at the offending Penguin that had dared to fulfill the final requirement. In an instant, the already-almost-dead avian was engulfed, the flames wreathing its feathery form with screaming heat as the Dwarves beating it dove for cover. The creature was reduced to nothing but smoldering cinders in an instant, as the lion's share of the power contained in the ritual was emptied into it.

But the majority of the power being gone didn't mean it was *completely* used up. As the initial blast dissipated, the residual energy fragmented and scattered, morphing into a dazzling field of fireflies. Thousand-degree sparks flew together and formed countless fireballs, each pulsating with fiery brilliance. They shot out, leaving trails of rapidly-refreezing vapor as they arced through the air.

The sky became a canvas ablaze with trails of vibrant light, leaving after-images along their parabolic paths. Seemingly slowly, the bolts rained down upon the battlefield, each ball of fire greatly reduced in power due to expending the energy to move and survive in the arctic chill. Sounds of combat were replaced by various cries as feathers were lit ablaze, hair burned, and fat sizzled.

It was a symphony composed of the clash of fire and flesh. The attackers could only scream in terror as the relentless barrage from an element they had never before been exposed to decimated their ranks.

Scents of burnt ozone, hair, and cooked meat lingered as the last echoes of the ritual faded into the night that seemed somehow darker after the incandescent ritual vanished. Joe let his hands drop to the side as he released a long, unwilling sigh. "That's what I get for wanting to test it. At least it turns out that Socar had the right of it… I would've never figured out how to convert it to fire like this without adding additional components or some kind of alchemy. So, I guess I've got that going for me… which is nice."

He could only watch as the ritual slowly stopped turning, then winked out like a burst soap bubble as soon as it was out of either targets or energy. Joe's eyes trailed down to the first Penguin that had been crisped, grimacing at the mere ashes that remained. "Super effective, but not much in the way of material left if we burn them. I suppose it's called the Ritual of *Slaughter*, not the Ritual of Easy Butchery and Material Collection. Live and learn, I guess."

CHAPTER THIRTY-THREE

Quest updated: Student Ritualist III. Monsters slain by the Ritual of Slaughter: 183/1000 (914 Marked before activation.)

Experience gained! Calculating experience…

Your Village has completed the second Beast wave needed in order to upgrade into a Town! Beast waves remaining: 23/25.

"The second wave had hit during that? They can *overlap*? Abyss." Once again, Joe anxiously watched the 'experienced gained' notification, hoping for a new outcome and a surge of points for his next level. It wasn't to be: the words continued to spin his hopes up without ever allowing them to be fulfilled. Resisting the urge to scream his frustration at the sky, Joe remembered that the system was, if not alive, then at least controlled by an intelligent entity.

At moments like this, the Ritualist had the intense sensation that something was watching him, and that feeling intensified every time he glared at the spinning message.

Taking a deep breath, Joe slapped a smile on his face and shifted his focus to his companions, getting ready to share their excitement over the results of the battle. But his smile fell away as he realized that he was utterly alone in his jubilation.

Searching more and more faces, he quickly understood that this was the norm for the vast majority of the people around him.

Nearly every individual looked grim, and Joe finally realized that he'd *drastically* underestimated the potential damage these Beast waves could inflict, even at such a low bar for completion as moving from a Village into a Town.

Not just in the physical destruction, but in the impact it would have on the mentality of the people trying to keep the Village intact. It was clear that the aftermath of the assault had left everyone shaken to some degree.

That wasn't to say that the destruction was *not* extreme. The truth was, the area lay in ruins. Its once… if not *proud* walls, then at least proper defensive barriers, had been reduced to barely more than crumbling remnants. All they did now was serve as a visual reminder of the deadly battle that had just unfolded.

The sounds of combat had long faded away, and weary and fearful civilians began emerging from wherever they'd been hidden away. Even without having been an active part of combat, their faces were etched with fear and exhaustion. All too soon, they stood among the debris, and a swift check told Joe that there was practically no building between here and the entrance to the walls that hadn't suffered some level of damage.

Soon accusations and shouting erupted, and demands to flee the failing Village were being thrown about. Joe did his best to resist holding any resentment toward them, knowing that their concerns were valid. As the situation of a lack of walls, massive numbers of monsters to go, and nearly all of their trump cards having already been played sank in, more of the calls and shouts shifted to the population questioning the very foundation of the Village, the viability of the settlement as a whole.

"We should abandon this place to its fate, start over somewhere else!"

"Why'd we even bother to set up a Town Hall? All that does

is put restrictions on how much we can build and where! Now it brings such strong Beast Waves like this?"

As he had been the one to initiate this dilemma, Joe's heart felt heavy with the weight of responsibility. He stood next to the walls that had been reduced to gravel, allowing the blowing wind to strike him with full force as he tried to get his thoughts in order. His gaze traveled over the buildings, and Joe realized that the structural damage of the buildings was actually the *least* concerning aspect. After all, a simple Ritual of Repair, an investment of mana, and a small amount of time would be able to completely restore the area into a pristine condition.

No, it was the loss of *life* that shook Joe to his core. His steadfast allies, the Legionnaires of the Dwarven Oligarchy, had borne the brunt of the battle. They had lost many of their warriors and gained very little in return. Already, their anger was palpable, and gruff voices snarled for recompense or wailed as they realized their loss. The tense unity that had been created in this Village had been fractured, and it pained Joe deeply knowing that he was the tip of the spear that had guided—forced—this disaster.

"I'm not gonna blame myself for this. I was just trying to make a haven, a refuge against the encroaching monsters, a-" The Ritualist forced his mouth shut with a **click*, stopping that train of thought when his Wisdom allowed him to intuit his true reasoning at that moment. "No… all of this was done so that I could fulfill *my* desires. I just wanted to be able to escape as soon as I wanted, to move on when it was convenient. I wanted freedom… but this isn't… this isn't the way. Running away isn't *freedom*."

Closing his eyes, he adjusted his thoughts then and there. "I've been saying I want freedom for so long, but what does that even mean to me? What's there to gain from unfettered freedom? I'm not… this was *not* about freedom. Is *meaning* what I've been missing? I've been searching for meaning in my life, and I still believe that it lies within my capabilities, my magic especially. But if I truly want meaning… then I need to accept responsibilities. Can I truly have one without the other? I think… I can't."

Opening his eyes once more, he swept his vision around the devastated area, committing to memory everything that he was seeing at this moment. The broken terrain, buildings that looked like they'd gone through an earthquake, and citizens mourning the loss of their friends or family; teetering on the brink of despair, already prepared to abandon the Village they had established, their new home.

He knew what he needed to do.

As he was already standing next to the Town Hall, he simply walked over, opened the door, and stepped inside. He found a group of solemn-faced Masters surrounding a table, glumly staring down at the feeble map of the area they'd been able to compile. Joe's eyes were locked on Grandmaster Snow, and he stepped forward and offered a salute.

"Grandmaster. I'm still not entirely certain where I went wrong, but please allow me to fix what I've broken. I know that I'm no longer officially a Major General, but my heart still lies with the Legion. Seeing my adopted people hurting like this is… it's almost enough to break me."

For a long moment, only silence was returned to him, and Joe felt his head bow forward in shame. Then a sigh of discontent reached his ears, and Snow snapped at him. "Oh, stop wilting like a flower. You want to take responsibility for this fiasco? Fine. But wrong. All I see is a man who finally realized why we were so hesitant to invest into the Village. Why we wanted to move slowly. Perhaps you even have an inkling as to why we're wary of humans and their strange attitudes?"

"They all act like their lives are as fleeting as they once were," Master Stu grumped with a heavy tone. "Until your people realize that your lifespans are essentially endless, and death is merely a waiting game until you're returned, you are going to put us *all* at risk! I just don't get why you can't get it through your-"

"Enough, Stu." Snow's words were filled with resignation as

she watched Joe take the verbal beatdown without a single complaint, hint of bitterness, or flash of arrogance in his eyes. "Frankly, Joe, I don't know what came over you when you got here. It was like you were infected with paranoia and saw enemies where none existed. For the first time since you were hit in the face by a chill wind, you're stepping up and offering to do what is needed. Perhaps you've reached puberty for your race?"

Joe let out a soft groan as he did his best not to grumble in annoyance or snap at her. For all he knew, she didn't actually understand... then he saw the mirth dancing in her eyes and recognized she was messing with him. That allowed him a moment of relief. If she were open to debate and discussion, as well as inviting humor into the mix, hopefully not all was lost.

"I'll admit my own fault. I could've handled the situation better. I'll explain some of the reasoning your detractors have been highlighting right now. You lost every title that bound you to us, that gave you position, while also helping you to see us and our actions favorably. The fact that you don't even have the same restrictive title that's been placed on the rest of us as well as your fellows, well... it made some of this Council... concerned. I'll tell you true, there are still several among us that think that you've become a traitor to our people and aren't to be trusted."

Snow seemed to be speaking as though she didn't feel that way; her words were reluctant and apologetic. "It is my duty to represent all Dwarves, and unfortunately, *not* all Dwarves trust you even a fraction as far as they could throw you."

With this clear explanation, Joe searched over his previous interactions with the Council, realizing how his annoyance with them and refusal to adhere to their requests could be used against him as evidence proof that he'd turned against them. He could even see where Snow had been attempting to guide him to an answer that would assuage their concerns. But he'd seen that originally as her calling him out or specifically attempting to infuriate him. "I can only hope that we'll be able to move past that."

"Joe. Hundreds of our warriors were just killed, and our defenses not just breached, but in large part eradicated. I personally trust that it was simply beyond your control." Speaking gently for the first part, Snow's words shifted to be as icy-cold as her namesake.

"Yet, I still hear the demands of our people, and they're even more concerned about your loyalties at this moment. I've already received dozens of appeals for this location to be abandoned, and they're well thought out and carefully reasoned. It seemed the erstwhile leaders of the civilian factions had nothing *better* to do while they were hiding in their buildings than write up demands and petitions."

Joe was aghast at the whipcrack turn this conversation had taken and attempted to pull his thoughts in order. Before he could state his case, argue, or fly into a rage, depending on which of his Characteristics took hold of him, Snow finished her thought with a long-suffering sigh. "Frankly, Joe, I am beholden to the whims of my people. I'm not seeing a good reason *not* to go. To build our people's City up as *we* need it to be. Over decades, if need be."

"I fully understand. But there *is* another way, what I believe is a better way." Joe gathered himself, fighting down his inner greed hamster as he forced out the words that he was holding within him. "First off, I'd like to gift the council *sixty* percent of all of the monster corpses that I'm due for the slaying of creatures moving through the killing fields—less upkeep costs—when they're defeated and destroyed by the ritual towers I'm placing on your walls. I believe it wouldn't be unreasonable to assume that number would soon reach thousands, perhaps even tens of thousands of corpses that are slowly increasing in rank."

Joe could see surprise on the face of every person in that room, and it appeared that Havoc was about to reach out and strangle him. He wasn't certain if they'd made a different decision beforehand, but the Ritualist knew that even forty percent would be enough for him to continue his work at a decently fast pace. "Second, I propose to create a path of safe escape for the people who choose to remain within this Village. Everyone that we know, as far as the eye can see, got here because they stepped into a bubble and trusted that it would take them to the bifrost. I can't guarantee it would get them there, but I can certainly send them somewhere within fifty miles at high speed."

"They were only going to set a *twenty-five* percent tax, you daft-"

"Simple, but perhaps an effective solution." Snow sharply cut Havoc off, then paused and debated on her next words, hesitation clear on her face. She seemed torn between her longing for safety and security versus the unknown perils that awaited them if they remained within the confines of this Village. "If there's one thing that's easy to trust, it's self-sacrifice and the willingness to do what needs to be done at great personal cost. I think… I do believe that *perhaps* this could…"

She paused and once more considered her words extremely carefully. Tense silence remained with the remaining Masters, which was slowly replaced with hesitant nods and tentative agreeing murmurs. All except for a few of them, whose faces turned a deeper crimson as they realized that the council was going to cave and trust this outsider, this *human*, once again.

Master Dreamstrider, one of the few Masters on the council that Joe had previously directly engaged with, was finally unable to contain himself and gently slapped a palm on the table to pull attention to him. "I am *sorry*, but I won't be remaining in a place that allows this walking disaster of a human to run rampant! You may make your case to as many as you would like, but I will be leading the faction that desires to thrive in our *traditional* ways, far from here."

"Dreamstrider!" Grandmaster Snow barked with great shock as the current member of the council stood and refused to meet her gaze. "You forget your place!"

"*I* forget my place? *My* place was atop a mountain, a world away, molding the minds of those who dreamed for more!" He didn't stay to argue, and slowly, four more of the Masters stood and joined him in this small exodus.

Joe watched as the departing Dwarves disappeared from the room. He knew their departure was a loss, a crack in the foundation of this new civilization they were trying to build. He could only hope that the citizens and warriors who *did* remain would recognize the truth of his words and actions and would be filled with the flame of determination: a resolve to rebuild, to forge a path forward into the unknown, no matter how difficult the road ahead was.

Before they could get too far, Joe chased after the departing Masters and handed them a stack of Ritual Tiles. "I'm sorry for the part I had to play in the loss of… I don't even know how many members of the Legion."

His words trailed off as he collected himself then gestured at the tiles. "Please know that I'll never say a word against you leaving, and I'd only ever greet your return with open arms and a smile on my face. I know it isn't much, but please accept these so you have somewhere to survive the cold night that is falling on us, until you're able to create the home that you desire."

It took a few moments before the tiles were accepted, and no further words were exchanged. But Joe had seen the stony glares being sent at him soften, and he knew there was no more he could do at this point. Once more alone, Joe glanced into the distance where a gaping hole in their protections was practically begging monsters to swarm through.

Instead of walking over and diving into the work by himself, Joe steeled himself to once more work as a team. Perhaps, eventually, he would be confident in leading, but for now, he decided to content himself with following the needs of the many. Turning around once more, he stepped into the Town Hall and joined directly into the discussions of how to move ahead.

Joe could only hope that, going forward, the relationship he'd strained would be able to heal. It was time to do more than seek the fastest route forward, working around the Dwarves as though they were *obstacles* to his success. They were far more than that: they were friends, companions, brothers-in-arms, and even customers.

It didn't matter if he would be able to try again as many times as this world demanded, perhaps every once in a while needing to explore the far reaches of the planet. The Ritualist would never be able to live with himself if he didn't make every effort to ensure that the people around him not only survived, but *thrived.*

CHAPTER THIRTY-FOUR

The once-bustling Village Square now echoed with a solemn emptiness. This was all thanks to the departure of a huge chunk of civilians and a concerning number of the Legion who had marched away with them. Ostensibly, the troops had gone as an escort, but by the way each of them was carrying supplies, it was unlikely they'd be returning. Joe looked at the report he'd been handed, wincing as he saw that their overall population, which had been over ninety thousand, was now below forty.

Of that amount, a surprisingly large contingent of humans had remained, nearly twelve thousand of the original twenty. The Ritualist supposed that he shouldn't be surprised by this fact, as the humans would be returned to the nearest friendly Town Hall if they were slain. Joe hadn't tested this fact himself, but there was a rumor circulating that, if they tried to come back, and all available Town Halls had been destroyed, they'd be respawned at a random place on this planet.

Joe was fairly certain that this single continent was larger than the entire surface area of old Earth, so he had no interest in testing the random respawn mechanic. Momentarily, he debated on whether he should create a shrine or a temple, as that would give them a secondary option for a bind point, but right now, he had other tests that were more urgent. "Just another reason to make sure this place stays safe."

The council had awarded him an honorary title of Master Coordinator, not something that would show up on his character sheet, but simply documentation to show their favor and ensure that he could work, requisition materials and assistance, and act in their name as he secured the defenses of this area.

They'd even promised him that he'd be allowed to name the Town if they managed to reach that settlement rank. Joe already had an appropriate name picked out: Novusheim. It had seemed appropriate to incorporate some Dwarvish highlights into the nomenclature, and an easy translation would just be 'new home'.

Taking a deep breath, he surveyed the damage once again, trying to determine where he needed to start. In just under eight hours, they would have yet another Beast Wave coming at them, and two sets of their walls had been destroyed for hundreds of feet in either direction. That would still give them a bit of time as creatures were forced to march through the preceding ones, but it would allow the monsters to enter in a dense pack instead of spacing them out, depending on their speed and ability.

Joe had also checked on his ritual towers, finding that over half of them were currently fully out of mana in their Mana Batteries. The ones that still had a charge were on their last legs, and those might only get off two or three attacks before failing.

"All of this is bad, but what's the most important task for me to focus on right now? The walls or the towers?" He tapped on the paper, pulling out the map and scanning it to see what sort of gauntlet the monsters would need to run through with the current defenses breached. "Over a quarter of the rituals will be flat-out ignored, unless we do something about those walls, and there's a good chance that the outer walls are going to fall in the next few waves, thanks to those Salamanders."

When he'd originally arrived in this world, Joe had been

appreciative of the flat landscape and the excellent view it afforded them. He'd initially assumed that this was just an abnormality, but it appeared that the monsters actively worked to flatten the land across the entirety of the world. The Ritualist wasn't certain if that was just so the wind could blow more consistently, keeping the world cold and icy, or if they simply hated being obstructed in any way. "I suppose I could get the remaining earth Mages to work on the walls, but that's just slapping a bandage on a gangrenous wound."

Deciding on his course of action, Joe hurried to request aid from the material manager, Max. That was likely the most highly visited location in the entirety of Novusheim, and he was sure that he'd be able to request help and send people out on behalf of the city from there. A small smile touched his lips as he moved, realizing that he'd already begun thinking of this Village as 'Novusheim'. It flowed off the tongue well for him, and he hoped it would someday be spoken of as a beacon of resilience, a shield against the creeping chill of the world.

Joe chanced a glance upward as he realized that the actual darkness of the night was likely going to start inhibiting the vision of some of the residents. He resolved to ensure that, every time there was a Beast Wave, he would switch the sky barrier to daytime so they had everything they needed for success.

As soon as he arrived at the warehouse, the Ritualist began paying a few people around him to act as criers, shouting out what he needed and what skillsets he was looking for. It was a slow process, as everyone was scrambling to do what *they* felt was necessary, just as he was. But he was able to hire a dozen people to get to the towers, retrieve the Mana Batteries, and return them here for charging.

The most difficult part of that was managing to get it through their minds that pulling the battery out wouldn't cause either the enchanted Core nor the tower itself to explode in their faces. He shook his head at the fact that this was a serious concern for them, thanks to the Dwarven propensity to use raw Cores as the energy source for their war golems.

Convincing the Earth Mages to do the work he needed was significantly more difficult. Most of them simply wanted to raise another simple earthen barrier, but Joe decided that he wanted singular blocks of stone, almost like massive, oversized bricks. His plan was to leave small gaps between the stone work, so that if one section was destroyed or collapsed, it wouldn't bring down everything else around it, not to mention being easier to replace. The main objection to this was that this required a multitude of spells instead of a singular spell with a flat mana expense per side.

Luckily, he had a simple and easy answer for their whining. "Do you want to take the easy route, or do you want to be *dead*?"

Only a few extra salty Dwarves announced that they were ready to give up the ghost, but for all of their grumbling, they still moved out when the others started walking. Joe could only shake his head and hope that they'd do a proper job, or else he'd have to figure out a way to punish them properly. He even knew how he'd do it: all Joe would need to do was to point them out and loudly announce that their work was sloppy and unprofessional. That would be enough to send them into conniptions, as well as ensuring they never again slacked off, simply because it was *him* giving the orders instead of someone they respected wholeheartedly.

With people moving to do the tasks he needed, not on his behalf, but on behalf of their settlement as a whole, Joe found that he had a small amount of downtime. With time being the most precious resource of all at the moment, he accessed his spatial codpiece and began flipping through the blueprints contained within it until he finally came upon the one he was looking for.

Joe tentatively pulled it out, looking around carefully to see if anyone was going to pop out of the shadows and attack him simply for its possession. He had a history with this particular structure, and he could only hope that being two worlds away from Midgard, specifically the Kingdom of Ardania, would mean that he could create it without increasing his 'Despised by Humanity' title or inviting assassinations.

"The city wall of Ardania..." Joe looked over the complicated blueprint that he'd once upon a time used without knowing that it was considered taboo to do so. It had everything he needed at the moment. Somehow, among all of the gear and items that had been grabbed and brought along during the desperate escape to Jotunheim, no one had thought to visit the ancient records vault of the capital and take the blueprints for their majestic, enchanted, practically impervious walls.

His needs were fairly simple at this moment, at least. "Curved wall, modular, plenty of space for enchanting, and can be set up to easily be removed as the city ranks up and better versions are found. Pretty much perfect."

Heavily enchanted, costly walls would be much worse for this area, as the enormous monsters in the future would likely have a penchant for smashing through them if they were more intelligent. They had been warned that the larger the monster was, the more intelligent it would be.

Even the Rhinosealus had shown signs of excellence in combat in the form of strategic thinking, but it had been limited by its form. Something told Joe that the final boss that would be coming in this assault wouldn't be quite as simple to bring down. "Now all I need to do is determine what material I should make the walls out of, so I can rest easy that the cold won't be able to bring it down on its own. Something that won't degrade on Jotunheim..."

Burble!

"Oh. Yes, thank you, AutoMate. A coffee at this moment would be divine." Joe took a long sip of the steaming coffee, warming his hands on the excess heat of his mug. As he only had room in his thoughts for the current task at hand, he interpreted the motions that his coffee elemental was making of tapping on the metal sides of its home as a show of affection.

He smiled at it, and AutoMate shook its tiny liquid head in apparent exasperation before unsummoning itself. "I should try making a section of this wall next to my workshop. A little bit of extra durability there and the ability to easily repair it with a ritual would probably make that the best location to get started."

He started selecting sections of the blueprint that he would be using, eliminating all gates, portcullis, and other barriers that would simply cause the encroaching hoard to begin smashing their way in. Going with a simple, twenty-foot section book-ended by crenellations that he could place ritual towers on, Joe started drawing up a copy of that on another blueprint so he could transfer it over to the ritual for rapid construction. Before he reached the halfway point, the first of the runners came back, holding a handful of Mana Batteries.

"I grabbed as many as I could, and I'm still first! That means I get a bonus, right?"

"Absolutely." A sack of Uncommon Cores dropped with a clanking thud on the table between the two of them, and the Dwarf peeked in curiously, eyes flashing with avarice as a sly smile graced the space under her mustache.

"Anytime you need more work done, make sure to call for me. Here's my card; it has a mana signature on it. Just send in a point of your own mana, and it'll act as a beacon for me to find you. Should work anywhere within the Village." She held out a fist, lightly rapping her knuckles against his before sauntering away, holding her reward in front of her to showcase that she'd completed the challenge Joe had given them.

He had five of his Mana Batteries, but Joe looked at them with a hint of despair. "Abyss… I forgot to figure out a recharging station!"

CHAPTER THIRTY-FIVE

"This next wave is going to be a rough one." Joe muttered to himself as he put the finishing touches on the ritual that would inscribe enchantments on his behalf, making the careful and precise changes to the structure of a Core to turn it into a Mana Battery. "I really need to figure out how to make a recharging station… making a new battery so it has a full charge right away isn't exactly *efficient*."

Joe had gone through his notes, almost positive that he had the information he needed in order to make the recharging station somewhere. Sadly, to his growing dismay, it was nowhere to be found. He'd only ever *discussed* making one before now… apparently. "Didn't I make one back on Midgard…? No, that was just one of these battery makers. Huh. Wild."

Most of his regeneration was going to the largest battery he'd reclaimed, though he had dozens of other people working to fill the others. Frankly, his mana pool and regeneration was absurd for his level, a direct boon from Occultatum. Even while devoting his strength to multiple projects, he still had plenty for the creation of this ritual, if not enough to actually *activate* it on his own. "If I remember correctly, this one is particularly finicky, already unstable, and this world is only going to exacerbate that situation. I'd better put this in the back room of my workshop."

Joe put action to his words immediately, going into the back, locked vault area of his workshop and setting up the ritual, which would act like a rapidly swirling gyroscope when it was active. As a testament to his familiarity with the diagram, the ritual itself had undergone a remarkable reduction of its overall size. What once had occupied nearly ten feet of floor space now fit in the distance between his hands when they were positioned just in front of him with his elbows bent and tucked to his side.

The dense spell hovering in the air put a wide smile on his face. "I don't know what it is about human nature that makes us want to miniaturize all of our creations, but it's always either a focus on making them super huge, super tiny, or super fast. Not a terrible thing, I suppose, but an odd observation."

Beast wave 3/25 will be starting in 24 minutes!

"Yeah, I get it, stay focused." Joe couldn't even be annoyed with the intrusive message, as he'd been letting his thoughts wander off on a tangent. "Focus… follow one course until success. I should write that on the wall somewhere. Or, *or*, I could activate this ritual and get my batteries filled."

The Ritualist had recognized an uncomfortable truth. As the Beast waves grew larger, going from hundreds of monsters to thousands of them, he was either going to need to add a mana recharging station directly to the ritual tower—hopefully that would work with the Rare towers that Socar had specifically designed to be modular—or he was going to need someone on standby next to the tower, ready to switch out the drained battery for a full version as soon as it failed to generate another attack.

"I wonder if I could convince an enchanter to make me a battery pack, so I can stuff a bunch of these onto a tower and not worry. Otherwise, I'm going to have to convert an *enormous* Core into a battery just to get through a single wave." The realization that he had a multitude of choices made Joe calm down, somewhat surprisingly. Somehow, having *four* distinct options felt freeing and filled him with a deep sense of relief. "Huh. Finding out new things about how my brain works every day."

Cutting off the flow of his mana to recharging the battery, Joe waited a moment to reach full capacity for himself, planning to empower the ritual that was currently motionless and enervated. After ensuring that his stabilization cubes and alchemical candles had been properly aligned and lit, the Ritualist poured power into the activation sequence. Ever so slowly, the ritual circles were converted from glowing lines of aspects into eye-catching, bright blue, swirling lights. Upon completing the project, Joe double-checked to ensure the stabilization was holding properly, then tossed a Rare Core into the center of the swirling energies.

Its momentum vanished as soon as it reached the center of the diagram, and a bright light traced its way along the shining gemstone. Joe let out a held breath he hadn't realized he had been holding as the ritual showed that it was working properly.

"That Rare Core could be converted into six thousand experience. If I recall correctly, that means it'll have a total mana capacity of twelve thousand." Joe did some quick mental math, forehead furrowing with concern as he realized how close he'd come to disaster. If he hadn't recognized that the batteries of his towers were about to go out, they would have been forced to deal with an entire wave unassisted. At this low level, that might not have been enough to overrun the Dwarves, but the waves had combined, and the Boss Monster had come early.

If the Boss had joined instead on the *third* wave, that would certainly have been enough to bring down the Town Hall, unless the Masters or Grandmaster Snow intervened directly… and they had made it *quite* clear that they would not.

According to Havoc, even though everyone still in the Village was back on good terms, the Dwarven Council wasn't opposed to joining their fleeing brethren and building out their base more carefully if this place were destroyed. Joe had been able to extract a promise that Snow wouldn't actively seek the loss of this Village, but none of them would engage unless they were specifically pulling their people out of harm's way.

Apparently, even though Joe hadn't seen it, that was what they'd been doing during the previous attacks. Anytime one of the Dwarves was about to be slain, they tried to fully remove that person from combat. Still, there were only so many warriors a double handful of powerhouses could save at a time, and losses had been high.

Back to the issue at hand, Joe recognized that imbuing a ritual with Dark Lightning Strike to blast the swarming mobs would cost the tower one hundred mana per lightning strike. He could also overcharge the tower, allowing it to strike again without coming off of the standard cooldown. But each time that happened, the cost would increase by ten percent. "You know, that might not be a terrible option for the last little bit of the labyrinth, but putting that at the start would drain the tower down to uselessness as soon as the wave began."

If he were to take this Rare Mana Battery when it was finished, that meant the tower could strike a hundred times—standard attacks—before the battery needed to be replaced or recharged. As the damage was based on his personal skill level, that meant the tower would output forty-seven thousand, six hundred and forty damage to the target it struck directly, while also dealing approximately twenty-six thousand damage to every creature within… checking the description of the skill again, Joe realized that the splash damage would actually spread for twenty-seven and a half feet.

That was better than expected, but unless the monsters were crawling all over each other like they had been in this most recent wave, likely only up to four or five additional targets would be damaged. "Still, substantial damage output. I think I'll make at least five more of these-"

A horn was sounded at that moment, signaling that the monsters had been spotted moving toward them. Joe was forced to run out of his workshop, slamming the door behind him as he gently cursed. Running around like a chicken with its head cut off for a few minutes, he collected as many fully charged Mana Batteries as he could. Knowing he was out of time, the Ritualist was forced to entrust a few other people with the task of collecting and replacing the others as soon as they'd been topped off.

Then he ran as quickly as he could, Omnivaulting to the top of the walls and bounding along until he got to the outermost tower, the first one the monsters would need to pass. He opened the panel on the side that housed the energy source, placing the Core carefully, then closing the panel gently. Above him, the inert ritual flooded with blue light, then spun in place. Joe's tense shoulders loosened as a quick sigh of relief escaped his lips: there was never any guarantee that everything would begin working perfectly again after a ritual had been without power for a time.

The wall he was standing on began to tremble lightly as the high-level monsters sprinted toward the entrance of the walls as quickly as they could. Unwilling to waste any time watching them thunder toward him, Joe hurried ahead, following the same path the creatures would need to move along. As carefully and rapidly as possible, he replaced the Mana Batteries and moved to the next, until he was out of supplies. "I really hope someone else is working toward me from the other direction!"

But, at this point, he'd done everything possible to help bring down the monster density that would be able to reach the Village. Everyone had planned for a larger-scale, pitched battle, digging trenches and erecting barriers that would not be enough to fully block any monsters coming through. But those defenses would afford the Dwarves themselves some modicum of safety and security.

Joe descended to the final tower, his mind teeming with ideas for what he could do to improve the setup of defensive towers that would crown the walls. Lightning and acid were his current goto's, but he needed to either bring in support that could assist in the creation of fire-based attacks or find someone who would train him as rapidly as possible to get a fireball spell or something similar up to snuff and converted over to a ritual.

Fireballs and other spells of that nature had been more than plentiful back on Midgard, and he cursed at himself for avoiding them. At the time, he had slightly looked down on the sheer *commonness* of those spells, and he had intentionally not dedicated any time to learning them. Certainly, his lack of fire affinity at the time would have hindered his progress, preventing him from quickly advancing, but he had not even bothered to acquire the most basic Novice version.

He internally chastised himself at the realization that he didn't grab the spell because it would have been 'hard' to learn. It was an oversight, as he had never anticipated gaining a natural affinity for fire. But, at this point, acquiring additional spells, enchantments, and similar abilities seemed out of reach, thanks to the influence of Jotunheim. "Bleh… I'm probably going to have to leave this world entirely in order to find ways to learn the spells that would be the most useful here! A little bit of 'hard' work back then would have been useful for the current me."

Joe promised himself that he would one day delve deeper into his own research and unlock the secrets of volatile elements, but as with all learning, he needed a starting point. As he rushed back to the central area of the Village, he hoped silently that Havoc would have an answer for him or at least be able to offer guidance. "Ooh… maybe I can use one of my 'Apprentice' slots with him to get this! Where else had I been offered Fire spells? The engineers of The Shoe offered training with fire, but I don't remember if that was proper blastin' magic."

The thought that he might be able to undergo some intensive training with Havoc and get past this block simultaneously excited and concerned him. On one hand, he would be able to have powerful spells that he *absolutely* needed. On the other hand, the last time he had done something to that effect with

Havoc, the Dwarf had brought him to the edge of death at least eight times a day and called it 'proper teaching'.

Howling from the frigid monsters followed him, and the bitter-cold air swirled around him as the enormous volume of the horde impacted the air pressure. For once, he was glad for the noise. Joe could only be thankful that the current icy conditions helped pull him out of his shiver-inducing memories.

Then he frowned as he realized that their presence felt more menacing than usual, as though they recognized the fact that the defenses had been weakened, the towers weren't at capacity, and an enormous number of people had fled. As he got closer to the nearest thing they had to safety, Joe realized that the bloodlust was being diluted then fully shoved back by the intense defiance radiating from the Village. Joe took heart at that thought, even if the sensation was just a placebo that he was creating within his own mind.

Novusheim *needed* to be filled with silent determination, refusing to be brought low and trampled flat like every other attempt at civilization on Jotunheim had been. Rather... *he* needed the town to be defiant. It was frustrating to him that he was so bad at balancing the needs of the town against his own desires, but the first step in being the requisite amount of empathetic was working to recognize that difference.

Far behind him, an acid-filled bubble was launched forth with a whistling shriek, impacting the front ranks of the horde. He could imagine it well: a bubble roughly the same size as one of the Penguins striking the frontrunners, a geyser of acid sprang forth, corroding the hides of the invaders with a malevolent **hiss**.

As he launched himself over the final barrier and came down into the open area of Novusheim, the first notification of a monster being slain reached his eyes. He pushed it to the side without bothering to read over it. A Defeatist Penguin had to have just been slain for the kill to happen that quickly.

There was no time for casual reading of system notifications right now. The remaining forty thousand defenders were currently bracing themselves for the coming storm, weapons gleaming in the ever-darkening dusk of Jotunheim.

Joe couldn't join them, not for this. He'd need to trust them to break the tide against their shields, to bring it low with their weapons. There was a *proper* wall that needed to be built, and there was not another soul with the ability to erect it before the horde was upon them.

CHAPTER THIRTY-SIX

The Ritualist spent the entirety of the Beast wave in his workshop, perfecting the buildout for a single section of wall. He'd forgotten how *ruinously* expensive the wall was by itself, but he had to merely grit his teeth and accept the burden of creating it. "Can't say I'm unhappy that my bargain for resources handed over to the council was *after* expenses. Otherwise, I'd be a whole lot less willing to invest. But now? Now it's just using up resources I'd lose to them anyway. Heh."

He had all of the schematics he needed in order to make a Tier *five* wall, which was what had been in place around Ardania itself, but he'd only ever made a Tier two version, the Beginner version, back at his guild-owned Townie McTownface. At the time, it had been due to his shocking lack of resources. Well, not particularly shocking at the *time*, but now?

Looking back at how little he had, even with all of his presumed wealth, as well as what his Guild could provide? *That* was the shocking part. If he were to convert his aspects to material right now, he could probably buy half of the entire human capital city with the Legendary aspects alone.

The most difficult part of creating these walls wasn't going to be the actual structure itself. No, it would be the enchanting, and everything that went with setting up what the Dwarves would consider 'genuine' defenses. Currently, although Joe had the ability to create enchantments, his skills in that arena would be of extremely limited use in this environment. He'd need to rely on other people to pick up his slack, and he only hoped that being back on good terms with those in charge would elevate that need to a higher priority.

Strolling out of his workshop, Joe made his way determinedly through the charnel house that his front yard had become. Every step was a stab at his pride, as most of the monsters of this wave had been easily brought down by the tens of thousands of defenders. Perhaps it was the fact that no one had been relying on his ritual towers to take down the creatures, or it could be the fact that the temperature in the area had risen to the point where no one was getting the 'chilled' debuff without standing outside for at least twelve hours… but he felt that the truth of the matter was that there was a *fraction* of the fatalities that had occurred during the Boss wave. Even then, that number was close to ninety-eight percent *human* deaths.

Conversely, there were *thousands* of wounded. Various healers were moving throughout the makeshift medical area, and Joe paused for anyone in his direct path to heal them as needed. His presence alone was enough to stabilize anyone with severe debuffs, his Neutrality Aura giving them a small but constant amount of Health while actively targeting and removing the issues that arose from open wounds, poisons, and poor hygiene.

He powered forward, knowing that others were handling this situation at least as well, if not better, than he could. But if the walls didn't get built and the gaps in their defenses went unfilled, the next wave of more, stronger monsters, would cause the same—or worse—issues.

Within minutes, he had his survey tool out and was preparing to replace the Trash stone barriers serving as barriers with actual, proper *walls*. "There's fifty feet of open space on the first, leftmost section. The right side needs multiple fortifications, making an 'L' to cut off this path leading directly into the Village, instead forcing them to circle one more time. Across the corridor, we need two sections of one hundred feet each… no, let's turn that into four sections of fifty. If we leave a six-inch gap between the walls, that should be enough to account for attacks and shock on them."

That would also lead to greater visibility for the defenders, and as he listed the positives of this type of building in his head, he became ever more sure that this was the best path forward. The supermassive monsters wouldn't be able to fit through that small of a hole, but his allies could have archers and spellcasters peppering the onrushing forces as they swarmed down the corridors. "After this, I'm going to have to work with the engineers and city planners then coordinate with the geomancers, so we can knock down and replace the simple stone directly adjacent to the town."

Eyeing the aforementioned rock critically, he continued murmuring to himself as he made his plans. "We need all of it to get sunk back in, then we raise the entire inner wall in one go. That means I'm going to have to measure that space and prepare a ritual for each section, so we can rush over and activate it as soon as we complete the previous one. We'll build it with a constant, fairly gentle curve. That'll force the monsters traversing it to slow down or at least not be able to build the wildly destructive momentum that they're managing currently."

Deciding he'd wasted enough time planning for the future instead of pushing for success in the present, Joe looked at what would be the most important thing to fix at this moment, rightly deciding on choosing to fix the 'L' bend of the walls. Partitioning off an entire section would grant them valuable time to whittle down their enemies. "I'll have to do this in two separate rituals. Luckily, those are at the Journeyman rank, so I can make a full, tier five wall section."

The main expenses for this ritual came from the fact that crafting a Journeyman ritual meant substituting Rare aspects—

as aspects at the Journeyman rank were 'Special' aspects. Because of this, the highest cost of completion was the one thousand Rare aspects needed for every hundred feet of wall. Even then, that was a rough estimate between the cost of the actual formation of the wall, as well as the creation of the ritual itself.

Joe could only soldier on with a grimace, doing his best to ignore the fact that he could create a fully functioning workshop at the Journeyman level for the same cost as forming what was essentially a huge stationary shield, excellent for blocking direct attacks, but useless for anything else.

He tried not to let any miserliness sink in. There was no doubt in his mind that these barricades were the linchpin to their continued survival. After positioning everything exactly as he wanted, heavily relying on the survey tool, Joe turned and faced the large crowd of gawkers that had gathered around to see the pretty lights he was making. "Excellent! *Volunteers*!"

Many people tried to break and run, and he chastised them lightly by sending a ritual orb **thunking** into the back of their head. Joe was able to bring down a few of the most likely candidates for high mana pools, rushing over and dragging them back to help him as they fought and clawed at the ground.

"No! I've seen what happens to people who build these things with you! I just ate lunch!"

Joe casually dodged a weak punch sent his way, though his shadow coalesced into a clone of him and smacked the offending Dwarf right in the face. "Enough games, people! This will start the expansion of our city, or at least our eventual city! Don't you want real walls? That's what this is! You saw what it'll look like, mostly. At least you saw a framework for it. Get over here and help out! If you have nothing better to do than watch me set it up, you have nothing better to do than help me finish it off."

No one had a good argument against his logic, though a few tried to beg off on account of being wounded or the like. Joe had no mercy, simply chucking a ball of healing water at them and watching as it froze on their skin before dissipating into motes of healing energy. "Great, now no one has *any* reason to avoid their duties!"

So saying, he positioned everyone and activated the ritual. Over the next few minutes, the wall built itself from the top down, hovering in the air as the ritual circles spun around and generated the stone wholecloth. The creation traveled down until it reached the ground, firmly ensconcing itself in the frozen surface of Jotunheim. Once complete, Joe inspected the wall section with a critical eye, eventually finding no issues and declaring the ritual a success.

Then he turned and released the Dwarves that had been volun-told to help and cheerfully shouted that he was looking for more people to help him set up the next piece. With the bright white stone glistening and reflecting the brightening daylight that Joe's sky barrier was creating, people were much more apt to join in on the process. The Ritualist helped that mindset along by reminding everyone that they would be able to directly claim that they'd been involved in creating the majestic walls of the city—hundreds of years from now, when they were showing off a proud, successful city.

Being a living part of history was a point of critical success for Joe, and soon he had people lining up all the way back to the edge of his workshop to join in on raising the walls to higher heights. In what seemed like no time at all, the first two most critical sections had been completed, followed by the couple hundred feet of bulwark he'd been hoping to get done. At that point, there was only a one-hundred-foot stretch of wall that needed to be constructed before the breach had been fully repaired, but it was in a manageable position, the hole merely allowing a huge opening into the Village.

At that point, Joe had already burned through twenty-five hundred Rare aspects, and he wasn't particularly *keen* on continuing further until this operation had proved its worth. Still, after looking at his remaining Cores and aspects, he simply kept his mouth shut and charged onward. He had already committed this much, and he wasn't going to stop just because it was getting expensive.

Realistically, did the safety of the people he was trying to protect have a price tag he wouldn't be willing to pay? He mulled over that thought as he erected the final two sections of wall, deciding that… yes. Joe did, in fact, have a few hard lines. First and foremost, he refused to put himself in a permanently bad position. The reason he was willing to continue at present was because that wasn't actually a huge concern–monster material would be flooding into his coffers sooner, rather than later.

Pushing those thoughts out of his head, he inspected their efforts and felt a deep sense of accomplishment. The walls exuded security and durability, sharply contrasted to the Trash-tier stone palisades that they were erected next to. By the disgruntled words and furtive motions his assisting Dwarves were making between the two structures, the Ritualist realized that he likely wouldn't have any issue getting up the next sections. Most likely, he would never need to literally hunt down volunteers again.

"*Now* we're talking." Puffing up his chest, he softly voiced the words that were crawling through his mind at that moment. "When it looks this good, people are going to *fight* for the chance to join in."

Horns began sounding, and Joe looked out at the true night sky, realizing that he'd been working on this project for nearly an entire work day. He glanced around at the people who had helped him with a deep sense of affection, knowing that he'd have still been working on the second piece if they hadn't been willing to jump on board with him.

Exhausted but accomplished, full of feelings of gratitude for those around him, Joe made his way back to his workshop to sleep through the next wave of monsters. It was the best way to prepare himself to complete the next of his never-ending duties.

CHAPTER THIRTY-SEVEN

Five days, or more accurately, one hundred twenty-eight hours had passed since Joe had finished working on the initial chunks of wall. The Village had settled into a rhythm, and Joe in particular had dived deep into the peculiarities of defending this place.

He now had a devoted group of people who were charged with refilling the Mana Batteries at the end of each wave. They were paid in beast Cores, an expense that Joe passed along to the city by simply holding onto the materials that were processed in his aspect tower. All of the Rare or better Cores he was able to obtain went right into his pocket, though he planned to use a boatload of them to recreate a huge chunk of the wall very shortly.

As the Beast wave counter ticked higher, they as a town had been getting more and more nervous. They had already defeated two additional sets of elite monsters, but the second boss of the challenge had not yet reared its ugly head. With wave twenty approaching, they knew that the boss that had been holding back would soon be forced to take the field. Joe was doing everything that he could to take advantage of the extra time he had before all of his preparations would be tested to their utmost.

He'd been frantically creating as many wall-section rituals as possible, preparing for the inevitable moment that a supreme monster would start knocking on them. With the timer currently ticking down towards zero until the watershed wave started, the moment was ripe for them to topple the inner Trash-tier stone walls and replace them with Tier five, pristine protections. Double-checking his aspects, he confirmed that he had everything he needed to finish off the inner circle of wall.

Joe had also been taking careful note of how many resources on average he was able to bring in for himself. Even though the number of monsters increased fairly drastically with each wave, having directly doubled from wave ten to wave eleven, he'd been seeing a fairly consistent increase of approximately eight percent Rare aspects per wave instead of the enormous jump he'd been hoping for and secretly expecting. "In total from wave four to now, I've been able to capture about forty thousand Rare aspects... that's the opposite of bad."

It was a delightful number, and it had been very fun to see, even if he had been constantly siphoning from it to create the as-of-yet inert rituals. With that many resources and a much larger bank of the lower-tier aspects, he'd be able to create forty one-hundred-foot sections, nearly four-fifths of a mile of dense, immensely durable partitions. Sucking in a deep breath, he threw open the door to his workshop and exited at a sprint.

Everyone was moving quickly, trying to prepare for what was coming. Most of them were doing things that were small in scale yet personally important for success. For instance, he saw hundreds of people polishing armor, sharpening weapons, warming up, or just meditating in the cold. Joe wasted no time standing around to observe them, knowing that every moment was extremely precious.

He ran to the first part of wall he was going to be replacing, situating the ritual perfectly then dropping a large stone block as a marker to announce the presence of the Ritual Tile that was laying there. He could only hope no one would step on it or walk away with the strange magical memento he had left lying around.

Carefully positioning the rituals took time, a frustratingly *large* amount of time when he was on the clock. But eventually, he did finish and found that with that amount of resources, he'd be able to replace just over two-thirds of the entire wall, since sections of it would be trimmed down to be turned from square to curved. That meant there'd be *slightly* less room to build in the city, and Joe hoped he wasn't going to be messing up too many plans by making this adjustment.

Happily for himself and everyone else involved, the Ritualist had shared his overall plan and was assured that, when he was ready to put it into action, he'd have access to a large contingent of people ready and willing to change the walls over to the better version. As he rushed back to his starting point, Joe was greatly relieved to see that he wasn't the only one moving that direction. Dozens of Dwarves—accompanied by the odd human here and there—were running to the stone markers he'd placed, forming up into ranks behind each of them.

Seeing so many people ready to participate, ready to be a part of things that he *knew* were important, nearly made a tear come to his eye. It was a beautiful event, something he'd have never been able to orchestrate on his own. Feeling a swell of gratitude for the council, as well as a brick of shame forming due to his resentment of them when he first arrived, the Ritualist hurried to the first of the wall sections and started getting people into position. When everyone was ready, he gave a sharp nod to a group of brown-clad Dwarves standing just to the side.

With what appeared to be practically no exertion of effort at all, they ripped down fifty and a half feet of stone, dropping it to the ground in the killing corridors before leveling their hands out and directing the stone to sink into the earth. Joe watched that lack of effort with a great sense of unease. Most of the maze they were relying on was that same material, and only the compulsion to walk around the barrier instead of destroying it was keeping the monsters from simply *slapping* their way into the meaty center of their Village.

He'd been told by a reliable source that the lowest-level Penguin they had seen was the approximate of level twenty and that the strength of the elite monsters was closing in on the equivalent of a level twenty-five to twenty-eight human. People had been bandying those numbers about as if they didn't particularly mean much, though he'd heard plenty of betting going on that the Boss monster would be quite a bit stronger—likely topping in at the equivalent to level thirty-five.

As far as Joe knew, even Grandmaster Snow was only approaching level forty. If the Boss monsters were as strong as predicted and were going to keep increasing in strength… the Ritualist was concerned that, even *if* the Grand Master decided to step in, she would be fighting someone on an equal playing field instead of simply crushing them, as he would otherwise expect.

"Don't borrow trouble from the future, Joe," he told himself as he carefully re-centered and channeled his mana into the ritual circle. Mana and aspects flowed out of him as Dwarves all around him grunted in exertion, their mana pulled out of them at an exorbitant rate. Seeing their strain, Joe looked back on many of his previous challenges. He realized that, although he'd been through many painful experiences, he'd gained equal if not greater rewards because of them.

For instance, back before he defeated the Archmage on Midgard, Joe had been captured by the Mage's college and forced against the magical device that powered that building. At the time, the experience had *sucked* in more ways than one. Still, it *also* afforded him the capability to channel massive amounts of raw power without burning out his body. Having front-loaded the pain, even as extreme as it had been, he could now channel mana far beyond anyone at his own level or experience.

That was just one example among many, and now that he was looking at them with fresh eyes, it occurred to Joe that those deadly, challenging experiences had actually been precious moments that forged the tools he needed to succeed. "Back when I first entered Eternia, and I told the game I wished for power, I never thought it would look like pain, suffering, and needing to fight through that to gain the strength I wanted. Gotta remember to be careful what I wish for."

The first section of wall for the day was completed, and Joe nodded at the group of exhausted Dwarves around him as he Omnivaulted over to the next one, his speed easily matched by the Earth Mages who were coming to drop the wall. It was the moment of truth, when he'd see if he'd properly placed the ritual. If his calculations were off by too much, he would need to change every single ritual slightly as he moved along. Then, dependent on those changes, the others would be an even more extreme adjustment.

Joe touched his survey tool to the ritual, waiting with bated breath as the Trash stone was scattered, leaving behind a glowing framework generated by his tool. Grabbing a ruler out of his storage, he measured the distance, concerned for a moment before nodding slowly. "Good, that's within tolerance —only about a quarter of an inch off. Six inches was an arbitrary choice on my part, anyway."

Returning to the group, he lifted another section, another, three more, before finally the horn was blown and the attack on the city was announced to be underway.

The Boss monster of the second ten waves has joined the battle for the survival of the Village! As this is the 20th wave, it will be accompanied by a group of elite monsters! The Frozen Cyclops strides toward you!

"Oh no…" a Dwarf next to Joe muttered with great concern. The human glanced over as the Dwarves shared knowing looks amongst themselves, and apparently his confusion was evident. The same Legionnaire who had spoken originally recognized Joe's lack of knowledge and happily filled him in. "Bro, don't you know what the difference is between a named monster and one that isn't? The first boss wasn't a named monster, even though its like, race and such had a *name*, if you know what I mean."

"If it's named, it's intelligent… would be my guess." Joe watched his conversation partner carefully until the bearded Dwarf bobbed his head.

"Yep. Pretty much that. Depending on the type, they can also use tools just like we can. You know. As force multipliers, bro." The Dwarf shrugged, standing from his half-prone position, where he'd dropped from mana exhaustion after helping Joe complete the most recent ritual. "Strong, tough, and smart. If it wasn't a monster, sounds like my ideal girlfriend."

"Ayy!" A half-dozen of his squad mates fist-bumped the Legionnaire, but Joe only rolled his eyes and politely nodded before walking away.

Keeping his thoughts to himself, Joe subvocalized, "I swear… every time I talk to an active member of the Legion, my Intelligence temporarily drops by five points."

Even with the imminent threat, Joe merely continued to focus on the rituals. They worked as fast as they could, pausing only when they were certain that monsters were in the mazes. Even the lowest-Intelligence private among the Legion realized it wouldn't be prudent to open a giant hole in the walls while monsters were running along the other side of them. Deciding to test his assumptions, the human moved closer to the actual section he'd just put in place, watching through the gap as the first of the monsters flashed by.

"Mmm. Too fast for me, but maybe Heartpiercer Mcshootypants could get a shot off." Knowing that they wouldn't be able to finish the project while the assault was ongoing, Joe and the remaining groups returned to the entrance of the Village, prepared to meet whatever enemies would be coming for them. In the distance, his ritual towers were flashing, and monsters were howling. Joe's notifications were piling up, but as the minutes turned to nearly an hour, and not a single monster managed to enter through the gap, everyone began to shift nervously.

Double-checking his notifications, he saw that they were indeed monster kills and not some other accolade he had achieved. Joe was as stumped by the situation as everyone else… until a deep, guttural bellow washed over the walls and into their ears, resolving into words when his brain processed that a noise this loud could actually be a creature speaking.

"It. Is. Time. To. Kowtow!" The words came from a creature so immensely large that there was space between each of them, and it still took a moment for Joe's perception to decode the noise that could've been mistaken simply as thunder in the distance. As the rumbling speech continued, Joe slowly became better able to translate the message coming in. "Destroy. Your. City center and. We will merely vent our wrath. On your walls and structures. Leaving your lives intact."

"Yeah, enough of this. I'm going to go see what's going on." Getting a running start, Joe leapt to the top of the walls and started running along his well-beaten path toward the entrance of the city. He slid to a halt on the icy surface instead of going farther, as he'd originally intended. There was a simple explanation: he could already see the monster from here.

'Monster' was truly an accurate title befitting this Cyclops. The only other descriptors Joe could possibly come up with were massive, mountainous, gargantuan, or even perhaps the rarely used and surprisingly simple to pronounce 'brobdingnagian'. An avalanche's worth of snow was kicked up with every single step it took forward, though it was covering ground at a snail's pace in comparison to what its size indicated it could achieve.

Nearly as concerning was the fact that the vast majority of the Beast wave was moving in tandem with the Cyclops. That was surprising, as it was apparent even from this distance that most of the monsters, especially the smaller and less intelligent varieties, had quite a bit of trouble reining in their base instincts.

"If I need to humiliate myself by walking the path that you have laid out for the Children of Jörmungandr, I will reply with humiliation in kind. We will spare no life of those from the summer realms. We will leave no stone unbroken. I will feast upon the marrow of your warriors by the hundreds to sate my appetite for vengeance."

Joe watched the glacially approaching hoard with confusion. It was obvious that this Boss monster had the means and intelligence to charge in and inflict a massive amount of damage on the Village even if it *might* not outright have the power to take it all down by itself. Joe clasped his hands behind his head and rubbed his shiny head as he tried to understand why it wouldn't simply lead an all-out assault.

"Could it be that it's just wanting to keep the entire horde together in order to smash against us with a united army? What is…?"

The Ritualist's eyes went wide in horror as he recognized the truth of the matter. The Cyclops was still miles away, moving toward them at a slow pace, yes, but it *was* moving. Joe was almost certain that was enough to fulfill the compulsions that drew it in to attack the Village.

"It can apparently force the monsters to gather around it and move together…" Joe's eyes flicked over to where a string of numbers were constantly flipping. "…and the countdown to the *next* Beast wave is already ticking down."

CHAPTER THIRTY-EIGHT

The ever-swirling storm clouds hung low in the sky, seeming to sink lower, as if to get a better view of Novusheim's impending doom. While Joe had convinced the Dwarves to set scouts, and ensure that they weren't taken by surprise by a sudden surge, his main focus was completing the inner set of Journeyman-ranked walls. The only creatures to escape the commands of the Cyclops were the least intelligent, most feral of monsters. Fodder, in other words.

So long as the main force was held back, Joe was confident in his capabilities and had the Dwarves with him smash the walls that were in place, immediately beginning work on the replacements. Each time he heard one of his ritual towers strike a creature down, he had to grimace at the sheer *waste* of the Mana Batteries. "That could've damaged *fifteen* monsters…!"

The countdown had continued apace, and already the twenty-fourth wave was set to begin. Joe had given up on watching the monsters accumulate around the Cyclops: he already had such a desperate sense of urgency that he was practically drowning in it. Acting quickly to defend the Village was one thing. Seeing close to ten thousand monsters surrounding a massive behemoth in their midst?

That was enough to cause urgency to shift into despair, and Joe wasn't about to let that happen. "Gotta stay busy, and I've gotta keep everyone else busy as well. Idle hands means a mind focused on things that are out of our control. Fight that anxiety!"

The last section of wall he had a ritual for finally went up, and Joe sent an extremely relieved smile toward the Town Hall. Every corpse in town, every scrap of raw material had been donated to the cause of upgrading the walls. The town would need to pay back the appropriated materials, but that should be a blip on the radar compared to the sprawling field of creatures that were going to be coming in the next few hours. A slightly dark thought made Joe realize that perhaps the town also wasn't too concerned about repayment… perhaps they thought they might not make it through the attack.

"*Incomiiiing*!" An undulating call went up, causing the fresh smiles to slip and removing the feeling of relief that the intense walls had created. With a simple nod at the people who had been helping, Joe shot into the air, flipping over and using his motion to gain a panoramic viewpoint of the situation. From this distance, he could only make out the fact that a subset of the creatures had broken away from the main forces and were zooming along the ground toward the walls.

"Why now?" the Ritualist grumbled to himself as he stared at the snow that was being kicked up into a cloud around the approaching monsters. "If he has control of them, why not wait until wave twenty-five has officially begun? Is there a limit on how many he can control? Or is this something more sinister?"

He waited as patiently as possible, having no other options at the moment. The rituals were as charged as they could be; the inner walls were complete. That meant his role in the situation was now only to watch and support as needed. Time passed quickly, and the monsters were exceedingly fast. Only the vast distances involved made the procession seem slow—

that, and Joe's mounting anxiety. Yet, even as the kicked-up snow got closer, Joe found that he still couldn't see the individual monsters leading this charge.

That could only mean one thing, and the rapid-fire shouting from the scouts only confirmed his fears. "The entire attack force consists of Salamanders! Prepare to engage; they're after the walls!"

Like a German sausage festival, this was a wurst-case scenario for Joe. His rituals would be effective against the cluster of deadly, chill-exuding lizards, but there would still be a lot of wastage. In practically no time at all, the maelstrom of Ancient Ice Salamanders crashed upon Novusheim, each step the icy creatures took sending more intense shivers down the spines of the defenders. Both figuratively—as they prepared themselves for a battle more against the elements than against the creatures they could easily dismantle—while also literally, since the movement of the beasts caused a shift in the air itself, rapidly decreasing the temperature of the early night of Jotunheim.

The Trash-rank barricades of the Village—already weakened by previous assaults—groaned and cracked in places under the strain of the creeping frost. The super-chilled air clung to the walls, moment by moment increasing their fragility.

Joe realized that this was an effective tactic that the Cyclops was using against them, creating a vulnerability simply by having these physically weak Salamanders lead the path forward. The incoming monsters would cause layers and layers of the walls to fall, simply by walking past them and engendering enormous vibrations to shatter the now-frozen emplacements.

Unsure of how he would handle the situation, the Ritualist was taken aback as the Legion called for a charge. Thousands of Dwarves rushed forward, swarming up and over the walls like an ant hill that had been kicked. Even with their speed, by the time they reached the enemy, the Salamanders had completed two circles around the Village, enormous fissures ready to fracture further and leave holes in the defenses.

Taking the fight directly to the enemy proved advantageous, even if the Dwarves had to be mindful of the splash damage Joe's rituals could inflict on them. The defenders had split into three groups: the main body of fighters had remained in the Village, while the attacking force had split into two groups, one to go forward farther and one to handle any Salamanders that managed to escape the vanguard.

With the speed that the creatures could move, it almost proved not to be enough, but Joe's Ritual of Dark Lightning Strike managed to snipe the last few that escaped their clutches long enough for the aggressive Legionnaires to fall on them. The final Salamander fell, and soon the last of the Dwarves that had been trapped by the breath weapons of the monsters were chipped out of their icy prisons. A quick headcount later showed that they'd taken no permanent losses, and the healers were already moving to assist the worst damaged or debuffed of their comrades.

A resounding cheer went up as the announcement was made that they had won without any losses, which turned out to be a grave mistake. As the shouts reached a crescendo, harmonizing with each other, chunks of the Trash-walls in multiple places around the city shivered and shattered. Joe could only clutch at his head with both hands, letting out a deep sigh of frustration as the now-sheepish Dwarves simply shrugged and scrambled swiftly to the semblance of safety they sought.

Joe counted eleven enormous gaps in the walls and quickly mapped out the path that would allow for the quickest entry into the Village proper. He could only groan as he realized that, without fixing the issues that had just been created, over two-thirds of the total defenses would simply be ignored by the oncoming horde.

"There's no way. There is absolutely *no way*. Even with everything that we can throw at them before we have to have blade meet flesh, it's still going to be a rough battle. If they don't even take a ball of acid to the face? Yeah, we'll be overrun in no time flat."

The Ritualist wasn't one to give up, and even on the brink of defeat, understanding the likely destructive power of the impending Cyclops attack, he wasn't ready to evacuate or throw his hands up and surrender. Joe simply couldn't shake the feeling that there *must* be a way to salvage the situation. With that in mind, he sought out answers by walking atop the walls, inspecting the damage, and comparing it with what he knew he could do and what the people around him could provide. "The attack could come at any time... but I'm betting the Cyclops is going to wait until the start of the next wave, when he maximizes his forces."

There was a thick layer of ice on the walls, and over half of all of the Earth Mages had left with the group of civilians to set up their own defensive encampment. The likelihood of fixing these long stretches of wall with the same magic that had raised them in the first place was, to put it gently, *low*. "I just don't have the resources to set up effective walls out here with my rituals, not to mention how complicated that version is compared to practically anything else."

The sound of skittering Salamander claws caught his attention at that moment, and he unleashed his Ritual Orbs without another thought, following up the physical attack with every magical option at his disposal. The nearly-invisible Salamander that had been creeping through the area, apparently sent to weaken the foundations of the walls, was pinned in place and torn apart by the swirling combination of attacks.

You have slain an Ancient Ice Salamander! Experience gained: 100.

As though that notification was a rough kick into the slow-moving system, several other notifications Joe had been waiting for appeared.

Experience calculations complete! Due to special circumstances and the recursive rewards that you are able to gain, you have been given an option. While on Jotunheim, you may choose to either:

1) Gain 5% of the standard experience and 100% of the resources that you reduce into aspects when using rituals to slay your targets.

or

2) Gain 10% of the resources that you reduce into aspects and 100% of the standard experience given for a kill when using rituals to slay your targets.

Yes, this will limit you greatly. These rules apply here due to the sheer quantity of targets and are to help enforce balance.

As soon as the words entered Joe's eyes, he could only see red. His mind began spinning in circles as he weighed the two options presented to him. With option one, he'd be leaving this world nearly as weak as he had entered it but with a surplus of materials. It seemed like a reasonable choice, certainly the best choice for him with his magical lifestyle. Still, Joe couldn't shake the feeling that he was being short-changed, as if the world were deliberately attempting to hold him back.

His eyes flipped to the second option, promising a more generous return of experience... but it would mean losing ninety percent of everything he was owed. The allure of faster progress and greater awards also was enticing, but the sense of unease settled deeper into his mind. He hunched over slightly, so disturbed by this strange imposition that he instinctively curled into a more defensive position. Attempting to take deep breaths, Joe tried to think of what he should do.

In a moment of clarity, Joe activated Query for the first time in weeks. "Tatum, what should I do here?"

With his divine spell at Beginner zero, the feedback was almost enough to drown out the near-instant answer that came to him. Still, it was clear enough to understand. A single word answer from the in-game deity that he followed made Joe's eyes go hard.

"*Refuse.*"

"It *is* giving me options... I see. I think I understand." The Ritualist's back straightened, and he firmly stared down the message, trying to swallow his anger and spit out his thoughts. "You're not giving me choices. You are asking me to willingly accept a lesser reward for the work that I'm doing. This isn't about trying to make balance... this is someone realizing that they messed up along the way and didn't expect us to be this successful this fast. No. I will not accept this neutering. I will *not* go along with it."

When he turned his head away, the system screen he had been seeing remained locked in its geospatial coordinates, as though it were frozen there by a bug in the system. He could only assume that was the world's way of saying that it was in shock, but frankly… it wasn't Joe's problem. He glanced back at the screen every once in a while as he walked away, until it faded into the distance.

Then it appeared in front of him again, three times as large as it normally was, replaying a message he'd grown to hate.

Experience gained! Calculating…

CHAPTER THIRTY-NINE

Trying to leave the oddities of the system behind him, Joe turned his attention to the task at hand. There were huge, gaping holes in the walls. Without some immediate intervention, the Village was likely to be destroyed. As far as he could tell, there would be no nice, easy, uniform solution to the issue, as the walls were entirely different shapes and sizes. "Come on, brain, I know you're trying to race, but you're just spinning your wheels!"

The Ritualist continued his journey, traversing the entirety of the remaining simple maze without running into a single idea. He looked at the hole he'd come to a stop in front of, his mind blank as he let his eyes wander along the jagged edges of stone, traveling up until he saw the leaning tower that somehow was holding on, if barely. Joe muttered to himself, "Well, *that* has to be throwing off the formation. I bet Socar would be losing his mind and ordering me to put a new tower up right away."

His thought process sparked something in his mind, and as he pulled in his awareness, it lit into a bright fire of inspiration. Going over his own abilities, his spells, the innate power of his rituals given to him by his base class, Joe realized he did have a potential answer… his talent didn't lay in creating bulwarks and defensive gear. It wasn't about generating enormous weapons of war to lay siege to the oncoming enemy. No, those were merely a byproduct of what he could do, and they were at best on the fringes of his specializations. "I design rituals to make *buildings.* Everything else is only a subset of that or using similar skills!"

He didn't have the time or resources to construct solid walls, and since that was what had been here, that was the only solution his mind had seen. Until now. "I could set up a Trash rank structure in something like… what? Five minutes a pop? Abyss, even now the idea of doing that makes me queasy. Why would I *intentionally* make Trash?"

After considering his options for a few fleeting seconds, he firmed his will and swept around, sprinting toward his workshop in the distance. Jumping over the steep drops between walls, sprinting along the tops of them, and soon catching himself with his ritual orbs as he came in for a landing outside the main door, Joe slammed open his workshop and rushed over to the table.

"It's gotta be huge, and it needs to be something that can easily expand to fill any hole out there. Size is the only thing that matters, not at all how I can use it. I'm sure I got my hands on *something* that can…"

Joe rummaged through his codpiece for a long moment, using both hands to reach in and pull out… "Yes! A Trash-rank warehouse!"

Energized by his idea, Joe sprang to action, piecing together the series of enormous Trash warehouses that he would need. He had eyeballed the distances and hoped that any gaps remaining would be small enough to block the majority of monsters. If only a few got through, that wouldn't be much of an issue, as they would be the smallest of their brethren. In fact, as he realized that, Joe resolved to leave one or two holes Penguins could move through in order to help spread out the threat level of the creatures that would be coming after them.

"These are going to be pretty dang makeshift, but if I don't need to have the resilience of the traditional Common or better warehouses, I can make practically an infinite supply of these."

Using his Student-ranked Architectural Lore to its maximum potential, Joe stripped the ceiling off of the blueprint he was creating for his ritual. Everything else was copied over, and he ensured that the building wouldn't fall apart until at least after it had served its purpose. "As a Trash warehouse, it's going to be a rank below Novice. That means we're going to have constant degradation of the building, so I'm going to have to time all of this perfectly."

A glance at the countdown timer showed him that he had several hours until the twenty-fifth and final Beast wave, when the enemy forces would be on them. He was going to make that time limit with ease, as these structures were essentially going to be four-sided stone boxes without a lid. "Triple the size of the door, make sure it goes all the way up and into open air… you know what? No door. Only the door*way*."

Carefully coordinating the placement of walls, floors, and exits, Joe used his power and deep understanding to instruct the magic exactly on how this would be built. He finished in record time then stared at the clock as he tried to think of what else he could do. His eyes narrowed, and he turned to look at the building plans laid out in front of him. "These are going to be constantly weakening… I can use that."

Setting out his stabilization cubes and candles, Joe swept everything off of his table and got to work creating a new and enhanced Ritual of Slaughter. Following the instructions he'd been given by Socar, Joe planned for the worst-case scenario and set out meticulous instructions for the activation of this ritual. His words were barely intelligible as he whispered to himself, deeply focused on his task. "The more narrow I can make the requirements, the deeper the power of the final activation will cut."

By the time he was done, and the ritual only needed to be powered in order to be ready to go, he was down to the last precious hour before the main assault. This close to the brawl, he had difficulty finding anyone who was willing to weaken themselves by donating mana, but he finally convinced enough people that they would be fully restored long before any fighting reached them. Nearly half of the time had passed when Joe found himself striding toward the Town Hall, towing the completed Journeyman rank ritual circle with his mind.

There, he was met by a cadre of Masters, with Grandmaster Snow once again looking at Joe with deep confliction in her eyes. "Haven't we been over this? We don't want you putting untested magics onto this building. You may end up causing more harm than good."

The Ritualist paused in his movement, thinking over the positive engagements he'd been having with the council recently. He didn't want to lose that, but he also needed this to be in place. "Grandmaster Snow… you've already shown your hand in telling me that neither you nor your other members will raise a weapon to aid in the defense of the Village. I *fully* understand that you are instead planning on rescuing your people, perhaps pulling everyone back and into the Ritual of Bubble Travel that I've set up for all of you. All I can ask is that, if you aren't going to help, you at least don't stop me from doing my very best to keep everything intact."

After a few more moments of the weary standoff between the groups, the Grandmaster simply shook her head and stepped aside, waving her hand at the building. "I suppose you should just go ahead and do whatever you want."

Joe didn't move, though his eyes certainly focused more sharply on her. "I'm not trying to cause further issues, Grandmaster. If we manage to make it through this, it certainly won't be unscathed. I hope… I hope that, in the near future, we'll be working hand-in-hand once more. When we have a proper Town, the next step up is a City. All we will need to do is hold out, prepare our foundations, then go for a mighty push. I don't want to have to shoulder that burden alone."

"Well, perhaps we can-"

"But I *will*, if needed." Joe coldly interrupted her. "Let me ask you this, Grandmaster. Do you *want* to be a part of the city? Do you want to have ownership of who can come and who can go? Will you allow outsiders to decide that they need instruction from Elven teachers and allow them to import them? Not everyone in my Guild joined the same side I did, and I'm certain they'll have their own goals. If I have to do everything myself, I will exclude *no one*. Everyone will be welcome into the city, and the laws created will be mine—and my Guild's —alone."

He waited a beat before stepping forward, once more dragging the ritual circle. "I don't want to cause issues with you. I'm not asking for much, only for help in creating a city worthy of *our* people. If I can get that much, I'm done. I'm ready to make my stand here."

There were many frowns being sent his way, and Joe could see that arguments were raging behind barriers that blocked sound and blurred lips. As the ritual circle settled into place, it seemed that they'd come to a consensus. Joe turned to face them, and Grandmaster Snow stepped closer to him.

"You have been good to us, Joe." She sighed deeply, seeming to sink in on herself as she shook her head. "We will return that with trust. If we are able to hold this Village without catastrophic losses, then we will agree to your plan. But you *must* trust that we are going to attempt to do the very best for our people, to ensure the continuation of our species. You brought an empty field up to the edge of a Town in under a month's worth of time. That simply won't be possible when attempting to create a city, and if we don't have everything ready for a months-long siege, any other preparation will be wasted. Do you understand?"

"I am *so* more than ready to get some help and listen to advice," Joe expressed with a much-relieved smile. "All I want is to be able to travel around as I need. Once all of this is behind us, I'll vanish into my workshop for who knows how long and leave the decisions and running of things to the people that *should* be in charge."

"As all Master craftsmen do," Snow stated wryly, glancing over at Havoc. "I am looking forward to the time when we're able to sip tea and go over the finer points of an item's creation, instead of scrambling to survive while also withholding suspicion and letting go of our deeply held prejudices."

With that, her eyes flicked over to Master Stu, who had remained in the Village against all of Joe's expectations. Now it made sense to him: the Master had remained in order to spread disgruntlement over Joe's rising influence as a civilian. While he had his suspicions, that gesture confirmed where this strange malaise between the two groups stemmed from. Stu met Joe's eyes directly, a hint of challenge in them as he firmly held his gaze.

Joe simply lifted an eyebrow and walked away. There were rituals to enact, buildings to create out of nothing, defenses to place, monsters to kill, and his new home to protect. The human wouldn't allow himself to be caught up in strange power plays and politicking of the Dwarves: those were the pastimes of wealthy and bored Oligarchs.

CHAPTER FORTY

Joe stood at the breach in the wall farthest from the city proper. His ritual was active, and the warehouse he was making was nearly complete. The far wall fit directly into the hole, jutting out slightly as he had repositioned the warehouse to ensure that there was the maximum amount of room for the creatures to wander through it. "I really hope the narrowing of walls doesn't count as a blockage. This thing will fold like paper if they run into it too hard."

The Ritualist had gotten far better at planning for the future, and he leveraged that to his advantage now. Jotunheim's chaotic field would rapidly force the building to deteriorate, so he saved the innermost sections of wall to be filled for last, just to ensure that they would remain long enough to break up the flow of monsters as needed. Certain that it was just his imagination, Joe still twitched, his eyes flicking back and forth as though the monsters were hidden in the shadows nearby. The air was heavy with the metaphysical stench of bloodlust and actual decay, wafting in from the immense horde.

It was here, at this most vulnerable point, that he needed to prove that this would work. If the monsters were able to push right through the building, Joe would be forced to concede the Village and issue a general evacuation order. The escape Bubble Beam was up for the test, and he could only hope that the Cyclops didn't have a ranged option that would allow it to eradicate the fleeing citizens.

"No, stop. I can't think like that."

Joe took a deep breath, steeling himself for the impending battle. It was going to be rough, but he was going to work his butt off to make sure he had no regrets at the end. "Warehouses, Ritual of Slaughter, then build ritual towers like a crazy man wherever Socar tells me to put them."

The ritual completed, barely a strain on his resources or mental acuity in the slightest. Keeping an eye on the building, he saw that the durability counter on it began to tick down immediately. At its current rate, it would lose five points of durability per minute. That was even faster than he had expected, and Joe tried to do the math. "Will it hold long enough to serve its purpose? That's all that matters… so long as the monsters have to still walk down this hallway, instead of circumventing all of those towers, I don't care if it falls after that."

As this was the nearest warehouse, which should have the greatest number of creatures moving through it, Joe placed the first section of his Ritual of Slaughter and checked that it was keyed to a very, *very* specific requirement. "Any creature at all that moves through this building while it's losing durability will be marked."

Relieved to see that the powerful ritual was still able to take effect on such a low-ranked building, he decided that there was nothing else to be done. Joe simply had to work with the hope that everything would work out.

With a flick of his wrist, he channeled his mana into his feet and activated Omnivault, bounding into the air as he rushed to his next necessary location.

As this is the 25th and final wave, a group of elite monsters has joined the battle! You're so close. Just fight off this last wave, and the Town is secured!

As soon as that announcement had appeared in his vision, the monsters in the distance howled with excitement and broke into a sprint toward the Village. Joe pushed himself farther, reaching the hole in the outer wall that needed to be fixed. The one that all of the monsters were currently rushing toward.

He arrived when they had only crossed a quarter of the distance and heaved for breath as his adrenaline forced him to set up his ritual with shaking hands. Slapping everything into position, Joe activated the ritual, and the weakest aspects he owned flooded out of his storage device.

If there was one notable thing about creating literal trash heaps of buildings like this, it was how absolutely *rapid* the process went. Without the delicate managing of aspects, the intricate flows of mana, or needing to take into account the aesthetics of the final product, the process just flat out *finished.* Joe stared at the final product, the draw of mana rapidly fading, and considered how he could use this more effectively. "You know what? I bet I could use this as a gigantic shield, if I have something flying at me. What did that take… twelve and half seconds?"

Even so, the monsters were nearly upon them, and it was the moment of truth for his defenses. Penguins shot across the ground, closer, and closer… rushing directly past the building and toward the original opening that they should have been targeting from the start.

Joe let out a whoop of mixed joy and relief, recognizing that he had just gained nearly half a minute to continue doing what he needed to accomplish. Now, instead of going directly into the walls, the monsters needed to circle the Village and find the entrance once more. This caused the group to split around the city, the two halves of the stream meeting up once more when they reached the entrance, pouring in even as enormous orbs of acid rained down on them.

With time inexorably running out, Joe moved on to the next warehouse, and the next. Soon, each of the holes were plugged, though as planned, he left gaps to allow the Penguins to get ahead of the other monsters. He did, of course, ensure that all of them would need to go through any of the buildings where he set up the markers for the Ritual of Slaughter. That was imperative for their eventual success; even if they managed to take out the over ten thousand weaker monsters in this wave, the Cyclops alone was more dangerous than all of those combined. Still, using these warehouses as conduits, he hoped to be able to draw upon the power each of them was imparting to his ritual and unleash it in a mighty final strike against the boss.

It was going to be a delicate balance. This wave was going to be the dance between life and death for not only the Village, but thousands of Dwarves. Humans, too, but those would come back with only a small penalty. He blinked several times at his lack of concern for his fellow man. Perhaps it was just that his mind always focused on the things most likely to be lost that were irreplaceable, but he didn't want to lose sight of the fact that he needed to care for his people, as well. Still, no matter how he got there, this work would be of great benefit to his people as well.

The night deepened as thousands of monsters queued up to enter the maze, the sheer density of the horde preventing rapid entry and causing the creatures to be severely punished by the ritual towers raining death down on them. At this moment, the bravest human volunteers were standing next to the ritual tower, refilling Mana Batteries by hand and swapping them out whenever the attacks of the ritual tower slowed to a halt. So far, as long as they were not completely barricaded off, the walls had been essentially ignored, treated as natural barriers that all monsters needed to go around.

Only when the defenders didn't follow the rules of this world did monsters attempt to go over or through them, which was enough for the volunteers to brave the danger. That, and a significant bribe.

Joe worked tirelessly until the final warehouse was up and slowly degrading. Were he not protected by his Neutrality Aura, he would be covered in dirt, sweat, and the stink of fear. He wasn't too proud to admit that the presence of so many monsters, some of them even coming within a dozen feet of him, had caused him to break out in a cold sweat more than once. Knowing that he was barely staying ahead of the leading edge, Joe set up the final piece of the Ritual of Slaughter, hiding it carefully and innocuously against the wall of the warehouse before sprinting away.

Squawk!

A Penguin zipped directly through the building, in one door and out the other, right on Joe's heels. He leaped up and away as its beak closed around his foot, yanking off his shoe as he flew through the air. "No!"

Landing on the wall surrounding the city, Joe dropped onto his rear and dangled his feet over the edge as he stared down at the Penguin who was looking up at him and slowly chewing on the leather shoe.

"Penguin! You *suck*! Do you have any idea how difficult it's going to be to get new shoes *here*? I'm going to have to create a building specifically for it, find someone who can make those shoes, get them to sign an agreement with me, and wait until they can process leather and anything else they need. All of this while standing there awkwardly in my socks!"

Of all the things that frustrated Joe at this moment, all of the bizarre Charisma games he had been playing with the Dwarves, the struggles he had been facing, the strange betrayal-but-not-a-betrayal from a lady who he had thought he might have a future with… somehow, for some reason, this minor inconvenience was the tipping point. "Jotunheim is the *worst*! *Dark Lightning Strike! Dark Lightning Strike!* Die, you feathered menace!"

Breathing heavily, clenching his hands, the Ritualist could

only watch as the Penguin took the attacks, clearly in pain, but otherwise ignoring him as it started zipping off down the path. Joe's breathing slowly evened out, and the rage clouding his mind faded while his purpose remained. Still, as he raced along the top of the walls with uneven footsteps, he had to control his breathing so as to stay in the moment.

Pulling out the updated map that Socar had given him, Joe looked over the scribbles and markings. For some reason, the Mage had absolutely horrendous handwriting, and luckily Joe had recognized this, asking him to mark each type of tower with a different symbol. There was a little star, a heart, and an 'X', to denote which type of tower it should be. Magic drained out of him near-constantly from that point forward, as he erected towers and placed the pre-built ritual tile on them, in conjunction with the stabilization cubes.

Even with as fast as he could build them, as rapidly as he could power the rituals, it still wasn't fast enough for him. Upon activation, every single one of the rituals began delivering its payload within seconds, blasting out lightning, acid, or a combination he had worked out that allowed a bolt of lightning to pass through the bubble of acid—causing a chunk of it to convert into a corrosive gas in hopes of making it bypass the outer defenses of the monsters. The fact that every once in a while, that gas would remain in the air long enough to explode upon contact with the follow-up magical attack… that was just icing on the frosted cake.

There was a constant stream of monsters all around him, luckily scores of feet below, but as Joe finished activating his most recent ritual, he realized that he was almost at the entrance once more. Devoting the touch of mana required for the final step, the Ritualist had to dodge to the side as a bubble of acid formed and launched nigh instantaneously. "That was new…! What in the world could have caused that to be a straight-line shot instead of an arc?"

Joe, mind foggy from the time spent in the cold, as well as the consistent pushing of his limits, turned and found himself at a perfect height to stare directly into an enormous orb. The rapidly-blinking Cyclops had acid streaming and bubbling over its only eye, but the damage could be qualified as an irritant at best.

"Ah. *That* would do it."

CHAPTER FORTY-ONE

"You dare to assault the son of the son of the grandson of *Brontes*?" At this close range, the air-shuddering quality of the words coming from the enormous Cyclops' mouth made the sounds nearly unintelligible. It was only after several long seconds, when the echo came back to Joe, that he was able to understand what was actually being shouted at him.

He had larger issues than the linguistic limitations between his foe and himself at that moment. Namely, the fact that upon looking straight into the eye of the Cyclops, Joe found that he simply couldn't move or pull himself away from the visage. It was an intense draw, comparable to Essence Cycle in that his mind seemed to be submerged in minutia. Details were irrelevant, yet they seemed to hold a depth and mystique that-

The Cyclops blinked again, trying to clear the remnant acid from its eyes, and Joe jerked his head to the side and forced his gaze not to slide back to their original position as the enormous lid closed over the nearly perfectly circular eyeball. "Well, *that's* not good."

Feeling that not being here was absolutely the way to go, Joe turned and sprinted away, making him unable to see the enormous hand that was shooting out at the tower that had so offended the Cyclops. Still, he could *feel* the howling whirlwind that preceded the enormous appendage. Before the actual gauntlet-clad hand touched the tower, most of the stonework had been stripped away by what was essentially terrain damage. Instincts honed by hundreds of battles screamed at Joe to continue his run, and he Omnivaulted into the air just as the leading edge of the concussive airwave struck him.

Damage taken: 252 terrain (wind) damage! Exquisite Shell: 11,417/11,669

He was expecting to be sent tumbling through the air, but his jump—combined with the wind moving in the correct direction—sent Joe soaring up, higher and further than he'd been expecting. Instead of needing some assistance to reach the next wall over, he instead passed over *three* of them before needing to push off something to reach the next landing safely. To his surprise, when he kicked his legs, Joe was able to push directly off of the wind howling along behind him. "It has a thin layer of water! Yes! Master-rank Jumping to the rescue!"

The condensation had collected mist and compressed it directly to water as the cold-air shockwave pressed in toward the comparatively well-heated Village.

"That's right, you *brute*! I can jump off of water in all forms! Fear me." Joe cackled as he got ahead of the swirling wind and took cover. That meant he needed to deal with the concussive wave all over again, but that was much easier when there was a bulwark of stone blocking it. After the worst of it had passed, Joe peeked his head up over the stone top of the wall and watched as the Cyclops, grumpy, started marching along the path that had been set out.

It was angrily grumbling the entire time it moved, but its nearness combined with the echoing quality of the twisting maze meant that the words that Joe was able to understand were fragmented at best. Every step it took meant another ritual tower could reach it, and some of the attacks began diverting from the monsters below to the enormous monster in range, thanks to the tower picking the most dangerous targets.

Joe, ever the studious craftsman, noted this as a flaw in the design of the rituals and resolved to specify the targeting sequence *much* more carefully on the next go-round. Right now, he was reaching his limits. Every muscle in his body was screaming for a break, and his mind was begging for the respite of a bed and sleep. But he forced himself to push through. The fate of this Village and its defenders relied at least in part on his continued efforts.

"I just don't understand why it isn't *smashing* its way through." Joe winced every time the Cyclops got close to a tower. That meant the behemoth humanoid would reach up and crush the tower with a swift motion, but not smack it with its weapons or do anything to expend serious energy on removing the obstacles in its path. "It's clearly intelligent, and it knows that these trashy walls wouldn't actually stop it. So why…?"

Standing fully upright, Joe stretched his weary muscles and prepared to get closer to the Cyclops once more. As it turned to follow a new corridor, Joe Omnivaulted along behind it, doing his best to stay on its blind side, out of the direct line of sight of its stunning, enrapturing eye. Moving stealthily atop the wall wasn't something he was used to, but it was utterly necessary at the moment. If he presented himself as a target, there was a good chance the Cyclops would turn and swat him like a fly, possibly demolishing a wall or two at the same time. Joe couldn't afford to take that chance, and so had to play the waiting game.

Each time the Cyclops reached the end of a section and started to turn, Joe repositioned himself, until finally he was directly behind the invader. Then he rapidly closed the distance, Omnivaulting over the seething tide of monsters that swarmed around the feet of the Cyclops. A single mistake would almost guarantee his death, then Joe would have no possible way to assist until the results of this battle had already been determined.

Something about the way it carefully took wide turns at sharp corners brought up a memory in Joe's mind, but it wasn't until he closed in and the monsters parted for a long moment that he understood what was going on. "It's the club! Every time he takes a corner, he's making a wide turn with his arms acting as a hitch. It's almost as if he were a semi truck getting off the freeway and onto residential streets."

The weapon was glowing with a dark, malevolent energy, and the Ritualist couldn't help but notice the fact that, no matter how annoyed the Cyclops became, or whatever else it was doing, there was at least one part of the weapon that was always touching the ground. An enormous furrow had been dug all the way through the maze, and if he checked, Joe was certain that it would extend all the way out to where the Cyclops had originally been standing.

Watching for a few more moments, Joe realized that the club seemed to sap the momentum of the Cyclops, forcefully slowing it down and causing the monster to strain with every step it took. However, by the increasing tempo of the magical pulsating, this must have been a calculated sacrifice. If the Ritualist had to guess, there was an immense reservoir of power building up in that weapon, but he had no idea what it would look like once it was unleashed. "What's this? Is it sapping his momentum, building up a charge the longer he touches it to the ground, or a combination of both? I wonder if this is the real reason that he took five entire waves to reach the wall…?"

The air around the weapon seemed to be boiling due to other-worldly power, and it was nearly as entrancing as the eye of the Cyclops itself. As his eyes roved the creation, he beheld the runes and symbols etched into its surface, the markings whispering that they contained untold ancient power. From what Joe recalled from the Mythos of the Cyclops, the original beings had been descendants of the Titans and were lauded as exceptional craftsmen on par with Hephaestus himself. They created Zeus's thunderbolt, Poseidon's trident, and the helmet of Hades.

"If this is the son of... no, don't do that whole list." Joe counted up the generations, coming up with the great-great-great-grandson of Brontes and realized that it was nearly as long to say that as the title the Cyclops had shouted. "If he has even a fraction of *that* power, and made this club himself, I shudder to think of what it could accomplish with an attack. What kind of magics are imbued into it...? Yikes."

With a deep breath, Joe decided on his plan of action. "No matter what else happens, I need to make sure that the club comes off the ground before the Cyclops is ready to use it. Only problem is... how?"

He didn't need to figure all of this out by himself. There were other, older, potentially wiser people that might've seen something like this in the past, and they just might have a solution for him, so Joe turned and ran. It was only at that point that the Ritualist realized how close they already were to the center of the Village and that the dug-in Dwarves were fully engaged with the enemy.

As he leaped over the battle, he scrutinized every detail that he could wrap his mind around and learned one disturbing fact. The only reason the Dwarves and humans guarding the path forward hadn't been slaughtered already was because the monsters simply didn't care about them. The beasts were throwing themselves into the Legion to be cut down, just to give the next monster in the wave a chance to slip past the defenders. The Dwarves had adjusted to this swarm tactic, but it was clear that a considerable amount of their might was being devoted to this task.

Even with the Defenders still numbering in the tens of thousands, the smallest of the beasts stood more than twice as high as the tallest Dwarf and had a Constitution score akin to a pure granite boulder. Coupled with the fact that the beasts were using each other as springboards, the Dwarves were being overrun and taking losses by the second. A few light hops later, Joe was closing in on the commanders of the battle, and he was met by a double guard who watched him warily.

"I have news about the Cyclops! I've got to tell the commander and plan a countermeasure!" Joe shouted to be heard over the din of battle, only to be met by two solemn shakes of the head.

"He needs to focus. No interruptions, not right now." The guards were adamant on this, and they bodily shoved Joe back as he tried to push past them anyway. After the first warning, blades were out, and the threat was clear. If he wanted to force his way through, he'd be showing himself as a traitor and would be cut down as one.

Casting around for a solution, rubbing his left hand over his bald head, Joe's eyes landed on the Council of Masters that had decided to take the field, coming out of the Town Hall well in advance of the Boss monster's arrival. Joe sprinted to them, shouting and waving his arms to get their attention. "Grandmasters! The Cyclops coming in is building up an attack; that's why it's moving so slow! When it hits, I'm sure that whatever it touches is going to be obliterated. We need to prepare a countermeasure!"

"We *did*, Joe." Grandmaster Snow reached out and patted Joe on the shoulder in a conciliatory manner. "We are-"

Master Stu broke into the conversation, sneer leading the way. "Oh, look, the human thinks he saw something that our experienced scouts specialized in their craft didn't! He thinks that there's an *easy* solution to a problem of this scale. He doesn't realize that the club in question will hit with the force of a moon impacting a planet when it's drawn, moving so fast his eyes won't see it. Point and laugh at the human who'll be dead before he even realizes the attack is coming!"

"That is *more* than enough, Master Stu." Despite the annoyance in her voice, the reprimand was still soft, compared to the frosty bite Snow could imbue her voice with. "Joe, we have assessed the threat and determined that it's not within your capabilities to handle. We're calling for an evacuation, effective immediately."

"You *can't-*" The Ritualist cut off his own words, closing his mouth against the tirade that he wanted to let free. "Okay. Okay, I understand. There are things more important than winning right now."

Embracing their choice, he opened his eyes and gave a firm nod. "I'm here if you need any help getting things set up. If not, I'm going to go and join the fight, hopefully giving some of the Dwarves extra time to make their escape."

Snow stepped forward, drawing Joe into a slow hug. "Thank you, Joe. Yes, I would greatly appreciate it if you could help us activate the ritual. I can do it, but you can do it faster. You would save the most lives by taking over that task."

"Then why are we still standing around?" Joe turned slightly and led the way to the square next to the Alchemy Hall, patting the Ebonsteel block of metal he had left as a landmark in passing. After he'd realized that nothing would be able to easily damage it, he had decided that it looked like a nice monument and helped break up the monotony of the landscape. "Let's blow these bubbles and get you out of here. I'll miss you."

"You won't be coming?" Stu had a great deal of surprise and suspicion in his voice. "*Why?*"

"I'll be setting up my own city after this one falls," Joe stated heavily, his eyes dim and his words lackluster. "I can no longer ask you to put your people at risk, but I'm not going to give up on creating the first city and taking control of the bifrost."

They reached the edge of the open area that had been planned as a plaza in the future. The group spread out, quickly getting into position as Joe began laying the groundwork for the ritual's activation. "I wish you great success and endless safety."

CHAPTER FORTY-TWO

There was no need for Joe to add additional stability to the ritual, as it was a high enough rarity that it could weather the chaotic pressure Jotunheim placed upon it. Under the careful observation of Grandmaster Snow and Master Stu, Joe began altering the ritual ever-so-slightly so it would drop all who entered it among the Dwarves who had left to start over with a new Hamlet.

Joe described the process that he was undertaking to give Master Snow a better idea of what was happening, as well as to hopefully mitigate the sheer suspicion that was pouring off of the Master of Sarcasm. "Changing this vector sigil will allow us to send you south, which should put you into direct contact with the group that left previously. Moving this section will change the speed at which the bubbles travel, but setting it too high will cause issues for you."

He grunted as he activated the ritual, then paused it immediately, leaving it primed for the next person who would be taking it over. "Remember, they're not made of water, not exactly. They have water *in* them, but that acts more as an insulating layer for the outer and inner shell of force. Think of it as a cushion so that, if you hit something very suddenly, that takes the blow for you while popping the bubble."

The Ritualist's words washed over the Dwarves, and the Grandmaster nodded along solemnly, focused on everything he had to say. He knew that for a fact, as he earned a skill increase seemingly out of nowhere.

Teaching has reached Student I! When a student is teaching a Grandmaster something new, that has benefits, too!

The increase made him pause in his words, and Master Stu took that as evidence that he was done giving them instruction. The Dwarf got *very* close, to the point where Joe had to step back or risk draping himself on the stout form that was now in front of him. "Everything is ready there, and we'll take it from here. I've got plenty of practice with those bubbles that you gave us for little houses. I know that all I need to do is add mana into this spot, and the ritual will power itself up. I suppose you can go back to your desperate flailing against a monster too strong for you to defeat."

While the interruption and condescension was annoying, Joe had to acknowledge the Dwarf: he knew his magic. The human simply shrugged when Master Snow didn't intercede, and he began moving away from the area. Seeing as they were still his erstwhile allies, if he thought that the Dwarves would cause an issue with the ritual, he would've stayed and forced his help upon them.

However, with everything set up, the Master clearly knew how to control the diagram, and Joe wasn't worried for them. He did not care if Stu didn't want him here; there was plenty for Joe to do. For instance, a Cyclops to topple.

Even if that seemed completely unthinkable at the moment.

As he started to return to the active combat zone, Joe found that his heart was pounding his chest. In the distance, he could see the top of the Cyclops's head as it slowly walked through the maze of walls surrounding the city, large enough that it was visible over the tops of the partitions even without the enormous mirrored surfaces that he'd created to give them forewarning. Now that it was closer, the **screech** of the club it was dragging behind it scraping against the frozen earth caused the ground and the air to rumble, even between each step the monstrosity took.

For the first time, Joe realized that the small gaps and mirrors he had left between sections of wall might come back to bite them. Even in the reflective rituals in the air, if the Cyclops glanced up and someone managed to meet its eye, they'd freeze in place momentarily as its power caused them to fall into some kind of paralysis—or hypnosis—which the Ritualist knew wasn't a pleasant experience.

The only thing that was saving them was that the Boss itself was lumbering forward with a measured, determined gait. After merely a moment, they were usually safe enough from that strange effect.

Yet, if they were mid-combat, that moment of hesitation could prove dangerous, and it would've been considered extremely life-threatening if the monsters themselves were focused on attacking the people in front of them instead of reaching the Town Hall and wreaking havoc. The chilly creatures were continuing to surge around the Boss monster, some of them even failing to have enough situational awareness to avoid getting stepped on and pulverized by the enormous, falling feet of their leader.

Even as things became more dangerous, Joe started to recognize habits and patterns of the monsters that were swarming towards them. The Penguins had continued waddling with surprising speed, beaks snapping hungrily as they passed by Dwarves and humans. But now they all were skimming along on their bellies, indicating that the vast majority of them had been destroyed during the onslaught to this point.

Joe paused his other spinning thoughts and focused on that fact for a moment. "If I remember correctly, that means that at least eighty-five percent of the Penguins that took the field have been slain."

If most of the weaker creatures had been destroyed, that meant they were likely approaching the end of the assorted, collected waves of creatures. Even so, Joe could tell that there were thousands remaining. If they could eliminate the fear of a Penguin bouncing over the lines of battle and managing to arrive at the Town Hall, they should be able to handle the creatures that ran, slithered, or plodded along. At least, they would have… if it wasn't for the general retreat being called at that very moment.

"Abyss!" Joe cursed darkly as the Dwarves, having an escape route—and with their leaders deciding that the odds were overwhelming—slowly began falling back, obviously intent on regrouping at the ritual that would send them careening from this area and leaving everyone else behind to deal with the aftermath. The human paused in consideration as he realized that *not* everyone was turning and running immediately. Instead, they were continuing to funnel monsters and bring them down.

He snapped his fingers as he made the realization. "Of course… if they simply leave and allow all of the beasts to roam free, as soon as the Town Hall is destroyed, *they'll* be hunted by the monsters."

That helped to shore up one of his major concerns, which was the fact that if he was left with only the human defenders, they wouldn't be able to stem the tide of flesh that was rolling over them. The Legion was buying him time, even if they didn't mean to, and he was going to use as much of it as he could. A surge of determination filled him just as the Cyclops arrived at an area too narrow for it to move through and slapped a wall.

Chunks of stone erupted away from the center of the town —which meant monsters didn't surge directly into the Village, but instead were able to bypass a double row of walls as the bitterly cold structures crumbled from the blow. Joe Omnivaulted into action, racing toward the walls that had just been destroyed and leaping to the top of the inner wall after pushing off one of his buildings. Sprinting along the top of the panels of stone, he swiftly approached the openings that monsters were already pushing through.

As more of them came through the open wound in the defenses, more and more of the wall around them continued to crumble, and it was obvious that the entire section would likely soon fall.

From his elevated position, Joe could see the maze stretching out before him, the lackluster walls that created the labyrinthian path rumbling and collapsing. He could see the smug grin of the Cyclops and knew that the casual attack hadn't interrupted its plan for the destruction of the Village. "Let's see if I can wipe that grin off your face."

Though his words were laced with venom, he kept them quiet, as he didn't actually want to draw the attention of the Boss monster, not when he was close enough that it could *flick* the air and cause a shockwave that would send him hundreds of feet through the sky. Taking a deep breath, Joe began pelting the area with Dark Lightning Strikes, softening up the creatures, often making them stiffen in surprise as pain zapped through their body.

Hoping he wasn't making a colossal mistake, he pulled a Ritual Tile out of his codpiece and held it in his left hand as he continued to direct his spells toward the landing space he was scoping out. Joe did a flip in the air to arrest some of his momentum, impacting the ground and rolling forward to disperse any of the damage that wasn't sent out in a shockwave around him, thanks to his 'Superhero Landing' title.

Joe slapped the ritual to the ground, grunting as he forced enough mana into it to fully activate the barrier ritual. A wall of force sprang into existence in the huge gap, not perfectly closing it off, but also not being well-placed. As the energy tried to spring up, the Ritualist found that it was trying to appear within stone, and his body was rudely yanked to the side, along with his Ritual Tile as the structure rejected the power and forced it to materialize off to the side.

Now the hole in the area was *better* covered, but Joe himself was completely off-balance. The vast majority of the creatures on the other side of the wall ignored the tiny opening and continued sprinting around the city following the path that was laid out, but as the snow settled around him and Joe tried to regain his footing, he locked eyes with a Hoardling that was bearing down on him. Saliva was rushing out of its mouth, coating its fur and granting it a secondary maw of icicle-teeth. It opened its jaws wide to clamp down on him, likely planning to bisect him with a single **chomp**.

Joe hadn't been forced into close combat in quite a while, having had the luxury of being able to choose his battles. It showed in his poor reaction time, and he got to experience this creature up close—while it was alive—for the first time.

Its face was adorned with a heavy, ridgeline brow that would likely help with blocking blows coming from above, a trait that its growth had clearly selected for in a land where its predators were much larger than it was. Its barrel-like chest was rising and falling with every excited breath as it thundered toward him on all four limbs, revealing not only its raw power, but also its excitement for a new flavor of meat.

A denser pattern of frost-laden fur adorned its neck and shoulders, almost resembling a regal mantle coated in diamonds made of ice. As it bellowed in his face, starting to clamp down in preparation of a thick slab of man flesh in its mouth, Joe finally got his wits about him and mentally panic-threw a half-dozen ritual orbs into the open orifice. The jaws slammed closed, but only part of the way.

Metal weapons wedged in its mouth, forcing the jaws to stay open with a grinding **crack**. Shards of sharpened teeth erupted from its muzzle, saliva from the wounds freezing in an instant and turning into shrapnel that pelted Joe's body, even as the blood remained fluid and rushed away to the ritual spinning in the distance.

With a mental tug, Joe took control of the Intelligence orb in its mouth and forced it to start spinning. The weapon brushed against the remaining teeth, releasing superheated bone dust and a sound like a dentist drill turned excavator. Joe jerked his chin up, a somatic reaction to his mental instruction of the orb, and the weapon blasted up and out of the top of the Hoardling's skull.

It collapsed, not dead but in extreme pain from all of the frayed nerve endings that had just been exposed. Knowing that he was in a bad position, Joe forced himself not to try and end the fight. Instead, he pushed up and away, landing atop the wall once more as he glared down at the creature that had been fractions of an inch from swallowing him.

"As soon as this battle is over, I'm finding your body and turning you into a fur coat and matching pair of shoes," the Ritualist promised the creature that was already getting to its feet and rejoining the assault. Rethinking his plan, the human ran along the ramparts and threw himself over the gap, coming down on the next wall over. This time, instead of dropping to ground level, he held the Ritual Tile in his hand and activated it, then he carefully dropped it in the center of the hole as he leaped over the damaged section.

The ritual sprang into existence, once more cutting off the flow of creatures, even if it was poorly placed. Joe eyed the barrier, which was several feet out from the actual hole, grimacing at his terrible aim. "That's not going to last long, but it gives us a chance."

Feeling that he'd done everything he could, Joe turned and watched the lumbering figure of the Cyclops once more. For a moment, the human deflated as he saw that it was on the final stretch and would be entering the Village within the next few minutes.

His head fell forward, but his eyes landed on the soap-bubble-thin barrier of energy that any of these creatures could destroy with ease but instead chose to move around. Joe's eyes widened fractionally as a crazy plan struck him, and he began sprinting along the wall in hopes that he could return to the Village center before the Cyclops arrived.

The Ritualist began chuckling darkly to himself as he gained speed. "There's only two outcomes that could happen next. Either this works perfectly and everything is fine, or it works *not* so well, and I have an angry Cyclops *and* Dwarves coming after me as I wipe out the last, best hopes for Dwarvenkind. Fun times."

CHAPTER FORTY-THREE

Joe backflipped to disperse his momentum as he approached the ground, coming up to his feet and Omnivaulting forward on the first roll, doing what he could to maintain his speed without sending out a shockwave that would cause his allies to stumble. At nearly the same time, the Cyclops reached the entrance to the Village, maintaining its heading and slamming directly into the illusion Joe had created of open space.

A wide smile appeared on his face as he saw the Cyclops stumble back, only for the smirk to be wiped out a moment later as a closed fist impacted the wall hidden behind the illusion, failing to destroy it but causing what appeared to be hundreds of thousands of pounds of force to echo through the magical rock face Joe had raised. Cracks appeared along the entire section, the force traveling along it perfectly before blowing out the last half-foot of stone from the entire ten-foot-thick section.

Joe spared it a glance, seeing that the six-inch gap he'd left was now a full foot, but it was still too small for other monsters to squeeze through. "Yes! Not leaving it as a single, connected structure was the right idea!"

Before he could be too pleased about his forethought, the

illusion that he'd generated at the entrance to the Village sputtered and failed as the magic was forcibly disrupted and dispersed. There was a comparatively small explosion as the ritual warped too far and detonated, failing to do more than send a blast of icy cold air across those near it. Frankly, Joe was surprised it had lasted even this long. It had been inscribed on a Ritual Tile and left in a small alcove along the wall.

It seemed that the grumpy Cyclops's punch had collapsed that area, but if they made it through this, he could correct that issue later with minimal effort. As he flung himself in the air once more, he held his breath as the Cyclops turned and looked into the Village for the first time, surveying the forces arrayed against it. The air was thick with dread and anticipation as the colossal Boss turned its single blazing eye toward the Legion sprawled out before it.

As it perused the defenders valiantly standing before it, the enormous being let out a chuckle as every fighter was frozen in place from the intensity of its stare. Wide smile in place, it lifted its foot and stepped into the open area around the Village…

…only to jerk to a halt in consternation as its shoulders and the club held at a strange angle forced it to get stuck in the opening like a cork in a wine bottle. It looked back to see what had happened, releasing the thousands of combatants from their hypnotized state at the same moment. With a scream of valor tinged with fear, nearly every human in the area unleashed spells, arrows, or threw themselves forward to begin slamming their weapons into the outstretched leg of the Cyclops.

The defenders were using the corpses of fallen creatures as improvised barricades, having carefully ensured that they died in clumps or in mounds that now stretched dozens of meters into the air. As the beasts were so large, they provided excellent protection and good footing for Dwarf and human alike, while impeding the movement of larger creatures greatly. Joe could hear the battle cries echoing out to him, and he had to chuckle at his favorite.

"That's right! Strike, then hide behind the mound of dead Penguins! Rinse and repeat until this big boy goes down!"

Only the very closest of the Dwarven Legion joined in the attack, the others continuously falling back toward where Joe was sprinting, a stream of bubbles arcing up into the sky rapidly carrying them away.

As far as the Ritualist could tell, the attacks landing on the Cyclops were doing next to nothing in terms of damage. Fireballs would strike exposed skin and erupt into a massive gout of flame, only to leave a slightly scorched hair follicle in the spot it had landed.

Lightning crackled along its skin, eventually dispersing as though it had been grounded out with a lightning rod. Weapons struck flesh, practically *bouncing* off the iron-hard icy surface of the Cyclops. Even warhammers and other blunt instruments failed to create cracks or obvious points of failure in its body, as it likely had a layer of dense blubber beneath the surface, similar to the Penguins.

Still, they must have been doing something. The Cyclops snarled in fury and began to struggle harder, using the hand not holding its club to reach over and slap at the stone perimeter in a motion Joe could only describe as someone slapping at a mosquito that was landing on their chest and annoying them.

The attacks became more frantic as the wall failed to be destroyed, merely groaning and rumbling with each heavy blow that it took. Soon, the open hand shifted into a closed fist. As spells and weapons were exhausted against its leg, the wrecking ball of a hand continued to pound into the Journeyman-rank fortification Joe had put in place.

"Tier *five*, sucker! It takes more than a couple hits for even *you* to take it down!" The Ritualist crowed excitedly as the wall held from another attack coming down on it. The Cyclops bellowed in rage, as if it had somehow heard Joe's taunt, the air shaking hard enough that any windows in the area shattered under the intense reverberations it created. It thrashed madly, slamming its closed fist down on the stone continuously, sending enormous plumes of dust and debris flying with each blow.

Every strike brought it closer to freeing itself and gaining access to the softer targets laying siege to it, and its effort quickly began to bear fruit. An enormous divot in the wall began to form, and each repeated strike caused multiple feet of stone to collapse. With a grunt of triumph, it brought its fist down one last time and sheared off a massive slab of stone, managing to pull more than half of its body through the opening. This gave it all the leverage it needed to increase its frantic strikes. Finally, the not-yet-enchanted blockade was strained beyond its limits and could no longer stand firm against the creature's brute strength. That section of wall finally gave way fully, sending a cloud of dust out into the suddenly silent defenders.

A nearly tangible sense of desperation exploded outward from the ranks of soldiers and humans, and as the Cyclops shifted to face them, they broke.

The Dwarves turned and charged toward the rear as a unit, while the humans scattered to the wind as the Cyclops howled in triumph. A single point of light grew brighter in its enormous eye for a few seconds before coalescing into a beam of energy that shot out and caused a path of ice to form wherever it touched. Any living creature hit by that Stellar Ice Beam wasn't merely trapped within ice: Joe estimated with near certainty that they were frozen to their core.

"Faster!" Joe threw himself forward one more time, reaching the edge of the ritual he'd set up. He skidded to a halt, looking around desperately for Grandmaster Snow but only finding Master Stu guiding the members of the Legion into the entrance point of the ritual. "Stu! Where's Snow? I have a plan, but I need to stop this ritual for it to work!"

"Are you *insane*?" Stu bellowed in reply, not bothering to look at Joe as he continued directing the efforts to evacuate. "Are you finally admitting to working against us and came here to kill us all? I know for a *fact* that you've been consorting with the enemy!"

"No, you-!" Joe cut himself off and blinked rapidly in surprise at the strange accusation. "Stu, what are you even talking about?"

"We *saw* you!" The Dwarf finally turned and shoved an accusatory finger at the Ritualist. "You were working with a human that was revealed to be in the employ of the Elves! When you found out the truth, you didn't cut all ties! We *saw* as you struck a deal to be released! Now, with your messages coming through the Town Hall, we have proof that you've been maintaining contact with her! Plotting against us! Exposing our secrets! Planning to bring her here and let a known agent of the Elves have access to everything that we build!"

"*What*?" Joe physically reeled back from the snarling Dwarf, his mind whirling but only managing to settle on a single thought. "Hold on a second… you've been intercepting and reading my mail?"

"This is *war*, human." Stu pulled something out of his pocket and nestled it in his right hand, looping a small section of twine around one of his fingers as he did so. "War is something that we're very experienced with and know well. It's funny how you betrayers never seem to understand that we're onto you, even when all the signs are there. The cold and distant leadership, the stifling of resources… we gave you every chance to come clean, and now, when we are at our weakest with the monsters at our throats, you try to cut off our escape? I *knew* you'd try something like this. That's why, when everyone else left, I stayed here and waited."

"I'm not trying to betray you, Stu! I'm trying to help all of us!" Joe sputtered as he thought over his conversations with Daniella and tried to find the pattern Stu was pointing at. While it had certainly seemed like he'd been on the outs with the council, he'd assumed that was a repercussion of losing his title, not that they were intercepting his private messages and making wild assumptions based off of them.

The Dwarf pointed at the Cyclops in the distance that was swinging its hand back and forth, sending Dwarves and humans alike scattering into the air, broken and destroyed. "Go play with the monsters that you called here to destroy us and don't look back. Otherwise, since I know you'd just come back to life, I'll do more than slay you right here. I'll make you suffer! Then, I'll make sure that your sins are never forgotten among my people! *Incite rage*!"

Unlike the bravado-filled shouting, the last two words were practically whispered. With all the other commotion going on, Joe was certain no one else heard them spoken. All of the confusion Joe was feeling coalesced into a single bar of white-hot *anger* as Stu activated his mastered Bardic skill to force him to send out the first noticeable attack.

Master rank 'Incite Rage' has overpowered your Mental Manipulation Resistance (Apprentice II)

"Oh no, the human is attacking me! *Traitor*!" the Dwarf shouted as he easily dodged the clumsily thrown ritual orb, wearing a smug, dark smile on his weasley features. "With that… the Cyclops will destroy this place, and as they've no reason to back you or work with you ever again, not a single Dwarf will stand against my version of these events. I'll be able to ensure that my city is only ever filled with *my* people, and yours… yours will finally learn their place. Thanks for the assist, Joe."

The Dwarf made his move, his weapon flicking out toward the Ritualist, who had to push himself to activate Omnivault in order to dodge the erratically moving weapon. Stu's hand followed him, and only then did Joe realize that the string was connecting the flying weapon to the Dwarf's hand. With a **crack**, it swung around and slammed into the side of Joe's knee, sending him tumbling heavily to the ground, even though his Exquisite Shell took the entirety of the damage that would have been done to his body.

But then he realized with horror what the Master of Sarcasm had meant about making Joe suffer.

Damage taken: 0.

A Master-rank bardic debuff has been applied: The Emperor's New Clothes!

Your Leggings of the Silkpants Mage have taken all the damage that would have been applied to you as durability damage!

Your Leggings of the Silkpants Mage have been destroyed!

Pushing himself up into a plank position and kicking forward to get back to his feet, Joe's eyes tracked the weapon as it shot back to the Dwarf's hand and his assailant readied another attack. "Are you seriously attacking me with a *yo-yo*? You're destroying my *gear*?"

Stu snorted derivatively as he whipped his hand forward once more. "What would you expect a Master of Sarcasm to wield? *Razor*-sharp wit? A sword made of *iron-y*?"

Joe felt a debuff slam into him, dulling his reactions and causing the yo-yo to crack off his Exquisite Shell just in front of his nose. He stumbled back, managing to maintain his footing as he glared at the Dwarf. "Actually… yes, that'd make sense to me."

Your Half-mask of the Silkpants Mage has been destroyed!

"*Fool.*" Stu muttered as he lashed out once more, pulling on the string just before the yo-yo would have hit Joe in the face, causing the weapon to drop to his chest and a circular saw to pop out of the edges and shred his torso coverings right through his Exquisite Shell.

As the Ritualist put maximum effort into evading the next attacks, the ground beneath them began to once more rumble as the Cyclops came ever closer to destroying the Town Hall, and with it, Joe's only hope for redeeming himself with the Dwarves.

CHAPTER FORTY-FOUR

Joe's mind was having trouble processing the stream of events that was occurring around him at this moment. The Legion was in full-blown retreat, a Cyclops was bearing down on them with the intent to destroy their home and then their bodies, and here he was, dodging a yo-yo as a Dwarf who was a master of annoying people tried to use the situation to sabotage humanity's reputation with the Dwarves.

The entire Village was a chaotic frenzy of clashing weapons, swirling spells, and the thunderous sounds the Cyclops made with every step or attack on the warm-blooded creatures that got in its way.

Staring down his unlikely opponent, wielding an even more unlikely weapon, the Ritualist rubbed at his head, which was reflecting the light of the fake sky he'd created above them. "This is weird, Stu! Knock it off, and get out of the way. You're absolutely going to need to replace my gear, but I'll bring that to the council to handle."

"What're you going to do?" the Dwarf taunted him as he swung his yo-yo off to the side like a flail, "Tell on me? The

Grandmaster has already evacuated, and by the time you would find her, you'll be fully cut off from all contact. After all–"

He interrupted himself at that moment, whipping his weapon forward hoping to get off a cheap blow while the human was distracted. Joe let the yo-yo whistle through the air above him, buzzing slightly as its blades spun ferociously around the tiny implement. The Ritualist was quick on his feet, and even quicker on the uptake. As Stu shifted his positions, Joe abruptly dodged at an oblique angle and let the returning weapon bypass him. Then it completely stopped in the air and shot at him to tear up his socks.

"You know, I'm only an Expert with this weapon. I'll just have to keep practicing on you until I rank up a little bit." The Dwarf was sounding somewhat manic at this point, and his eyes were flicking from Joe to the Cyclops bearing down on the Town Hall. Both of them knew that as soon as that final structure was out of the way, all of the monsters in the area would turn on the invaders to their world with all the ferocity starving beasts could bring to bear.

Joe saw that motion for what it really was: fear. "You never served in the Legion, did you?"

"I never needed to," Stu sneered at him as he whipped his unconventional weapon around once more. "I was always more effective in a position of command, helping direct the minds of the brightest of our people! Can you imagine it? Me, wasting my time on the front lines using a sharpened piece of metal to bring down a slathering *beast*?"

"A great scholar once said that a society that separates its scholars from its warriors will have its thinking done by cowards and its fighting done by fools... *bro*." Joe lifted his hand into the air, middle finger and thumb pressing against each other. He didn't need to make any motion in order to complete the action he had in mind, but it helped to drive the point home. Snapping his fingers, he mentally deactivated the ritual behind the Master Dwarf. "I don't know about you, but *I* think every single Legionnaire brings something to the table."

"You've killed us!" Stu screamed as he thrust a finger at Joe, his eyes wide in fear as he looked at the totally still ritual behind him. Spittle shot from his lips as he screamed at the bald-headed human in front of him. "You've killed *me*! *Me*!"

A greataxe came down on the Master's head, turning at the last second so that the flat of the weapon—instead of the edge—slammed into the side of his head. As the Dwarf slumped to the ground, Joe was greatly relieved to see Major Cleave standing behind the fallen member of the council, instead of someone he didn't recognize. "I think I've heard enough to make an official report on Master Stu's behavior."

"Cleave! I have a plan; help me collect the Ritual Tile!" Joe didn't waste a moment thanking her or explaining himself. The Maniac Dwarf had already distracted him enough that he was uncertain whether he was going to be able to put his plan in place before all was lost.

He dashed over to where the confused members of the Legion were beginning to panic, their escape route cut off as a Cyclops closed in. He scooped up the tile, ensuring with a brief inspection that it hadn't sustained any damage. Then he turned and sprinted toward the Town Hall. Cleave stood in front of him, crouched down, hands cupped. Joe ran forward, lifting his foot and pushing down into an Omnivault as she hoisted him into the air and added her own strength to the skill he was using.

The human absolutely *blasted* into the sky in a sharp, parabolic arc, his loose clothes flapping around him in the arctic chill and sapping the heat from his body as he rapidly closed the distance. He only had eyes for the building or the Cyclops that was approaching it more slowly with each passing second.

Joe didn't need to wonder why it had slowed, as it seemed that the club it was wielding was growing heavier and *heavier* the closer that it got to its goal. The Ritualist landed atop the Town Hall, swinging the Ritual Tile into position, adjusting the targeting and velocity sigils in the same smooth motion. With a scream of effort, he activated the ritual, causing a series of swirling ritual circles to appear in the air in front of him. Then Joe made the mistake of looking up to assess the distance between himself and the Cyclops; meeting its eye as it stared at him.

Instantly, his body froze up like a mouse staring up at a snake that had already coiled around it. Across the entirety of the craggy, mountainous face in front of him, a wide smile was present. The Cyclops recognized him and fully understood the effect that its presence had on lesser beings.

It was moving along at a snail's pace, its front foot trying to force itself to the ground so that it could pull the colossal Boss forward. The club behind him resisted every bit of momentum possible, but finally, almost softly, the Cyclops's foot reached the ground, and Joe made a horrifying realization.

The weapon was now in range of the Town Hall.

It began to shine, brighter than Joe had seen throughout the travels of the Cyclops, and it was vibrating at a frequency that made his teeth numb at this range. The weapon itself began twitching around, and the Cyclops grimaced slightly as it reached with its other hand to grasp the handle so it didn't fling itself out of his grip. Still staring Joe down, the Cyclops opened its mouth to release another thunderous noise that would eventually be translated into words, only to go stock-still as a sound that sounded like the world itself splitting apart echoed across the area.

Snap!

On the heels of the calamitous sound came a shout from a voice that Joe knew far too well.

"*Adjust!*"

Ever so slowly, the Cyclops's head shifted to the side as his neck turned and twisted. Three seconds into this strange motion, Jaxon came into view, riding on the shoulder of the Cyclops and already pumping his fingers into the same spot on the redwood-tree-trunk of a neck once more. Then the Cyclops tensed up, forcibly resisting the motion and bringing its face back toward its target once more.

By then, Joe had shaken off the paralysis and fully activated the ritual. Bubbles streamed from the top of the building, slamming into the upper body and face of the Cyclops in an unending stream, bursting upon impact but arresting its forward momentum as it began to lean forward. The tiny amounts of water in each bubble splashed onto the Cyclops and froze instantly. Normally, this wouldn't have been an issue, but there were thousands of bubbles per second striking the monster, and a thick layer of ice began collecting across the surface of its body. This only slowed its incoming attack by fractions of a second, but those added up quickly.

"Ha, ha! *Ice* to meet you!" Joe taunted the beast as he rushed to the next phase of his plan.

The Boss monster unleashed yet another otherworldly roar, the thunderous sound waves reverberating the air. Any message it would have carried was rendered utterly incomprehensible to his ears, but even so… the Ritualist knew what it was trying to say.

It was the same message that every creature bent on destruction tried to monologue to its prey. It was mocking him, telling him about what it would do next, when it didn't have the restrictions that were holding it back at this moment. But Joe didn't care about that. All he cared about was that the Cyclops's view was blocked by the bubbles frothing the air around its enormous head.

As soon as the first part of his plan had been enacted, Joe had immediately Omnivaulted to the side of the building, springing off the ground a single time in the direction of the Pyramid of Panacea. There was another ritual set up over there, which he'd left in place, and he might be able to change the outcome of the attack with it. He didn't look back, not even when he could hear the Cyclops intoning its final words. Even as the air began to shudder from the pent-up energy of the heavily enchanted artifact of a club, Joe simply maintained focus on the ritual he had landed next to and was now *dumping* mana into.

It was fully active, he just wasn't certain if he or it was going to be fast enough. The energy behind him reached a crescendo, and the sound of tens of thousands of bubbles being popped reached his ears a moment before a shockwave of air tried to knock him flat. Joe only maintained his balance thanks to his 'Immovable Object' title, which allowed him to resist eighty percent of any knockback effect. His eyes were closed as he hoped for the best.

Then his world was swept away as a wave of dirt, snow, and force shifted the very landscape around them.

The Ritualist's eyes flung open, and he found himself upside down in midair, still clutching the enormous Ebonsteel block of metal. At some point, he'd lost his hearing from the enormous explosion at close range, but he was unable to state exactly when, as his head was spinning as though it wasn't attached to his body.

Joe forced his eyes to focus on the ritual in front of him, then at the slew of notifications that had popped up. He ignored the damage notification, which told him that his Exquisite Shell was broken, and that most of his health was gone. Even though it was greatly interesting to him, he ignored the chiming notification informing him that he'd finally earned experience again—and he *really* wanted to see how that one had been worked out. The only one that mattered at this moment was a durability notification that he'd just received from the Town Hall being damaged.

Damage received on Town Hall (Village). Durability: 394/100,000.

"*Mend.*" Just before the ground rushed up to greet him, and his vision was blocked by a surprisingly mild terrain damage notification, an explosion of air shot out of Joe's lungs in three syllables. "Ha. Made it."

CHAPTER FORTY-FIVE

He was buried beneath a thin layer of snow, but the Ritualist's body was broken, and his lifeblood was pooling in a sanguine puddle around him. Unable to move his arms, his legs, or his head, Joe was utterly uncertain how he was still conscious. Even though his mind was screaming with pain, the fact that he could think at all meant that he had a chance. Working to channel every ounce of his Battle Meditation skill, he put all of the alarms his body was hollering at him to the side and focused on his Ritual Orbs.

One of the orbs, which wasn't bound to his Characteristics, floated out of its position in his tattered bandolier and drifted up to rest gently on his face. Even though he was freezing to death at this very moment, Joe was still surprised at how cold the surface of the orb was. Focusing his intent, before his mind drifted further and he was sent to respawn, Joe activated the spell captured in the weapon. His body was flooded with the healing power of his spell, Lay on Hands. His neck snapped back into position, sounding far too reminiscent of what Jaxon had done to the Cyclops only moments prior.

Health gained: 457

Current Health: 647/2,344 Caution! You are bleeding / freezing / chilled / stunned / deaf–

"Ignore remainder of debuffs!" The human groaned, even though he couldn't hear the words coming out of his mouth. With the healing, Joe felt the remainder of his body come back into alignment, which unfortunately allowed him to *fully* appreciate all of the pain that he was in at the moment. He wanted to get to his feet immediately but forced himself to wait until Lay on Hands came off of cooldown. Then he pumped another heal into himself, followed by a Mend from his own hands.

Current health: 1,361/2,344

As his ears were fixed, the sound of combat, screaming, and an unending bellow of abject fury that continued far longer than it should nearly deafened him once more. "That's going to have to be enough for now!"

Struggling to push through the snow, Joe whipped around and got his legs under him, Omnivaulting straight up and exploding out of the surface of the snow like a porpoise showing off for a group of tourists on a canoe. His eyes immediately went to the Cyclops, which was now moving at its regular speed, flashing through the open area as fast as any Dwarf could sprint, thanks to its enormous limbs and lack of weapon impeding it.

It was still holding its club, and both the Cyclops and the weapon appeared completely undamaged, unlike the once nice, level surface of the Village. From this angle, Joe couldn't even see the bottom of the hole that had just been gouged out. "I guess we can just put a pond there. Maybe a lake."

Without hesitating any longer, Joe tossed a hasty Exquisite Shell on to himself at approximately a quarter of the power it could be even as he sprinted into the distance, targeting the far corner of the open space. He had originally planned to build his workshop in the far back corner of the Village but had realized that was a bad spot and set up shop right next to the entrance of this area. Even so, there was now a building in that location.

The Town Hall.

It was practically rubble, large chunks were missing from it, and it appeared that a stiff breeze could knock the entire structure over. There was a gaping hole in the side that Joe could see, where the club had come down and smashed into its side before he could transfer the *entire* building, using the Ritual of the Traveling Civilization.

"I can't believe how cost-effective that is when I'm not trying to pull an Artifact from another world onto this one." Joe tried to see the humor while he could, because the Cyclops was ahead of him, bearing down on the building with a cohort of monsters coming along for the ride. He was hoping that the next stage of his plan would work, but it was going to take a few seconds before… there!

Like a pilot light igniting a larger flame, a ritual circle sprang into existence above the shattered remnants of the Town Hall. It began to spin and shifted from a bluish-white coloration to a deep, metallic silver. Power began to condense in the center, looking for all the world like a swimming pool's worth of mercury suspended in midair. It sloshed back and forth, shaping itself and being pushed into place by continual surges of power coming from all directions.

Tiny gray specks of this near-liquid material were rising up from the bodies of every monster that had come through the walls, some having as many as four liquid motes of energy lift off them before rushing into the greater collection. They moved practically at the speed of light, hovering in the air for only an instant before streaking to the center of the ritual like a shooting star. Finally, only ten steps before the Boss monster would arrive and be in range of the building, five motes of grayish energy lifted off of it and shot into the center of the expanding energy.

"It's too late!" Joe screeched in fear as the club went up, poised to strike. The Cyclops bellowed in exertion, but as its foot landed, a massive detonation shifted the ground and blew off two toes. The ankle of the Boss rolled, tendons snapping like steel cables as it stumbled and fell to a knee. The creature tried to inhale and ignore the pain, forcing itself to its feet as all the light coming from the sky winked out, showing only the darkness of the true sky above them.

"Ha! I'm so glad I forgot to move that Ritual Tile!" Joe wasn't too worried about the loss, so long as the Ritual of Slaughter came through, now that it had been given enough time to fully activate. "I really hope Socar was correct."

Joe shifted his position, flinging himself to the side instead of trying to chase down the Cyclops. "Come on, formations… activate East Small Metal or whatever the Abyssal final effect was supposed to be for a single-target piercing effect!"

The ritual didn't disappoint, the practically molten metal already condensing down to a flat plane. For one brief moment, the liquid became perfectly reflective, a shining sheet of a mirror hanging in open air. The Cyclops stared itself down, its movement slowing to half speed as it was forced to fight against its own debuff.

"Why didn't I think of that earlier?" Joe shouted in the air as he gripped the sides of his own head. "It literally had a debuff that makes anyone who sees its eye get paralyzed! This is fighting a gorgon one-oh-one! No, it's fine! It's all notes for the future: use the active effects of monsters against them."

Then the sheet of metal collapsed to a single point, a singularity of power shining brilliantly enough to create false daylight. The ritual circles containing it flared a single time, so lightning-bright that Joe was forced to blink instinctively. By the time his eyes were open again, the energy was gone. He looked around frantically to see if it had missed its target, as the Cyclops was still moving.

It took two steps forward then came to a halt and slowly sank to its knees. The son of a Titan fell forward, its face slamming into the ground. A high-pressure stream of blood shot into the air above it, arcing up nearly a hundred feet in the air, only to come down and be captured by the still-active blood collection ritual weaving through the air like a sanguine snake. A flash of light like the glint of moonlight off an unsheathed blade at midnight caught Joe's eye, and he whipped his head to the side in time to see the remnant power of the Ritual of Slaughter continuing its deadly work.

It flashed to every monster in the area, starting with those nearest the Town Hall, as they were the first to gain the Mark of Slaughter on them.

The larger monsters had holes blown through their skulls. The smaller monsters had their heads directly ripped off by the force of the flying power. Quick as chain lightning, the now much-reduced power flew off into the distance toward the entrance of the Village, vanishing into the masses of monsters still congregating there. Joe tracked it as best he could, but the remaining energy wasn't even enough to enter the maze, simply clearing the open area before dissipating, leaving nearly a quarter of the assembled monsters alive and well.

Joe sucked in a deep breath, filling his lungs to the absolute maximum capacity, before bellowing at the top of his lungs: "The Boss monster has been defeated! Fight off the others, and we win!"

The clamor of battle reached a new crescendo as his call was taken up, but Joe didn't approach the site of the extermination. He ran over to the building and immediately got to work setting up a Ritual of Repair. He focused on the area between himself and the entrance of the Village, ready to drop the ritual and throw everything he had into blasting anything that made it past the waves of defenders.

Excellent use of Dark Charisma! Incite that violence! Charisma + 1!

Your call across the battlefield has improved the morale of the remaining fighters! Charisma + 1!

Your announcement has caused 1,000 additional fighters to join combat! Charisma + 3!

Your announcement has caused 10,000 additional fighters to join combat! Charisma + 5!

The notifications rang out every few seconds, seeming to stabilize at a total of ten additional points in his Charisma. Joe nearly let his trickle of mana flowing to the Ritual of Repair sputter out as he sucked in a breath out of sheer surprise. "Celestial feces, there really *are* some good benefits to aligning to Dark Charisma. I wonder what I'd need to do if I had somehow managed to align it to light, or whatever positive is?"

He considered that for a few seconds as the building to his left continued to reassemble itself, brick-by-brick. Then he shook his head, "I likely would've needed to convince people to stop fighting or connect with them on a deep personal level. This is probably for the best."

Remaining at his post for the next several hours was an enormous test of his willpower, as he wanted to go and see what was happening. Yet, no one else was coming over to help him guard the building nor help repair it. That meant that he had to stay wary, alert, and ready for anything. Finally, two and a half hours after the Boss monster had fallen, an alert swept over him.

Congratulations! Your Village has successfully defeated all 25 Beast waves! Your Town Hall is automatically undergoing an upgrade in rarity to reflect its new status as a Rare monument structure! Town Hall (Uncommon) → Town Hall (Rare). Please note, this will not fully or automatically repair the building. If it has sustained damage, you will need to find alternative ways to repair it.

Joe read that message as 'if you do not have a Ritualist with you who can magically repair this building, you are going to need to find all new materials at the rank of this building and hope for the best'. That was fine with him; in fact, at this moment, he would have been fine with another Cyclops coming toward them. They had succeeded, survived, and reached the official rank of Town in under two weeks of being on Jotunheim!

He celebrated alone for a few minutes, until a trickle of people started coming over to inspect the corpse of the Cyclops and look over the upgrading Town Hall. Jaxon came sprinting directly over to Joe, screaming in excitement as he threw himself into a full tackle hug.

"Joe! You magnificent *crazy man*! I've never considered

having a building dodge an attack! That was a work of art. You saw the attack coming and *adjusted* the situation to our benefit. I can't express how much I love that idea… perhaps, some day, *I* will be able to adjust concepts! Maybe I can even adjust the air and have an attack land somewhere else instead of on me? So many ideas!"

"Technically, it didn't *just* dodge… it counterattacked." Both of them laughed at that, and Joe wasn't entirely certain when it had started raining, but there were droplets on his face. Luckily, his Neutrality Aura whisked those away before they became annoying. "Jaxon! We won! We have a *Town*!"

A harsh voice crashed over the jubilation of those in the area, sweeping away Joe's smile like a tidal wave. Stu was stomping toward him, cracking his knuckles as he eyed the building that was being repaired. "All that means is that *we* have a *problem*!"

CHAPTER FORTY-SIX

The Ritualist shifted his position, ready to bodily block the Dwarf from approaching the Town Hall. His words came out dripping with condescension. "What're you going to do, Stu? Destroy the Town Hall in front of your entire people? Smash it so we can't build all of these fine people some better places to live, work, and thrive? Go ahead! *Be* the reason that all of their effort, all of their losses, are thrown away."

The Master's furious strides slowed to a halt, and he stared at Joe without looking around, his hands clenched into fists so hard that blood began leaking from his palms. Finally unable to take another moment of the situation, Stu spat out, "You… filthy *human*! We don't *want* you here! We don't want you around, messing up our lives and changing how the world works!"

A low murmuring started to fill the air as the celebrating defenders began listening in on the conversation. As the Master of Sarcasm continued shouting at Joe, the murmur turned into a susurration that rapidly grew louder and more unaccommodating. Finally, another Dwarf walked forward and asked Stu a question, his voice filled with confusion and concern. "Council bro, didn't this guy save our butts? Like, a whole bunch? With the Elves, now with this hefty eyeball boi?"

"He didn't save us; he broke the *balance*! The Elves would take a fortress, and we would take it back, slowly building our knowledge, based on how they defended or attacked!" Now the Master of Sarcasm thrust an accusatory finger at Joe, his eyes filling with madness. "All this bald human did was mess up the good thing we had going! He's a *traitor*!"

Joe remained silent and merely continued repairing the Town Hall, giving the Dwarf plenty of room to build up momentum for his swan dive off the approaching reputational cliff. It didn't take long, as practically the only people that had remained this long were veterans of the Legion or other humans who were certain to take Joe's side in this matter. A contingent of military leadership started forward, their hands on their weapons, their eyes narrowed as Stu stood there fuming, heaving for air as he barely held himself back from throwing himself at the Ritualist.

"You mean to tell us that… our losses, our friends, all of the work that we've been doing for centuries… all of that was a front so that you and the Elves could test out weapon ideas and new iterations of defenses?" Joe wasn't sure what rank this Dwarf was, as he hadn't spent enough time learning the military lore. But going by the respect of all of the Dwarves around her, this mustachioed non-commissioned officer had been on the front lines more often than not. "Was this how you ran your sector? Feeding information to the Elves that they eventually used to wipe us out? I don't know about the rest of you–"

Here she was raising her voice to the crowd around her, and their angry silence spoke for them as she continued, "--but to me, it sounds like *you* were the traitor. How many weapons did you give the Elves? How many of our defensive plans did you hand over? Somebody get me a strategist; let's map out the route the Elves took to carve through our fortresses. Something tells me… something tells me they practically *danced* directly through Stu's sector."

Finally recognizing that he was as good as on trial at the moment, the Master paled and backpedaled furiously. "No! That's not what happened! I'm not a traitor; I'm a wordsmith! It was never meant to make our people fail, only to succeed. I swear, I didn't know they'd come through my territory so easily! I thought we had a deal!"

"Oh look, 'I'm not a traitor, I'm just incompetent'!" Jaxon cheerfully called out, getting a few eyes flicking over to him, but they all quickly returned to the Dwarf. "That *is* an extremely novel defense, but I'm pretty sure it's not a very good one."

Stu closed his eyes, took a deep breath, and relaxed. A moment later, he looked around the crowd and spoke again. This time, his words were carefully crafted and oozing the Charisma that he'd worked to build up over the centuries.

"No, none of this is what you think it is. Let's all take a few minutes to come down from our battle high, take a few moments to regroup, and I can clearly explain the situation. My apologies, I was out of sorts. I think I was struck with some kind of insanity spell for a minute there. Likely from earlier, when this bald human attacked me. You all know about that, don't y–?"

His final word was cut off as Major Cleave sprinted into the area, her axe held high. "*There* you are! You're as slippery as an eel! I have no idea how you got out of the ropes I tied you up in."

"No, not the *face*!" Stu squealed and lifted his arms to protect his head as she swung her axe. Moments later, he was unconscious on the ground with a furiously breathing Major holding her weapon above him in preparation to directly execute the man that could apparently slither out of bindings.

"Hold on!" Joe called out before she could strike the man down just because rope wasn't holding him. "I'm fairly certain he has a high affinity with ropes, twine, and the like, because he uses a yo-yo as a weapon. Most likely, he just used some kind of skill that unknotted the ropes you tied him up in. Try chains!"

"I don't have any chains." Cleave ignored Joe as she lifted her axe high. "He practically admitted to working with our ancient enemy, and–"

"Are you going to send him back to them as an Elf with a ton of accolades to his name, as a Dwarf?" Joe's words cut through her focus, and Major Cleave paused then let her weapon fall to her side. "Don't give him what his alternative self would want. Hand him over to Grandmaster Snow, have him removed from the council, and put him to work on behalf of the Dwarven society until he clears his name."

No one seemed to be listening at the moment, and Joe furrowed his brow. Then he remembered that he was aligned with Dark Charisma and was attempting to tell people not to be violent at the moment. Of course it was ineffective! "Forget that! Beat him within an inch of his life and throw him into a mine to break rocks until he clears his name!"

"*Yeah!*" The mob cheered and began to break up. They'd been running on pure adrenaline from the battle and were finally starting to cool down. Joe let out a sigh of relief, knowing that the brisk air around them likely helped save the situation. Every once in a while, he forgot exactly how warlike, hierarchical, and *direct* the Dwarves were when it came to major issues like this. To his great relief, everyone began to disperse, the issue at hand seemingly having been decided.

"Oh, wait, no. They're running off to loot as much as they can before someone stops them." Joe cursed lightly, sending a Dark Lightning Strike at a group attempting to steal his Cyclops. "Back off! That's mine! I'm already planning to donate most of it to build up the city!"

"Then I'm taking your Penguin, bro!" The Dwarf that had taken the brunt of the lightning strike was shaking uncontrollably as his nerves reset. He scooped up a snowball and whipped it at Joe's face in retaliation. The human didn't flinch.

An instant later, the packed snow puffed against his Exquisite Shell, and the Dwarf took a shadowy slap to the face.

Joe smirked as the Dwarf flinched and ended up slipping and falling face-first into a snow drift. "I feel like that worked out well."

The next few hours were a blur of activity as thousands of people worked together to haul carcasses, fix the Town Hall, and even participated in moving it back to its original location after a handful of geomancers filled in the massive crater that was in the place where it had originally stood. That worked out extremely well, as they were able to firm up the foundations under the building to a much higher degree by repurposing the failing Trash walls. They made the stone as dense as possible, in order to hopefully protect against any burrowing creatures that might attack them in the future.

Just as everything was resetting and seeming to settle down into a standard routine, thousands of Dwarves marched toward the city from the south, led by none other than Grandmaster Snow. Her expression was grim, and her visage was thunderous as she looked for Joe. Eventually, she did find him. Joe watched calmly as she stomped toward him, coming to a halt and staring into his eyes silently.

Then she pulled her hand back and slapped him across the face with a crisp **smack*. "If your hair-brained idea had failed, nearly half of the entire remaining Dwarven race would have been wiped out! It was an unnecessary risk! If you're willing to gamble with our lives so casually, how are we supposed to *trust* you in the future?"

"Well, let's be as rational about this as possible." Joe turned his face back to examine the fuming Grandmaster, gently spitting a bit of blood from a split lip to the side. That strike had been enough to eradicate the rest of his Exquisite Shell and deal a few points of damage through it. Somehow, she'd even managed to cause his Retaliation of Shadows to fail, the automatic spell dissipating as soon as it began to manifest in the air next to her.

He saved that realization to think about at a later date.

"Fact is, *you* ran, evacuating even before your people. That doesn't scream that you had a lot of trust in me in the first place. Or that you were too worried about them."

"It was a level *thirty-five* Cyclops! It was over forty feet tall and had the potential to wipe out everyone!" Before she could build up a full head of steam in a rant, Joe held up a hand to forestall her.

"Just tell me one thing, Snow. Would you have been able to easily defeat that Cyclops if you had joined combat?"

"Easily?" She shook her head sharply. "Absolutely not! It would have been a hard-fought battle, but it's likely that I would have won. That's not the point."

"It *is* the point." Joe gestured to the side, where Stu was being dragged toward them by two members of the Legion, a couple of large bumps protruding from the top of his head where Cleave had bonked him to knock him out.

"If you had joined combat, or the rest of the Masters had, there's no way that Cyclops would've been able to casually build up enough power to wipe out a chunk of the town in one hit. If you had gotten involved ahead of time, it may have taken out a few walls, but it wouldn't have threatened our settlement. The question is... why *didn't* you? I think I know now."

Joe walked over to the captured Master of Sarcasm, mimicking Snow's actions from a moment before by rearing back and slapping the Dwarf across the face. He came around with a shout and immediately began struggling against the Legionnaires holding him. "Stu is a coward. He's been working against your best interests, *our* best interests. To be fair, I don't think he thought his actions, through... he just didn't want to give up his eminently comfortable, profitable life. Ever since we arrived on Jotunheim, the biggest impediment to his being able to be lazy... was me. Think back. Why'd you make the decision not to trust me or Havoc when we had ideas?"

Grandmaster Snow opened her mouth to speak, then turned to blink at the Master of Sarcasm, who was staring at her with wide, pleading eyes. Her brow furrowed in confusion and consternation. Joe saw that and let out an internal sigh of relief. "Good. Now, think back to what happened on the last world. I will let the Legion explain that situation to you. I'm sure they can give a better accounting for his actions—or rather, lack of action. I hope this is enough for us to move forward as friends and without his whispering against us behind closed doors, for us to trust each other again. I really liked it when we had that."

"Because then you were able to make a cool turtle that caused a super volcano to erupt!" Jaxon cheerfully butted into the conversation. "When is the next time we can do something like that? I feel like an active volcano would be useful as a neighbor. Heat up the air, create a few lakes, be a natural terrain advantage..."

"You've given me a lot to think about. Not *you*, Jaxon, I'm talking to Joe." Snow slowly stated, her gaze slowly trailing along the assembled groups of intermingled Dwarves and humans, who had never, to this point, had an issue working together.

Then she looked out at the rest of the town, where a small but robust economy was starting to develop, thanks to Joe's efforts and his willingness to turn the means of production over to the people around him. "No more of this. Our lives have changed, and we need to adapt, or we'll fail once more. I'm going to do what I should've done back on the summit, when you defeated Master Stu. I'm invoking my right as a Grandmaster. As of this moment, humans will have representation in the city... in the form of Master Ritualist Joe."

A cheer went up from the crowds around them, as the Grandmaster had used some form of skill to project her voice so that everyone could hear it. Even though he was still leery, Joe accepted the recognition with an uncomfortable smile. His eyes lit up as a new title appeared in his vision. "Oh! It comes with a useful title? In that case, I suppose I'll accept."

"Hold on, can I be on the council as well?" Jaxon offered

with a winning smile. "Or Major Cleave? She brained this guy twice; that has to count for something!"

"No chance," Snow hastily denied, though she softened the words with a smile and an explanation. "Unfortunately, there's a maximum limit on how many counselors can be in charge. Only ten-a-city."

CHAPTER FORTY-SEVEN

Watching carefully as a hacked-off Cyclops finger was fed into his aspect tower, Joe had to take deep breaths so he didn't feel too queasy. It wasn't that the actual process of watching a body get converted into aspects was an issue. More than anything else, it was the fact that this had been an intelligent monster that spoke to him directly. Something about that made this process more… personal.

"Can't complain about the results, though," Joe breathed to himself as he watched Unique aspects flooding into his Natural Aspect Jars. He was going to be able to turn this creature that had created such devastation and led swarms of monsters against them into the very thing that it was trying to prevent: a civilization. He was already demarcating sections of the monster for his projects. "I think I'll need half a foot in order to build a greenhouse, a couple of fingers in order to set up the rest of the quality of life rituals. I wonder if I can make a ritual efficient enough to only need a fingernail per apartment building? Hmm…"

He made some notes in his notebook as he waited for the

rest of the finger to dissolve. When that was done, he closed it with a snap and motion for the next chunk to be brought in. Joe flinched away as he looked to the side and saw the enormous eyeball being rolled toward him. For an instant, it'd seemed to be staring directly into his soul, and he froze up. Not in the debuff way, but just in a natural reaction to seeing an enormous, freaky eye staring at you.

Unfortunately, whatever effect the eye had on intelligent creatures had faded with its death, or he would've fought to turn the grisly organ into a defensive structure.

It was rolled into the opening, rapidly dissolving the exterior of it. Then it deflated like a balloon as a large hole was punched in one side, and the thick gel within it spurted out into the tower. Joe directly gagged at that, stepping back a few feet. "Abyss! what in the…! Okay, at least it went in there and is being dissolved. That would've been a nightmare to clean up."

As it deflated, it stopped moving into the tower of its own accord, and they had to work with a half-deflated eye flopping in place as they tried to force it deeper into the opening. Joe didn't even touch it with his hands, instead pushing with his ritual orbs to get a nice even distribution of force across its surface. Then the cleanup crew left with a wave, off to chop off another chunk. Joe went back to his notes, once again waiting for the next piece to start arriving, when he heard a sharp **clink**. He looked up with a slight frown, trying to find what had made that noise. When he looked into the aspect tower, it was like looking into a spotlight, his ears filled with the astral scream of a magical item, thanks to his Magical Synesthesia—it was painful to listen to, heavily distorted because of its Beginner rank—and he realized what had happened.

Joe had just found the Core of the Cyclops, and he needed to tuck it away before anyone noticed. He deactivated the ritual with a thought, Omnivaulting head-first directly into the half-dissolved goo that was filling the tower and swimming through it until he grasped the shining object. He got to his feet, half-submerged in aqueous humor as he triumphantly sucked the luminescent gem into his codpiece. He stared into the distance as he read over the notification of the item, already knowing exactly what he wanted to use it for.

Item gained: Monster Core (Artifact). This Core can be converted to 12,000 experience or used for other crafting purposes.

"You're going to be my first Artifact-ranked aspect jar. As soon as I can convert you over, I'll be able to start constantly accumulating bright orange aspects. What a beautiful addition!" Joe was muttering to himself furiously as he made his plans, nearly quivering in excitement to get started on the process, even though he was nowhere near having enough aspects to begin the conversion process. But, as soon as he did… he would never run out of them again, at least not permanently.

"I think he finally lost it." A hushed voice echoed in the building, reaching Joe's ears and causing them to twitch and burn bright red in shame. "He's just standing in that sludge, slapping his hands up and down on the surface of it like a child in a bathtub."

"I needed crafting materials!" Joe shouted back, his entire bald head now bright red. He swam out of the muck, stepping out of the tower and reactivating the permanent Field Array the aspect tower generated. He couldn't bring himself to meet anyone else's gaze, and they were all grinning at him with only a *hint* of concern nestled beneath the mocking smiles. "A-*hem*. Anyway, what's the next piece you brought me?"

"We brought the rest of its big ol' head, but I'm pretty sure it won't fit in there. It's too hard for us to chop up without dulling our weapons, so we just sliced through the brainstem and rolled it this way." With that description, Joe carefully didn't stare directly at what they brought him, instead simply nodding and setting up an extremely thin Field Array. He was going to have to slice this into chunks but didn't want to waste all of the valuable aspects that would be lost in the process, if he made a full-sized one.

The grisly work continued for days, even though the

Cyclops was the first and most important of them. Tens of thousands of monster corpses in various states of 'destroyed' were brought to him, thanks to being considered his kills, though he ensured that he parceled them out correctly for taxes, as well as what he owed his other assistants and employees. Eventually, Joe looked up and didn't see another body waiting for him, and he allowed himself a breath of relief. It was wonderful to gain so many crafting materials, but the gore of the situation had practically numbed him to the excitement of it all.

Finally, with all of that out of the way, Joe turned his attention to all of the notifications he'd been holding off on reading. After all, letting the corpses rot would have meant fewer aspects gained. The system messages came to him in the form of Town first, system announcements for him personally, then changes to his skills and stats. He assumed they had been arranged that way on purpose, so he didn't brush past any of them.

Settlement upgrade to Town complete! Every person who actively defended the city has gained 10,000 experience! Your town has been given a 100-hour monster repellent, and no monsters will be able to approach your walls unless a member of your settlement initiates combat. New building slots are available; expand this section to peruse those updates!

"Well that was a nice little bonus." Joe shook his head slightly, "More experience than I've seen in a while—no, don't get grumpy. There's a lot more messages."

He took a breath and moved to the next section, which had a strange border of gold around it, indicating that it had come from an administrator or moderator team that were still in control of the system.

It filled Joe with a strange sense of relief to know that this place was still being actively directed, and he hoped that they were working for the good of the people trapped in this world.

Congratulations! Your request to have the issue elevated has brought direct administrator attention to your actions on Jotunheim. Your non-direct combat prowess has been noted, and restrictions upon skill gain, experience gain, and aspect gain have been unlocked, allowing you to further refine and enhance your unique method of not-exactly-combat. From now on, your encounters with monsters will yield greater rewards.

Thanks to your faction leader (Occulttatum) arguing on your behalf, we are pleased to inform you that you will gain a full 50% of the experience and aspects from Monsters defeated through non-direct combat methodology. We hope that you understand that this enhancement in value is entirely in recognition of your ingenuity and resourcefulness in dispatching foes beyond your true combat capabilities.

We hope that you will keep up the good work and continue to explore innovative ways to overcome challenges. Your strategic thinking and mastery of unconventional methods will be key to your future success, or the reason for your eventual downfall. Happy hunting, may your victories be as overreaching as your methods.

Joe read that message several times, tasting the words by saying them softly, and eventually coming to recognize the message for what it was: he'd just made some moderator extremely angry. They were giving him his rewards, even while doing their best to craft the message in a condescending and insulting way. His lips curled up, and Joe chuckled softly. "Looks like, no matter how powerful you are, there's always someone above ya. I'll keep that in mind. Sorry if I caused you trouble, Mod."

The Ritualist flinched as another message intruded in his line of sight, blocking the others that were waiting for him. This one flared with the light of the sun, and he read it with some trepidation.

Don't worry about that, young one. Within the intricate web of life's tapestry, there is always someone perched upon a higher rung of power. Never forget that true strength lies not solely in one's position, but in how that power is wielded.

It is the compassionate and wise who rise above, inspiring unity and lifting others toward greatness. So long as you remember to strive, not just for power and lofty positions, but for the noble character that defines true leadership, you'll be just fine.

-A.

That was the second time Joe had seen a message signed off

in this particular way, with that particular flavor of notification burning his eyes at the same time as filling him with warm and fuzzy happiness. He took a deep breath, nodded a single time in recognition, and let the message fade away so he could see what else was waiting for him.

EPILOGUE

It appeared to be a message from the first entity once more, going off the grumpy undertones.

Joe, Tatum's Chosen Legend, behold! The moment you've been waiting for has arrived: the final calculation of your undeserving experience gains. After extensive calculations, deep sighs, and countless eye rolls, we have calculated that you have received anywhere from 5-8% of the total experience for the monsters you had a hand in slaying. As we are being carefully observed by the administrator, note that you can see the full breakdown by clicking {here} if you would like to check our math on the 12,741 notifications.

I dare you.

No? Fine.

Experience gained: 101,335

Congratulations. You have reached level 27.

Remember that this is not a reward; it is simply a begrudging acknowledgment of your progress. We suggest you savor it, as it is extremely likely that the road ahead will be filled with frustration.

Battle Meditation has reached Student V!

Dark Lightning Strike has reached Student VIII!

Exquisite Shell has reached Student IX!

Mend has reached Journeyman IV!

Neutrality Aura has Journeyman V!

Retaliation of Shadows has reached Expert II!

Combat Ritual Orbs and Mental Manipulation Resistance have both reached Apprentice IV!

Somatic Ritual Casting (Student) has broken through to Journeyman 0! Congratulations! You are now able to create ritual circles up to the Apprentice rank in an instant if you have a deep enough understanding of them!

Omnivault has reached Master I! All characteristics except Karmic Luck have been increased by 5!

Name: Joe 'Tatum's Chosen Legend' Class: Reductionist
Profession I: Arcanologist (Max)
Profession II: Ritualistic Alchemist (4/20)
Profession III: Grandmaster's Apprentice (14/25)
Profession IV: None
*Character Level: 23 → **27** Exp: 399,593 Exp to next level: 6,407*
Rituarchitect Level: 11 Exp: 64,000 Exp to next level: 2,000
Reductionist Level: 5 → 6 Exp: 23,541 Exp to next level: 4,459
Hit Points: 2,463/2,463
Mana: 6,078/8,327
Mana regen: 71.87/sec
Stamina:1,914/1,914
Stamina regen: 6.68/sec

Characteristic: Raw score

Strength (bound): 176 → 182
Dexterity: 178 → 183
Constitution (bound): 171 → 177
Intelligence (bound): 185 → 190
Wisdom: 173 → 178
Dark Charisma: 126 → 141
Perception: 173 → 178
Luck: 110 → 115
Karmic Luck: 23

Quest reward ready for pickup: Return to Occultatum at 25 and earn a ''super spell' variation.

Quest complete: Student Ritualist III. Monsters slain with a Ritual of Slaughter: 1,000/1,000. Reward: Slaughter was its own reward, if you took the loot.

Quest complete: Journeyman Ritualist. Coven Established: 1/1. Student-ranked Ritualist: 1/1. Reward: Knowledge that you have brought others on the path, as well as a Journeyman-ranked utility item that will be customized to your needs.

Item gained: Mana Condenser Diagram. This utility diagram shows how to condense mana from the environment into a usable form. Gathering that mana is your problem! Excellent for creating rituals that require constant channeling of power and necessary for the creation of Mana Battery recharging stations.

Utterly flabbergasted by how sharply his level and skills had increased, Joe resolved to make a shrine at the bare minimum in the near future to commune with Tatum. He was *going* to get that reputation reward, and he was certain there would be other, additional cleric powers that he would be getting access to. "Also, that Student Ritualist quest was a bust. That'll teach *me* to finish quests that don't have a reward listed."

He couldn't *actually* bear the thought of being angry right now. Obligatory grumbling out of the way, and with a smile crossing his face, the Ritualist turned to the final message: which appeared to be standard mail. The only confusing part of that was the fact that almost no one would have sent him a message, as they all lived within the same square mile. He opened it up, his smile fading away into serious concern as he read over the contents.

Subject: Urgent plea for help - Desperate Need for Rescue

Joe, I hope you are reading your mail more often than you usually do, as I think time is running out for me. Something I did set off the Elves, and they banished me to Jotunheim. They phrased it as a promotion, as a way to build an entire skyline with my talents, but I know it's an exile. As soon as I crossed the bifrost, I was assigned a menial task and cut off from all resources or study material. There's no escape in this place, and the distances involved are so vast that I have no idea how, or if, you could help me.

Frankly, I don't even know that you would. But I hope you will.

Somehow.

-Daniella.

"Well, that's a kick in the teeth." Joe slowly lifted his hand and rubbed the back of his head, trying to think of anything he could do to help her. The message had come in days ago, and another one had not followed it. "I bet they were reading her mail, too. No wonder she got exiled. But… how in the world would I be able to find her? This planet is as large as the surface of the sun!"

He stood there for a short while, thinking over his options and coming up with nothing that could help him in this scenario, short of capturing the bifrost and using it as a beacon for her to eventually follow. While he was lost in thought, Havoc came strolling up and saw the bizarre expression Joe was making, hurrying over to slap him on the back. "Are you choking? No? Then snap out of it! Celebrate your victories, who knows how many of those you're going to get in the future?"

"Yeah, absolutely." Joe agreed, trying to swallow down the confliction he was feeling at the moment. "Just got a letter from an old friend, and… I'm not even sure if she's a friend or not."

"Put that on the back burner and remember to forget her for a minute." Havoc's metaphor felt like a gut punch to Joe, who winced from the butchered old Earth quotes. "Look around you! Less than two full Jotunheim days, and we have three *years'* worth of growth! The walls are getting fixed up, proper this time! The buildings are full of people working hard, and everyone gets to live under the stars."

"Yeah, about that-"

"No! No apartments, no houses! Tents! Tents for everybody!" Havoc cackled at him, the arm he'd casually thrown around the human now turning into a vise-like grip. "*Finally*, my people are getting back to their roots. Their determination is as strong as a mountain, their persistence as unyielding as a diamond hammer! Something you've done has had a great impact on their grit, their determination, and I think it's a combination of the bubble tents and sheer tenacity."

"Havoc, it's cold outside. A few apartments-"

The Dwarf clamped a hand over Joe's mouth and leaned in to whisper in his ear. "No homes! No apartments! *No luxuries*! Not until we have a full City! Even then, I'm fine with it being a tent-a-city!"

ABOUT DAKOTA KROUT

Associated Press best-selling author, Dakota has been a top 5 bestseller on Amazon, a top 6 bestseller on Audible, and his first book, Dungeon Born, was chosen as one of Audible's top 5 fantasy picks in 2017.

He draws on his experience in the military to create vast terrains and intricate systems, and his history in programming and information technology helps him bring a logical aspect to both his writing and his company while giving him a unique perspective for future challenges.

"Publishing my stories has been an incredible blessing thus far, and I hope to keep you entertained for years to come!" -Dakota

Connect with Dakota:
MountaindalePress.com
Patreon.com/DakotaKrout
Facebook.com/DakotaKrout
Twitter.com/DakotaKrout
Discord.gg/mdp

ABOUT MOUNTAINDALE PRESS

Dakota and Danielle Krout, a husband and wife team, strive to create as well as publish excellent fantasy and science fiction novels. Self-publishing *The Divine Dungeon: Dungeon Born* in 2016 transformed their careers from Dakota's military and programming background and Danielle's Ph.D. in pharmacology to President and CEO, respectively, of a small press. Their goal is to share their success with other authors and provide captivating fiction to readers with the purpose of solidifying Mountaindale Press as the place 'Where Fantasy Transforms Reality.'

Connect with Mountaindale Press:
MountaindalePress.com
Facebook.com/MountaindalePress
Twitter.com/_Mountaindale
Instagram.com/MountaindalePress

MOUNTAINDALE PRESS TITLES

GameLit and LitRPG

The Completionist Chronicles,
The Divine Dungeon,
Full Murderhobo, and
Year of the Sword by Dakota Krout

Arcana Unlocked by Gregory Blackburn

A Touch of Power by Jay Boyce

Red Mage and
Farming Livia by Xander Boyce

Ether Collapse and
Ether Flows by Ryan DeBruyn

Dr. Druid by Maxwell Farmer

Bloodgames by Christian J. Gilliland

Unbound by Nicoli Gonnella

Threads of Fate by Michael Head

Lion's Lineage by Rohan Hublikar and Dakota Krout

Wolfman Warlock by James Hunter and Dakota Krout

Axe Druid,
Mephisto's Magic Online, and
High Table Hijinks by Christopher Johns

Skeleton in Space by Andries Louws

Dragon Core Chronicles by Lars Machmüller

Chronicles of Ethan by John L. Monk

Pixel Dust and
Necrotic Apocalypse by David Petrie

Viceroy's Pride and
Tower of Somnus by Cale Plamann

Henchman by Carl Stubblefield

Artorian's Archives by Dennis Vanderkerken and Dakota Krout

Vaudevillain by Alex Wolf

Made in United States
Troutdale, OR
04/22/2024